To the reader with an inquisitive mind
and a fearless disposition,

You are invited to embark on a quest, a treasure
hunt, if you will, down a path only a puzzler
may dare tread.

Within this book lie pages from a diary — ripped out and
hidden by a woman in love, terrified for her life.

Inside the diary she concealed a trail of clues, all pointing
to a book, The Birdcage Library, a faded tome found
in her possessions after she disappeared.

The clues, once solved, lead to the location of a secret so
prized a man might go to any lengths to find it…

What was the fate of the diary's owner?
And what of the treasure she guarded so fiercely?

Curious reader, can you unlock the mystery?

Will you set her secret free?

Acclaim for Freya Berry's writing

'Fascinating…utterly gripping'
LIZ HYDER

'A remarkable talent'
ANTHONY HOROWITZ

'A gripping, intelligent thriller'
EMMA STONEX

'Compelling, atmospheric, brilliant'
MARIAN KEYES

'Richly imagined'
THE TIMES

'Sumptuously written'
GLAMOUR

'Spellbinding'
JANE SHEMILT

'Darkly compelling'
STYLIST

**The answers to a puzzle lie hidden
within an old book.**

It's 1932 and adventuress and plant-hunter Emily
Blackwood accepts a commission from Heinrich
Vogel, a former dealer of exotic animals in
Manhattan, living now with his macabre collection
in a remote Scottish castle.

Emily is tasked to find a long-lost treasure which
Heinrich believes has been hidden within the castle
walls. But instead she discovers the pages of a diary,
written by Hester Vogel, who died after falling from
the Brooklyn Bridge.

Hester's diary leads Emily to an old book *The Birdcage
Library* and into a treasure hunt of another kind, one
that will take her down a dangerous path for clues,
and force her to confront her own darkest secret...

**Open *The Birdcage Library* and let
the treasure hunt begin...**

UK Marketing Contact
For marketing enquiries, please contact zoe.giles@headline.co.uk

UK Publicity Contact
For publicity enquiries, please contact joe.thomas@headline.co.uk

International Contacts
International Publicity Contacts
Australia: publicity@hachette.com.au
Facebook.com/HachetteAustralia
@HachetteAus

New Zealand: contact@hachette.co.nz
Facebook.com/HachetteNZ
@HachetteNZ

India: publicity@hachetteindia.com
Facebook.com/HachetteIndia
@HachetteIndia

THE BIRDCAGE LIBRARY

FREYA BERRY

REVIEW

First published in 2023 by Headline Review
An imprint of HEADLINE PUBLISHING GROUP

1

Cataloguing in Publication Data is available from the British Library

Hardback ISBN 978 1 4722 7635 3
Trade Paperback ISBN 978 1 4722 7636 0

Typeset in Sabon by
Palimpsest Book Production Ltd, Falkirk, Stirlingshire

Printed and bound by CPI Group (UK) Ltd, Croydon, CR0 4YY

Headline's policy is to use papers that are natural,
renewable and recyclable products and made from wood grown in
well-managed forests and other controlled sources. The logging and
manufacturing processes are expected to conform to the environmental
regulations of the country of origin.
HEADLINE PUBLISHING GROUP

An Hachette UK Company
Carmelite House
50 Victoria Embankment
London EC4Y 0DZ

www.headline.co.uk
www.hachette.co.uk

For Rachael, the truest adventuress I ever knew
And for Rory, my co-wanderer, always

'The songbird in its cage sings not for joy but rage.'

Italian proverb

'Exposing an illusion is not the same as uncovering a truth.'

P. T. Barnum

Welcome, dear reader. You have found me, and I you.

The diary you hold in your hands is a treasure map. It will lead you to what you ought to seek. Like all such maps, the trail is cryptic. The reason for this is simple.

The man I love is trying to kill me.

CHAPTER ONE

Every life has its own lie. I think of them as like plants – lies, I mean; doubtless this is due to my botanist's profession. Some are tame and neat: cottage garden geraniums, sprucing up the exterior. Others are subtler, wilier, their roots sunk deep.

There is a third kind: the creepers, the vines. Plants of the jungle. Parasites. Lovingly they reach up and in, entwining themselves with their host, slowly but surely leaching its life away.

The train snaked up Scotland's west flank, coiling through the peaks of Argyll, winding its way around Loch Linnhe. The landscape grew bleaker, green bowing to red bracken not dissimilar in colour to my hair. My skin gleamed pale in the window – paler since our arrival. My father and I had spent seven years absorbing the Australian sun, only for it to disperse in a matter of weeks. I felt guilty for leaving him, though I could hardly have refused the fortuitous employment offer I'd received.

The train was a rickety-looking thing with an air of frontier bravado. I'd changed onto it at Glasgow and made sure to request my stop with the gaunt conductor, as my new employer had directed in his letter. The handwriting was elegant, flared.

'They're all request stops here, Miss . . .'

'Blackwood. Emily Blackwood.'

He nodded bleakly, returning my ticket as a bishop dispenses a wafer to a sinner. His lugubriousness was at odds with the countryside's vaulting magnificence, but it seeped in as we left tourist country with its viaducts and waterfalls, pretty train stations and tamed lochs; the winding roads that led nowhere and the white crofters' cottages pebbling the bracken like roc's eggs in a giant nest. The sky outside grew greyer, draped over humpbacked hills that somehow both crouched and loomed; the stations grew smaller, or perhaps the hills reared higher. This far north, nature had different rules. I saw it in the passengers: iron under their skin. It was easy to believe that wolves had lived here once, sleek shadows winding through the pines.

It was a long way from the cloud forests of Papua. I'd been on expedition there, collecting new and rare plants, not five months since. It was on a brief visit to Port Moresby to pick up an insulin shipment that I received a frantic message from my childhood friend Daniel Loewe. It said that the small but adequate funds he had been managing for my father and me had been lost, all of it, in the roilings of the Depression.

I'd returned immediately to Sydney to organise our affairs, then booked us a cargo ship back to England – all we could now afford, though at least I talked us into a cabin. My father, Edwin Blackwood, had been blind for seven years now, since I was twenty-three, and I could not accept his discomfort. Still, when we disembarked at Southampton, I had been glad of his blindness. Along the dock the well-heeled men and women glided down from the great liners;

at this end, I led my last living family member through a maze of pigs, sugar bags and Marconi telegraph machines. He clutched my hand hard enough that tears sprang to my eyes, refracting in the vicious January sun.

I'd thought I'd found a home in the new world, but the old one had made the truth perfectly clear. The cage had never relinquished me – only hidden its bars awhile.

As the conductor's congregation dwindled, he came over again, gripping the seat opposite like a lectern. I'd spent the journey searching for some trace of familiarity. We had been born in Scotland, my twin sister and I, on St Kilda: a tiny archipelago flung far out to the west, as though God had dropped it in a hurry and forgotten it. We left when we were eleven, never to return.

The conductor asked again for my destination. I repeated myself.

'Yes, and from there?'

I'd memorised the address, a habit picked up on expedition. Perhaps it was the sudden rain thrumming against the window panes, but my answer produced a strange effect.

'Castle Pàrras?' The Gaelic tugged at me. 'Nobody goes there.'

'I suppose I do.'

'On whose invitation?'

'Mr Henry Vogel.'

'Heinrich Vogel, you mean. He is German.'

His voice carried no warmth, but I was intrigued that he knew of my new employer. Lord Rothschild, through whom the offer had been conveyed, had never heard of him. I'd been working at Rothschild's natural history museum at Tring, the first job I'd been able to get: the great collector was selling his vast bird collection to an American museum, a decision that had appalled the British birding community, and indeed beyond. It was 1932, and the general public were

3

drunk on natural history. Nobody knew why Lord Rothschild was selling. There were whispers of a pressing need for money, and even of scandal. The latter might have explained why we worked for some weeks in secret, and why the man himself avoided the process entirely. The Americans had branded him unfriendly; I thought him shy. Regardless, I had spent the last few months packing dead birds into crates for a meagre salary. I could picture the newspaper headline: *Adventuress turns warehouse worker.*

The work for Mr Vogel was similar – the letter Lord Rothschild had given me declared that he had a large collection of taxidermied creatures that required cataloguing as a precursor to sale – but the fee was generous, almost absurdly so. The task was expected to last at least a month, and the applicant was to live on site at Castle Pàrras for the entire duration. No holidays or visits – apparently a function of the remote location, and the urgency of the project. What was so urgent about a collection of stuffed animals, Lord Rothschild had been unable to inform me.

A month was a long time to leave my father. We were accustomed to substantial periods apart while I was on expedition, but then I had been able to equip him with the care of a nurse, a maid and a housekeeper. Now he was left alone in the miserable cottage we had taken, apart from the grouchy old female I had part-cajoled, part-bullied into visiting twice daily for a meagre sum, and the flies that scuttered at the windows no matter what I did.

There was a terrific bang: the train slammed to a halt. Even with the months of stabilising myself on a canoe in Papua, I was flung back in my seat. The conductor recovered with impressive speed.

'We've hit something.'

He went to speak with the driver while I checked the leather tool belt I always wore, ensuring nothing had slipped

4

from the various pouches. Satisfied, I peered through the window. The rain still came: the landscape flickered, here one moment, gone the next. There was a small loch, dull and grey, encircled by bracken the colour of dried blood. The ground looked boggy and treacherous.

'A deer.' The conductor had returned and was pointing out the other side. I went to look. The corpse had been flung off to the west, little more than a scruffy mess of flesh, a sad travesty of Lord Rothschild's immaculate stuffed specimens. Its neck was terribly twisted.

'My mother knows Heinrich Vogel's delivery boy,' the conductor said suddenly. 'He has lived there these five decades. Never any visitors. No.' He held up a skinny finger. 'There was one, about a year ago. What was her name now?'

He could not remember. The train clattered into life again and we spoke no more.

At last we drew into the lonely stop, the mist slinking around us, pulling the train into itself. The station was huddled atop a windswept plain, its small stretch of platform as alien to the landscape as the primitive Papuan airfields I had seen, narrow strips torn from the jungle. Once I had watched villagers swarm over a cargo plane, petting it and trying to feed it sweet potato. No villagers here: there was nothing and no one, not even a ticket office.

I gathered myself and my bags, the insulin bottles within giving a faint clink of protest. The conductor opened the door and I stepped out into the murk.

'Are you being met?' he asked abruptly.

I glanced back, surprised he cared. 'No, but I am told it is not more than a mile.'

He pointed north-east, to where the horizon ended. It was three o'clock, but the sky was dim. 'Down there, though the road is bad.'

Of course.

'Well,' I said. 'Goodbye.'

He nodded, his mouth a thin line. 'Good luck.'

And though I had traversed Papua, Sumatra and the Daintree alone with less than half a map, venturing through crocodile-infested swamps and among strangers bearing knives longer than their forearms, I shivered.

The conductor wasn't wrong: the road *was* bad, and long months indoors had softened me. I picked my way along the pitted holes, bags banging against my hips. Odd tufts of grass had forced their way from bare rock; I thought I saw a fossil, some swimming thing long since turned to stone. There must have been glaciers once, and before that, the deep black sea.

At the point indicated, the land dropped away and I found myself atop a steep embankment overlooking a valley encircled by peaks, my path the only way in. At the far end, where the land pinched into a deep V, the sea thrashed; between it and me ran a long, thin sea loch. This water was matt black and calm as calm could be. At its near end it met a stony beach, from which issued a rather beautiful, ancient-looking stone causeway, its arches skimming back out across the loch. My stomach turned, for at the end of the causeway was a small island, and upon this was a castle.

It was not a fey, fairy-tale creation. It was a real castle, built for keeping things out, or in. A longish main section fed into five hexagonal towers, connected by ramparts, all built of a curious reddish stone. A low but sturdy wall surrounded it. Both this and the castle were pierced with arrow slits. It looked as it had been designed to be: forbidding.

At the island's northernmost edge the earth had eroded into a cliff. The tower here jutted perilously over the loch, and while the rest of the building was in fair repair, this one was falling apart, its roof riddled with holes, its windows loose and damaged, toothy stone visible. At some point the waters would wear its perch away and the whole would topple into the depths.

It might seem strange for a collector-explorer to hate the sea, but I had my reasons, good ones, and it was by deliberate omission that I never studied aquatic plants. I had not dipped so much as a toe in the ocean since I was eleven, and I spent any voyage upon it firmly in my cabin with my specimens, pickling this or that, ignoring the vinegar in my own stomach. But here the waters had caught up with me: for as long as I stayed, they would surround me on all sides. A liquid cage.

I do not know how long I stood there before I realised I was gripping my bags painfully tight. I shook myself free and picked my way down the slope, towards the loch, and the castle, and the mysterious Heinrich Vogel therein.

CHAPTER TWO

'Miss Blackwood!' The man before me seized my hand with unexpected vigour. 'I feared the road had run away with you.'

I blinked. The vaulted ceiling arched over my head like a cat's spine; the rug beneath my feet was worn to a shine. Dreamlike, I could not remember quite how I had got there. Ah: I had passed across the causeway, the loch lapping throatily at the stone. Green eyes momentarily flickered at me from the dark water, and I quickened my steps until I reached the island, ascending the path that rose from the loch and passing under the ancient arch that bent, crone-like, above the encircling wall. The massive castle door opened for me, beckoning me inside, and I stood now in the great hall within, a stuffed buzzard spreading its wings above the enormous fireplace. It felt subterranean, and though I knew we were in the long, straight portion of the castle I had seen from above, I would not have been surprised to learn we were beneath the level of the loch. It was here that I had been cheerily met by the elderly man before me. Heinrich Vogel.

I was taken aback by his upbeat demeanour: from his

castle, I would have expected someone forbidding. This man reminded me of a salesman whose wife despaired of him ever retiring. He was old, very old – 'ninety-two next March, my dear' – and his skin had acquired the greenish tint of the aged. Yet his eyes sparked with surprising life, and his movements, though slow, gave the impression of sprightliness. He was impeccably dressed, in a black suit intricately embroidered with deep purple.

I was ushered into a low sitting room down a flagstone corridor, where a fire leapt as cheerfully as he. Tea and crumpets were already waiting, and while I tucked in, he nodded politely through my references and dismissed my compliments about the castle.

'Pàrras means "Paradise" in the Gaelic, though I cannot say whether the namers ever stayed here in winter.' His eyebrows fluttered. 'And you are just come from the jungles of Papua? Fascinating. I read of you in the *Times*.'

I nodded. I'd been collecting orchids and other rarities for the University of Sydney on my latest expedition (in grimmer moments I now thought it might also be my last). Before the news of our ruin and my subsequent departure, I had given, on request, an interview to a *Times* reporter who had come to follow the gold prospectors in the island's secretive valleys. 'An Adventuress in Paradise', the headline ran. A small follow-up article a few weeks later had noted my return to Sydney and that I was travelling thereafter to Britain upon the Orient Line's RMS *Otranto*.

'Ah, the jungle,' Mr Vogel said regretfully. His accent was Germanic, though faint, and there was something else mixed in too. Not Scottish. A twang.

'You have been?' I missed that realm, and the freedoms it brought. We'd built ourselves a cage and called it civilisation.

'My brother found it enthralling. Though he always said he saw more of the heart of darkness in the cities than he

9

ever did in the jungle. We had an emporium together.' He frowned, then passed his left hand across his face, as though wiping something away. 'But I am getting ahead of myself! Come. You must see the collection.'

With the aid of an elegant cane, he levered himself to his feet and led me slowly but surely through the cool, dry air of the corridor, back into the great hall. Without the fire lit, the cold lapped from the reddish stones: I trailed my fingers along them for a moment, then removed them.

'Castle Pàrras has only been taken once,' he said, nodding towards the great door, now barred by unseen hands. 'There was a siege – the invaders starved them out, said they would be treated with mercy. Well, we know how *that* turned out.' He twisted round, smiled slightly. 'They say the castle stone was white before the invaders came.'

We emerged through a smaller door into a courtyard. In the daylight, the skill of the embroidery upon his jacket became clear: it was intricately wrought, spiralling across the back and breast in fantastic shapes. Flowers, beasts, and things somewhere in between. There was a word for those twisting patterns – but I was distracted by the courtyard, glowing in the sun. Five red stone towers rose above us, a different wrought-iron ornament spiking from the roof of each. Some towers had doors leading directly onto the court-yard; the rest seemed only internally accessible. We were entirely surrounded, yet I sensed the loch beyond. Mr Vogel told me it was tidal and went by the name of Loch Leithe.

'The water is moving underneath the island.' He gestured to a well at the courtyard's centre, explaining that the loch had penetrated it some years before, poisoning the source. 'For that reason, this tower' – he indicated the northernmost, the one that leaned perilously over the waters – 'is unsafe. Access is strictly forbidden. On pain of . . .' he smiled, 'I believe "death" is the traditional warning.'

10

I raised my brows. 'Death?'

'The foundations are slipping. It is extremely unsafe. So perhaps that is not too extreme a pronouncement.'

Less a pronouncement than a threat.

'Do not mistake me – we are not sticklers for rules, Miss Blackwood! It is for your safety. This is the only law around here.'

'And remaining always at the castle,' I could not help but add.

'I am sorry for that. I hope you will understand that I needed somebody serious. The job must be a quick one. I will explain the reason in just a moment. *Ja?*'

'*Ja.* I mean, yes.'

I was distracted as we arrived at the eastern tower, one of those accessible from the courtyard, its door old and cracked. The handle was held in a lion's mouth. I waited for him to produce a key, but instead he said, 'The last intruders needed siege weapons. Apart from the broken tower, and the main door, we do not trouble ourselves with locks.'

He hauled at the handle with surprising strength. 'My menagerie.'

My jaw dropped. The hexagonal room was absolutely crammed with animals: all of them dead, all of them stuffed. It was like Tring, but smaller, and even more tightly packed. I might have been in God's workshop. Creatures reared from wooden pedestals and snarled from glass cases. There were lions and tigers, porcupines and pheasants, zebras and gnus. Most impressive of all was a whole stuffed grizzly bear, snarling in one corner. All of life was here, except that it was dead.

'My life's work.'

Menagerie. An unusual descriptor. 'It is extraordinary. How did you come by it?'

'The collection is my own. I said that I ran an emporium. New York. My brother and I sold animals – living ones.'

His expression darkened momentarily, like a scudding cloud. 'These are all that is left. It continues on the upper level.' He motioned upwards, and now I noticed a spiralling stair, black metal coiling up into the ceiling. 'My creatures need cataloguing. Perhaps boxing, we shall see. A month should be sufficient. We do what we can to maintain them, but . . .'

'We?'

'Lynette, Yves and I. Lynette has been my housekeeper for many years. Yves is my uncle's grandson – my first cousin once removed. I think of him as my nephew.' His eyes had lightened again. 'He works in Munich but summers here.'

'May I ask a question?'

'Naturally, Miss Blackwood. Though answers – answers are another thing, eh?'

'Why do you have all this? Why collect?'

'You have just come from one of the greatest collectors in the land. Why do *you* think?'

I thought for a moment. 'Lord Rothschild enjoys science, but he adores discovery. He seeks more, always more. Sometimes I think he will not be content until he has gathered all the earth under his roof.' I was suddenly conscious of the closeness of Mr Vogel's gaze. 'It is not wonder, or passion, or knowledge that drives him. It is hunger, though for what, I cannot be sure.'

There was a short silence, then the old man sighed. 'The truth is, my mother collected.'

'Animals?'

'Dolls. My brother and I were still young when she died. After that, we went to New York, leaving my father behind. We set up as animal dealers. Our big break came after Charles took thousands of canaries to California and sold them to gold-rush miners, homesick and wanting their songs. It went so well that we were able to set up our Manhattan emporium.'

I looked about me as he spoke. The room did not contain a single canary.

'And another question, Mr Vogel, if I may. Are you really planning to sell? If so, why now?'

'I make that two questions, Miss Blackwood. I shall have to watch myself around you.' He smiled again, fiddled with his cuffs. 'I wish to provide for my nephew. He is my sole inheritor and finds his circumstances recently . . . straitened. Scottish castles do not attract a healthy return. By selling my collection, I wish to provide for him.

'As for the timing, well, you are not blind. Death holds his coat forth for me.'

I waited.

'But as you will be staying here for the foreseeable,' he went on in a rush, 'I believe we must have no secrets from one another. Therefore I will tell you mine.' Cuffs adjusted, his hand slid into his jacket pocket. 'It is this: I know exactly when I am to die.'

I gazed at him blankly.

'Oh! Do not mistake me – I do not know the manner of it, only the timing. But I do not speak of some vague premonition. I know the precise day and hour of my death.'

A slight smile; the hand in the pocket shifted.

'So now you comprehend my reason for haste. The moment approaches, and I find myself almost out of time.'

CHAPTER THREE

With this extraordinary pronouncement, Mr Vogel showed me to my room, or rather, to the base of the relevant tower.

'I no longer care for the stairs,' the old man said ruefully. 'Lynette will have taken up your luggage.'

I frowned, but said nothing. I did not like other people touching my equipment. It had too often saved me from this or that disaster for me to enjoy any interference. At least, as always, I had kept on my tool belt with its assorted compass, knife, vasculum, Thermos flask, notebook, et cetera. Those were the essentials.

It was arranged that I would start work the next morning, and I bade Mr Vogel farewell. The sun had come out and would stay out for days and days to come; when I look back at that first, innocent period, I see that sunshine once more, punctuated by cool shadows.

I set off up the coiling stairs, the ceiling low enough that I had to stoop. My room was at the top. I went up the first flight, where I passed another door, the dark wood soaking up the shadows, and continued on up. Later on, I would note how the stone at a certain level had worn smooth from the passing of so many other shoulders, other lives, and this their only trace. Light came through the arrow slits punched in the wall, but not brightly enough for me to spot the rusted metal spar protruding from it until I felt a stab in my shoulder. I stopped, soothing over the tear in my clothing. I was lucky it had not punctured the skin.

The stairs spat me out into a hexagonal room, entirely of stone. Small alcoves were cut into the wall, uncomfortably reminiscent of a catacomb; at the far end was a window, and despite myself, I went immediately to it. It was as I had feared: the tower was uncomfortably close to the sea loch, black water loitering below.

Well, I would simply avoid the window. Otherwise there was a dark wooden bed and a small desk, the latter bearing a vase of fresh-cut sea pinks. From the invisible Lynette, I presumed. Pinks were the first flowers my sister and I ever pressed. My father taught us to use blotting paper to wick the moisture away, then put them quickly in the press. You want to capture them in the moment, he told us, as though they might flee. We turned the winch with hot childish hands. I worried that the flowers would be crushed to death, before I realised that was precisely what we were doing.

That's it, my father said. As tightly as possible.

Three weeks later, we opened the press. The plants were there, beautiful, changed to mere drawings of themselves.

Careful, my father said, but we had already snatched them up, fascinated by their new crispness, our fingers caressing them to pieces.

I unpacked, checking the contents automatically. They were an even more motley assortment than usual. In his letter, Mr Vogel had desired that I bring any pieces collected on my travels, particularly in Papua, for which he had a passion. He was willing to pay handsomely for items of interest, and I felt sure I could oblige. I had been on four major expeditions to date: the Australian interior, China,

15

Sumatra, and lastly Papua. The first had been the shortest, lasting four weeks; the longest was Sumatra, where I'd been gone eight months. I had brought curiosities from each, including several Papuan bamboo arrows, tipped with cassowary bone and wrapped in a picture tube; an ancient terracotta statue of a Buddha from Sumatra's Minangkabau Highlands; and a beautiful urn purchased from an Aboriginal man deep in Australia's empty burning heart. Last, and (I hoped) most intriguing to Mr Vogel, was a stuffed Count Raggi's bird of paradise in a glass box.

I had come across it in Papua, in a village that stood on stilts amid the yellow clay and pitpit grass. The bird was about a foot long and its plumage was stunningly beautiful, its head yellow and green, its body a rich brown. But the truly riveting thing was its cascading tail. It was fantastic, a daydream, a smoking cloud of sunset red several times longer than its body, the colour a perfected version of my sister's hair, and my own. I'd seen many paradise birds by then, though I never grew accustomed to these daytime comets, their tails unfurling sprays of light. The people in Papua thought they were the origin of the world, and at least one naturalist, supposed to be shooting specimens, had instead found his rifle slack in his hands as he gazed agog.

I'd encountered it in the house of a chieftain whose wife had a wound on her foot, and to whom I had given a small tube of antiseptic ointment. More valuable than gold in those parts – anyway, gold was of little value to them. Their currency was in Nassariidae shells. Yet it was not the bird itself that captured me, but the method of its preservation. Very unusually, it had been stuffed. That was not the style of these people: they skinned the birds and smoked them so the bodies were rendered immune to insects, the prized tail kept safely intact. Generally the feet were cut off too, leading early traders to conclude that the birds remained always in the air, feeding on dew, only brought to ground by death.

Yet this bird was taxidermied in an entirely Western style. I'd examined it thoroughly, running my hands over its sleek, hard body, over the unusual stitching that ringed its neck. It even had black glass eyes, gazing intelligently at me from its case.

The case . . . it was well made, of wood and more glass. There *was* no glass in this part of the world. The emptying insulin bottles that I carried were a reminder of this, along with my specimen vials containing mould-preventing alcohol. For this reason I had to return every two months to Port Moresby to collect further shipments. Always I felt the thread of my illness running through me, a leash against which I strained. At the final return, six months in, just before I learned that we were ruined, I had cut it particularly fine and was beginning to hallucinate by the time I stumbled to the harbour. Perhaps that was why Daniel's news had seemed for so long like a bad dream.

I asked the chieftain if I could inspect the case, and he consented. I examined it, but could not discern any signs of where it might have originated – at least not until I gently lifted it up and looked underneath.

SPECIMEN PREPARED BY THE UNITED STATES NATIONAL MUSEUM.

How on earth had it come here? The chieftain told me it had been given to his father by a wandering ghost. It had lived with a companion spirit for as many rainy seasons as accounted for half the number of feathers on a bird of paradise's tail, happily occupying a spirit house built for the purpose, even tending a garden. Every so often they would depart for long periods, but always returning to visit the bird.

The chieftain's father died in this period and the box passed to him. Then one day, another ghost arrived. The

17

first ghost came to the chieftain, glowing, and told him the bird was his to do with as he wished. Then they departed, never to be seen again.

The chieftain insisted on giving the bird and its box to me in return for the antiseptic, and though I protested, I privately knew that if he had not offered, I would have attempted to buy it. It felt somehow familiar – necessary. Fate caressed my shoulder, and though it was hopelessly impractical, I carried the thing about thereafter, strapped to my horse; and when the terrain grew too rough even for him, in my canoe.

I sewed up the tear in my sleeve from the iron spar, then unpacked. It did not take long: I travelled light, mysterious bird boxes excepted, and preferred simple, practical clothing, tending to plain. I was already nearly six foot, pale with red hair; I did not need more ways to draw attention to myself. In Papua, villages I had never set foot in before greeted me with cries of 'She comes!' I had passed into legend, which was useful, since legends, as everyone knew, were beyond question.

It was questions that had kept me in Tring's library until long after midnight the previous week. Ill-paid though the temporary museum job was, its end date had loomed large in my mind, and my father's, though he would not admit it. I'd lingered in the library to evade such worries, as well as the gin bottle concealed in the cabinet beneath the gramophone. My colleagues disliked the museum at night-time, but I loved these silent hours, surrounded as I was by every species under the sun except for *Homo sapiens*.

I was perusing the botanical books, telling myself I was picking new texts to read to my father, in truth simply spending time with the specimens described, when I bumped into Lord Rothschild, a man who enjoyed human company

18

as little as I did. He held a book, which he tucked behind his huge back, but I saw it was on birds – the same creatures he was so mysteriously selling.

This was my opportunity to ask for permanent employment, and I took it. I told him of my expeditions; of my botany degree and my doctorate from the University of Sydney, not mentioning that the latter was only the second ever awarded to a woman. I took no pleasure in being a rare specimen. I saw enough of those in my work.

But he cut me off. 'No need, Miss Blackwood. I received a letter this morning, specifically requesting your services. I have it in this very pocket.'

I blinked stupidly, not only at the coincidence but at the fact that he had opened the letter at all. For a man who had been the named recipient of the Balfour Declaration, he was notorious for never reading his mail. It was a miracle the Jews ever got their homeland.

'An enquiry from a man who desires help with his own private collection. Animals, I am afraid, but the work is not especially skilled. A Mr Henry Vogel. You know him, I assume.'

'I never heard of him in my life.' I unfolded the letter he handed me. Mr Vogel cut straight to the point. He required assistance in cataloguing his collection, had heard of my expeditions and my recent work at Tring, and thought I would do the job admirably. I was about to declare that a botanist was surely not the right fit when my eye fell on the salary.

'I'll do it.' And that was that.

I finished my unpacking. Much of it was botanical equipment that I was unlikely to require here, but I had come to take an embarrassingly unscientific comfort in the accoutrements of my profession. In one of the alcoves I lined up my vascula – botanical boxes for storing specimens without crushing them – and some of my glass bottles. Several contained essential oils from my father; the rest (even more essentially) insulin. The diabetes had begun seven years ago, in the aftermath of the accident in which my sister died. It was hard not to link the two, though I knew that was ridiculous.

The largest bottles contained gin. These I stashed under the bed, though not before I had poured myself a measure. I managed, mostly, to keep the alcohol under control enough not to exacerbate my illness. Long periods away from it while on expedition helped, but of late I had been oft-reminded of my dependency.

Task complete, Lord Rothschild had made to hasten away, but I stopped him.

'Sir, I must ask: I cannot see why you must go through with this sale unless there is a great need. *Is* there a great need?'

He took the bird book from behind his back and gazed down at it. I had to lean in to catch his next words.

'I concealed something for too long, and this is the result.'

And once more I was in the jungle, wet leaves slipping like serpents past my legs and everywhere the vines growing up around me, through me: a greeny cage from which I could never be free because it came from within. Lord Rothschild's deception had caught up with him. I could only hope that my own never would.

I think I knew even then that it was only a matter of time.

CHAPTER FOUR

The next morning my new employer was nowhere to be seen, but someone – presumably the unseen Lynette – had left bread, jam and coffee on a tray at the base of the stairs. I ignored the jam but took the rest out to the courtyard, where I ate it standing up, chased with a long drink from my Thermos, eager to inspect my new kingdom. The clock on the southernmost tower showed that it was still early. The day was crisp and new with a faint snap of salt.

The menagerie tower was cool and dry and, surprisingly, had electricity – I pressed a switch and the animals awoke in silent greeting. I'd watched Daniel wage numerous battles with his father over installing electricity at Butterworth: Harold Loewe had vehemently fought against anything that might damage his stucco work. In the end, Daniel put a live ferret under one end of the ballroom floor and a dead rabbit at the other. The ferret's path around the ancient joists showed him the most effective route for the new wires.

'Progress!' Harold said bitterly to me, just before he died. 'He insisted upon those lights, and now, when I look out of the window, I can no longer see the stars.'

An unusual moment of vulnerability. Daniel's father was

not accustomed to showing weakness; as a Jew, he could not afford to. (He was not in fact Harold, but Harel, come to England from Germany in his youth.) Only through Daniel did I know of his desperate ongoing efforts to cling to life: the endless doctor's visits, the Train Bleu to the south of France, the folk remedies cooked up by the village wives. Even now, the faint smell of linseed oil, mixed with raw eggs, permeated the air.

At least I understood what he wanted, and the voraciousness of it. He reminded me of a lizard I had seen once, half picked apart by a bird, flopping and wriggling in the blood-streaked dust yet clinging to life with a ferocity far greater than that of its assailant. My father had met Harold at university, a rich man's son who saw lectures as an unfortunate hindrance to his education in shooting, whisky and women, in that order. It was thanks to my father that Harold scraped a pass, and Harold never forgot it. When his wife died in childbirth, it was to my father that he wrote for comfort; and when my mother too passed away, my father did vice versa. Harold immediately invited him to Oxfordshire, to take up the parish priest position at Butterworth. It was highly unorthodox for a Scottish minister to join the English church, but Harold was an influential man, and conveniently close to the bishop. We moved into a cottage in Butterworth's grounds for a laughable rent.

In his later years, Harold became the kind of elderly gentleman who loved to hear about the fortunes, or preferably misfortunes, of other elderly gentlemen, his conversation feeding on gossip like a moth on clothes, wearing holes in the thing in question. He did my sister and me the favour of being frank, and we returned it. Around the Loewes, the divisions among my family disappeared for a few hours and we could be at ease with one another again. It was always just Daniel, Emma and Emily: Daniel was four years older,

22

but did not have many friends his own age. It was years before we twins thought to ask why.

'*Jude*,' Harold said bitterly. The only time we ever heard him speak German.

Daniel laughed it off. 'I don't mind,' he said, on a solitary weekend down from Oxford. 'Besides, I have my hands full with you two.' And he stirred up the mirror pond with his stick until the carp hid in fright.

Only gradually did I realise how much he did indeed mind. How it caged him. How it followed him through university and into the City. Though his office was well wadded with his father's money, nothing could insulate him enough, not his hard work, not his talent with figures, not his easy laugh or considerate nature. Sometimes I wished for him – and myself – to be more like my Wardian cases, the glass boxes in which I sent live plant specimens to institutions across the world: sealed environments in which the plant was sustained almost entirely by itself. Nothing could get out or in.

I had in fact once sent such a case to Daniel, containing a single orchid. I did so on a whim, lonely upon arriving in Sumatra, then kicked myself about it during the long expedition that followed. He kept it in his office, he wrote to me, still in its case. A Chinese Character Phalaenopsis, its markings flourishing beautifully while the filthy air beyond ate itself away.

It feels as though I could read it, he wrote, *if only I could understand the script.*

There had been a time when we had understood everything about the other. He had never known his mother; Butterworth's garden was her only legacy. Still, he managed to be whole, a state I both admired and envied. Initially he threw himself into making my sister and myself competent fisherwomen; then, realising he was doomed to disappointment, found other diversions for these peculiar twins who had never seen

23

a tree in their island-bound lives. Our families were enmeshed from the beginning, and that made our first meeting after my return to England all the more painful.

I went to see him at his office. I insisted on the location – refused to ever let him visit the tiny cottage we had taken. It would have been like stuffing a sovereign into a ragged purse. He was so untouched, Daniel Loewe, or had been. He was utterly wrecked at how he had ruined us, though I had vowed from the first to absolve him. It was the only way not to pity either of us, and pity would have ripped me in two.

Officially the purpose of the meeting was to discuss the decimation of my family's funds, how the rot of the Wall Street Crash had spread unavoidably throughout each and every one of the investments made by himself and his firm; how, in his desperate belief that he could fix it, he had not told us until it was much too late. Unofficially . . . well, everything about that meeting was unofficial, from the sweat on my palm as we shook hands to the apologies that poured from his lips. It had been hard not to glance at that Phalaenopsis in its case, at the glass-walled soil and the roots woven thickly through it, twisting as the conversation did in my hands. At one point I became angry. Not at him – most of the City had suffered the same losses, or worse. He had done his very best. It just hadn't been enough. No, I was angry at the world, at myself, for focusing too much on making my father proud and not enough on our financial security.

Daniel's dark eyes flickered, but he let me rage, accustomed from childhood to my temper. When I was done, he embraced me, murmuring comfort into my hair. His freshwater scent had not changed; my eyes blurred with sunshine and the chalk stream where the three of us fished as children. I'd thought I loved him, before it all went wrong. He drew my

24

sister and me together, his presence soothing the raging silence between us. I would have loved him for less. But it was more than that: his constant enthusiasm and energy belied his kindness and honesty, as well as the belief that the world also possessed such qualities, despite its many assurances to the contrary.

As I left him, I realised the Phalaenopsis was positioned against the wall directly before the desk. Whenever the office's occupant glanced up, he would see it.

I got to work in the menagerie, deciding I would make a basic tally of all the creatures before beginning a proper catalogue. Wildcats, four; hyenas, two; baboons, one; et cetera, et cetera. It was not unlike being at Tring again, the work a comforting monotony of wonders. On many a lunch break I had watched the butterfly ladies at work: charming unmarried village girls who pinned and set Lord Rothschild's massive lepidoptery collection. At first they seemed as fluttering as the creatures they worked with – Miss Britton was particularly pretty – but like their preparations, on closer look their delicacy was belied by the presence of steel. I'd watch them pushing pins skilfully into the corkboard around their specimens, avoiding the wings by scarcely a hair's breadth. The creatures would be dried on the spreading board for a week or so before the pins were removed and they were mounted in one of the cases specially designed by Lord Rothschild himself. Actually they reminded me of my own Wardian cases, though Lord Rothschild's designs were glassed below as well as above, so that examining the hidden underside of the specimen was simply a matter of turning the box over. I was terribly glad the same principle could not be applied to human beings.

I ran my palm down the grizzly's flank, enjoying the illicit thrill of handling a wild thing. It glowed with apparent life, yet the falsity was revealed with a touch. A far cry from the aliveness of Papua. I sharply missed paddling down the lazy Sepik, crocodiles observing me from their reedy beds, while the fluffy yellow flies I never managed to identify pulled their newly hatched fellows from the water.

I concentrated on compiling my survey. And realised there was a serious problem.

I could only hope it would not invalidate my entire reason for being here. It seemed foolish to do myself out of a much-needed job. I decided to continue with the tally, then speak to Mr Vogel that evening.

In the meantime, needing a break from that dusty silence, I left the castle and sat on the crumbling wall outside, keeping my distance from the loch. It was calm, though in the distance small waves came in serried rows, like crocodile's teeth. My hand went involuntarily to the tooth at my own throat, given to me by a pastor in Papua. While collecting specimens, I had befriended some local women, who invited me to use their village as a base. They were preparing for a skin-cutting festival, where boys were ritually marked to represent their passage to manhood. The candidates had been kept in a house together for months, resting and being fed. The fatter and happier they were, the softer their skin became and the less they would feel the pain. (I was surprised by this: was not tougher skin better? I asked, and was gently mocked for my foreign logic.)

During my stay, a man was found dead, killed by the laughing death, a mysterious and incurable sickness not uncommon to those parts. His wife was accused of sorcery and sentenced to execution. I had not yet worked out how to intervene when the pastor was brought in: the villagers wanted him to pray for her departing soul. Instead he performed an exorcism. The evil spirit was driven out and, fortunately, she was pronounced saved. During the pig feast

26

that followed (originally intended to mark the execution, but the villagers sensibly saw no reason to waste a party), the pastor took me aside.

'You have a spirit too,' he said.

By that time I could get along pretty well in their language, and I looked down at myself, my skin browned and covered with mosquito bites. The pig hissed and spat on the fire.

'Your lookalike is standing behind you.' He indicated a point behind my left shoulder. 'But you knew that already. She has been there for a long time.'

Despite the fire, a chill spread down my spine.

'You worry that perhaps you can only see her because you are mad. But that does not mean she does not exist.'

I twisted round, knowing already what I would see: nothing, only the pig, and the tattooed villagers, and the blackness of the forest beyond.

'You must choose what to do.' He touched the tooth necklace he wore. 'You keep her with you and you die. Or you ask her to go and you live.'

I did not bother denying his words. 'How do I do that?'

'It is different for each person. I cannot order a spirit out. It will cling there, like crackling to pig flesh. You must find a way. Here, take this. It will give you protection.' He tugged off the tooth on its cord and gave it to me, despite my protests.

'From what do I need protecting?'

'The great question. Is it the dark out there' – he gestured beyond the fire, out at the mazy black – 'or in here?' He tapped his chest lightly, then gazed over my shoulder again. 'You must decide. Only then will it depart.'

I could not help but glance again at the corkscrewing flames. When I turned back to ask how I would know when it was done, nobody was there.

*

27

The wind picked up, ruffling the loch's perfection. Time to go. I went back inside, through the front door and the great hall and out across the courtyard, the decrepit tower before me. Unlike the others, a large padlock held this one shut. Its base was solid – only in the upper layers had the stones torn themselves free.

On pain of death, Mr Vogel had said. Well, I'd lived through my fair share of danger. I just wanted to look inside – I didn't have to go in. And should Mr Vogel challenge me, I was fairly confident I could assert myself against a nonagenarian.

I withdrew from my tool belt the thin knife I always carried, and quickly inserted it into the padlock.

It would not turn. I withdrew it, or tried to, and found I could not. I jiggled it cautiously, then again, harder, with an odd panic. I looked around again: no one to be seen, yet there was a rising pressure in the air, a feeling of something coming, something frightening. A gull screamed, and in a panic, I gave one desperate yank. Miraculously, the knife came free.

I hurried away, hastening for the menagerie, just as the door in the long, straight portion of the castle opened and a woman emerged.

'Lynette?' I asked, my voice calm even as I shoved the knife into my trouser pocket.

'Miss Blackwood. Gracious, you're tall.'

She was plump, tidy, about fifty, her skin pale and her dress drab, though freshly pressed. She would have been entirely unremarkable had it not been for the flesh of her forehead. It had *melted*, folding like wax over one of her eyes.

'I did not know anyone would be here.'

'I brought your lunch.' She carried a tray of egg sandwiches, her hands wrapped neatly around it, almost moulded to it.

28

'Thank you.' A burn, I realised. The tallowing flesh was the result of a burn.

'You must be the famous explorer. The Blackwood orchid. I have heard of it.'

That first discovery. It lived exclusively inland, far from the sea. 'Parasitical plants are my specialty now.'

She nodded. 'Like small cow-wheat. It was all around the woods where I grew up.'

I was surprised. 'Yes, though technically that is hemi-parasitic. It steals nutrients from other plants, but it can also obtain them from its own root system.' Botany was full of such frauds. Plants that masqueraded as other plants. Fungi that could enslave ants to their will. Mother Nature was a gleeful deceiver.

'Then why take from others?'

I was surprised again, this time by a sudden ferocity in her features. Then she smiled. 'Your new employer would like you to dine together this evening.'

I told her I was diabetic and had to avoid anything sweet.

'Don't you worry. I will see to it. It would be good for you to spend time with Mr Vogel before Yves arrives.'

'His cousin?'

She looked pleased, as though I had identified a rare and impressive species. 'Yes. He will be here tomorrow.'

'Does he come often?'

'Just for the summer, but he is coming early this year. We had the unusual pleasure of having him here in January as well. You will like him, Miss Blackwood. Everybody does.'

That evening, I descended the staircase, its centre worn thin, twisting upon itself like my twin's plait that I used to weave around my fingers. We were obsessed with each other in the beginning, ignoring our mother in favour of snuggling up to one another like wolf cubs. Even when we fought, screeching, neither of us would leave the other. We had both understood that to be alone, as other people were, was the worst punishment of all.

Adjacent to the great hall was a more modest dining room: here the floor was covered by a green tartan rug, quite new, while an ugly iron chandelier hung over the table laid for two, the places cosily adjacent. It felt rather like someone playing at castles: on the walls were stags' heads and paintings of old hunts. Mr Vogel had told me about the siege; doubtless there were other ghastly stories associated with this place. Scotland mined its own mythology like other countries extracted gold or oil. I asked Lynette when she entered a moment later, carrying a flask of wine, and sure enough:

'Oh, it was terrible, Miss Blackwood. The lady's son had been killed by a rival clan in a skirmish. She pretended forgiveness and invited the chieftain and *his* son to dine, along with their men. Suckling pig, it was. She kept a herd as pets. That is one of her creatures.'

She pointed to a painting, dim with age, where a coddled porker gazed fondly into the middle distance.

'The chieftain's favourite was blood pudding. She promised to serve them her secret recipe. Then her soldiers rose up and slit the son's throat before his father's very eyes, along with the rest of his men. The blood ran across the tables and filled the tureens!'

I nodded, satisfied. It was a miracle any Scot ever accepted an invitation to dinner. 'What happened to the chieftain?'

'No, madam, it is too dreadful.'

'Oh, *go* on.'

A sharp voice interrupted us. 'Go on with what?'

Mr Vogel entered, dressed again in a fine suit with another intricate pattern, this time in deepest navy, and a waistcoat of the same. I was intrigued by his finery. Why did he bother, locked away in this castle with only Lynette's plain dress for company, and now mine?

'Lynette is telling me tales of the castle,' I said.

'Gruesome ones, I imagine.'

I looked to her for confirmation, but she had disappeared. I don't mean that she had left the room. It was as though she had emptied herself out, any personality instantly erased from the eye that had not been damaged beyond repair, replaced by a devotion that mirrored the pig's.

She poured the wine – only for me – then served us a rich soup and bread. I did not finish it, though not because of the diabetes. In Papua I'd lived mostly on fish, yams and boiled water-weeds, and still missed the lightness of that diet. My employer did not eat much either. This surprised me: as I'd told him, the collecting mindset was linked firmly in my mind to appetite.

What I had not said was that I disliked it, this unstocking of the world to fill rooms like Mr Vogel's menagerie. I had never planned to become a plant hunter – I'd wanted to work in conservation, but there was no money in caring for the earth's treasures. A jungle seemed endlessly abundant, but the botanist in me understood its fragility, and I could not comprehend the failure, or refusal, of educated men to see it. A professor in Sydney had once told me that the specimens we found would one day give answers to questions we did not yet even know existed. Perhaps that was why I sometimes felt an unscientific weariness, a sense that our race had seen everything yet understood nothing.

Which brought me to the issue with the collection.

'Mr Vogel,' I said between mouthfuls, 'we have a problem.'

I spoke into his frown, informing him how in natural history, the labelling of specimens was essential. Not just with the species' name, but the date it was collected (i.e., killed), the location, the collector's name, et cetera. Without such data, the collection was virtually useless to a scientific institution, little more than a toothsome *Wunderkammer* for children. I could not think how he had not considered this before.

He did not blink. 'They are not labelled because they were not *collected*. At least not in the way you would consider them so. Often my emporium had animals that were sick, or died in passage. These were stuffed.'

'Even so, your collection would be worth considerably more if it possessed adequate information. Even the basics would help. Do you have sales records? Ledgers?'

His eyes closed briefly, his hand going to his jacket pocket, working away at something within as though in consolation. 'The collection is extraordinary in itself. Why should pieces of paper make it more so?'

'The animal on its own is not enough to tempt purchase. Museums label everything down to the last ant. Lord Rothschild would pin a label to the earth if he found one large enough. I do not think an unlabelled creature would be accepted even as a donation.'

He spread his hands. 'Is it not enough for a giraffe to be a giraffe?' So many of his actions had the echo of a flourish. His emporium had brought marvels to men: he had lived in the age of spectacle, and these dusty specimens were now its only remnant. It made me rather sad.

'Wonder is no longer the operating mode of our world,' I said. 'The force of the age is knowledge. Precision, categorisation. Today's collectors are not dilettantes seeking freaks. They are men of science. There may be enthusiasts whose requirements are less stringent, but not many.'

A long pause.

'Very well. You may examine the ledgers. Perhaps you will have some luck cross-referencing the animals, though I doubt it. Half of Africa passed through our doors.'

I said what I had been thinking. 'Forgive me, but I cannot believe your attention has not been called to this issue before.' He said nothing, only regarded me intently. 'I think you must be straight with me, Mr Vogel. What is it that you really want for your collection?'

His gaze still assessed me. I felt like one of his menagerie.

'All right. I will be straight with you, Miss Blackwood.'

'That would be preferable.' My voice was even, but a thrill ran through me.

'I am not interested in cataloguing the collection. Nor do I seek to sell it. Once a thing is mine, it is mine for ever.'

I frowned. 'Then why create this job at all?'

'I created it,' he said, 'for *you*.'

CHAPTER FIVE

I remained in my chair, staring at him. Lynette came in and cleared the table; we both ignored her. I felt as I had in Sumatra when I had almost fallen into a pig trap.

'I shall explain,' Mr Vogel said quickly.

'I think you'd better.'

He said nothing further, only withdrew a *Times* newspaper clipping from his breast pocket and pushed it to me. The creases were worn, as though it had been unfolded and refolded many times. A shiver down my spine: the photograph was of me. It was the article detailing my Papuan expedition. I was frowning out from the docks of Port Moresby, my luggage piled up beside me in preparation for the voyage. I disliked being photographed, sympathising with the so-called primitive belief that an image took a piece of your soul. My own could ill afford the sacrifice.

'We get little enough news here, so I always pay attention to the papers. I was interested to read of your exploits. But I was far more interested in *this*.' He stabbed at the photograph. There, in the extreme left-hand corner, was my bird of paradise. 'I recognised it immediately.'

'What? How?'

'It once belonged to me.'

My mouth fell open.

'I found the bird on my travels in the Papuan jungles.' My subconscious frowned at this as he continued, 'I gave it to Charles's wife – alive – as a wedding gift. When it died, they had it stuffed and put in this very case.'

'How did it end up in Papua?'

'My brother's wife . . . how shall I say this? She decided to end her life. In a fall. My brother went mad with grief and disappeared shortly after. I never saw him again.'

'I am sorry.'

He brushed his left hand across his face. 'It was nearly fifty years ago.'

'How can you be sure it is the same one?'

'A simple matter. The box bears an inscription, does it not? I will tell you what it is.'

I waited, keen to see if he could substantiate this extraordinary claim.

He moistened his lips. 'It reads: "Specimen prepared by the United States National Museum".'

I sat back, stunned.

'I am correct, am I not?' Mr Vogel was watching me closely.

'Yes. And when you said in your letter that I ought to bring something of value to sell . . .' This was what he had been after. How neatly the trap had been set! 'Why the covert method?'

'I am sorry for it. After your return to England, I had no idea where you had gone, until the news story about Dr Murphy's work at Tring.'

I knew the article he spoke of. It had been published barely a fortnight previously, declaring that the packing of the birds was nearly finished and they would shortly begin their voyage to America. The piece had named Dr Murphy's team in full. Including me.

'After nearly four months, I had found you again. But what would you have done if I had written to you out of the blue? You would have thought me a crank, or perhaps a thief. I could not risk losing the creature. It is the only new item of information to come to me in almost fifty years.'

'Information about what?'

'Tell me first – did you bring it?'

I hesitated, then gave in. 'As a matter of fact, I did.'

His eyes gleamed, but he did not appear surprised. Lynette had brought up my luggage when I arrived. Had she searched it?

'Tell me everything about how it came into your possession,' Mr Vogel said. 'Leave no detail out. In return, I shall tell you all.'

I did so, then slumped back in my chair. So that was that. I would hand over the bird and my time here – my job – would be at an end. The best I could hope for was to sell it to him for an acceptable sum. Not without bitterness, I said, 'So you do not require me to catalogue the collection.'

'Ah! Not so fast. I would not be so dishonourable as to bring a capable young woman so far only to dismiss her again. I had another reason for wishing to see you at work, Miss Blackwood. You see, after my sister-in-law died, Charles disappeared and the emporium business collapsed. I was left a bankrupt. I never saw my brother again, but a short while after his ship departed New York, an unknown person entered this castle.'

'How do you know?'

'Three indications. The first was a freshly-dug grave.'

My eyes widened.

'Charles buried his wife here. This castle belonged to her family. He must have brought her body on the ship.'

'And the second indication?' I hoped it was less macabre.

'The groundskeeper saw a light within the castle.'

'Did he investigate?'

'Unfortunately, it was during a storm. The situation of Pàrras is such that when the winds rise, even opening the door is a battle. We get storms in all seasons, including in summer. All one can do is wait. Besides, it was also the solstice.'

I did not understand the connection.

'The groundskeeper visited next morning. The front door was locked. There was no sign of forced entry, but he knew what he had seen. It is a castle: it is built to keep people out. The only way in is with a key, and only two people alive possessed such a thing: the groundskeeper, and my brother's wife. I searched the belongings she had left behind. Her key was missing.'

'What was the third indication?'

'*The Birdcage Library.*'

'Which is . . .?'

He waved a hand. 'Nothing of importance. The vital thing, Miss Blackwood, is what Charles was *doing* here. I believe he was hiding something. Something that was in his wife's possession before she died and has never been seen since.' A deep breath – the sound of a theatre curtain being drawn aside. 'I believe he was hiding my treasure.'

I blinked. Behind us, the fire crackled. 'What treasure?'

'Something I discovered on my last sourcing expedition. Foolishly I brought it to my brother and entrusted it to him. He was the elder, and I wished us to share my good fortune and take our business to greater heights.' His eyes turned black. 'But it was not to be. My sister-in-law died and my brother fled with his prize, leaving me with nothing.'

'What was it?'

'Forgive me if I do not share that information at present. But I will tell you this: I believe the bird of paradise is a clue to its whereabouts.' He smiled, leaned in. 'So here is my true proposal: help me find this item, and I will reward you handsomely.'

I did not know whether to believe him. His expression was deadly serious, but it was all too strange. Besides . . .

'I am no detective, Mr Vogel. I am a botanist. You ought to hire a professional.'

'But you *are* a detective, Miss Blackwood. First, what is species discovery if not treasure hunting? Plant collecting requires an exceptional attention to detail, a highly trained visual memory, and of course considerable ingenuity. I read of your tracing of the desert flower you found in Australia, based only on the scattered recollections of a hunter half crazed with thirst.' He paused. 'Second, you have done what no one else has in fifty years: you have found a clue.'

I shrugged. 'Anyone can be lucky.'

'Do you believe in fate, Miss Blackwood? No? Perhaps you should. Every puppet ought to be aware of its strings. I have searched for decades and found nothing. You are caught in our little hunt now, whether you like it or not.' His fingers drummed on the table. 'There is also the matter of your character. You raised the matter of labels, knowing it might sacrifice your job. Your mind is not only thorough, but honest. What do you say?'

'You have not even told me what the treasure is. Nor what the reward would be.'

But Mr Vogel sat back, his energies drained. 'That is enough for this evening. Bring me the bird tomorrow. I shall explain everything when my nephew arrives.'

I left him. My interest was piqued, yet it was all so peculiar. A dead woman – a stuffed bird – a lost treasure. In my bedroom, I could not stop myself gazing for some minutes at the loch, gleaming in the dying light.

To quiet myself, I read awhile, an old favourite of my

father's on cryptogamic parasites. The author was also a fair artist, his velveteen mushroom sketches almost tangible. I missed the outdoors on my skin, the sheer *thinginess* of things. In nature, one was never alone.

Slowly I realised that I was reading aloud. I had become so used to doing it for my father, working through book after book while his head bent in sightless concentration. He had himself studied botany before turning to theology. Somehow he held both the world and God in his head, a double vision I never managed to master. He used to believe no such doubling was required. Look, he would say to my sister and me, pointing out liverwort or sea campion. Marvel at His creation. His sightless eyes still shone when I described this or that discovery:

'It is wonderful, Emmy. You are seeing the world for me.'

But he no longer saw God in the corona of a *Passiflora*. The Lord abandoned him with my sister's death. It changed him utterly. He was an Old Testament kind of man, large and bearded. We were hopeless sinners, his righteous anger forcing the congregation to its knees, hot enough to boil the water in the font. Only my sister and I stayed as we were, backs straightened to the exact same degree. Emma and Emily, though we were often both called Emmy, as though we were interchangeable. Our four eyes bored into the pulpit with the relentless gaze we had inherited from him. Our spines did not bend, because we well knew that for some deeds there could be no salvation.

CHAPTER SIX

The day that one of the twins kills their mother is sunny. Soft brown sheep's wool drifts through the air, caressing the laundry. Not their family's, though; their mother is having one of her days again, their father busy preparing that week's sermon, so the clothes fester lankly in the tub and the garden starves for water.

The garden is their mother's joy: she has a witchy ability to cultivate, though the strength of the St Kilda soil fades with every passing year, dwindling along with the population. Mostly she grows herbs. There is no doctor on the archipelago and the islanders come to her for their cures and poultices. 'Cultivate your garden,' she says to them. Though they are eleven now, Emma and Emily have never thought to ask what she means. Nor do they wonder at the fact that the only thing she cannot heal is herself. That day, all they know is there is no breakfast, and her eyes are empty. Recognising the signs, they go off in pursuit of guillemot eggs to blow out and sell to tourists.

It is hard to say exactly when things go wrong. They are on the other side of the island to where the men are doing the real hunting, where they know they will be chased from the tempting edge. They are supposed to be too young for this, though everyone knows they do it anyway. Everyone here can climb. Few can swim. The seas are so wild there is little point.

It never bothers the twins. They have spotted a particularly rich nest, on a ledge of the rearing cliffs. One clambers down to get it, her sister holding the rope. She climbs alpine-style, barefoot, ignoring the roiling waters beneath. There is a rocky shelf she can edge along, before a fault raises the continuation to some fifteen feet above.

It is while ascending this latter portion that the rope catches in a fissure. She stops, pulls. It's stuck. She loses her nerve – unties herself and somehow scrambles up to the ledge. Her twin yanks the rope free, throws it down again, but her courage has failed her. She is gripped, clutching the unforgiving stone, unable to move. She can no more secure the rope to herself than throw herself into the sea.

Her sister runs to the village for help. Their father is nowhere to be found and all the men are away slaughtering fulmars, assisted by the women and children. Only their mother is there.

She comes, her daughter's plight clawing the day from her green eyes like so much ivy. Born on St Kilda, small and slight, she has always been a champion climber. She descends, confident and rope-free, in her element and entirely beautiful. Reaching the ledge is nothing, nothing at all. She whispers into her daughter's ear, words that slowly lift the girl's chin and uncurl her fingers from the rock. Words that soothe her pounding heart. Then she ties the rope around the girl's waist against the thirsty sea. Calls up to the other that it is all right.

She gives her shoulder to her daughter, who clambers up to the next ledge, from where it is an easy climb to safety. Something makes the girl stop and glance back: her mother is looking up at her, hair blowing across her green eyes, obscuring the expression therein.

She reaches out to haul her mother up. The twins are only eleven, but already possess a climber's wiry strength, and their mother is tiny. Her skeleton must resemble a sparrow's. Her mother's hand stretches to meet her own – yet in the milli-second before their fingertips meet, there is a strange step backwards, a stumble. The girl snatches, wild, desperate, but it is too late – her mother is falling, her hand closing on empty air as a scarlet streak tumbles into the boiling sea.

It's her fault. In the years to come, she will replay that day over and over. Her fault for getting stuck. Her fault for failing to seize her mother's hand when she slipped, for failing to save her. Her family know it. So does the island. Green eyes watch from between each curling wave, fixed upon her in accusation.

A fissure cracks within the family and slowly expands like ice in rock, swelling with their father's grief. From that day he has only one daughter. The other is a stranger, a murderer: tolerated, but always at a distance.

As for the twins, for the first time they are different to one another. There is nothing secret about the guilt and who bears it. No longer can Emma be confused with Emily, Emily with Emma. No longer are their lives and souls jumbled together, inseparable. Their mother's death tears them asunder. One becomes two. It nearly kills them both.

I did what I generally did when the memories rose up: took my insulin injection, stabbing myself in a thigh permanently raddled with yellow and purple bruises. The pain was, as ever, a reliable distraction.

The next morning, I returned to the menagerie. Mr Vogel's cousin would be arriving in a few hours. I would then show my employer the bird and learn more about this mysterious treasure. In the meantime, even though cataloguing was no longer my responsibility, I wanted to locate the ledgers he had mentioned.

I found them in a forgotten corner, tucked beneath the scaly feet of an armadillo. Handsome things, leather-bound, with the dates embossed in gold on the spines, each spanning several years, running from the late fifties to 1883.

I opened an early one. The entries were all birds: white cockatoos, condors, egrets, bustards. I picked another, even earlier: canaries, only canaries, imported in their thousands as Mr Vogel had said. I was once again struck that while there were many birds in the menagerie, I had not seen a single canary. The records showed the date, the provenance (always Germany for the canaries), the collector, the duties paid, and the signature of the person who had received them. Some were by H. Vogel, but most were by C. Vogel. The brother. I wondered what their relationship had been like before Charles's betrayal.

I flicked through the other ledgers, flitting effortlessly through time. The goods slowly morphed, grew teeth. Lions, both of land and sea; wildcats, monkeys, a python. Even an elephant, which someone must have liked, because there was an exclamation mark beside its entry. Eventually I took up the final volume. The data was much the same as elsewhere, but in 1880, a new name appeared.

Hester, it said, the writing clear and confident. Taking its time, in contrast to the dashed scrawls elsewhere. *Hester Vogel.*

I regarded it for some time. Was this Charles Vogel's wife? The one who had killed herself, the treasure vanishing with her? In the middle of the following year, her name gave way to another, which I could not read, though it seemed a man's. Then, less than a twelve-month later, the entries ended entirely. The remaining pages were blank.

A knock – the door opened before I could answer, and a young man flooded in like so much sunlight. I took him in, my expression unchanging: he was tall and fair-haired, handsome, with eyes a white-blue that glittered. I guessed him to be about my age. On his temple was a cut that looked unexpectedly fresh.

'Emily Blackwood.' He leaned easily against the doorway. His skin was bright and glabrous; other than that wound, he looked well fed, well bred, like a pedigree lamb. He held a wicker basket covered in cloth, as though he had just stepped from a mountain pasture. 'I brought you lunch.'

'Yves?' I noticed that his accent was rather thicker than his cousin's. More glottal. I could have spread it on toast.

He nodded lazily. 'Lynette tells me you are joining us on our treasure hunt.'

'Apparently. Although what that treasure is, no one has yet explained.'

'My uncle – I call him that – is most protective. So would you be if you had searched for something for fifty years.' A shadow skittered across his features. 'It is not so healthy. He should be out of doors.'

'You are close?'

'I come every summer.'

'And this winter.'

He did not blink. 'Yes. And this winter. As a child, I used to help him with his hunt. I thought it was a game, but now . . .' He broke off, hefting the basket. 'Come. I have a picnic.'

We stepped out into breezy sunshine, and he led me out of the castle, around the walls to the grassy edge of the cliff, where a blanket was already spread. I was uneasily conscious of the loch below, but showed nothing as Yves methodically laid out the food in neat lines, sausage, cheese and hard-boiled eggs.

44

'Army training,' he said, catching my gaze. 'Hard to shake.'

'No longer?'

He shook his head, deeper gold sweeping his features. 'I had a fit. Epilepsy.'

I was surprised: he seemed so uncannily healthy, well put together as though by a master craftsman. I would have said I was sorry, but I hated other people's apologies for my own disease.

'You can't help it.' He shrugged, rather violently, and I changed the subject. 'Your profession?'

'Teaching. Biology and the social sciences.'

'You are on your holidays?'

'No. I am taking some time out.' A lazy smile. 'Though you probably think we teachers have enough holiday already.'

'Not an easy job, I imagine.'

'Exactly. It is an important thing, to take the young minds and mould them.' His hands made a twisting motion. 'You are a scientist, my uncle said. There are so many ways that a mind can become poisoned, especially in this modern age.'

I told him of an English bishop who had proposed that all scientists stop their work until society had taken stock of its growing trove of knowledge and worked out what to do with it. He nodded approvingly.

'Ideas grow up like . . .' He sought for the word. '*Parasiten.*'

'Parasites.' A Greek word originally, meaning one who ate at another's table.

'Yes. It is important to root them out. To cultivate only the flower.'

I did not point out that several beautiful flowers were in fact parasites. Instead, I finished the cheese – it was delicious – and asked about Mr Vogel's family.

'They were rich German aristocrats in Hamburg. My mother remembers visiting their splendid house as a child.

45

But the father – my great-aunt's husband – he spent it all. Drink. His wife died of the grief. My uncle and his brother restored the family fortune years later, but she did not live to see it.'

'And then Charles took it away,' I said thoughtfully. 'Are you sure what you seek is in the castle?'

'Hester Vogel – Charles's wife – grew up here.' That firm hand I'd seen in the ledgers. I was right. 'After she died, they found an envelope in her rooms, addressed to Heinrich. The note inside had just one sentence.' He sat subtly straighter, reciting the next words like a child. '"The path to the treasure lies in Paradise."'

Paradise, or *Pàrras*. Interesting. It had been a long time since I'd thought in Gaelic. 'How did your uncle come to possess the castle?'

'When Hester died, it automatically passed to Charles. But when he vanished, the executors determined that it should go to my uncle. She had no other kin.'

'And some day it will be yours.'

'Yes.' He smiled slightly. 'Though if I were to live here, I would first find the monster.'

My brows raised.

'The monster of Pàrras. An old story, but you know how stories are. Like parasites, yes? Ask Lynette, she will tell you. They say that many years ago, on the summer solstice, a rival clan came to dinner. They were slaughtered. All except their leader.'

I nodded drily. 'Lynette may have mentioned it. What happened to the leader?'

'The residents had built a secret chamber years before. A hiding place, should they ever need it. They dragged him there and locked him in. Rumour says that he lies in that chamber still.'

'Rumour?'

46

'The room has never been found, if it ever existed. Of course, the villagers gossip. They say that as the clansman died, slowly, with neither food nor water, he swore he would exact revenge. They say that twice a year, at the solstice, he roams the castle, seeking to slake his terrible thirst.'

The solstice. Mr Vogel had said that when visted by the mysterious intruder, the groundskeeper had not entered the castle because of the storm, and because of the solstice. I had wondered at his mention of the latter.

'My uncle does not approve, of course, but every castle needs its ghost story.' He grinned, and the whiteness of his teeth was so immediate, so real, that the gloomy tale seemed ridiculous. He rose, brushing crumbs off him until he was as clean as before. 'I will go find my uncle. He can tell you all.'

While Yves was gone, I collected the bird in its glass box from my room, still wrapped in its protective cloth. I treated it like I did my tool belt, as a necessity I could not afford to lose. The habit had been reaffirmed after my father and I disembarked at Southampton, bird and all. I'd spent nearly the last of our money on someone to help with our luggage: my father was still a bear of a man, but the strength had vanished from his limbs, so it was me and our hired companion who struggled up the hill, past the threepenny stores and a pub where a crowd observed a man with a terrier and a caged rat; a cheer went up as he released both down an alleyway to whatever fate awaited. Not much further on was the long queue for the employment office, undulating down the street like a great snake with precious few ladders in sight. An unhelpful reminder of the precariousness of our position.

I left the porter and my father and spent the very last of our ready funds on a coach ticket. Returning, I found the porter on the floor. He had been knocked down and a trunk stolen – my trunk, which bore my name stamped in black ink.

I was furious, though of course it was not his fault. 'Did you see who did it?' I asked, helping him up. He was a thin, starved creature – I rather thought I could have knocked him down myself. He shook his head.

'Ah!' My father let out a shout of frustration, almost causing our assistant to collapse again, this time in fright. My anger instantly ebbed. My father hated his disability, though over time he seemed to bind it to him, if only to loathe it at closer quarters. I embarked on a search, combing the area in ever-widening circles as though the trunk were a plant. I found it thirty minutes later, dumped in an alleyway behind a fried-fish shop. Nothing had been taken, but it was an inauspicious start to our homecoming. The bird of paradise had never left my side, hidden away in a travelling case.

Yves entered, followed by Lynette, plump hands clutching an envelope. 'A letter for you, Miss Blackwood. A Daniel . . . Daniel something or other. I cannot read the surname.'

Yves watched as I took it.

'Thank you.' I didn't open it. Unpacking on my first night, I had discovered three letters I knew I had not put there, for the simple reason that I was avoiding them. I glared at them. One envelope bore the emblem of the Royal Geographical Society. The other two were from Daniel Loewe.

My father had been blind for approximately the same amount of time as I had been diabetic, but he'd soon learned there were other ways to see. His dream while we grew up had been for one of his daughters to become an RGS fellow. Restless on the ship from Australia, at his suggestion I had written up an account of the orchids of Papua and Guinea and sent it off to them in neither hope nor expectation. The RGS might no longer be closed to women, but it did not

48

mean they'd have any interest in a no-name botanist living in distant Australia. In any case, I knew the thinness of a rejection slip by now. I'd shoved the envelope down into the bag, where I could no longer see it.

As for the ones from Daniel, I'd stuffed them down even further, but it was too late: the three of us were before me, knee-deep in the trout stream, cool water pouring around our legs and light glittering in our eyes. My sister was laughing with that same cold sparkle; Daniel bent close to me as I probed the moss for secrets. I saw the fat trout he'd caught, flopping and gasping on the weedy bank until my twin bashed their heads in. Their scales shone up and down our arms and turned up in unexpected places for days afterwards.

That was the worst thing about memories – like lies, you never knew when they would catch you out.

I would not read the letter Lynette had handed me. It was not that I could not forgive him – he had done what he could. I really, truly did not mourn our lost comforts. What I hated was the shifting, shapeless mass that overhung my father and me, the gnawing worry for his future. The night before I left, after helping him to bed, I'd emptied more of the hidden bottle beneath the gramophone than I intended. Just as I was considering whether a better woman would attempt sleep, someone had knocked at the door.

It was Daniel. From the dark glaze of his eyes, I saw he was in a similar state, perhaps worse. That must have taken some doing. Harold had loved liquor but hated drunks, and as a youth, Daniel had been strongly encouraged to take alcohol to teach him how to handle it.

I'd been there shortly before Harold passed away. As night fell, I had his man Reynolds open the curtains and turn off the lights. Though the eyes of the man in the bed were closed, I hoped that somehow he could see the stars. I never told Daniel what his father had said to my sister and me some years previously, after Daniel had begun work at his father's business.

'He is too good-hearted.' He sounded sad. 'I have not brought him up correctly.'

We replied that surely a good-hearted adult was not a matter for disappointment. Harold snorted.

'Ha! To succeed in this life you need iron in your soul. Daniel does not have it. I have not smelted him properly – he is but half-made.'

Quietly I said, 'Surely kindness is not a weakness.' My sister elbowed me in the ribs.

'It is if one cannot afford it. The City will either be the making or the breaking of him. I fear it is the latter.' He exhaled, a long, rattling breath. 'Look after him, you two. Please.'

As I regarded the man who stood drunk before me, I thought that Harold might have been right. Daniel tapped my nose with unusual levity. 'You have been avoiding me.'

It was the first time we had touched since my return, other than that crushed embrace in his office. Before I could snap at him, he'd ducked past, through the cramped hall and into the sitting room.

'Oh *Em*,' he breathed. I winced. I hadn't allowed him to the cottage before. Suffice to say it made me glad of my father's blindness.

Daniel pressed his fingers into his eyes, then turned to me.

'Don't,' was all I said. I knew that he was about to plead with me to bring my father to Butterworth, that he would share with us every remaining scrap. I knew equally that I could never allow that to happen. I pressed past and scooped up the gin, passing him a glass before he could speak again. He took it. I chinked mine to his, and whether it was that familiar motion, or the hissing of the ice, or the gossamer swirl of the Noilly Prat, the walls retreated. For the remainder of the bottle we swapped stories as though we were just two friends, I of the jungle, he of the funds, cackling at the absurdity of each.

When the last drops had disappeared, the room grown kind and smeary, it felt natural for his hand to wrap round mine and help me up. I was as tall as he and found myself meeting his eyes. There was a . . . a shock between us, and suddenly I was not in that miserable living room, so lately grown warm and alive, but in a greenhouse seven years previously, sun glowing through the misted panes.

'Good night, Daniel,' I said quietly, taking my hand away. He stared at me for three heartbeats, then departed.

He came again the next morning to say goodbye. A mistake, we both knew it. My tongue felt several inches thicker, as though I had chewed dumb cane, and it was not because of the gin.

Tap, tap. I heard Mr Vogel's cane on the flagstones a few seconds before he entered.

'Yves. When did you arrive?'

'Two hours ago. I did not wish to disturb your work.'

What work? I wondered as they embraced – familiarly, yet I saw Yves was avoiding his cousin's eyes. Mr Vogel gripped him on his shoulders, and though I could not hear, I read the words on his lips.

We will talk later.

Yves, it seemed, was in trouble.

Mr Vogel's attention turned to me. 'You have it?'

I gestured to the covered shape, shadowy in the light of a single paraffin lamp. He approached it quickly, eyes shining. Before he could lay a hand upon the cloth, I said, 'Before we go further, I insist you tell me the nature of the treasure.'

He frowned, but stopped his approach, passing his left hand across his face. 'The item my brother took . . . it is a diamond. A diamond of rare size and quality.'

A diamond! Even the meanest stone could assist with my father's care.

'I will find it,' I said seriously. Then, as he resumed his approach, 'We must also agree on my reward.'

His eyes darkened. 'Reward?'

'You appointed me for a run-of-the-mill cataloguing position. You cannot expect me to trace this item for the same rate.'

'I shall extend your salary to cover the period of your work, of course. The rate itself is already generous.'

I smiled grimly. 'Then I would expect an arrangement regarding something you have sought for fifty years to be even more so. You are to sell the diamond, I presume? Then I suggest a finder's fee of fifty per cent.'

He emitted a bark of laughter. 'Ten.'

I toyed with the corner of the bird's cloth, watching how his eyes flew to it. 'I cannot imagine that I am the first seeker you have brought in. Evidently they have failed. If I can track a flower the size of my thumbnail in the desert, I can certainly find your treasure in a castle. Forty.'

'Twenty-five.'

I did not hesitate. 'Done.'

We smiled faintly at one another. I ought to have wondered then how easy it was to persuade him.

He did not move towards the bird again. 'I have some stipulations of my own. Now you are let in on our secret, you cannot tell anyone. Not a soul. I cannot risk others trying to find the diamond.'

I promised I would not.

'Second, I must insist that you do not leave Pàrras until it is found.'

'I beg your pardon?'

'I cannot have you locating the stone and spiriting it from here.'

'Mr Vogel, I will not become your prisoner.'

He spread his hands theatrically. 'Who is a prisoner? You may still go to the village, walk the hills as you please. Yves shall accompany you.'

'I cannot agree to indefinite confinement.'

'Then let us say . . . the summer solstice. Eight weeks from now. At which point, should the stone *not* be located, you will be permitted to leave.' A wry smile. 'After a thorough search of your person and possessions.'

It was a long time to leave my father in his reduced circumstances. My heart cracked to think of him alone in that cottage, which the landlady had equipped with little more than dust and slimy satin cushions. Still, if this diamond could change that – not for a few weeks or months, but permanently . . .

'All right,' I said.

'Good. Now, if you would not mind . . .' He motioned towards the box. Behind him, Yves leaned forward, his casualness gone.

'Ready?' I asked.

Mr Vogel gave a half-smile. 'These five decades.'

Like a magician, I whisked the cloth away.

'Ah . . .' He bent forward until his nose nearly touched the glass; then, without looking, he located the catch with the practised nature of one who had either done it many times or imagined himself doing so. Gently he prised the bird from its fastenings, lifted it out and turned it over in his hands. Some deep-held emotion rippled across his face.

Eventually, reluctantly, he passed it to Yves. 'Run it through your machine. Be *careful*.'

'What machine?'

But Yves had already gone. Flushed, Mr Vogel paced back and forth, fingers moving inside his jacket pocket as though seeking comfort.

'Do you have siblings, Miss Blackwood?'

There was no right answer to this question. 'No.'

'Then perhaps you will not understand. I knew my brother as well as I knew myself. Better. Those early years, as young men – boys, really – alone in a tenement in New York, we went through things we never shared with anyone, never. Perhaps you doubt that the diamond is here. But I *know* it is, Miss Blackwood, through that connection with my brother. I feel it just as you feel a piece of grit in your eye, even though you cannot see it.'

'Did you ever speak to the police?'

'No.' His voice was steely. 'No police.'

'Yves told me about your sister-in-law's note. It sounds . . . ambiguous.'

His eyelids fluttered. 'I would not spend decades on an ambiguity. You know about that mysterious visitor. After their departure, nothing seemed to have changed. Except one thing. They had left something on the table in the great hall.'

'What was it?'

'It was a book.'

Yves reappeared, breathless, bird in hand.

'What did you do?' I demanded, at the same time as Mr Vogel said, 'Well?'

'There is something, Uncle. It flashed up on the X-ray. Clear as anything.'

X-ray? I thought, even as Mr Vogel's chest heaved. 'Bring it, boy, quickly. And fetch a knife.'

I withdrew mine from my tool belt: he snatched it without comment, eyes never leaving the creature. Yves set the bird on the table and Mr Vogel approached, wielding the knife like a surgeon.

'Where?'

Yves pointed to the right side of its breast.

Slowly, with trembling fingers, Mr Vogel laid the blade against the feathers. I watched, glad that I had already negotiated my commission. It looked as though my search would be over before it had begun.

With a faint tearing sound, the blade sliced into the bird's delicate breast. It felt barbaric. The knife went in – but no further. It had hit something hard.

Mr Vogel's breathing quickened, but he kept himself together, widening the incision until he had cut a hole around the hidden thing. Then he reached in – probed, grasped – and pulled it free. Yves let out a shout; I gasped. Slow triumph spread across Mr Vogel's face.

It was a diamond.

CHAPTER SEVEN

It was beautiful, it really was. About the size and shape of a gobstopper, it nestled snugly in Mr Vogel's palm. I would never forget his expression then: that of a man who was finally free.

'I don't believe it,' Yves whispered. He snatched up the paraffin lamp. 'Let me see it, Uncle.'

Mr Vogel did not appear to hear him. He was gazing lovingly at the diamond. I watched as Yves approached with the lamp, light leaking across the stone's multifaceted surface . . .

Which failed to sparkle. I frowned, tilting my head, waiting for it to catch fire in the illumination. But it remained flat and dull. Mr Vogel apparently had the same thought: scrubbing it against his sleeve, he held it up again, twisting it back and forth, brandishing it like a talisman. Nothing.

'Uncle.' Yves' voice was low and desperate. Slowly Mr Vogel raised the stone to his mouth. I had the bizarre impression that he was going to kiss it, and he did indeed press it to his top lip. Then I remembered the old test. A real diamond remains icy to the touch. A fake one, on the other hand . . .

'Warm,' he whispered, his face ghastly. A rat shoved back into its cage.

The energy, the life went out of my employer: the salesman with all his possibilities disappeared, and in his place was only an old man, bent, finite. He left us, taking the counterfeit with him.

Paste. The diamond was nothing but paste.

'Best to leave him for now.' Yves returned the bird to its box, its tail washing up against the glass like firewater. Strange to have one's hopes dashed by something so beautiful.

'Where are you taking it?' I asked as he picked it up.

'To the kitchen. Give Lynette something to look at. In the meantime, you must help my uncle.'

'You have an X-ray?' I said, ignoring this last.

'I have a laboratory above the library. A few years ago I installed an X-ray machine.'

'Why?'

'To examine the castle's contents. See if we had missed anything.' He hesitated. 'Actually, at first it was for my uncle. He . . . he gets unwell sometimes. He was convinced that part of him was not right.'

'A sickness?'

'Not exactly. He thought there was a hollowness, in here.' He gestured vaguely at his own chest. 'I set up the machine to show him that this was not the case.'

'Why not go to the doctor?'

'He hates leaving here. And doctors, for that matter.'

I nodded. 'Why was he angry with you earlier?'

'Uncle thinks a life is not properly lived unless it is done like a veal calf. Hidden away. I say that life is for the opposite. It is for the outside, for the big movements. And that we Germans *eat* veal calves.'

The malapropism was oddly endearing. 'It is good of him to hunt so hard for you.'

'Hmm. He wants the stone found before he is dead because otherwise he shall never rest. He does not like that life is the one possession he will be forced to yield.'

'He told me of his theory. When *does* he think he will die?'

'The summer solstice. Why else do you think he chose that deadline for your work?'

'But that's just a couple of months away.'

'Don't worry. I know you shall find it.'

'How can you be so sure?'

Yves smiled. 'Because Lynette tells me he believes you have something to hide. And the best hiders make the best seekers.'

'Blueprints,' Mr Vogel said the next day, unrolling a parchment of extreme age. I examined him carefully, but there were no signs of yesterday's crushing disappointment. He had wiped away its traces entirely.

I on the other hand had hardly slept, bad dreams bubbling up from beneath. My father once bought a pressure cooker for mountaineering expeditions. (The lower boiling point at altitude otherwise meant longer cooking times.) He brought it on Alpine trips, taken with the daughter he could still stand to look at after his wife's death. The lid would begin to quiver, then judder, and just when you thought the whole thing would explode, he'd calmly turn a screw and it would subside again.

Lacking screws, I used gin to freeze my anger, my guilt. The lemon was still there when I awoke, half-cut, its insides gone pearly overnight.

Tiredly I gazed at the blueprints, the castle's insides spread before me like one of Lord Rothschild's butterflies. *The path to the treasure lies in Paradise.* Would Pàrras really surrender its secrets?

'I will do my very best,' I told Mr Vogel, 'But really, the success of this enterprise will come down to luck.'

'Luck, Miss Blackwood? I think not. It is not *luck* at work here. It is fate.'

I began in the great hall. Under Mr Vogel's sharp eyes and Yves' curious ones, I divided the room into a grid and started to go over it with a fine-tooth comb. Every piece of wall and floor would be searched for hidden openings, every item of furniture inspected for hollow parts or other irregularities. I opened every drawer of an antique cabinet: a dusty hip flask, a whole drawer of corks, a ring of wire, twisted round a finger in an idle moment. I cracked open the door of the grandfather clock, clutching its pendulum briefly. My hands were soon thick with dust, leaving ghostly prints.

The first day ended without result, and the second. But I was settling into a rhythm. Mr Vogel was right: I *was* good at my job, and this hunt was not so different to my usual work for the University of Sydney, or Kew, or any of the other institutions for which I had collected. I hummed as I pushed a tapestry aside, pressing my knife lightly into the mortar behind it.

As I worked my way around the hall, I learned that my employer kept to a strict routine. He slept little and arose early, breakfasting on oatcakes and kippers. Then he returned to his rooms, where Lynette told me he tended to a private collection of creatures. Lynette herself was mostly in the kitchen, cooking up whatever it was the delivery boy brought on his bicycle. Always there were steams and smells emanating, suffusing the stones. I had wondered whether her injury stemmed from a cooking accident, but before dinner one evening, Mr Vogel, without giving specifics, told me that her fisherman husband had beaten her two decades ago and thrown her out. He had offered her a position and she had been at Pàrras ever since. She worked very hard for him, that slavishness I had seen on the first night never quite disappearing.

To my surprise, she also turned out to be a capable taxidermist. Mr Vogel had her going through the menagerie, keeping it as good as new, or nearly so. On my fifth afternoon, entering the kitchen to grab a cheese sandwich, I watched her plump white fingers tuck into a kingfisher's feathers with a farming needle.

'Mr Vogel taught me,' she said in response to my compliments of her skill. 'It was he who formed this collection in the first place. Twenty-four years it took him. I would swear he never looked up until it was done.'

'What about the embroidery on his clothing?'

'Also his own doing.' She nodded approvingly at my impressed expression, then told me that another treasure seeker had come the previous year, a widow called Phyllis Briggs.

'She stayed in your tower. The one with the rose finial.' The iron ornaments that topped the roofs. 'Each one is different. Pineapple, thistle, mistletoe, rose, heather. Your room was the old mistress's childhood bedroom, you know.' Her needle pressed into the feathers. 'Hester Vogel.'

'But Phyllis Briggs found nothing?'

'No.' The needle came out again, and before I could ask more, she had embarked on yet another tale of clannish atrocity, her cheeks growing pink with pleasure. I wondered again at this latent ferociousness, then considered that, had I had a violent husband, I might feel the same.

At one o'clock, Mr Vogel lunched. Fish again, this time the haddock soup known as Cullen skink. Interesting that a German, then American, had so thoroughly absorbed Scottish habits. Like a chameleon. Then he returned to his rooms again, this time for a siesta, followed by a walk around the castle walls. He completed this circuit exactly three times, then retired to the low sitting room for tea.

I found him here after discovering a loose flagstone, and invited him to the great hall to watch its disinterment. He was reading when I interrupted, the pile of books beside him diverse: works of anthropology and zoology in far-flung territories alternating with practical books on craftsmanship and embroidery. In the weeks to come, these brisk modern works would give way to peculiar musty things on folklore, witchcraft and other fancies. I never saw him with a novel.

There was much excitement as I dug up the flagstone, Yves helping me drag it aside under Mr Vogel's scrutiny. But beneath it was only dust and the slender bones of a small animal.

Disappointed, I finished with the great hall and turned to the cellars, which I guessed would take four days. These reminded me of Poe's Amontillado, and I had to scold myself for being silly. No one was going to bury me alive. Mr Vogel sometimes came down to watch as I ferreted around dusty corners or pored over the blueprints, hunting for irregularities. Despite the disappointment of the paste diamond, he was always genial, occasionally interrupting to ask about this or that point of interest, or about a previous expedition. He took a great interest in my work, and it was difficult not to be flattered. Still, he always knew the exact moment at which his presence began to intrude, at which point he would retreat to his own rooms. By now, I knew these to be in the western tower.

By contrast, Yves quickly lost interest in my activities, busying himself in his laboratory or out on the moors. I bumped into him outside the gun room one morning and discovered he was stalking deer.

Despite the hard work, I almost felt I was on holiday. I'd forgotten the summer light in Scotland, so different to the butterscotch of England or the heavy mead of the tropics, washing the air with a fresh primary brightness. That first week I wrote cheerfully vague letters to my father – though not to Daniel – hoping the village woman could read them to him. I missed our rituals. In Sydney, he had a little room that he called his spirit house – so named because of all his specimens and concoctions in jars. One could not spend too long there: the fumes of the preserving alcohol induced light-headedness. I sometimes stored plants there, but most were his, collected over the decades. He knew exactly where every specimen was, and under his direction I would check each one, taking notes, topping up the alcohol where needed, or monitoring the progress of the essential botanical oils he made. Since completing my doctorate, we both of us knew that I no longer needed his instructions. We'd kept on anyway.

Sunday was my day off, a welcome break amid long hours in the gloomy cellars. At breakfast, Yves caught my eye over the coffee pot and we made a plan to go to the village, which I had not yet visited. Good. As I had told Mr Vogel, I would not play prisoner.

'It is not much,' he warned as we set off across the causeway. The tide was lowering: we had a few hours to make the three miles there and back. In spring, Yves said, the causeway was often drowned for days and they had to use the boat.

'What about when the storms come?'

'We wait. And hope that we do not run out of milk.'

It was a fishing village, and true to Yves' word, it wasn't much. Boats clustered in the harbour, beside a large patch of waste ground. The few people around were either much too fat or much too thin. We passed a couple of shops selling cough mixtures and cheap furniture, and entered a single, empty café whose proprietor apparently did not appreciate our disturbing his solitude. We drained our tea and left: immediately it began to rain. Yves swore quietly in German.

'I'm not going back to that café,' I said.

He grinned. 'The church, then.'

Before I could protest, he had taken my hand and pulled me along. It wasn't far, beside a village hall threatening bingo every Tuesday.

The church was quiet, and cold compared to the warmth of his hand. I released it and we stood in the gloom, listening to the rain. I exhaled sharply.

'What is wrong?'

'Nothing.' I walked distractedly down the aisle. It had been a long, long time since I'd set foot in a church. There were flowers, half dead, excessive for such a small place. A recent wedding, or a funeral.

Yves seemed quite comfortable. He inspected the brass eagle supporting the Bible, then sat in the front pew, flinging his close-cropped head back to gaze at the ceiling. I briefly surveyed the gold of his throat. Strange to think that he might at any moment have an epileptic fit. If he did so in here, it would probably be taken as a sign – possession, either divine or malignant. I liked him for the unexpected flaw, like the painter's fingerprint visible on a work of art, even if I agreed with his unspoken view. It would be better to be perfect.

The rain kept relentlessly on, water pouring down the glazed saints' cheeks. A stained Eve held out a fruit to Adam, each apparently heedless of the serpent coiling up the branch behind. Old stories. Old gods. Once, in the jungle, I'd found what I thought was a temple. Just a few stones tumbled about, swallowed by tangling vines and enormous roots. That was what I liked about plants. They kept your secrets – unlike religion, which sought to expose them.

'I always hated church,' I said suddenly.

'So did I,' Yves said, standing up. 'All that rubbish about sin. There is no such thing. Only weakness.'

63

He began to prowl the perimeter, pausing to read this or that inscription, fingering the wax of an extinguished candle, and all the while nearing a door in the corner of my eye – a door that I knew instinctively would lead to the bell tower. I could not stop the memory sounding in my head, its echoes tolling through my very being.

It's a hot summer's day, seven years ago, the day my life comes crashing down for a second time. The flies have pursued us, Emma and Emily, drifting down the lanes, past the fat slow-worms lolling in the hedgerows, the air like warm wine. Hot and irritable, we seek the refuge of the church, where our father is preparing that week's sermon; as we come up the path, we hear him declaiming to the empty pews. The sun beats upon our shoulders and the old yew tree, bent and exhausted, stoops over the church door as though it would bar our way.

Inside is dark and mercifully cool. The only time I ever feel religion's clemency. One of us dips a hand in the font, red hair flaring in the gloom. 'Don't do that,' our father says irritably, though his expression alters when he sees which of us is the culprit. Even when not behind the pulpit, his voice always resounds with the same enriched solemnity, as though God himself is listening.

'It's too hot,' my sister says. 'Let's go on the roof.'

The church tower was constructed sometime in the fifteenth century. The great bell is still there, its name long forgotten, reached by ladders ascending through layers of ancient wooden scaffold. We have not been up in years.

We go together now, the three of us utterly unaware of the danger. There are five ladders, each one rising to a rickety floor that supports the next, the huge bell hanging above like a sword. In the sunbeams piercing the occasional slit, I can just make out my father and sister's dusty footprints as

I make my way up behind them. Where the light hits, the stonework is worn and crumbling.

My sister makes the summit first and tries to bring down the lead-covered trapdoor that opens onto the roof. I hear a curse – the Lord's name, taken in vain – and a gentle reprimand, along with the faint dragging of my father's leg. Shrapnel.

I reach the last scaffold, and here is the bell, a huge smooth alien back, as though a whale has flung itself down from heaven. My father and sister are at the opposite wall, a thin plank reaching between us, laid alongside the bell's wheel. My father moves past my sister towards the trapdoor. And it seems to me that those toothy wheels suddenly move in response, welcoming us, and the great bell starts to toll all on its own, a huge noise, an infinite noise, beginning in the belly and filling the lungs and throat, a sound beyond mere hearing. As my father and sister turn to look, the scaffold on which they are standing simply dissolves, as though we have been imagining it all along, this floor and the one below it and the one below that. My world crumbles away, and as they fall, I leap forward without even thinking, until there is only me, cocooned within that wrecking ball of sound, clinging to the back of this metal leviathan.

Then it falls too, and I crash down with it.

When I eventually awaken, I feel nothing but pain, see nothing but a long tail of red hair streaking in the rubble. Like a comet brought to earth.

In the village, they hear the peals and think there is a wedding.

'Miss Blackwood?' Yves was closer than I had realised, watching me.

I gathered myself. 'Call me Emily. Emmy.'

His mouth lifted. 'Emmy. It has stopped raining.'

We went outside again, walking along the small harbour:

a boat had come in, and we watched the fishermen unload their catch. A shack sold whelks and clams.

'You should come stalking,' Yves said suddenly. 'On the moors. With me. Can you shoot?'

I had carried a pistol on my expeditions ever since my Australian professor had advised me to when exploring the interior. The trackless wastes hoarded the bones of many men. It wasn't a desert, but an ocean, old and deep. There were even boats marooned out there, the only survivors of hopeless searches for an inland sea. I told the professor that I would have to practise if I wanted to hit a rabbit or a snake.

It is not for the animals, he said. It is for you.

There were worse things than dying; the living death of extreme thirst was one. I'd read of those unfortunate men who crawled out of the desert with their lips withered, black chunks for noses, the skin sucked against every bone.

Yves began to tell me about stalking. It seemed considerably different to hunting plants, I thought, as he described positioning himself downwind, crawling on his knees through bogs and stream beds. You did not need to sneak up on vegetable matter. Nor did you need to kill the object sought in order to claim it.

What was I doing here? I was neither a stalker nor a treasure hunter. I was a botanist. Was this really the best way of providing for my father, chasing an unlikely gemstone hundreds of miles away? My singleness of focus suddenly unspooled.

Perhaps Yves guessed something of my thoughts, because he stopped speaking. Gently he laid a hand against the middle of my back, as though to usher me through a door that wasn't there; I surprised myself by not moving away. We stood like this for a long time, gazing wordlessly out to sea.

CHAPTER EIGHT

Quite naturally, I began spending more time with Yves. We slipped into a routine, spending our mornings at our separate pursuits – I learned that he was studying part-time for a doctorate – then meeting at lunchtime. He'd purloin sandwiches from Lynette and we'd sit out in the courtyard, or above the loch. We did not visit the village again, instead walking around the castle walls in the manner of Mr Vogel, the stone warm to the touch. I hardly noticed the ebbing of my desire to leave the island and its encircling sea.

One evening in the third week, after Mr Vogel and Lynette had retired, we found ourselves alone and by unspoken agreement moved to the low sitting room and its armchairs by the fire.

'Whisky?' he asked.

'I didn't think you drank.' I had never seen him with alcohol at mealtimes.

'My uncle doesn't.' He opened a small cabinet. It was empty. 'Watch this.'

He jimmied the back and the wooden panel came away in his hands. Behind it were several amber bottles. I smiled. It was so nearly similar to the gin in my gramophone cupboard.

'You're lucky I haven't searched this room yet.' I made a mental note to be extra thorough with the Pàrras cabinets.

He smiled back. 'I found it when I was younger, helping my uncle with the hunt. I used it to store marbles at first.'

'He doesn't like alcohol?'

'He hates losing control.'

And yet . . . just as my father had discovered other kinds of sight, there were other breeds of intoxication. Twenty-four years Mr Vogel had spent creating his taxidermy collection. Stripping life back to its bones, rebuilding it again. What did that do to a person? He'd spent even longer searching for the diamond. I sighed, taking a long gulp from the glass Yves had given me. What were my own chances of finding it?

'Your hair,' he said. 'Has it always been that colour?'

'We were blonde at first. It ripened over time.'

'We?'

I flushed. It had slipped out. 'My twin and I.'

'I did not know you were a twin.'

'She died.'

I realised my glass was already empty. He leaned across and took it from me, his hand momentarily wrapping around mine.

'I do not think we want one another's pity,' he said softly. 'But I am sorry all the same.'

We said no more after that, only stared into the fire and drank. It could have been a desolate scene, but instead I felt myself growing warm, as a forest fern uncurls in the sunshine.

There were two ways to extract a secret from someone: with force, or with understanding. From necessity, I'd tried to render myself impervious to both. Which method would prove best against Pàrras? Yves and his uncle had tried ransacking the place. They'd found nothing, beyond a convenient hiding place for whisky. If I were to succeed, I needed to find a different way.

'Yves?'

'Yes, Emmy?'

'What was the book left on the table?' At his frown, I clarified, 'The one Mr Vogel said was left by Charles the night he entered the castle.'

'Oh, that. I can't remember. It was a mouldy old thing. Why?'

'Can I take a look?'

Yves' room was directly below mine. We ascended the tower together: I was conscious of the whisper of stone on my shoulder, Yves' eyes on my back. I waited outside while he found the book. I'd thought it would be in the library – from the blueprints I had seen, this took up much of the eastern tower, though I hadn't yet visited. But his uncle did not like to see it there, Yves said as he emerged onto the tiny landing and pushed a book into my hands. I brought it up between us, though there was barely space to do even that: it was thin and aged, bound in morocco.

'Thank you.'

'Perhaps it is not wise to let my uncle see you with it.' His eyes met mine. 'Our little secret.'

I went up the vanishing stairs, my back painted with his gaze.

The hour was late, but the bedroom wasn't dark, not yet. I threw myself onto the bed and looked at the book's cover. The title was stamped in gold.

THE BIRDCAGE LIBRARY.

The third indication that Mr Vogel had mentioned of Charles's presence at Pàrras. He had dismissed it, but here in my hands it possessed a weight that went beyond its simple mass. My fingers tingled as I brushed them over the letters.

Below the title was the author's name. Herman Millar. I had never heard of him.

I opened it. It was a first edition, dated fifty-one years previously. On the frontispiece was a printed sketch of a cage; within this, in green ink, someone had doodled a bird with some hills behind. The next page was a chapter list.

Crossing the Line – An Introduction
Styles
Empty Cages
Antiques
New Cages

I turned to the introduction.

Crossing the Line

In recent years, cage birds have developed a marvellous hold among the general public. It has been wonderful to see the usual canaries and finches become an entry-point into a whole universe of brilliant captives. It was Audubon who first mapped our country's avian treasures, and he would have marvelled at the breadth of species available to-day to even the most disinterested collector. Such popularity is entirely logical, for who can fail to be moved by the simple twitterings of a parlour bird?

But a good bird is worthy of a good cage, and hence this little book has been formed. I flatter myself that the cage-maker is as important to the trade as the breeder or dealer, for the cage may be just as vital to their song as the provision of wholesome food and water. I have observed, for instance, that canaries prefer an enclosure of twelve inches by twelve inches, any larger being detrimental to its song, and any smaller deleterious to its health. All keepers ought to pay sufficient attention to management, for to supply our delight, these charming creatures must become our prisoners!

This compendium, however, is principally concerned not with the practicalities of bird-keeping, but with Beauty. The fancier naturally wishes to care for their pretty warbler and ensure its safe confinement; yet with a little thought, a birdcage can make for an exceptionally splendid prison. Therefore I beg the wise purchaser to consider the ornament as much as the enclosure and address himself to the display of beauty as much as its incarceration. He must place himself equally inside the cage and out of it. This I call CROSSING THE LINE. After all, we do not keep our songbirds in a box! The natural airiness of a cage is intentional, and indeed some very brilliant designs have been manufactured which shall never hold an inhabitant, being unsuitably ornate or delicate for the task.

I have worked long in the making of cages; and I trust the good name of MILLAR & CO. is not unknown to the enthusiast. Over the years, when a particular design and model has taken my fancy, I have kept a specimen for myself, and it is these designs that make up the contents of my BIRDCAGE LIBRARY. It is my intention to enumerate various styles of cage, their role in history, the principal considerations of their design, and their varying advantages. The examples shown have been chosen according to taste and fancy . . .

It went on for several more pages. I flicked to the main chapters. There were many drawings of cages, some technical, others decorative, many fantastically shaped: palaces, domes, pagodas, even a church. Some more resembled doll's houses than cages: 'perfect for the winged gentleman', the writer said.

71

Why had Charles left this in the castle?

My insulin was overdue. I jabbed myself, then made myself a gin martini. There was a small cut on my finger from my searches, and the juice of the lemon stung. I had no ice, but it would do.

In vino veritas.

The sun still nudged just above the horizon, reluctant to depart. I thought of the supposed ghost. The summer solstice, with its sliver of dark, seemed a strange time of year for a haunting. But perhaps it was not the creatures of night that were most terrifying – at least with those you knew that day would come. Worse, perhaps, were the monsters that rose while the sun was high.

I drank another glass and picked up the book again, my fingers by now rather clumsy. It opened again on the frontispiece, with the bird and the hills drawn within the cage. By whose hand? Charles's? I peered at it. The cage was not so magnificent as the ones in later pages. Just a classical dome. With the hills inked in, it looked almost like a window.

I glanced up involuntarily at my own window. It was the exact same silhouette as the cage. And the hills beyond . . . I held up the drawing. The hills were the same shape. Yet this window was not mine at all, but Hester Vogel's, from her childhood.

Had it not been for the gin, I would likely have ignored the coincidence. But with alcohol, different things seemed possible, which was of course exactly why I drank it. Rather woozily, I went to the window, bringing the book. There was no doubt about it. The hills were the same, pinching into that deep crevice where the loch met the sea.

A woman dead by her own hand; her husband fled; a brother left behind. And a book. Had Hester drawn this? If so, was it a simple doodle of a childhood memory, or something more?

72

Mr Vogel saw fate at work; I saw people, and long-held secrets. A trap, or a trail, or perhaps both.

I scrutinised the page again. The bird perched on a thin green shelf of ink. Almost like a window ledge.

I opened the window – the cold evening entered, an intruder awaiting opportunity – and inspected it. The frame seemed ordinary, though the old white paint was cracked, the glass ancient and warped in places. I ran my fingers down each side of the wood: nothing, though of course I had no idea what I was looking for. I did the same along the sill, absently wondering about a third martini.

A sharp pain made me stop. The small cut in my finger had snagged on something. I tugged the skin away, wincing, and bent to look. A smear of blood had appeared, staining the paint – no, whitewash, a thin veneer of it.

I rubbed at it, careful not to snag myself again. In its place appeared the head of a nail.

All thoughts of gin fled. The nail had not been hammered flush into the sill – the whitewash had only made it appear so. Without its coating, it looked like a tiny lever, waiting to be pulled.

I sucked the wounded finger, which was trembling slightly. Then I went to the door, wedged a chair under the handle, returned to the window and pulled.

I watched what happened next in slow motion. The sill began to tremble. As I eased into it, the whitewash slowly flaked – then, in a long straight line, it *cracked*. No, not one line, but two, meeting each other in a thin rectangle that slowly rose, the wood sliding out of itself to reveal a slender tray-like drawer about the size of a book.

And there, nestled in the casement, was indeed a book.

It was thin and old – not even a book, really, just a roll of unbound pages, its words written firmly yet in haste. The ink was green.

CHAPTER NINE

The Account of Hester Vogel

Welcome, dear reader. You have found me, and I you. I am Hester Vogel, wife of Charles. You knew that already, I hope, though that is the trouble with laying a path: with all the planning in the world, one never knows who will walk it.

Yet this is more than a path: this is a treasure map. It will lead you to what you ought to seek. Like all such maps, the trail is cryptic. The reason for this is simple.

The man I love is trying to kill me.

The whipcrack has sounded; the circus is ready; the audience holds its breath. Now we enter the first act.

I was born in the room you find yourself in, to a woman who, as soon as she had recovered, was banished from Pàrras and forced to leave me behind. She was exiled by her own parents, who were precisely the kind of people one might expect to live in a frostbitten, wind-chilled castle – that is to say, frostbitten themselves, and cold to the core. My grandparents were furious when their daughter fell pregnant to a lowly cage-maker. They had ordered a cage made for a canary, presented to my mother as an eighteenth birthday gift. My father was invited into the castle; he set eyes on my mother over the cage, a simple bell model with an iron finial in the shape of spreading wings; fitting, since he thought he beheld an angel. A secret passion ensued. After I was born, my grandfather half destroyed the northern tower in his rage. He and his wife exiled my mother and my father. She would never see her home again.

The chilly pair raised me as they saw fit, which was to say in the Calvinist fashion: some were destined for grace, others for damnation, and as such people generally are, my grandparents were perfectly assured to which set they belonged. My own fate was more doubtful, given my conception; however, they attempted to ensure what they could. Perhaps they loved me, in their own fashion. But what a fashion! I was educated at home, fed on righteousness and porridge without sugar. I was not allowed to play with other children, and so spent long, long hours wandering around Pàrras, probing it for secrets. The only visitor I recall was my grandparents' lawyer, Richard Heatherwick, a kindly gentleman who had adored my mother and who, I discovered much later, offered to adopt me on several occasions, seeing Pàrras and its inhabitants as unfit to raise a child. In this he was only half correct, for the castle and its environs became my true and only friend. The dear aged stones, the hidden crannies, the gannets that plunged into the loch beyond the windows, and the secret paths of the lichen across the stones – they put romance in my soul, and a necessary hope, one day, for something different.

Then, when I was nine, my mother died. She and my

father had never been allowed to contact me. I think they tried when I was five or six; certainly I heard my grandfather shouting one night, and the castle door slam shut. Pàrras had been designed as a fortress, and it served its purpose admirably until my mother's death. My father came to inform my grandparents, and I entered to discover a man I had never seen before, calluses on his elegant fingers and a fire burning so coldly in his eyes that I gasped.

He took one look at me and told my grandparents that he was taking his daughter with him. And whether it was that cold fire, or the shock of their child's death, my grandparents for once did not protest. Nor did I. Here at last was something new. I did not hesitate.

It transpired that my parents had been living in New York, unable to bear any closer proximity to the daughter they had lost. I traversed the Atlantic with this stranger, and on that voyage I was able to examine that fire of his, to gaze into its heart and see that it was broken.

We arrived in New York, and from there set up in the little town of M—, north of Boston, which my father adjudged a better place to raise a child. He had a small business making his cages, and it was a relatively simple matter to re-establish the company there. I loved it immediately, and while he did sums and consulted ledgers, I ran about on the pale sand beaches beside that subtle green sea. I did not miss my grandparents; only Pàrras, and that only sometimes – there was so much novelty to enjoy. From my earliest days I wished to be an explorer, though naturally that was impossible. Playing at the border of infinity was the closest I could come. Perhaps because of my heritage, I have always loved the cold – I never feel it – and sometimes the winters were so vicious that the very waves would freeze. What a sight that was, the icy waters turned milky, billowing under themselves like unfurling silk.

My father and I grew closer with time; I came to love him deeply, and to mourn the time we had lost. When he was not working, he would play the pianoforte – he taught me also, but my fingers never equalled his, and indeed I preferred to act as his page turner. At other times he rolled up his trousers and we walked along the beach, his pipe tapping onto the sand, black ash mingling with the grains of white.

In later years, he often watched in amusement as I used my bathing machine. This I had built myself, using techniques learned through observation at the cage factory, and with the occasional assistance of Robert Odlum, an endlessly restless boy who shared my ambitions for adventure. We took up a whole corner of the workshop for some weeks, and were immensely proud of the result: a small wooden hut, rather crudely hewn and mounted on wheels. These I had cajoled my father's foreman, Mr Sullivan, into making for me, from as light a steel as was feasible.

This lightness was necessary, since while most such machines were drawn into the sea by a horse, protecting the swimmer from view as she entered the water, I insisted on self-sufficiency. Therefore I built a trapdoor into the hut's floor, and once in my costume, it was a simple matter to put my legs through the aperture and *walk* the thing down the beach. I named it *Pequod*, after the ship in Moby Dick, but the townspeople insisted on referring to it as 'Miss Millar's contraption', finding it exceedingly amusing. I suppose it must have looked rather ridiculous, as though the hut had grown feet. My father knew better than to laugh at me, but I would emerge from the machine to find his eyes twinkling all the same.

Gradually, thanks to several patented improvements, his small cage business grew. We moved to a larger home, this with a long, low room of oak, and it was here that my father began his collection of cages, taking this or that model from the factory and keeping it for his amusement – or rather, mine, since when I was not at the seaside, I thought it a marvellous game to play in that peculiar birdcage library all afternoon. There were the usual designs in the shapes of bells and boxes, but there were some in the Oriental style, others with twin peaks, and many that were more outlandish still. Germanic churches, Italian villas, Indian temples: to be in that library was to see the world. This will seem strange, but among those cages I tasted freedom.

Then, when I was eighteen, the war came and the view from the beach filled with long, lean ships. I had always wanted to go to sea, but it was my father who did so, boarding the *Albatross*, and certainly as I watched him sail away, I felt it around my neck. He was gone for months; months turned to a year, and no sign of his return. The pianoforte remained silent. Meanwhile, the army consumed more and more steel, and eventually it was stipulated that there should be nothing for birdcages at all.

The company faced ruin. I could not consult my father – the fighting was at its worst, letters were scarcely getting through, and I could not bear to add to his torments. Since his departure, I had taught myself book-keeping, after discovering that our foreman, Mr Sullivan, while greatly competent in operational matters, could barely tell the right side of a ledger from the left. But even without accountancy, it was painfully obvious that zero could come from zero.

Mr Sullivan quietly suggested that the time had come to release our staff from employment. We had some fifty, the bulk of them at this time necessarily women.

'You know as well as I do, Mr Sullivan, that we have nine widows.'

'Ten.' His voice was low. 'Mrs Williams heard yesterday.'

I closed my raw eyes briefly. 'Ten, then. What shall they do if I abandon them? I cannot give them up.'

He looked at me for a long time. 'Then what do you have to give?'

What indeed? I was nineteen years old, and I vowed then that I would give everything. Over the next few weeks, I began selling what few valuables my father and I possessed. The house emptied around me, even as the factory filled with creditors. Vultures, it seemed, did not only circle the battlefield. I grew so desperate that I wrote to my grandparents, pleading for assistance. But I received a reply from their lawyer, Richard, who wrote with the news that they had both passed away just the month before, my grandmother dying within weeks of my grandfather. Perhaps their hearts of stone had loved one another, if no one else. My mother being dead, I was the heir to Pàrras, though there was no money to it beyond the stones themselves. He enclosed the key. It saddened me more than I can say to instruct him to urgently find a buyer, and though he warned that a decaying Scottish castle was unlikely to attract a good sum, he promised to do so.

But no buyer was forthcoming, and at last there was only one thing left to sell: my mother's wedding ring. If I sold it, my father would never forgive me; if I did not, I would never forgive myself. I sat up all night on his bed, rolling its smooth circularity around my palm.

Then, as red dawn broke, my eye fell upon one of the letters scattered on the floor, which I had earlier hurled across the room in frustration and grief.

It was from one of the steel suppliers I had written to in desperation. Like all the rest, they said their metals were being diverted to the production of weaponry. Unlike the rest, they added in passing that their resources were also going to another business – just one other. That business, it said, was corsets.

It transpired that while the government had indeed confined steel supplies almost exclusively to armaments and other warmongering, they had made one curious exemption: its use in the manufacture of corsets was still permitted. War, it seemed, had brought freedom to our birds, but not to our women.

I did not care. I brought the idea to Mr Sullivan.

'Only think of it. A corset is not so different to a cage. The structure, and indeed the purpose, is largely the same. I do not think it would be a matter of much training. Nor do we require more than the smallest capital investment.'

I knew I was right – knew that I had found our only possible salvation. Mr Sullivan sweated, frowned and finally agreed.

When my father returned, three years after he had left, it was to a business that was thriving. I wrote to Richard in London to cancel the search for a buyer for Pàrras as soon as it was clear that we could survive; he wrote back saying that he was glad to hear it, with the surprising, touching addition that he had written me and any descendants into his will. On his death, his London residence would pass to me.

80

I never told my father how close we had come to ruin, and Mr Sullivan and the employees were similarly sworn to secrecy. My mother's ring, thank God, remained in my bureau.

He returned different. Perhaps it was the icy sea, or perhaps his blood ran cold at what he had seen, for like my mother's family, he came back frozen. With a heavy sense of inevitability, I had a quiet word with Mr Sullivan, which led to my agreeing to run the company until my father improved. The word 'until' stuck in my throat.

The next morning, I made the usual walk to my father's office. This time, however, the women had lined up on the factory floor to meet me, and as Mr Sullivan and I passed the silent rows, that same stuck feeling lodged in my throat. At the end of the line, beside the office door, was Mrs Williams. Our tenth widow – but not our last. She stepped out of the line.

'I know what you did for me – for us, Miss Millar,' she said quietly. 'We all do.'

I shook my head, a quick erasing stroke. 'It was nothing.'

She put out a hand and gripped my wrist; the contact was an electric shock. I could not remember the last time someone had touched me.

'No, miss. You acted for us, never for yourself. It was *not* nothing.'

I looked at her, then around, and saw how they were watching: young faces, powdered faces, old, whiskery faces. This unlikely workforce of women. This . . . this *family*.

'Thank you,' I said, my voice low and strangled. Then I fled into the office, the door clanging shut behind me.

'Well?' I heard Mr Sullivan demand gruffly outside. Grumbling cheerfully, they set to work.

I remained in that office for the next thirteen years, occupying my father's chair in every sense. The women and their machines chattered noisily outside, while I sat within, buried in accounts and silence. My father remained company director, but spent his days in his birdcage library. Slowly he began making cages again, brittle, awkward things with little of the elegance of his former creations. The corset company expanded, yet despite our success, I felt a growing constriction, as though whalebone had found its way into my heart.

It was the sea that saved me. Every morning, once the snows had gone, I would immerse myself and forget for a moment – oh, only a moment – what and where I was. I still used the bathing machine, though it needed upkeep that I had not time to give. The townspeople were accustomed to this peculiar habit by now, but the brittle men returned from war found it unappealing. After their bitter privations and horrors, they wanted only an easy life and a woman who would give it to them. If you should be a fellow spinster, dear reader, let me advise you: cold-water immersion is rarely the way to a man's heart.

But perhaps that last is incorrect, for in fact it was my own *Pequod* that occasioned my marriage. I arrived one morning as usual, and there he was, a stranger staring alternately at my machine and the sea. Behind us ran the white porticos of the houses and stores; it was a sunny August morning and nobody was around, unless one counted the gulls and terns swooping over the calm sea, which I always did. He was slender if not small, his clothes well made if not expensive. There was nothing obviously extraordinary about him, yet an intelligence in his eye, a focus in his demeanour made him as alien to that beach as a tiger.

'Does this machine belong to you?' With a thrill, I detected a foreign accent. European.

'Yes. I built it,' I said, lifting my chin in a manner that my father had always decried as an advertisement of stubbornness. (But surely it is better to be forewarned? I would say. My father's smiles were rare these days, but on occasion I could still trick one out, carrying its warmth for those days when the cold grew too much even for me.)

I expected him to tut or smirk, which were the two reactions of the so-called gentlemen in this town, but instead he was inspecting the hinges of its front door.

'These are not well fixed. I can find you better.'

'I do not need better.'

He frowned as if he did not understand my meaning.

'You are in the bathing-machine trade?' I ventured.

'No, but I often deal with cages. This is a sort of cage, is it not, to carry you into the sea?'

I had not thought of it so; the analogy nettled me. 'I doubt the women where you are from would see it that way.'

Yes, dear reader, I *was* fishing, and on that shore I landed my catch nicely.

He shrugged, not loosely, but a tight little motion. 'They do not have them where I am from. New York.'

New York! 'Do they not have the sea there? I must reprimand my geography books.'

Now it was his turn to be irritable. 'By any measure I have many dealings with the sea trade, madam—'

'Miss,' I said hastily. 'Miss Millar. You are in the cage business?'

'In a fashion. I import animals.'

'Animals!' Instantly I regretted the idiotic repetition. 'Of what sort?'

'Birds, mostly. Anything from the hummingbirds of Brazil to the paradise birds of British New Guinea.'

I was so lost in the romance of it that momentarily I could not speak, consumed by those long-ago dreams of adventure and newness: of high seas, empty skies, and above all, freedom. 'For what purpose?'

'Anybody who wishes a companion, be they gentle-women or bachelors.'

'You trade in loneliness?'

For the first time, he smiled slightly. '*There* is a business that shall never be out of fashion. But we also sell larger creatures, principally to showmen and circuses.'

'We?'

'My brother and I.' His hand moved in an odd, reflexive gesticulation. 'We have an emporium in Manhattan.'

'I should like to see it.' The words slipped out, but he accepted them with perfect naturalness.

'Then you must. My card.' He gave it to me. Then he tucked that hand neatly behind him, bowed, and walked away.

I watched him go. When he had quite disappeared (never once turning back), I looked at the card, which I paste for you here.

Charles Vogel & Brother
Purveyors of exotic creatures
Aardvarks to zebras. No animal too difficult to find

On the back was an address on Chatham Street.

Do you believe in magic? You may think me foolish,

84

but it is merely the word for the moment when the world draws aside a curtain you had not known was there. That was what my non-existent suitors never saw: it was magic I sought in the freezing sea, magic that numbed my head and sparked my veins and allowed me to tolerate living.

I had never been to New York, not since our first arrival, and my father refused to go. He had no wish to return to the city where his wife had died, but it was more than that. The war had not physically wounded him, but nor could I be sure it had not killed him. Above the living room mantelpiece was a stuffed great auk, a species now extinct. In the first months of his absence I began cheerfully greeting it when I returned to the empty house. As the months turned to years, the greetings became long conversations. I would ask the creature questions, and it responded with my father's voice. At times I tried to give it my mother's tones, but the ventriloquism would not stick, perhaps because I could not remember them, or perhaps because something in the bird's rather stubborn expression reconciled it irretrievably with the other parent.

The man who had returned from war now said very little, so I had resumed the conversations, albeit in the privacy of my own head. At some point I began to fancy that his spirit had actually entered the bird. That thought occasioned a particularly long sea session, but it proved hard to shake. And perhaps I was not entirely mistaken, for as the years went by, the livelier the dead bird became and the deader the live man seemed.

So my father could not go to New York, but nor could I travel so far unchaperoned. Why should I go at all? I was not in need of exotic creatures, let alone that most exotic of all – a husband. There were better

85

companions, more charming cages. But as I greeted the great auk after a day spent entirely alone in my little office, it occurred to me that while I might not require an aardvark, nor a zebra, there was a rare creature of which I was in desperate need – that most exquisite of treasures, a friend. Perhaps Charles Vogel did not wish to be my friend, but he was unlike anyone I had met in this nice dull town, and besides, I wished to be *his*; and wishing, as any good reader of fairy tales knows, is half the battle. I persuaded Mr Sullivan that we ought to attend a trade fair, and not a fortnight later, we set out together.

New York! I had been to Boston, that grande dame of a city, old before its time; but New York was different entirely, continually replenished in the same way that the sea is simultaneously ancient and new, a single hour heaving with as many people and languages as one might expect to see or hear elsewhere in a lifetime. Our omnibus pressed past oyster saloons and coffee houses, milliners' stores and cigar-makers. There was rubbish, rubbish everywhere, tea chests without tea, hats without crowns, and coal ashes spilling from earthenware jars as if in reminder of mortality, though I never saw a city less requiring such prompting. Every fellow rushed along as though the Reaper himself were in hot pursuit. The ladies carried silver-topped vials of smelling salts, Englishmen went about their exclusive business, and I heard a ruddy German talking ruefully of the East River brothels, equipped with trapdoors to roll troublemakers into the waters. The whole world, in short, was here. I had been wondering where it was.

Mr Sullivan and I went to the corset-maker fair and exclaimed over the new improvements and the manne-quins in the latest styles. It was not wholly a spurious visit. I was becoming concerned about the company. The new loom-woven, ready-to-wear methods had arrived, and our competitors everywhere had already taken them up. We needed to invest. 'It is the future,' I had told my father, expecting the usual disinterested nod and 'You know best, child.' But this time he had actually refused me. Millar & Co. was what it was, he said; it was a mark of quality; he saw no reason to change. Mr Sullivan and I hoped to learn more here to sway him, though the foreman, a man of gloomy countenance in any case, only gloomed deeper at the sight of all this inexpensive modernity. After several hours, I suggested we repair elsewhere, and led him up the crowded Bowery towards Chatham Street.

There it was: Vogel & Brother. The emporium was painted black, its name embossed in neat gold. The only hint of the wonders within was a solitary cage in the window, in which fluttered a single canary. It was only a very slight way off the Bowery, yet as I approached, the street noise fell away. Without time for hesitation, I went inside, the bell chirruping in welcome.

Words cannot express the feelings that arose at the sight therein. So little in adulthood gives rise to wonder: we scarcely know the sensation. But Aladdin in his cave or Ali Baba and his 'open sesame' would know what I felt, that stupendous admixture of strangeness and joyful awe.

The room was surprisingly tall, and narrow, giving way to a vaulted ceiling. A window light above illuminated the walls. And what walls! No paper was ever so beautiful or dynamic, for the place was completely lined with birds in their cages, piled from floor to ceiling. Their plumage flashed jewel-bright, and it struck me that this was what it was – a jewellery store. How Audubon would have been charmed to see these treasures!

One might have expected such a place to be filled with birdsong, but it was quickly evident that the main chatter came from a very richly dressed lady, speaking to a shadowy figure towards the back. From the hop that my heart gave, it was the proprietor himself.

'. . . the bullfinches, the chaffinches . . . six nightingales . . . I *must* have a parrot. The canaries I am assured of, once they have altogether recovered their plumage . . . I am quite determined to be the envy of Fifth. My man shall come to collect . . .'

The speaker was being gently but firmly shepherded towards myself and the door, talking animatedly all the while. She had the insistent high-class voice that one automatically associates with tea parties and never taking no for an answer, particularly with regards to cake. She was middle-aged and magnificent. The feathers in her hat must have cost the modesty of two or three ostriches, and her little black eyes sparkled in the lively fashion easily available to those with a salad of jewels garnishing their throat. Mr Vogel at last saw me: our eyes met and his brows rose fractionally.

'The python, I am afraid, I cannot accommodate just now,' she was saying. Mr Vogel bowed elaborately. His clothing was as well constructed as when we first met. 'Mr Fish, contrary to his namesake, *will* have his cats, and we cannot have Tiddles consumed in a barbarous fashion.' Then, with a regretful air: 'Although after what that creature did with my counterpane, it *is* tempting. I shall work on an arrangement and then come for him.'

Her eye alighted on me. 'What marvellous hair you have, my dear. Positively Titian. I hope you are not here for my python?'

I smiled. 'Your python is safe from me, madam.'

'But perhaps not from *me.*'

A crisp voice killed the general hubbub. Another lady had appeared in the doorway, dressed, if possible, even more richly than the first.

'Vogel, *I* shall have the creature. Bring it here, boy.'

A small assistant, still in his teens, brought forth a cage, huffing under its weight. I could see why: the snake within could not have been under eight feet long, its body as thick as a man's arm. It appeared unperturbed by the sudden audience; as I watched, it let out a yawn.

The newcomer ignored this performance, instead turning and pretending to spot the first lady. In their mutual greeting, the women's voices performed some special high-society trick. They still sounded as though they were at a tea party, but suddenly I was sure the tea contained arsenic.

Mr Vogel looked uneasily from the first lady to the second. 'Mrs Fish . . . Mrs Vanderbilt . . .'

They ignored him. My eyes widened in recognition. Mamie Fish and Alva Vanderbilt. I had seen the names in the gossip pages. Mamie Fish was part of New York's Triumvirate, one of three old-money women who ruled the social scene. It was they who ensured undesirables were not admitted, a group that unfortunately included Mrs Vanderbilt and all her vulgar new millions.

Mrs Fish eyed her foe. 'You seek my python, Alva?'

'I was not aware it was *yours*, dear.' Mrs Vanderbilt was serenity itself. 'Pythons are vicious creatures. One has to know how to handle them. I should not want one near my cat, if I had one. But then again' – a sweet smile, a lunge – 'cats are so *very* last season.'

Mrs Fish parried, riposted. 'I too strive to keep vicious creatures from my company.'

89

A thrust from the other. 'And *I* avoid all that is last season. Out with the old, in with the new. Is that not the saying, Mr Vogel?'

Both women's gazes shot to the proprietor; there was a short silence while he wrestled with the problem of what to say. But one did not bring a short sword to a stiletto fight. It was time to attempt a rescue.

'I am just come from Mrs Astor's,' I said.

Three pairs of eyes turned towards me – four if you included the python's. Mamie Fish might have been part of the Triumvirate, but Caroline Astor was its spearhead. It was *her* say-so, I had read on numerous occasions, that had prevented Alva Vanderbilt from joining the blessed choir of the Four Hundred. Invoking her name was like invoking God: in New York, there was no higher authority.

'From Mrs Astor's,' I repeated, 'and she is particularly seeking a lemur.'

'A lemur?' Mr Vogel said, confused.

'A *lemur*?' Mrs Vanderbilt echoed, dubious. Mrs Fish remained silent, only observing me with a thoughtful air.

'Indeed. She herself was considering a python, but it seems that one was seen at a party last year.'

'A party where? Who are you?' Mrs Vanderbilt demanded.

'Prussia,' I invented madly, praying that country was both respectable and distant enough that a New York society lady could both conceive of such an event and dismiss her ignorance of it. 'And nobody,' I added, in response to the second question.

Mrs Vanderbilt appeared to accept this latter. Her eyes sank in thought. We waited. Even the python seemed to have bated its breath.

90

'A lemur,' she repeated, doubt lingering in her tone.

'Mrs Astor is of the view that pythons are not respectable,' I said. 'It is the feet, you see.'

'The feet?'

'They have none.'

We turned as one to the snake. It had the decency to look embarrassed.

'No feet,' Mrs Vanderbilt said. 'Indeed.'

'And the feet being vital,' I improvised, 'to keeping one's . . . feet on the ground. As all the *best* people do.' I caught Mrs Fish's eye.

'Quite,' that lady said gravely. 'I heard McAllister saying as much just the other week.'

If Mrs Astor was God, Ward McAllister was her Archangel.

That did it. The victim succumbed to our stranglehold: she shot a feminine glare at the python, as though admonishing it for its deceit. Then, with a studied air of nonchalance, 'Do you have any lemurs, Mr Vogel?'

'Two come in last week, madam,' Mr Vogel said energetically, 'and both the best specimens of their kind. Just the two,' he added, 'and not a specimen more in all New York. A shipment from Madagascar has been very much delayed. I cannot see anybody purchasing another for at least three months.'

'Two lemurs.' And three months. I hid a smile as I saw the sums being done in Mrs Vanderbilt's mind. Two lemurs was better than one, and one lemur was better than anybody, Caroline Astor included. I edged around slightly, blocking the python from her view.

'Very well,' she said. 'I shall take both.'

Mr Vogel sprang into action. I was impressed by the extreme alacrity with which his customer was parted from her money and nicely dismissed from the shop, delivery promised within the week. Only once she had gone did we draw breath, the python settling into its coils. Mrs Fish turned to me, her eyes sparkling with mirth.

'That was a very clever thing you did.'

'By no means.'

'Nonsense! That silly woman was wholly taken in. That is the trouble with social climbing,' she added regretfully. 'The heights are liable to induce dizziness in the weak-headed.'

'You knew I was not sent by Mrs Astor?'

'Caroline? You are hardly her type, dear. Too clever-looking by half. Besides, I myself just came from there.' She smiled. 'I must thank you for saving my python. I have not felt so strong an affinity with a snake since Sunday school.' Her eyes glinted wickedly, and I found myself laughing.

'Good girl.' She pressed a card into my hand and swept out. The songbirds, no longer awed by her presence, set a-twitter again.

Mr Vogel turned to me. His expression was guarded, but not displeased. I introduced him to Mr Sullivan, who had been standing there like a lemon. The two men bowed to one another; Mr Sullivan thankfully did not comment on my acquaintance. Indeed, I was surprised to see that the gloom in his face had lifted, replaced with a boyish enthusiasm.

'This is quite the collection, sir.'

Mr Vogel responded with a modest dip of the head. It was false – I felt his pride – but I was not repelled. I recognised it from the mornings when I arrived at the factory, all quiet before the employees arrived, the machines expectant. It was a little kingdom, and it was mine, and while a throne was only another kind of cage,

I believed that women ought to be allowed to rule just as much as men – whether a household or an empire.

'We received a shipment only last week, and most buyers have yet to take their stock,' Mr Vogel said. 'Though I regret that you are not seeing us at our best. Our birds are in moult. Perhaps you would like to see our larger specimens.'

He did not need to ask twice: Mr Sullivan positively skipped after him. I followed them out the back of the shop, and reader, if there were wonders behind, there were yet more ahead. We entered the surprisingly large yard and stopped short, as well one might when confronted by an African lion in its cage. It was in the act of yawning, and its barred magnificence astounded the mind. One might as well have enslaved a fire. Nor was it alone; to one side were crowded more lions, and leopards, and a Bengal tiger. On the other, a more ramshackle pile held monkeys, to be used either as pets or trained for organ-grinders, Mr Vogel explained.

'But is it not cruel, to keep them in such small cages?'

'It is only for a very few days more, and we make their situation as comfortable as possible. Indeed, it is our first duty. These monkeys are wholly in our power and can only look to us for their necessaries. A tame animal is like nothing else on this earth. There is feeling – there is affection! As to the other company,' he smiled, gesturing to the lion, 'well, I imagine you would not like very much to meet *this* gentleman without his enclosure.'

'I thought you dealt in loneliness. I cannot say that I have ever felt solitude might be cured by such a beast.'

'Loneliness, wonder, it is all of the same piece. The hunger of the human heart for something beyond itself.'

I gazed upon him with great respect. Well, I could not help it. The company I had seen my father keep, at least until the war, was limited, gay, and almost entirely devoid of thought. The men were not in the habit of thinking, and the women had never been taught. Oh, they were *cultured* – they all kept up with the latest novel from so-and-so and wept at the play by such-and-such – but the duck of society was large, and art but a little dampener upon so waterproofed a back. They travelled light, feet never needing to touch the ground. But with Mr Vogel, ah, it was not so. Like Dürer, turning from the saints and becoming the first man to paint the soil, he held up the earth and presented it to me so I could not avoid it. I was unsurprised to learn later that he was a jeweller's son. He was concerned with the birds and beasts, yes, but also their cages, the fabric of the store itself and of his home. He desired to know how a thing worked, what it was made of, and once he possessed that knowledge, he could bend it to his will.

That attention fell upon me now; like my *Pequod*, I felt its workings upon my own hinges. Reader, I was thirty-two, unmarried, caught in a business that had locked itself around me with the very efficacy of its products. Even with all that came after, I cannot feel shame or regret for what I desired in that moment – to be sprung open.

But Mr Vogel was no longer looking my way; he had taken down a cage containing a single bird, small, brown-white and drab. A nightingale, silent under our scrutiny. The roof of the cage was of green muslin. The creatures often flew sharply upwards at this time of year, he said. It was therefore ill-advised to have a ceiling of wire, as they would injure their heads.

I watched as he carefully adjusted the cloth, ensuring that it hung down over the sides, low enough to reach its perch. He did all this without opening the door, and I was struck by the gentleness, even tenderness, of his movements.

Only later, after we were married, did I discover why the bird was in the habit of flying upwards in its cage. The summer is the time of its migration.

CHAPTER TEN

I reached the end of the page and stopped, heart beating in my chest.

The man I love is trying to kill me.

Fifty years since Hester Vogel had died. This diary had been hidden ever since. Mr Vogel had said his sister-in-law had ended her life. But this was no suicide note. This was an accusation of murder.

I shivered. The room was cold. Hester's childhood bedroom. Tonight, perchance, we would dream the same dreams.

I was not sure I wanted to, but there was more to the diary, and while it was late, I could not resist finishing it. I would make sense of it, then shake it free.

But first I needed fuel. Quickly I made another martini, muscle memory curling my knife through the lemon's skin, producing a thin, coiling peel.

Hester Millar . . . I picked up *The Birdcage Library* and studied the author's name. Herman Millar. Her father?

I looked again at the diary, the ink jungle-green. One of the highlights of my professional career had come during my Sumatra expedition, where I had found and brought back the rare *Rafflesia arnoldii*. The corpse lily. The largest flower on the planet was in fact a parasite with neither leaves, stems nor roots. Nor was it beautiful: toadstool red with white spots, its petals five fat lobes around a gaping hole. I'd tracked it for months through the vines on which it fed, sniffing for its telltale stink of rotting flesh. (The odour was designed to attract flies.) Not an obvious crowd-pleaser, but the university had been delighted.

I felt like this now with those pages before me: the scent of something rotten. Fifty years since Hester had died. A long time for her map, and the treasure, to remain hidden. Who had put it here? Mr Vogel thought it was Charles – the same man Hester was accusing of murder. If he had killed her, why lay a trail on her behalf?

I did not like to think how she might have died. A fall, Mr Vogel had said, but it seemed there was much he did not know.

'There are no limits to the inventiveness of evil,' my father once told us, before he gave up the Church. 'Nature is treacherous; man more so.' I remembered the interview that had finally won me the Papuan assignment. The expedition's sponsors were doubtful about the capabilities of women, and I'd been grilled by a panel of moustaches who hoped to throw me off.

'If I have no weapon,' the largest moustache said, 'but I wish to kill a man and escape the law, what plant could I use?' They waited. 'Perhaps we have offended you.'

'Not at all; I am only thinking.' My tone was casual, even as my mind raced to the Minangkabau Highlands of Sumatra, its valleys filled with treacherous gold and people who had developed ways of dealing with unwanted seekers. 'I would wait until he was asleep, then insert a sliver of bamboo into the flesh of his arm or leg. The plant grows inside the victim. He would be dead within a fortnight, and the splinter would appear only as a bruise.'

The moustaches frowned. 'All other candidates have opted for a poison.'

I shrugged. '*Cerbera odollam*. Hellebore. Ricin from the castor bean. Nature offers many avenues; the choice of one over another is really about the character of the man.'

'Or the woman,' one bit back. 'Bamboo seems a vicious way to die.'

I shrugged again. 'Parasites are my specialty.'

The green ink beckoned to me. Hester had planted a seed, and already I could feel it growing. I knew how secrets could take one over. I must not forget the reason I was here at Pàrras.

And yet I swallowed the last of the gin and, pulse thrumming, reached for the pages once more.

CHAPTER ELEVEN

I was married; I migrated to New York. At the corset fair, Mr Sullivan and I had met a businessman who quickly expressed a desire to buy the company and transition it to the new loom-woven methods, making all the necessary investments. With Charles's proposal, my father and I agreed it was for the best. He remained in M—. So did the great auk, for as well as a husband, I now had all the avian companions I could wish for.

I had hoped for so much from New York. It was a true place for adventure, but I quickly found myself involved in Charles's emporium. My new husband's younger brother, Henry, had been away for more than a twelve-month on a sourcing expedition and was not due to return until the following year. Charles was under-staffed, and on learning of my head for figures, he asked me to assist in the store's affairs. I quickly made myself invaluable, handling the ledgers while he focused on imports and sales and his several employees ensured the stock's daily care. The business thrived. At times, I gazed at the curtains that covered the windows and thought of the world beyond, but as time passed, and with the restless sea I loved so far away, it grew easier to focus on the matters before me.

When my father was at last persuaded to pay a visit, some five months after the wedding, I believe he was proud to see his daughter so engaged. He seemed much improved since the sale of the company – Mr Sullivan told me the cage designs he still made in private had regained their former fluency. This new-found confidence resulted in an unexpected gift.

'I wrote this for you.' He passed me a slim volume, beautifully bound.

The Birdcage Library, I read. The room had always been a key to my past, a key to my heart. I almost felt the clank. There, in neat drawings, were the cages of my childhood, the ones I had run around, swung from, hid inside. The ones where I had been, always, safe.

'I owe you an apology, child,' my father said quietly. 'Do not think I have not seen the sacrifices you have made these years. I am truly sorry it fell to you to make them.'

I could only nod; seeing I could not speak, he took me up in an embrace, and it was not that of an invalid, or an absentee in his own head, but that of a father. I kept the book in my bureau, safe, nestled in a drawer with the key to Pàrras. On sunny days, I pressed my face into the pages and could almost smell the sea.

But that first year, there was little time for introspection. I soon learned that Vogel & Brother's customer base was not limited to Mamie Fish; it drew purchases from half of New York's glittering Four Hundred, animals at that time being all the rage in an epoch quivering with plumage and claws. The Gilded Age was in full swing, with all its glitter and spectacle. Rich men bought hippopotamuses, poets wrote odes to wombats, and the great animal dealers, Mr Reiche, Mr Jamrach, Mr Hagenbeck and my own husband, vied with one another to take stock of the world, importing the most extraordinary beasts. Yes, Charles and I were very close then, working side by side, interleaving with one another like overlapping feathers. Under our joint stewardship, the business attained ever greater heights, and if the work was a little dry and familiar, what of it? I had a greater purpose: a husband, and soon, I was sure, a family.

Winter was drawing to an end, and the New York season with it. Fifth Avenue had lately received electric lighting, and it was something to leave our small but respectable house and walk the rain-slicked evening streets together, or perhaps descend into the smoky warmth of an oyster saloon, where the flash of knives and crack of shell formed a sharp sensory percussiveness contrasting delightfully with the smooth slip of the shellfish down the throat. Sometimes we strolled to the Brooklyn Bridge, then nearing completion. Charles admired its marvellous engineering; he had rented a storage cellar in its bowels and filled it with cages, readily at hand for whatever stock might arrive. It was considerably more crowded than my birdcage library, but I liked it anyway, particularly in the shadow of that bridge, whose two sides had slowly inched towards one another until they finally touched, something I found terribly romantic. Charles knew this – indeed, in an uncharacteristic burst of sentiment, it was in that room of cages that he asked me to marry him. I had replied immediately in the affirmative. Our home was not far away, on the lower east corner of Manhattan, and while many of the more fashionable families had already moved north, enough clung to their posts for Charles to be happy.

Or so I had thought. In the last six months, the quietude of those cool, wet walks had grown restless. I realised early on that Charles had a hunger, an endless pursuit for more and better. In his domestic appetites he was the model of self-control; only in his work did it run rampant. No deal could ever be good enough, no hours sufficiently long, no competitor adequately vanquished. I worked beside him, and all was well until the alligators. Charles had imported the animals for the first time, building a tank for the purpose. It was embedded in cement and bound with solid iron columns, the glass more than an inch thick. The ungrateful villains destroyed it in barely ten minutes, and the sudden profusion of water and vicious reptiles in our backyard caused the neighbourhood some consternation.

'I cannot but admire the creatures,' I said, half in jest, but Charles frowned.

'Everything in its proper place, Hester dear.'

He decided we could no longer keep such quantities of stock in Manhattan, and began working to create a supply depot in Hoboken. His workload doubled.

Around this time he began bringing me gifts – dresses, hats, a travelling coat – insisting that I wear ever grander clothing in the shop, though it made me stiff and uncomfortable, the dress sleeves trailing in the ink and making a mess of the ledgers. I sometimes caught him looking at my clothing in dissatisfaction, as though wondering how he could improve upon it, or perhaps me. I began to discover red crescent moons on my palms that I could not remember leaving there.

Those moons mocked me in their increasing frequency, for while many different species arrived at our door

102

weekly, one variety never did: a human child. Charles's swelling discontent became audible as a dripping faucet to one lying in bed, a minor irritation that expands to be all-consuming. His approaches for lovemaking grew more frequent, desperate, his body a weight on mine. I saw a different side to him then: he became almost animal, all fingers and claws, his whiskers scratching my cheeks until they were sore. The first time, on our wedding night, I had felt that soreness in some way necessary: a small sacrifice made in purchase of a whole new life. But in those later months, when my husband was not looking, I would gently press those same cheeks, first with my palm and then the back of my hand: they were red, like the regular disappointment of the blood that came monthly without fail.

I heard Charles's displeasure in his clipped steps past the boot blacks and butcher boys; in the abrupt knockings-out of his pipe; in the scritch of his signature as he wrote off to yet another collector in yet another far-flung clime. I was ashamed, both of my age and its shortcomings. An emptiness rose between us like a ghost, and neither of us knew how to vanquish it. It did not help that he was tired of being treated as a mere salesman by his customers, and a foreigner at that. He liked that I had grown up in a castle, however bleak – he would mention it to customers in a manner that made me uncomfortable, as though he would prefer it if I were still there. 'Any blackguard can sell shoes,' he would say. 'Only a gentleman may sell God's own creatures.'

And then came Jumbo. It had not escaped our attention that Phineas Taylor Barnum was looking to purchase the famed elephant for his Greatest Show on Earth. The story had been talked of everywhere for weeks, but it had not been thought that Bartlett of London Zoo would actually sell. The creature was, after all, a sensation. Schoolchildren begged for his rescue; the courts did their best to block a sale; Queen Victoria even made a personal petition. But all the Empire could not prevent the purchase. I had never met Barnum – Charles refused to speak of him, referring to him only as 'that entertainer', or, colourfully, 'the Greatest Charlatan on Earth'. Perhaps this was not unrelated to the fact that that gentleman had never sought the services of Vogel & Brother. Still, in January of 1882, the news broke: Barnum had won out, and Jumbo would be shown at Madison Square Garden.

Charles was apoplectic. The greatest animal trade of the century, one that would have assured Vogel & Brother's place in polite society, and the company had had no part in it. It transpired that he had written personally to Bartlett to offer his services and been declined. Barnum became known as 'that underhanded entertainer', and Charles sank into a depression I could not lift. Around this time, I made the mistake of suggesting that we go on a sourcing expedition once his brother returned. Weariness flitted across his face, along with something I had not expected: scorn.

'Do not be absurd, Hester.'

I did not mention it again, but at night, staring up into the shadowy canopy, I tried to understand. He knew the importance of respectability, which itself meant nothing more nor less than security, and had a well-founded horror of the alternative. His father had acquired a repu-tation for drink, even by the standards of the hard-living German aristocracy whose jewels he had once cut for a living. Despite his lowly origins, they were nevertheless content to entertain him at their card tables, his presence fuelled by his wife's fortune. Friends and connections began to keep away, which only worsened both drinking and gambling; bare patches began to appear in the rooms of their mansion, as though it had fallen victim to some mysterious parasite. Eventually the house was sold to pay the debts.

Charles's mother, a lovely, weak woman, to whom the money and family home belonged, had been grief-stricken. But the last straw, he said, was her beloved diamond necklace with its chain of pearls. In her youth, as the principal belle of the day, she had worn it to meet a princess. The moment of breaking came when she discovered the necklace in her possession to be a fake, her husband having sold off the real one years before and inserted an imposter, made of paste, in its place. She had died broken-hearted. Two months later, a seventeen-year-old Charles coaxed his fourteen-year-old brother Henry out of the window. Under cover of darkness, they boarded a ship to New York.

I could have wept for those two young boys, and for the cigar burns I discovered early on upon the insides of Charles's forearms. He said nothing at first as I turned over one arm, then the other. The scars were a livid white, like the hottest part of a flame.

Then: 'When I was small, my father brought home a canary. He had won it at cards. And lost a whole lot else. He gave it to me. Not as a present, but as a discarded thing.' He smiled slightly. 'I learned what the creature ate, what it liked, what it disliked. What made it happy, and what made it afraid.

'One day, my father came home early from his gambling. Drunk, of course, but more so than usual. He had lost heavily. When he was in a good mood, he used to make beautiful things for us. Animals out of wire. But over the years he did this less and less, and the creatures he did make were strange and twisted.

105

'I was careful to keep the canary away from him, but his return that day caught me by surprise. I was cleaning its cage in the kitchen. Henry and my mother were not there. I was happy. Wonderfully happy, for no reason beyond having a companion and a useful task to do.

'Something about the scene enraged my father. He flew into a violent fit. In the end, I could only curl up in the corner with my little bird cupped in my hands. Trying to protect it. Much good it did. He broke my grip, and its neck.'

He had the canary still. He showed it to me: a small thing, the taxidermy not particularly well executed, but bearing all the signs of love and wear of a child's comforter. There was nothing I could think of to say, nothing at least that would be of use to this most practical of men. If only fixing human beings were as simple as fixing hinges! Instead, I took his arm and put my lips to a scar, feeling how the skin had grown thick, like a coin. I did the same with the next, and the next, on this arm and the other.

When I had done, he closed his eyes. We never spoke of it again.

One Sunday, Charles went out, seeing to an ostrich shipment at the South Street docks. The emporium was closed, but one of the birds had apparently died during the crossing. Sarah, the maid, brought in the tea, and I sat in our comfortable living room wondering what to do. Charles himself had furnished the room, a quirk that would have raised most servants' eyebrows to their caps, to see him choosing fabrics and myself at the business books. But Sarah had been with Charles a long while and knew his ways; we had liked one another from the first. She had a sweetheart in Harlem and a brother who worked on ships, spending the last two years in the eastern Orient. Besides, my husband had done well, paying the same attention to cabinets and coffee urns as he did to everything else. Occasionally I felt almost like one of his creatures, a thing he had acquired, though he treated all his possessions with the same firm attention and care.

When my father had visited, he remarked upon my new-found composure. 'You are even sitting differently, dear.' I must have looked discomfited, because he laughed (a new phenomenon, since the company had sold) and said it was a good thing. 'It appears as though nobody could knock you off your perch.'

'Did I not sit so before?'

'Perhaps. And yet . . .' he sighed, 'sometimes I felt as if you were less seated, more *tethered*.'

Well, I had thought a few months later, collapsing into bed after a long day at the emporium, my head dancing with figures. I was in the right place now, surely. I had embarked on this new life. It was an adventure.

I could not work out why my hand shook.

Sarah entered again, this time with a note from Charles. It said that he was having trouble with the shipment and would not return until evening. I sighed and poked the fire hard. Ostriches! Honking great snappish things. I remembered the hat of Mrs Fish, that first day in the emporium.

Mrs Fish! She had sent a message earlier in the week, asking to visit the emporium on Sunday, after church. Since she was one of our best customers, Charles had not refused her. He must have forgotten. I glanced at the clock on the mantelpiece, then fled to the door.

I knew the store would be quiet. It was never *actually* quiet, of course, the animals saw to that, but I had quickly learned to love its twitterings and flutterings, scritchings and scratchings, punctuated by the occasional yowl. It was an endless conversation, no less intelligent than that of the customers, and often a good deal more than that. There would be someone in, of course; there always was, tending to the animals. Today it would be Raymond, the youngest employee, who loved the Carolina parakeets best.

But when I entered the emporium to the now-familiar peal of the bell, Raymond was neither changing water nor cleaning cages. Instead he was fixed to the floor with a look of terror I had never seen before, not even when attending to the hyenas. Mamie Fish had already arrived and was grilling him over a slow flame.

'This is most irregular, boy. I have a *party* to prepare for, I tell you. So many mouths to feed, and they've gobbled up a baby elephant already. Caroline will be at her most Caroline-ish if I do not have something new. What is the *point* of animals if one cannot get one's hands upon them?'

I allowed myself a moment to enjoy the spectacle. A good harangue is not to be missed, at least when one is not its object. Mrs Fish was wearing yet another dress of extraordinary riches, and there was a bird of paradise, whole, on her hat. I had seen dozens of bird species with Vogel & Brother, but never yet a live paradise bird. Charles had told me they were exceptionally difficult to keep alive in captivity. They did not have the will, he said.

'Mrs Fish,' I said, when I judged poor Raymond to have suffered enough, 'an honour. And on the Sabbath, too.'

'Ah! Someone sensible at last. You may leave us,' she added to Raymond, who required no additional prompting. 'The urgency of the matter requires it.

108

Although I know one usually expects Fish on Fridays' –
here she let out a great hoot, loud enough to rival the
whooping cranes – 'I have a *serious* assignation.'

'The party.' I was careful not to smile. To the Four
Hundred, and to the public who read so avidly about
them, there was no topic more serious. Only last week,
Delmonico's had hosted a banquet featuring two hundred
choices of entrée, including forty-six of veal; the centrepiece was a specially created lake, thirty feet long, with
several swans gliding upon it.

'Precisely.' She leaned in. 'I must have a *show.*'

'What did you have in mind?'

'No, dear, I want what is in *your* mind.'

'You want my ideas?'

'Naturally,' she said, seeing my surprise. 'You have a
particular inventiveness. I observed it on our first
meeting. Yes, I *do* remember. Anyone who can persuade
Alva Vanderbilt that a python ought to have feet is not a
person I forget in a hurry. I *know* you will have ideas. A
party is a story, and an exotic animal tells it better than
any dress. In fact, the animal is a story unto itself.
Besides, Mr Vogel ought not to be allowed to keep you
caged up with those ledgers like one of his budgerigars.'

'I am not caged up,' I interjected hastily. 'I enjoy
it.'

'My dear, it is no more desirable to know the insides
of a man's finances than it is to know the insides of his
ears. In both cases it is enough to be aware that the
outermost organ is functional.' Her eyes flashed wickedly. 'Come along to my little house and we shall plan a
party.'

The 'little house', it transpired, was a huge and beautiful brownstone mansion in Gramercy Park. The butler
led me through the hall and into one of a fistful of lavish

109

drawing rooms. Tea was brought while I tried not to look too hard around me.

'Oh, go on, *do*,' Mrs Fish said. 'What is the point of it all if everybody pretends they are indifferent?'

I flushed at how easily she had read me, then stared around with intense interest. So this was how the truly wealthy lived: not in stony, desiccated castles, but marinated in a sort of sumptuous batter. The room had been crammed with damask, brocade, velvet and bronze; there were acres of mahogany and Hauteville marble. Portraits and tapestries hung on the panelled walls (I recognised Marie Antoinette), while crystal chandeliers and Tiffany lamps provided illumination and tiger skins covered the floor. The only thing the room did not possess was a bookshelf.

'Ready?' Mrs Fish asked. I assented. 'Then let us begin.'

Three hours later, I left, rather tired. Mrs Fish's dinner invitations, I had learned, always bore the famed line: 'There will be something besides dinner, come.' It was the *something* that we had worked on together, and she seemed pleased with the result, insisting on her own carriage taking me home and only twitching her nose slightly when I gave the address. After that afternoon, I could accept this as high praise indeed.

I disembarked to the usual acrid odour of coal smoke, and just then, sleeting rain. It had been dry in Gramercy Park: perhaps the water was ashamed of its own lack of fashion. Society! There was no more curious beast – and it was a caged one, I had decided, because it was gradually becoming clear that what money did was limit. Whereas the poor or middle class ask what they can do, real money dictates what one cannot do. I had lost count of how many times Mrs Fish had said, 'We cannot have

110

that', whether in reference to courses, or place settings, or guests – and she of a relatively free disposition. Of course, I doubted she saw it that way. But whether the bars were wrought of iron or gold, one was trapped all the same. The plan we had concocted meant that Vogel & Brother would be instrumental at the party in two weeks' time. Beyond that, I decided, I wanted little from society. It would be a necessary evil, like religion, or boiled chicken.

But Charles had other ideas. He was ecstatic when I told him the news; I knew it because of the gusto with which he clipped off the end of his cigar.

'I haven't over-promised, have I?' I asked, taking his hand, suddenly anxious that the idea I had given Mrs Fish might prove impossible.

'We have the stock,' Charles said, his eyes glinting as he stood, breaking my grip. 'This is our chance, Hester. For more.'

I suddenly realised what I had done. I had vowed to skirt high society even as I handed Charles his ticket into it. Still, I did not know then the disaster that would come from it, and seeing his excitement, how could I deny him? It would be denying the boy who had arrived in New York all those years ago. He and Henry had had nothing, so they had begun importing canary birds from the Harz mountains, living hand to mouth until Charles hit upon the idea of selling to Californian miners eking out the gold rush. He had left Henry and embarked on the notoriously difficult journey across the interior, the Old Nicaragua Route riddled with bandits and horses' corpses, the canaries a constant fluttering reminder of the enterprise's fragility. In the Californian desert, he had at last found fortune, the yellow canaries being exchanged for yellow gold as fast as he could sell them.

So, with an increasingly familiar shunting motion, I moved aside the unease in my heart and only said, 'Yes, dear.'

Fortunately, the next fortnight was so busy that I had little time for doubts. Charles and I rehearsed our roles over and over until there could be no chance of failure. I did not see Mrs Fish until the day before the party, when she swept in to examine what she called her 'centrepiece'.

'Marvellous. Quite marvellous. Would you like to see the invitation?'

It was as thick and heavy as a book, or nearly so, and printed on stiff white card.

This ticket for the Ball must be shown at the door
Not transferable – to be returned if not used
Admit ——

'A ball?' I said. 'I thought this was a dinner party?'

'Oh! It was, but there was no point wasting your idea on a mere dozen. The whole town shall be there. And there *will* be dinner. At one in the morning.'

I gulped, but Charles positively glowed. I turned the invitation over and saw that, as we had requested, guests had been told not to wear red. But then I saw something else.

Mr & Mrs Stuyvesant Fish present
A Chinese Costume Ball

'China?'

'Yes, dear. Can you believe it has never been done?'

I stared at her. She seemed intelligent and aware. Was

it possible she was so swaddled from the world that she had no idea?

'But what about the Exclusion Act?'

The Chinese Exclusion Act was expected to be signed into law any week now, all but eliminating immigration from China for a decade. Anti-Chinese violence was more common in the west, where they had long been blamed for depressing wages and hogging the gold, but it was not unheard of in New York, particularly around the Five Points slum, where large numbers resided. Five Points was not so many blocks south of Gramercy Park, though of course to society it might as well have been on another planet.

Mrs Fish dismissed my concerns. 'Parties not politics, dear.' Inconceivable that such vagaries should intrude on her doorstep. Besides, the invitations were gone out, the dresses made. And of course, not one of the Four Hundred were Chinese. What could I do but agree?

The great day dawned. Charles was as a-flutter as the birds, positively trembling as he did up his dinner jacket. I had already given about fifty answers to questions regarding the propriety of his clothing, at least forty-nine of which I had invented. I myself was wearing the dove-grey dress I had worn at our wedding, plain but well made. I had never felt shy in all my business dealings, not at the corset factory, nor at Vogel & Brother, but for some reason that day, I did not wish to be seen. It was only later that I realised I was afraid of looking up to find society watching me through the bars.

We were about to leave, Charles still fussing with his collar, when Sarah came in, flushed with excitement.

'What is it?'

'This just came. From Mr Vogel.'

I opened my mouth to tell her not to be ridiculous, that Mr Vogel was right here, before I realised who she meant. Charles took the letter silently, tearing the envelope open before I could reach for the knife.

'Henry is coming home.' His voice was low, unassuming, but I recognised the gentleness in it: it was the same tone he had used until recently with me when we were alone, or with the birds on those sunny mornings when the emporium was quiet and fresh. Another treasured thing returning to his possession.

I was excited too, of course, yet nervous. Charles and I had spent our marriage creating the tenor of our lives together, the most delicate kind of music. I was anxious about the introduction of another voice. Henry's ship was due in early June, barely a week after Sarah's own brother would return from the East.

Charles and I arrived several hours before the guests and ascended the curving white marble staircase to the ballroom at the top of the house. We arranged everything, then sequestered ourselves in an alcove and observed the hubbub. Enormous flower arrangements were parading back and forth, apparently of their own accord, their carriers entirely obscured. The parquet floor had been polished to a shine that almost hurt to look at, and trays full of petits fours, bonbons and marrons glacés whisked by. Later, silk fans and silver card cases would be given out as favours. In the kitchens below, oysters were being stewed, turkeys boned, terrapins scalded. Mamie Fish appeared with the butler, nodded briskly at us and swept on. Flowers now lined every side of the hall, all white, crocuses and daffodils and quince blossom. The lamps were coming on. I had never felt so giddy nor so far from home, and instinctively reached for Charles's hand for reassurance.

He was not there. I looked round and spotted him across the room, fussing again over the centrepiece, and was momentarily seized by a loneliness of a depth and sharpness I had never known before.

Mamie Fish reappeared with another man in tow. 'I must finish with Tom first, Mr Havely . . . Here, meet Mr and Mrs Vogel. They are *integral* to my entertainments this evening.'

She swept off, depositing the new arrival as the waves deposit driftwood. Mr Havely was a jolly-looking man of medium height, smartly dressed. I liked him at once. He introduced himself as a plumassier.

'Here to put the last touches on Mrs Fish's hat, you know. Not our usual way of service, but she is one of our best customers.'

'It is the same for us,' Charles replied. 'We have supplied creatures for entertainment on many occasions, but never participated until now.'

'Ah! You are in the animal trade also.'

'Yes, only our stock is alive, not dead.'

'You ought to diversify. That is the real way of it, you know. Dead things are far less trouble.' Mr Havely guffawed. 'Though I should hardly be encouraging yet more competition. The London market has never been so warm.'

'I thought your trade was centred in Paris?' I asked.

'Oh yes, as a centre of fashion. But the real hub is London. You ought to attend a sale, Mr Vogel. Hundreds of herons! Thousands of eagles! The array is beyond even your storerooms.'

Charles bowed and said it would be an honour, likewise inviting Mr Havely to visit the emporium. Mr Havely declared he would do so. Then Mrs Fish took

115

him off again, leaving Charles and me alone. My husband gazed after them.

'Diversify,' he muttered to himself, in a brooding manner that unnerved me.

'Never mind that now,' I said. 'Tonight will be all right, dear.'

He squeezed my hand – briefly, but it was enough.

The guests were due at seven, and we were under strict instructions to conceal ourselves beforehand, behind Chinese screens placed on either side of the great ball-room doors. We took our positions, and the first ones began to arrive, clustering beneath the gold ceiling. Mamie Fish was intentionally not there to greet them. Instead, her husband did so: Mr Stuyvesant Fish, the man himself lurking some distance behind a large and magnificent moustache. His wife would enter when everybody was assembled.

I was hidden behind the left-side screen, like Polonius behind the arras. Charles was on the right. I only hoped that he was correct about this stunt affording us the respectability and fashion he craved. I rechecked my station, knowing he would be doing the same, then risked peeking out at the gathering crowd. The Four Hundred, or the Four Horsemen as I kept calling them in my head, though there was certainly no famine or plague here. They were a riot of satin, and velvet, and chinoiserie. The ladies were resplendent in the costumery of the East; tiaras, diadems and aigrettes abounded. Authenticity did not matter; spectacle did. One woman carried a bag that doubled as a real Chinese lantern. Another wore a sweeping gold robe of crêpe de Chine, while Mrs Astor carried a young pig. I scanned the crowd, but mercifully they had all followed the strictures. Nobody was in red.

A Chinese gong, bought especially, was struck, the sound reverberating through the hall. The din died and everybody turned towards the doors as one. We readied ourselves. Charles and I both stood beside a cage five feet high: within each, two hundred hummingbirds whirred. I could only hope that tonight's result would be as successful as in our practice.

As the gong sounded again, I took hold of the cage door.

It worked perfectly. That was what I reminded myself in the days and weeks after the catastrophe. It worked perfectly. As the gong rang out, I opened the door: the tiny birds fluttered out and up from behind the two screens, lifted by the gentle *ahh* of the audience. A wing-beat later and white-gloved footmen opened the doors: Mamie Fish stepped through, resplendent in a gown of red velvet and silk, adorned with real Chinese cherry blossom. On her head was a hat covered in fifty dead hummingbirds. The live birds, which had been fluttering charmingly but aimlessly, spotted her and flew down, alighting upon the red colour and flowers that their species found so attractive, forming a living cloak of iridescent fluttering feathers.

It was exquisite; the crowd were ecstatic; yet in the split second before the first hands could make their applause, there was a shout outside, a tremendous bang, and something smashed through the ballroom doors, crashing into a bevy of hummingbirds, which simply evaporated into a red mist. We gazed stupidly. Then a woman screamed, and the world exploded.

It transpired afterwards that while Mrs Fish had planned the ball superbly with regards to guests, victuals and entertainment, when it came to politics, she had made a severe miscalculation. The Chinese theme had provoked the ire of certain anti-Chinese agitators bent on assuring the passage of the Act, and the philosophers among them had decided that a Chinese costume ball might sway the politicians into believing that society had alternative sympathies. As the first gong struck, they had overpowered the footmen and forced their way into the house. Terrified shrieks from both ladies and gentlemen ensued as they fought to escape, even as more bullets were fired into the ceiling, showering plaster and paint onto the crowd so that it rained gold.

My first thought was Charles. My husband was a resolute man. I knew he would come for me. Only when he remained invisible did I realise he must be hurt. I forced my way out from behind the screen and was glad I did, since the next moment two wild-looking fellows flung it to the ground, its lacquer smashing into pretty smithereens. In the confusion, I was able to dart across to where the second screen remained standing. Behind it, curled up in a corner, I found Charles, unhurt and oblivious, whispering reassurances to the stuffed canary tucked tightly in his hand.

CHAPTER TWELVE

I turned the page and looked hungrily for more, but that was it. The bedroom was dark, the paraffin lamp burning low, but in my mind I saw the images vividly: terrified birds and glittering tiaras, a scarred man and a lonely woman. I was gripped. Though I was unmarried, in some ways Hester reminded me of myself. Her father too had gone to war. She too had sacrificed much to look after him, her very capability ensuring her isolation. I pictured her rooted to the spot, staring at Charles with the stillness of a wild animal that, having been caught, had at last given up hope.

But how were these pages leading me to the treasure, as she had promised? The account had ended, and I was no closer to the diamond than before. I lay down, letting my eyes close and my heartbeat slow. I'd been right that Hester's father had written *The Birdcage Library*. That seemed important. If this was indeed a treasure map, it was a highly personal one. I'd found this diary through a clue hidden in that book.

What if that clue was not the only one?

The next morning, I began work early, the diary swirling in my mind. I had already realised that merely digging over the castle, like Mr Vogel and Yves had done a hundred times, was unlikely to produce results. I knew from my profession that people might search, but they rarely looked. To find something no one else could, you had to tackle it in a way no one else *would*.

If I was right about *The Birdcage Library*, I had stumbled across precisely such a unique approach. A treasure hunt within a treasure hunt.

Then there was the question of whether to tell Mr Vogel. As I'd dressed that morning I'd thought of the broken tower, the one Hester had said her grandfather had torn apart in his fury. There was old rage in this tale, and envy, and perhaps murder. Yves had said his uncle did not even like to look at *The Birdcage Library*. There were wounds here that ran deep.

I remembered the maimed, snarling tiger I had come across in Sumatra, staked to the ground, half dead from the torments of the village boys made confident by the thick rope around its neck.

I had returned that night with my pistol and shot it in the head.

Mamie Fish had compared stories to animals, but I thought them more like plants. You could put a beast in a cage. Vegetation was far less easy to control.

It was because of this that I would not tell Mr Vogel, at least not yet. There were hidden things at work here, seeds planted fifty years before. I had to understand what they had grown into.

So I said nothing and carried on with my work. I had been glad to finish the basement; today I was to examine the kitchen. I'd forewarned Lynette, but when I arrived, lunch preparations were scattered over the long table, a rolled ham in pride of place.

'I can come back.'

'No, no. We must stick to Mr Vogel's plans.' She wiped a thick hand across a glistening brow. I had seen Mr Vogel make a similar gesture, though not from the same cause. His was a brushing-over motion, as though his left hand was sweeping a thing away, or ushering another into its place.

Interesting that Hester had referred to him as Henry, not Heinrich. Well, I could have sympathy for those who remade themselves.

Lynette asked permission to have the ham cooking in the electric oven while I worked. I assented, but came to regret it as the smell spread its tendrils through the kitchen. It was not the only regrettable thing that morning. I had to search the huge chimney, so vast it could have hidden the crown jewels without trouble. Clambering inside, I probed among the old charcoal and smells. Nothing, apart from soot and the grease of animals long since dead. I emerged covered in it.

'Good heavens, Miss Blackwood. I thought you were treasure hunting, not coal mining. There's a pump outside.'

I went to wash. The weather was warm, growing warmer. In later months, the trees in the island's north-eastern corner would loosen into gold, but not now, not yet.

I realised then that there were stones among the trees.

'The Millar family cemetery.' Yves had appeared from nowhere. 'Shall we visit?'

Hester's family. Heinrich Vogel was her only heir, and he wasn't even blood. It saddened me.

'Another time,' I said.

After work, I pored over the diary until late into the night, looking for a clue that might lead me to . . . what? Another instalment, I supposed. But I found nothing, and the next day was the same. When I was not in my room, some instinct

121

made me keep the diary and *The Birdcage Library* hidden, stowed under the mattress.

It was not until the third evening that I made a breakthrough.

Both books were open before me, beside yet another untouched envelope bearing Daniel's handwriting. The seven years we had spent apart had frozen our relationship in time. No wonder I could hardly look at him, given what had happened between us.

I was discharged from hospital some weeks before my father. Daniel had visited us both every day, and after my return home he kept doing so, going first to the hospital, then to our cottage in Butterworth's grounds. To the outside world, he seemed all right, but I knew him well enough to see how utterly my sister's death had smashed him. The depth of his grief surprised me. He pulled himself together for our sakes, but I saw my own symptoms mirrored in him, every living moment a strain. I learned to expect a visit in the early afternoon: tea, condolences, kind enquiries as to my recovery. The playful insouciance with which we had formerly treated one another had gone, another casualty of the accident. We handled one another as delicately as china.

Still, as time went by, much as saprophytic orchids will sprout from dead matter, I began to exhibit signs of life, going so far one day as to make lunch. He went even further, pretending to enjoy the wobbly eggs and badly dressed salad. Porcelain manners for our porcelain hearts.

One morning I was in the greenhouse, listlessly watering our specimens, mouthing each species under my breath. Their Latin names had become a sort of prayer. I would never pray again, but I directed my words towards the hospital, in offering to my father.

Then Daniel burst in.

'I cannot do this,' he exploded, inarticulate with rage and

grief. 'I cannot be so around you any more. My whole life is an artifice. The people in the office, the starched suit I wear, the damned clock that ticks – Emmy, if we cannot be natural with one another then I don't know what I'll do.'

It wasn't the words so much as the volume that shook something out of me. In all the weeks since the accident, I had not once heard a raised voice – everyone went out of their way to speak quietly.

'Then *be* natural,' I snapped at last. 'You think I do not hate this also? You think that now I have lost a sister, I wish to lose a friend too?'

He made a helpless gesture that made me want to slap him; I stepped towards him to do just that. But he grabbed my raised hand and somehow the other flew to the back of his neck. Pulled him down. His mouth crushed into mine and then we were pressing into one another, his hands on my face, my waist, my breasts, and *Strelitzia reginae* smashed to the floor but I did not give a damn.

We didn't talk about the greenhouse incident afterwards. My father came home the next day, blind and weak, and all my energies were directed upon caring for him, and then the subsequent move to Australia.

I saw Daniel just once more. He came to say goodbye the night before we left. My father was in the corner, and when he heard Daniel's voice, he picked up the newspaper. Quickly he realised the obvious futility of this, settling instead for sucking on his unlit pipe. For the first time I was guiltily glad of his blindness, rendering invisible the flush in our cheeks.

I knew Daniel well enough to realise that while he hated our departure, he did not blame us. I also knew that he would wait. I did not know what to do with this loyalty other than run from it. With all that had happened, a life together was now impossible; still I could not help but notice the dark eyes watching me, the nose peeling slightly with sunburn, and the lock of golden hair that had fallen across his brow. Without thinking, I pushed it to one side. It was the last time we would touch for seven years.

Back in Hester's bedroom after an early dinner, I sighed and tore open the envelope. But I was only halfway through unfolding the pages when a word in her diary caught my eye.

Audubon.

Their plumage flashed jewel-bright, and it struck me that this was what it was – a jewellery store, she had written. *How Audubon would have been charmed to see these treasures!*

I did not have to be a zoologist to know the name. John James Audubon was the famed naturalist who had created *The Birds of America*, one of the finest ornithological works ever made. But it was not this that sent a frisson through me. It was the fact that I had seen the name written elsewhere, ever so recently.

The Birdcage Library.

I turned to that book again. There. Right in the introduction: *It was Audubon who first mapped our country's avian treasures, and he would have marvelled at the breadth of species available to-day to even the most disinterested collector.*

Hester had named Audubon, but that was not the only word she'd echoed.

Treasures.

Perhaps it meant something, perhaps not. But my thoughts went to the library of Pàrras, and whether or not it might contain a copy of Audubon's masterpiece.

The library was marvellous. It took up a whole two floors of the eastern tower, thousands of books coiling round and

124

round the hexagonal walls. The third floor was out of bounds: the wooden stairs led only to a trapdoor with a padlock. Yves' laboratory.

That was a mystery for later. I gazed at the shelves; the books gazed back, a crowd of spectators. Like any crowd, some individuals looked expensive, austere; others were rougher-shod. I rather thought the former class had belonged to Hester's grandparents, particularly the large case containing nothing but Bibles. Elsewhere, the collection was ordered by genre and author: hunting manuals, classic novels, textbooks, including a shelf on diseases of the mind. There were several enticing tomes on magic and witches – or at least the elimination of them, if the presence of the *Malleus Maleficarum* was anything to go by.

The Audubon was not hard to find. *The Birds of America* had been printed in the massive format known, charmingly, as Double Elephant Folio. It rested horizontally on the bottom shelf. Understandable: it was over three feet long.

I hauled it out. Little chance of hiding *this* under my mattress, or getting it there unseen. Best to have a look now, then.

I lifted open the cover – it took both hands – and lightly ran my fingers over the copperplate engravings, bright and gorgeous as any plumage. Was another diary slipped between the pages? I looked through, paper crackling in expectation. Nothing.

It was very quiet, though still early. I heard a noise from the windless courtyard: the distant sound of a door closing. Then footsteps. Someone coming. Here? I should not be caught with this book. Discovery would lead to questions, questions to suspicions. I lifted it upright, and it was then that I noticed its spine.

It was thick, old, and in the way of such tomes, the backing material had come away, leaving an open mouth of darkness down the spine.

The footsteps were loud now. Unquestionably they were coming here. I crouched down and shoved my fingers into the gap, mentally apologising to the book. They closed upon something, but I did not have time to look, only withdrew it, stuffed it into my pocket, closed the book and shoved it back onto the shelf in the same moment that the door opened and Mr Vogel stood there, carved in twilight.

'Can I help you, Miss Blackwood?'

I was scrutinising the Bibles case with affected carelessness.

'I came for something to read. I have not been sleeping well.'

He gave a wry smile. 'I am not sure that particular book will help. I too often have trouble at night. Still, at those times we know things and see things that others do not. In some ways it is a privilege.'

I was surprised. I had never thought of it so until now.

'But as for sin,' he gestured at the Bibles, their stiff backs to him, 'perhaps it is a miracle that anybody can shut their eyes knowing of what deeds we are capable. When you think of how the Lord made his kingdom perfect, only to be betrayed!'

'I have always thought Eden merely a beautiful prison.'

'Hmm! Have you read your Dante, Miss Blackwood? Nine circles of hell, and the deepest reserved for traitors.' He smiled, ran a hand along a dusty shelf. 'God's law maintains that betrayal is the greatest sin of all.'

I left him, the thing I had found burning in my pocket. In my bedroom, I withdrew my discovery.

Several sheets of paper, loosely rolled.

Carefully I spread them out, a smile spreading also across my face. The ink upon them was green.

CHAPTER THIRTEEN

The days after the Chinese ball disaster were dreadful. Charles and I avoided each other, nursing ourselves, though neither of us bore so much as a scratch. In fact, only a handful of agitators had made it into the Stuyvesant Fish mansion: Gramercy Park was not an address to be long overlooked by the police, so in a very few minutes the attackers were subdued. Two gentlemen had sustained serious injuries but were expected to recover, and many ladies had suffered severe shock. Smelling salts were at a premium for some days. Mamie Fish had escaped blame, doubtless due to her friendship with Mr Gould, owner of the *New York World*, but otherwise she appeared to be lying low; certainly she did not visit the emporium.

What did it matter? We were not friends. Mrs Fish would continue being rich and cosseted and well-to-do. Charles, meanwhile, was devastated to have Vogel & Brother's name associated with catastrophe. That was what he cared for – the business. Of course I sympathised deeply with him, that small boy once again protecting his feathered charge. But I had thought I had found a true

127

companion; and yet in this first moment of need, that companion had apparently forgotten I even existed. When Sarah found me crying in the linen closet, I told her it was the shock.

An invisible layer descended between my husband and me, one that only thickened as the days passed. He spent more and more time away, from both home and the emporium, and when he was there, he was frequently entertaining a new acquaintance. Hyatt Frost had been in business with the Van Amburgh Show, and had worked with Barnum on his Broadway museum. I did not approve of his thickset face and predator's eyes, but Charles began meeting him in his study, informing me – not directly, but via Sarah – that they were not to be disturbed. It was the first time he had ever excluded me from business affairs, and the thick door between us lodged in my heart. A few weeks later he informed me that Vogel & Brother was founding a circus.

I blinked stupidly. 'A circus? Do we have the money?'

'You know we do.'

I did, though my grip on the ledgers had been loosening of late. Charles kept removing them for his private meetings.

'With Hyatt Frost, I suppose.'

'Naturally.' He made that habitual gesticulation of his that I had noticed on our first meeting. 'He has more than three decades of experience.'

'He is not a gentleman. We don't need him, Charles. We are one of the principal dealers in America.'

His brow was dark. 'Precisely. And that is *all* we are. Merchants! How many more lions do you believe we can stuff down the public's throat?'

'We sell *wonder*, Charles. I cannot believe there is a limit on that.'

'Then you are a fool.'

I stared at him. He had never spoken in such a way before, at least not to me.

'It is the nature of our race to become bored and discontent. It is not wonder that people seek, but novelty. *That* is why this venture will succeed.'

'Charles, dear. I know you have suffered these last few days.' I reached for his hand. 'But you must know that I am perfectly happy with our life together. If it is respectability you seek, do not do so on my account.'

He gave me the strangest of looks. 'I am not seeking respectability.'

'Then what—'

'Do we understand one another at all, Hester? Did you marry me because you loved me? Or was I just the first person who was different?'

My hand fell away. We stared at one another. Then he gave a small, sad shake of his head and departed.

I paid another visit to the linen closet – it was in a distant corner of the house, where, unlike the main rooms, I had learned I was unlikely to be overheard. The visit would be one of many over the ensuing days and weeks, as I tormented myself with this scene. I loved Charles. Didn't I? I thought back to that day on the beach, how struck I had been by his clever hands and clear eyes. How different he was to all the other useless, respectable men I knew.

It is not wonder that people seek, but novelty. The words hissed and spat.

Charles and Mr Frost began creating their circus, deciding to situate it on Coney Island. I had no part in it. My husband's new business partner smoked an evil-smelling pipe, and his eyes followed Charles always about the room. He had his own accountant, and I knew he disapproved of my involvement in Vogel & Brother. It was therefore no great surprise when Charles told me that he thought I should no longer come into the emporium; that it was more proper for me to remain at home.

'I can manage the books from here,' I said, but I knew it was hopeless. Once I would have prevailed upon him, but those days were over. I had thought that our marriage would raise us both from our lonely underworlds, each of us drawn out by the other's music. But looking now, I saw that he had already turned to stone. He no longer sought me out at night; we lay beside one another, my body entirely cold but for the hot tears in my eyes. Deprived of useful work for the first time in my adult life, I sat listlessly in the drawing room, with only the smoking coffee urn and Sarah's interruptions for company. (She had taken to dusting the mantelpiece suspiciously often.) A short period later, Charles told me that he had taken a house uptown, larger, in a neighbourhood of fashion. I nodded dully, and asked Sarah, and the new, unfriendly maid Charles had hired, to pack.

The house Charles had chosen was as new and unfriendly as the maid. I disliked it immediately, with its modish black mansard roof and its furniture cloaked in muslin dust covers, as though it had something to hide. The presence of new cushions and up-to-the-minute drapery made me far more uncomfortable than a mere escaped alligator. No longer would Charles and I share a living room; I had my own on the second floor, which he furnished himself since I refused to evince an interest in the matter. He even equipped it with a pianoforte, which I declined to play, though I missed my father's music deeply.

The room became my residence, my study, my prison, and though the weather warmed outside, I kept the fire burning out of spite. (To what audience? Charles was nearly always from home.) Nobody called – I had no friends in New York, only business connections, and these had been removed from me. Charles hoped for us to ascend into society, but Mamie Fish was as likely to leave a card as Jesse James. I felt the loss of my work as acutely as a missing limb. And not just the work: all the little daily chores that had formed the rhythm of my pre-marriage life had also gone, vanished into the maw of wealth. I could no longer find solace in peeling a potato: the cook, Myrtle, would have had hysterics. Once I dug out the key for Pàrras from my bureau and gazed at it for a long while, weighing the old iron in my palm. I'd been lonely then, locked away with my grandparents. But somehow I had never felt trapped.

At last, to stave off madness, I began to read voraciously, emptily. Detective novels chiefly, losing (or mayhap stoking) my self-pity in tales of murdered duchesses and missing fortunes. Such books tell us there are answers, if only we have the wit to find them, and I longed to accompany Wilkie Collins' wily Sergeant Cuff, or Charles Felix's methodical insurance investigator, or even the swashbuckling Mrs Paschal, smoking, with a gun in her pocket. When such detective novels failed to solve my reality, I resorted to poetry – Thoreau, Blake, Keats, but chiefly Whitman, whose *Leaves of Grass* I found inexpressibly comforting.

And then, one drab Thursday, more than three months after Mrs Fish's disastrous party, it came.

I was alone in my living room, as usual. Summer had arrived but the clouds had drawn themselves in, huddling over the spiny city. I had abandoned the linen closet of late; it was no good, dampening the sheets like that; Josephine, the new maid, had made a sly comment about mould. I distanced myself from my thoughts and, in gothic mood that morning, put on my blackest dress and reached for Poe, 'The Raven'. Perhaps I should get one, I thought moodily, though Charles had never yet stocked that species. I realised that while my husband lived and breathed animals at work, he had never brought one home as a pet. Excepting myself, I thought darkly. It was that kind of morning. Yet no sooner had I picked up the book than the door opened and Charles came in.

I stared at him. I suppose it is not so very strange for one's husband to surface in one's own home, but we had become so alien, he might as well have been Mr Rockefeller. He was carrying something large, wrapped in a cloth, though as he set it on the table, I recognised the bell shape.

It was a cage.

Charles had brought me a gift. All the hurt fell away, snapping the steel bars that had encircled my ribs for months. I rose to embrace him.

Then, curtly: 'From my brother Henry. He has arrived on our shores but has been detained in Boston a few days. He sent this ahead. A late wedding present.'

He went out, leaving me where I was, my palms open and empty.

For the first time, I was unable to muster the strength to run to the linen closet. So I sat where I was, buried my face in my hands, and cried.

I don't know how long I sat in that attitude before the cage emitted a desultory cheep.

'Hush.'

I had just begun to relapse back into misery when I was interrupted once more. Another cheep. I hushed it again, louder. The occupant of the cage, whatever it was, continued to cheep.

'Leave me in peace!' I said, but the sound kept on, and in a fury, I crossed to it, flung the cloth aside – and froze.

The creature inside was a wonder. The *colours*. God must have painted them fresh that morning. Its head feathers were yellow in the upper half and iridescent green on the lower, encircling a blue-grey beak and a bright black eye that regarded me with an intelligent gaze. Its body was a rich chestnut brown. But its tail . . . ah, the tail! A long plume of fire, a beacon on that grey day, flowing from the perch in an easy waterfall. The most beautiful thing I had ever seen.

I knew what it was. A bird of paradise, cousin to the corpse Mamie Fish had pinned to her head. It cocked its head with a calm appraisal not dissimilar to my husband's gaze. Immediately I remembered what I had thought this gift was, and what it had actually proved to be. A paradise bird when I myself was in hell! Heat sprang to my eyes again and I went to fling the cloth over it, but something stayed my hand. It felt wrong to hide away such beauty; almost a sin. I summoned Sarah, who gasped.

'Perhaps my brother has seen such creatures on his voyages. He is lucky indeed if so. Mr Vogel is very kind.'

'What? Oh. Yes. Henry. Please take it away. Put it in the kitchen if you like it so much.' I paused. 'With some water.'

'Yes, madam. Thank you, madam.'

I returned to the Poe, but how could I concentrate on a drab, dark raven with such a creature under my roof? In the end, I sent Sarah to purchase seed for it, maw and hemp and rape. I had no idea what it ate, and I would not ask Charles. I told her to trial various food-stuffs.

'Shall I update you on its progress, madam?'

'No. Only see that it is fed.'

Her eyebrows lifted, but she agreed. I did not want to be reminded of the complete failure of understanding between Charles and me. I was furious at Henry, this brother I had never met, who had nonetheless managed to wreak such mayhem.

Some days later, a great fuss was occasioned when Stephen, a burly emporium employee, came by asking for Charles. I put my head out of my living room and listened to them in the hall. (This was what it had come to! Eavesdropping on my husband's business!)

'It's the fresh batch of ostriches for the Sells brothers. They have been vandalised, sir.'

'Vandalised? How?'

'Someone got into the pen and took the feathers. Plucked them right off.'

Charles exhaled. '*Thieves.*'

'Sorry for interrupting, sir, but they seem so miserable. Keep hiding in the corners.'

'I cannot understand it. Nobody knew those birds were there.'

'Our customers did.'

'Nonsense, Stephen. What customer of ours would do such a thing? Every one of late has been of the utmost respectability.'

They left together; I returned to my well-furbished prison. It was obvious why the birds had been targeted. Ostrich feathers, so requisite these days in hats and fans, had reached unheard-of sums, despite the African farms

134

established for the purpose of supply. I thought with a pang of the paradise bird. Likely that would have fetched a pretty penny.

My feelings had risen up again, so I took the poker and approached the anthracite fire. (I felt a little sorry for it, it having received so many vicious prods of late.) But before I reached it, the door opened and Sarah entered, a light in her features, followed by another.

Charles, I recognised automatically, but then my vision shifted. He was several inches shorter, his face wider, his nose a little more characterful. Unlike Charles's air of firm calm, this visage suggested something altogether more lively, almost to the point of impropriety – an opinion quickly validated when he strode to me, expression alight, and seized me in a bear hug. I protested immediately and vehemently, and gave him the vigorous prod I had intended for the fire.

'Mrs Vogel, is this how you greet your prodigal brother-in-law? With a poker?'

CHAPTER FOURTEEN

I looked up, releasing a long breath. The bird of paradise had made its appearance in the narrative; so had Henry Vogel. I had suspected this would happen, but it was bizarre to see the living man enter the past. Like a door that one forgets has been left open.

I realised what had given me pause, despite the intensity of my concentration. A melody threaded through the window. Lynette was singing, her voice unexpectedly lovely. The hairs on my arms rose as I recognised the lyrics. 'MacPherson's Lament'.

> Sae wontonly, sae dauntonly,
> O rantinly gaed he,
> He played a tune an' he danced aroon,
> Below the gallers tree.

A condemned fiddler stood on the scaffold, awaiting a pardon that would never arrive.

> By a woman's treacherous hand
> That I was condemned to dee

He'd played the song in the gallows' shadow, then offered his violin to the crowd. None took it. So he'd smashed it over his knee and thrown the pieces into his own waiting grave.

I thought of the stones I had seen among the trees. I tucked the diary under the mattress and hurried out of the tower. There was still light in the sky. It was time to see where Hester was buried.

It was not far, down the green hill, which would soon be dotted with harebells. After the solstice. Lynette had stopped singing, but that haunting voice trailed me, quickening my steps.

The family cemetery had not been looked after. I thought less of Mr Vogel for it as I stepped over a bent iron fence. The weather-beaten tombstones protruded at crazy angles, weeping moss into the long grass.

I had never visited my mother's grave – she was buried on St Kilda – but I had practically lived at my sister's once I left hospital. I returned to England expecting to find ivy smothering the stone. But it was as neat as it had ever been – neater. Someone had left fresh snowdrops in a tiny, beautiful vase.

Daniel. He'd never mentioned it. I'd never thanked him.

I nearly stubbed my foot on a tombstone that seemed newer than the rest. I bent down, my breath catching at the inscription.

HESTER VOGEL

Strange to see it wrought in granite. I'd felt her life force through the green ink, but this tombstone, plain, without even a date, brought home the reality. Her bones lay beneath. We would never meet. I did not know whether to be glad that she'd been buried where she grew up. For me, it would have felt like a failure.

A cry pierced the air. A golden eagle swept the sky, pursuing invisible quarry with visceral grace.

'I keep my father's grave much better than this.'

I rose quickly – I had not heard Yves' approach.

'Where is he buried?'

'In our town. We live near München.'

A tight pride in his voice, present whenever he talked of his homeland or of the school where he taught. Why had he left it before the summer holidays began? I'd tried to ask one evening. He had hinted there had been a fight, though over what and with whom he would not say.

'It was a matter of defence,' was all he would comment. I was relieved. Perhaps it was the military training, but sometimes I caught a whiff of . . . not violence, exactly, but force. It was there in his sleek jaw, in the tight veins snaking down his forearms.

I did not press him for more details. I was surrounded by enough ghosts, their presence forming a spectral cage that seemed to shimmer in the corner of my eye.

'Lynette was singing,' I said. '"MacPherson's Lament".'

'One of her favourites. She told me the legend. His pardon was en route – his executioners knew it and changed the time on the town clock. He was dead before it arrived. The magistrates were punished: for years afterwards they were forced to keep the clock behind the correct time.'

'Sounds like they got off lightly.'

'Perhaps. I think it would be rather destabilising. Trapped in the past.'

I looked at the tombstone at my feet. 'It does have a way of keeping you there.'

Our eyes met. I was suddenly glad of his presence. We walked back together, and when I tripped over a hidden grave, he stopped me from falling.

Despite it all, I could not bring myself to open Hester's diary until the next day. When the sun was once again high.

CHAPTER FIFTEEN

Henry Vogel laughed, the most infectious laugh I had ever heard. I stared at him a moment, still clutching the poker. Then a smile escaped me for the first time in weeks.

'Shall we have tea?' he said.

We did just that. The living room slowly came to life, the walls receding as he spoke of his voyages and I listened, scrutinising him over the teacup's rim. He had been to Senegambia and Madagascar, to Ceylon and to China; he spoke with as much ease of Massowah as I might speak of Madison Avenue. *He* had known true adventure, and the exotic names rolled over me like the waves on my beach, shaking me to life. His face was tanned beneath his beard, and there were faint white lines at the corners of his eyes. He was very well dressed, his clothing perfectly civilised, yet something savage lingered. He had come straight here from Boston, he said, and would later visit the emporium. I could not help the grateful flutter in my chest, nor noticing that he smelled of salt and some strange foreign spice I could not identify. If Charles was the first different person I ever met, his brother was more different still.

But I *could* help *that* thought, I reprimanded myself.

'But where is Charles?' he said at last, pausing a story of a hippo collected by his agents and brought to port suspended between two camels.

'I am not sure.' Then, unable to bear the faint concern that rose to his features: 'He is likely to be at the emporium; or perhaps at Coney Island, on his latest venture.'

'The circus.'

'You have already heard?'

'I stopped in London to bid against Jamrach; Charles left a message there. Just five weeks out of date.' He smiled. 'The most up-to-the-minute news I have had in years.'

'And you approve?'

'Don't you?' When I did not respond, he went on, 'Charles is the elder. It is my nature to go along with his decisions. They usually turn out very well. Like *you*.' He smiled, and looked me over unabashed. 'Though perhaps too pale.'

'I have not been outside much of late.'

He regarded me musingly. 'I did not expect Charles to choose an indoors sort of woman.'

'I am *not*.'

My tone prompted a second sliver of concern.

'Well then,' he said after a pause, 'allow me to accompany you on a walk.'

I did. Along our street, a cat sat on a fence post: as I passed, it swiped at me like a tiny Scylla and, surprised, I stepped away from it, pressing momentarily into Henry. We went to Central Park: he wanted to see how the planted trees were coming along and how the bird numbers were growing. He was disgusted, he said, with many of the animal trappers he had met in his line, their

140

avarice and their carelessness, without respect for God's creatures.

'Quietly, without hesitation, they see Noah's vessel – gaze into the muzzle – then take what they will, raiding His treasury with greedy fingers!'

Killing was unfortunately a requirement: you could not bring home a tiger mother and hope to tame it. Far easier to bring the cub, which meant killing its parent, though unlike others, he tried to leave as many alive as he could.

'It is far simpler to shoot a bird than to snare it.'

I sneaked glances at him as we walked and talked. There was something theatrical about him, an aura of the spectacular. He professed himself impressed by the progress of the park, pausing by a resplendent black tupelo tree. I was reminded of Blake: that to the eyes of the man of imagination, nature is imagination itself. Henry Vogel seemed someone to be delighted by any thing: not indiscriminately, but with a sure sense of its worth. It was a long time since I had encountered anyone who valued things merely for what they were.

'Surely this is nothing after the jungles of East India,' I protested.

'Why should you think so?'

'One is at the hand of nature; the other is at man's, and must necessarily be inferior.'

'Is that your view? That man's works are lesser to nature?'

Perhaps it is as well not to ask my views on man at present.

'You are correct, of course, in many respects,' he went on. 'But after so long in the lap of nature, I find myself refreshed among the world of men.'

'I would not know.' It was galling to hear a man grow

141

weary of his freedom. He did not take offence, though once again I felt him observe me.

'It is not enough, nature, at least on its own. One grows weary of magnificence, and misses conversation. But this . . .' he swept his hand around the park, 'this is man in dialogue with nature. You read Whitman?'

I started. 'I adore him.'

'Then you will recognise what I mean when I say that I see this park as a conversation both civilised and untamed.' A flash of white teeth. 'Which I find to be the best kind of encounter.'

By now we were in the Ramble. I had walked there a dozen times with Charles, yet I suddenly felt as though I were in the thickets of that East Indian jungle, full of places to get lost.

'Thank you for your wedding gift,' I said at last. 'It was very kind.'

'By no means. It was given to me. Have you named it yet?'

I ignored the question. 'You shouldn't have. I have no use for beauty.'

'That cannot be true. Joy is nothing less than the recognition of beauty; it is the bridge to the sublime, which is after all the greatest need of the soul. Those who do not recognise this requirement, and feed it, are condemned only to a kind of greyness. Not life – only existence.'

Something sank deep in my stomach. I believe he detected its ripples, for he went on, 'I gave you the bird because it is my view that we men cannot be trusted with beauty. Women are so much better at it. They do not seek to impose themselves upon it as we do.'

Bitterly I said, 'Sometimes I find beauty very hard to bear.'

He looked down at me, the liveliness in his eyes mingling with surprise, consternation, and something else entirely. I realised we had stopped, that we were close enough for me to scent the salt and spice scent that clung to his skin like a lover.

'Oh!' I exclaimed, and strode on. 'This is much too philosophical.'

In silence we exited the Ramble and walked along the straight path of the Mall. I was grateful to nod to one or two acquaintances, as a sailor catches sight of land. The rest of our conversation was trivial, and above all, perfectly civilised. At home, he left me; I did not watch him go, but in my mind I saw him round the corner and New York swallow him up.

Henry met Charles at the emporium, and that evening we all dined together. The younger brother had changed his clothing and was now as elegant as the elder. It had been arranged that he would stay with us for a few days, in the small bedroom off the second-floor landing. I supervised Josephine as she made it ready. I think Sarah was hurt that I did not ask her to do it – I soon realised she was immensely fond of Henry, having known him for some five years – but in truth I could not bear to. We both knew that room should have been the nursery.

Josephine, meanwhile, was all a-flutter from Henry's arrival. Even Myrtle rose to the occasion. She was not an especially good cook, but she was a persevering one, beating her ingredients into submission. I watched her descend the stairs with a bowl in which newly delivered terrapins floundered, and felt a grim sympathy.

Henry would stay while he organised his affairs and found appropriate lodgings, though Charles had apparently offered up his rooms at his new club. I had not

143

been aware he had joined it. Oh, how I hoped our reconciliation would come – yet how hopeless seemed every way to it! In any case, Charles was in a filthy mood: Sarah told me in an undertone that not only had a gorilla died of sickness, but Raymond had quit the emporium. Worse, he was going to work for Barnum.

At eight o'clock, we sat down to turtle soup. I had wine, as did Henry. He was on my left, Charles on my right, and I tried to reconcile the feeling of double vision. They were laughing at an old childhood game: Henry, the more mischievous, had liked to hide Charles's toys about the house and make his brother find them. I had not expected such warmth between them – Henry had never seemed particularly at the forefront of Charles's thoughts – and I felt betrayed by my husband's attentiveness, by how bound together they were and must have been since Charles smuggled his younger sibling out the window all those years before. What other passions had he hidden?

'I ought to have disciplined you better,' he was saying, a gleam in his eye.

Henry only smiled and said to me, 'Charles will never give up what is rightfully his. When I think of how long he searched for that tin elephant!'

He turned back to his brother; I felt the withdrawal of his attention like the sand does the sea. 'You know, I had no doubts about leaving the business in your hands. I see I was right to do so. It goes from strength to strength. Though if I were to find a fault' – and now his glance landed briefly upon me – 'I might consider the circus rather daring.'

'Daring! Why, there can be no safer industry. You may not have noticed in your absence, but the American people have concentrated themselves wholly on the manufacture of railroads, coke and wonder, in that order. Whether the Academy's operas or Broadway's freaks, the great and the low feed off it equally.'

'Yes,' said Henry drily, 'but I imagine the Swedish Nightingale is less expensive to feed than hyenas. It is not the *demand* I question, but the outlay.'

'We cannot trade in fur and feathers for ever. Diversification, that is the modern way.'

I was startled: those were Mr Havely's words issuing from my husband's mouth.

'Are we certain that Vogel & Brother is not over-extending itself?' Henry asked seriously.

Charles could not help himself. His eyes were dragged unwillingly to me.

'We have the money,' I said quietly.

'A woman who involves herself in her husband's affairs?' Henry's delight returned. 'You have a head for figures?'

Charles had not told him. 'I have done the books since we were married.'

Henry regarded me for a heartbeat, then said, 'Brother, it is even better than I thought. You have found both beauty and sensibility. I congratulate you for it.'

Both of us flushed, though without pleasure.

'Hester does not do the books any longer,' Charles said quietly. 'It is more proper that she remains at home.'

'What! The lioness does not leave her pride. No, Charles, it is very hard, once one has had a kingdom, to share it.'

'Or give it up altogether,' I said in an undertone, but neither man heard. It was not that I missed dancing that weary dance of figures, exactly; it was that I missed the work, the *purpose*. I'd been surprised by the smallness of

145

the emporium's world, despite the great distances its wares had travelled; but the house was smaller still, and with far less company. I thought of the python I had met, the coils that could wind around and around in loving constriction.

'Frost's fellow now does the books,' Charles said.

Henry went very still. 'Hyatt Frost? What has he to do with it?'

'He is our partner in the circus venture.'

I had thought Henry a man little fazed by anything, but he seemed stunned. 'That swindler?'

Charles's tone was cold. 'The very same.'

'You went into business with *him* without informing *me*?'

'What is wrong with Mr Frost?' I asked, at the same time as Charles said, 'You were on the other side of the globe, Henry.'

'Yes,' came the swift reply, 'working for our business. Not undermining it.'

'Mr Frost has decades of experience.'

'Yes, but *what* experience? I suppose you mean the Barnum museum? You are aware it burned down twice?'

'That is hardly his fault. Both lost a lot of money.'

'Who is to say they would not have lost more without those conflagrations? I heard very curious things about the insurance policy. Frost has a fondness for making his own fireworks, which he deploys recklessly at his venues.'

'Rumours are not facts,' Charles said icily. 'Our competitors grow stronger, our profits weaker. A circus is a welcome opportunity.'

'It is not the circus I object to.'

'Mr Frost is putting up his share.'

'An *equal* share?' Nothing. 'Brother, you are being

taken for a fool. Even leaving aside the rumours of his questionable tastes.'

'Charles,' I said quietly. 'Is this true?'

My husband looked from me to his brother. At last he said, 'I do not answer to either of you.'

Myrtle entered with chops; we applied ourselves in merciful silence.

'I am sorry about Raymond,' I said at last, attempting sympathy. 'I had not thought it of him.'

'It is none of your concern.'

Henry was watching us. Suddenly I could not bear for him to see me prostrate.

'I had thought to get up a little parcel for him.'

'In God's name, why?'

'He was a good employee, Charles.'

'He had no right.'

I tried humour. 'He has gone to work for Barnum, not the Devil.'

'He was mine!' My husband slammed his plate down on the table, and the delicate porcelain smashed, shards flying at me like knives. Breathing hard, he stood and departed, leaving his napkin crumpled in his place.

There was a chattering sound, and I realised the fork I still held was trembling against the table. I set it down. I could not look at Henry. Sarah, bless her, hastened in with coffee, and it was only after she had bustled about with milk and spoons that I looked up. Henry's expression was dark. He held one of the plate's shards and was absent-mindedly digging it into the table, scoring a deep hole in the wood.

'Henry,' I said in alarm, and the shard clattered from his grip. We drained our cups in silence. Afterwards he insisted on thanking Myrtle. I followed him to the kitchen; I had nothing else to do.

'A delicious repast,' he was saying to her as I descended the stairs, his tone again calm, urbane. 'But what is this?'

With a clench of the heart, I remembered the bird of paradise, hidden away in the kitchen. I hurried down the last few steps to find him bent over its cage.

'What are you doing down here?' he was asking, with a tenderness that pricked my eyes.

Before Sarah could reply, I said hastily, 'Staying warm. I was not sure what conditions the creature preferred; it seemed best to keep it near the stove.'

I did not know whether Henry believed me, but something in that appraising gaze told me he did not.

'I see. What are you feeding him?'

I looked helplessly at Sarah.

'Maw seed, sir, and rape, and I have tried niger mixed in.'

'Seed! That explains his dulled complexion. The poor creature must have fruit. See how his tail droops.'

He moved aside, and I saw with a pang that the bird had sadly diminished since its arrival. Its eye was no longer lively; its tail hung limp. I would not have let the emporium creatures be neglected so. I felt a sudden deep remorse. It was not *its* fault that I had mistaken it for Charles's gift.

'I shall remove it to my living room,' I said, and did so, carrying it myself, declining Sarah's overtures of assistance. Henry followed me in silence. He did not offer to help.

'Good night,' I said to him at the door, but he insisted on observing as I set the creature up beside the window closest to the ebbing fire. We watched as it took stock of its new surroundings; eventually it emitted a faint, satisfied cheep.

148

I turned back to Henry, who was regarding me with a grave expression.

'Poor thing. It seems to have been neglected of late.' At the suffusion in his tone, something rose in me, a complex mixture I could not separate into its parts. 'But it is a magnificent creature, and it takes very little love to restore something to its previous splendour.'

Half in a trance, I found myself taking a step towards him. The instant I did so, he gave a small bow, turned on his heel and departed, leaving me alone with the bird, each of us confused and a little afraid at the situation we now found ourselves in.

Perhaps because of the dispute with Charles, Henry moved to his new lodgings in very short order. I did not see him for several days, and my living room felt smaller and darker than before, as dark as the bedroom Charles and I shared, with its heavy blankets and the curtains smothering the light. Or rather, it would have, had it not been for the paradise bird.

That first morning when I entered, it was gazing out of the window. I crossed and looked out also. Already the air was shimmering with heat: small boys darted about like minnows, carrying neat paper boxes of fried oysters, their activity concentrated around a gentleman with a new silk hat proceeding down the street like a stately shark. Beyond them, its scorched grass dappled with shadows, was the neighbourhood cemetery. Guiltily I considered how far removed the creature was from its greeny jungle. I bent down to inspect it properly, then, after a moment's hesitation, knelt. Oh, it was an impossible thing, its beauty tussling with the senses. I was reminded of the first time I had tasted Swiss chocolate: the richness, the smoothness, that same

149

delight of discovering something so far from the ordinary course of things.

A shout from the street: one of the small boys had dropped his oyster box and was howling. I roused myself to go and give him a few coins, but as I did so, the bird turned to me for the first time.

I did not generally handle Charles's creatures, but a travelling man once came to town and I held his hawk, observing the pure murder in its eye. My bird's expression was not like that. Perhaps the cage made it unafraid, but its look hit me between the eyes, forceful precisely because it demanded nothing. How often could I say the same of my encounters with people? I learned later that its kind had no natural predators until man arrived; with survival not an issue, beauty had taken over. I desired greatly to touch it, but though my finger caressed the cage bars, I did not quite dare. I sensed the life coursing through it, and felt that same life in myself. For the first time since I had last swum in the freezing Boston sea, the raw fact of my own existence welled up like a spring, bringing tears to my eyes. I remembered how to be alive. I had not even noticed that I had forgotten.

Over the next fortnight, I found myself spending less and less time with books, and more and more with Henry's marvellous gift. The Malay people called these creatures 'birds of the gods': they lent themselves natur-ally to myth. Did my own bird mourn for its home? I wondered, then found myself debating why I had never considered this for the myriad other beasts that passed through our doors.

It was just as well that I had the bird as distraction. I did not know what had come from the circus disagreement, but there was no sign of the venture being discontinued. Since that dinner, I no longer dared to ask Charles about it, or the emporium. There was a certain set about his jaw, a flint in his eyes; I did not want to strike it and cause a conflagration. The new way of things was that I remained silent.

One morning I heard Sarah protesting on the stairs, and a moment later Henry barrelled in, pursued by her apologies. I had noticed that about him – he did not enter a room, but rather burst in upon it.

'Hester. A wonderful thing has happened. Or may happen,' he amended. 'You must come at once.'

He would not answer my questions, only hurrying me from the house and into the waiting cab. The heat was sticky: sweat glistened off the horses' necks, the coach-man's cigar like a small sun. At last we bowled up at our destination: Vogel & Brother's emporium. I turned to Henry, trembling in annoyance.

'I cannot be here. Charles does not wish it, and nor do I.'

Those eyes glinted. 'Charles is not here. I do not know what row it is you are having, but I do not wish any part in it.'

'Then do not bring me to the store!'

He stopped and regarded me with an intense focus, a focus I recognised as Charles's, except it had not fixed so upon me for many months.

'Hester. You put the bird I gave you in the kitchen. I will not embarrass you by asking why.' He sighed, flexed his fingers. 'Before I arrived, I had no preconceptions about what Charles's marriage might be like. Now I have observed it, I see that sending you a caged creature may well have been offensive. The mind of humanity, particularly a preoccupied mind, naturally runs to

151

metaphors. But you are *not* the same, Hester. The bird has no choice in the matter. You are a grown woman: you must not lock yourself up out of spite. Charles does not want you in the emporium. What of that? We only relinquish the power we allow other people to take.'

'You do not understand.'

'I understand perfectly.' His hand grasped my arm. 'I was the very first thing Charles ever collected. He loved me as an object, as is his way; it was the work of years to make him love me as a person. As a brother. But I *did*, Hester, and once Charles loves in the proper way, he never lets go.'

I thought I understood. Truly I did. At last I let out a long, shuddering breath. 'Well, what is this wonderful thing?'

Strange to step once more over the emporium's threshold. As Henry had promised, Charles was not there, but nor, unusually, was anyone else. He went and flung open the doors at the back: summer rushed in, along with that familiar rich furred whiff. I closed my eyes. When I opened them, I realised he had been watching, and did not want me to know it. A sudden awkwardness slid between us.

'So,' he said, busying himself at the counter, 'this wondrous thing.'

I gave myself a moment to imagine. A new animal, perhaps. Some curious hybrid, never yet seen on these shores.

'It is a customer.'

I was disappointed. It would be one of the Four Hundred. I had not thought Henry easily impressed by society.

He laughed. 'It seems I can bear anything, Hester, but your disappointment. Do not condemn me yet. Ah – here he is now.'

Somehow the bell had sounded without my noticing: an old man entered, bearded, his hat low on his brow and his eyes limned with wrinkles.

'Mr Whitman,' Henry said. 'How may we assist?'

In a daze, I watched Henry chatter with the ageing poet. In the darkest reaches of my time at the corset factory, and in these lonely months of late, I had read and reread the book he had published, and edited, and published again. I cannot count the times his words had forced back walls that had been sidling in. He could draw forth one's soul with gentle fingers and launch it into the air, those small lyrics he had worked over and over in a manner reminiscent of the women in my own former workshop, frowning as they repositioned a spar of bone, turning it this way and that with adjustments nigh invisible to the untrained eye; yet once they sat back, with a sigh of satisfaction, anybody could look and see that it was perfect. If the most vital achievement of poetry is to make us feel less alone, then . . .

He wanted a canary, he said, nothing else would do. Henry brought down cage after cage and he carefully scrutinised each. It occurred to me that he was a detective like any in my novels; that he too was a pursuer of truth. And I understood then that I was trying to find something. What it was, I did not yet know, but as I observed the two men from my once accustomed place behind the counter, I knew that soon I would discover it; that the quick rising and falling of my chest meant something, as did my sudden consciousness of my body as more than a daily tool; and as I watched the poet bend

153

over what I somehow knew would be the decisive canary, I realised that my own pet was in some way at the centre of it all, that the paradise bird would be the key to unlocking a gate that had confined me for as long as I could remember.

At last the great man made his selection. I had been right. The little yellow creature regarded him with cocked head, then poured forth a stream of rippling notes. Its new owner took up the cage and turned to leave.

'Mr Whitman,' I blurted. 'Your poetry book. Is it now finished?'

He regarded me thoughtfully. 'What do you mean?'

'Have we had the final edition? I suppose, are you . . . done?'

He frowned. 'I am as "done" with my poems as I am done with living. Just because a thing has been made does not mean it cannot be remade again. It is the only true way to live: we are always in motion. The tides of our days; the rise and fall of our breath. We are remade a thousand times over, if only we could see it. Look at this creature. Why am I, an old man, purchasing a bird that may well outlive me? For joy, of course, and for love, the only true refreshers of the soul.' He made a slight bow. 'Now if you will forgive me, I have a canary to feed.'

He departed; the bell tolled behind him, echoing in the sudden silence.

I turned to Henry, with his characterful nose and the mouth that was a little too wide; the bright brown eyes, just then wearing a serious expression that I knew would dissolve to liveliness at the slightest prompt. I saw his body and his mind; what he was, and what he exceeded: the Henry I could reach out and touch, and the soul that

154

towered huge in the room. Dust motes drifted through the air, enveloping him in a golden haze.

'Oh,' I said. 'You're beautiful.'

I returned to the house in the early evening. Unusually, Charles was there, in his living room. He called me in, and I entered to find him seated on one of the hard-backed chairs, working. For once there was a courteousness between us, and we sat quietly but companionably in the hour before dinner. At one point he looked up from his papers and saw me observing him, and whatever he caught in my expression softened his own. He rose, crossed to me and cupped my face gently with his hands.

'Dear Hester,' he said. 'We have been so very far away from one another.'

I felt as I had in the frozen sea, when my very jaw would ache.

Supper that evening was convivial, almost like our suppers used to be. He talked of the circus's opening night, of the 'woolly mammoths' that would be exhibited in the entrance after their supposed discovery in Malaysia. I found this showman aspect incongruous against his usual rational self: the capacity for deceit, I suppose, since deception lurks at the very core of spectacle. But I listened happily enough while I ate my mutton, and thought of those eyes, that brotherly nose, that wide mouth. I could not help it.

'Oh,' I had said to Henry through the golden air. 'You're beautiful.'

I took a step towards him, and another. We were virtually the same height: I looked directly into those lively, living eyes.

'Hester . . .' His voice had a snapped quality. There was a broken thing inside him too. The only thing to do about it was to go on living. 'Hester,' he said again, quietly, and this time I kissed him, and he kissed me back, his mouth warm and full, the two of us alive with joy, just as the old poet had said. I delighted in his warm flesh against mine, in the heat of the sunbeams dancing as the clouds came and went, in the hardness of the counter and the floor against my back, in the delicate tuft of feather I found afterwards in my hair. At some point Henry went and locked the door, and though we were both shut in, surrounded by cages, I had never known such freedom.

CHAPTER SIXTEEN

I set the pages down, the account over, already determined to find the next. Hester and Henry. Henry and Hester. I tried to picture Mr Vogel now against then. A most curious palimpsest. So he had loved his sister-in-law: was it this that had driven Hester to suicide? Mr Vogel had spoken in the library of his hatred of betrayal. Hester's betrayal of Charles? Charles's abandonment of him? Or was that hatred in fact directed inwards, towards himself, for his own betrayal of Charles?

I had thought Hester would lead me to the diamond, but it seemed she was also leading me towards something infinitely rarer than a gemstone: truth.

The trouble was, I now had to find the next notebook. The story was evidently incomplete; I was confident another instalment existed. It was oddly like searching the jungle. Such climes seemed chaotic, but they had their own secret logic, based on the sun and the soil, on eating and being eaten. Nothing was quite as it seemed: green leaves might be fringed with stinging indumenta, soft ferns embedded with spines. Here was that same hidden order.

But unlike the plants I always managed to find eventually, the diary would not yield itself to me. Over the next few days, I caught myself staring at Mr Vogel, hunting for his younger counterpart, green ink crawling across that wrinkled face. He was smiling at one of Yves' beer-hall tales at dinner one evening and I was reminded of the dried flowers I still found occasionally in my sister's books: the suppleness had gone, but the essence lingered, somehow surviving the years. To my surprise, Lynette had removed the bird of paradise from the kitchen; it was now perched on a cabinet in the low sitting room, and after a whisky with Yves, I lingered there, feeling the touch of Hester's fingertips upon my own existence. The longer I spent with her diary, the stronger that touch grew. I found I did not mind. I might have been hunting for the diamond with the same methodology as I did plants, but this was different. I never really had to look after the specimens I found, merely keeping them alive long enough to transport them to clients. Tracking the diary felt more like those days battling the Dutch elm blight. Like here was something I truly cared for – something worth saving.

The bird's black glass eyes regarded me impassively. Hester had done this – gazed at this very bird. As with her childhood bedroom, I was following in her footsteps. My thoughts roamed. The first clue had been marked by a direct quote from *The Birdcage Library*. What if the second was, too? Though searching the entire work would take a long time . . .

I went up to my bedroom nevertheless and opened the book again. Nothing in that introductory chapter. But what about the second chapter? This was, after all, the second clue.

Styles, the chapter heading said, outlining the basics choices available to the bird keeper. I began to read. Several pages in:

When choosing his cage, the fancier may initially be dazzled by the range of choice available. It is natural to seek to keep up with the latest fashions, yet such a personal choice of ornament is also a matter of INTUITION. Consider it akin to choosing a home, for this, of course, is what you are doing, and therefore the process may have all the little agonies, all the hopes quickly raised only to be dashed, of finding one's own residence. This is the exquisite joy of the civilised collector – we take what we will, raiding God's treasury with greedy fingers – yet every treasure must have its chest!

A slow smile spread across my features. There it was. Hester herself had written: *Quietly, without hesitation, they see Noah's vessel – gaze into the muzzle – then take what they will, raiding His treasury with greedy fingers!* She had echoed the book again. But to what end?

I removed my expedition notebook from my tool belt and wrote out the sentence, then tried to make sense of it. If I took the copied text merely as the marker, the remaining piece must be the clue. Noah's vessel – that must be the Ark. Did a 'muzzle' refer to one of Mr Vogel's beasts? Perhaps a *pair* of beasts, given the Ark association? But there were many such in that deathly menagerie, and it would be both impractical and destructive to start shredding their noses in search of a clue within. Besides, what did that have to do with quietness, or indeed hesitation? I tried to be clever, working the words and letters backwards, acrostically, anagrammatically and any other way I could think of. Gibberish.

A slow ray fell across my paper. The sun was coming up. Without realising, I'd been up all night, and not a drop of gin in sight.

I rubbed my sore eyes and looked again at the green ink. All was silent. Lynette alone would be up at this hour, making bread. Sometimes the scent drifted through the window, as tangible as her lament had been.

Music . . . Hester had loved music, though she did not play. Loved it like she did her detective novels. Had she ever thought her own afterlife would come to resemble the latter? We were living in a golden age of detective fiction – she would have enjoyed it very much, though they were not the kind of puzzles I had grown up with. Before Harold passed away, he had fallen in love with a new kind of crossword in the papers.

'Cryptic!' he'd said, thumping the floor for emphasis. 'There is nothing else!'

He'd tried to teach Daniel, then my sister and me, but we rarely evinced much interest. We preferred to run amok in the garden, stirring up the mirror pond, folding the waters over the reflected sky.

Twist your mind, he would say when we did sit down with him. Break it open. Reassemble.

My pulse began to beat. Cryptic puzzles had not been invented in Hester's time, but codes were old as mankind – language *was* a code. I wrote down 'ark' in a space by itself, then turned my attention to the rest. I would confine myself initially to the words before the dash, which perhaps acted as a marker of separation.

Language was a code; so was musical notation.

Quietly. I was no musician, but I knew their term for it. *Piano.* Or simply, *p*.

Then the second part, 'without hesitation'. I wrote down several suggestions before I remembered that 'without' could be a place marker, positioning it on the outside. So perhaps it came at the start or end of the whole word. And it *was* a word, I was reasonably sure, containing 'p' and 'ark'.

Park. I bent lower to the ink, willing it to relinquish its secrets. Central Park? But what was the allusion to hesitation? My lips moved, mouthing more gibberish.

Pause. Delay. Falter. No, it couldn't be a whole word.

Um. No – *er.*

Parker.

What the hell was a Parker? And how could I gaze into the muzzle of it? I knew of no animal species with that label, though to my ears it sounded rather like some sort of obscure gazelle.

Which meant it was time to consult the ledgers in the menagerie.

All was silent as I crept downstairs, past Yves' room. The stone was cold under my bare feet, dawn poking through the arrow slits. I hadn't bothered with shoes, so caught up was I in discovery. Through the rosy courtyard, and then I was creaking open the menagerie door, the animals baring their teeth in welcome. I went straight to the ledgers and began combing through the entries, searching for any species bearing the name Parker. Parker's gazelle still sounded good. Or Parker's parrot.

But I found nothing.

The sun had well and truly risen when I set the last ledger down, neck aching. Time to return to work. Perhaps my deciphering of the clue was wrong or incomplete, but try as I might, I could not parse the 'muzzle' part any further.

I spent the day searching the low sitting room, then awoke again at the next dawn, already chewing my lip. Perhaps Hester had counted on a zoologist or other animal expert to find the diary, one who would know immediately what was meant.

Who *had* she intended to find it? Not me, that was for sure. Perhaps I was on the wrong track. What else had a muzzle?

My jaw dropped. Could it be?

I crept out of my bedroom again, but did not head for the menagerie. Instead I went down the corridor that led to

161

the great hall. I passed the kitchen, and the pantry, and reached the gun room.

A muzzle was not just the nose and mouth of an animal. It was also the barrel end of a gun.

I had only seen the room on the blueprints, and now found myself in a narrow, dark chamber, a deep gimlet window at one end through which the whitening light was visible. Not long before the others awoke. I scanned the furniture, the walls and the bare stone floor. It was functional, devoid of decoration save antlers on the wall and a ferret snarling from a glass case. I opened up its box, ran my hands over it, peered into its mouth. Nothing. I inspected the deer skulls, tapping the antlers in case they were hollow, but came up similarly empty. Otherwise there was a coat rack bearing a single coat, which I recognised as belonging to Yves, and a dark wooden table with a binoculars case.

That left the gun cabinet itself, a tough-looking antique with a glass front, containing perhaps a dozen shotguns. Mr Vogel, it seemed, had a rather beautiful collection.

I tried the handle – locked, and I could not pick it. But the brands' names gleamed through the glass, elegantly wrought upon the sleek, menacing objects before me.

Holland & Holland. Westley Richards. Purdey. And Parker.

I turned and ran back to my tower.

CHAPTER SEVENTEEN

Yves was awake when I knocked.

'Come in.'

I entered. His room was very, very neat, the bed already made. It seemed lighter than elsewhere in the castle, as though the stones themselves had been scrubbed.

'Something wrong?'

'Will you take me stalking?'

I could not alert him to my search, and this was the only way I could think of to get that cabinet unlocked. It did not take much persuasion. Upstairs, I changed into outdoor clothing and almost ran into him as he emerged similarly dressed.

'Look out,' he said, stretching, the lazy grace at odds with the neatness of the bedroom behind.

The gun room was brighter now.

'We had better be quick. Dawn is the best time.'

I watched hungrily as he unlocked the cabinet.

'What about that one?' I dared to point at the Parker, but he laughed.

'That is an antique. We do not use it.' He passed me another, newer model. And a knife.

'I have my own.' I indicated the one strapped to my tool belt.

'Already a hunter. I forgot.'

I could only watch as he relocked the cabinet and pocketed the key.

The tide was high, but Yves led me down to a small stony beach where a wooden boat awaited. Someone had painted it white, though they'd neglected to give it a name.

I insisted that I take an oar; the loch was covered in mist and we plashed along like Charon. At least no green eyes watched me: the exercise, as intended, helped distract from the intense discomfort of being on the water.

Yves steered us to the bank from which we would climb the hill, past a few storm-gnarled pines. We would be hunting red stags. He knew a good place, though he had not been there for some time. The deer were clever – would pick up on a man's routine and change their own accordingly.

We tied up the boat: the fog here was mercifully thinner. Before we set off, Yves took a cardboard box from the vessel and placed it a hundred yards away.

'Try it,' he said, nodding at the gun.

I lay on the springy ground, not letting myself wince as damp soaked into my clothing. I had not told him of my pistol, or the sheer amount of time I had spent in the dirt yard of our house in Sydney, my constant restlessness craving a bullet's release. I brought the thing into position. The telescopic sight was of the post variety: no cross hairs. It wavered up and down, fluttering with my heart. I took a deep breath and found that familiar control.

'That's it,' Yves said quietly.

I ran my finger down the trigger, the tip touching the curve of the tine. Then . . .

*

Yves brought the box back, an odd look on his face.

'Perfect,' he said. 'Absolutely perfect.'

I turned away, but not before I had glimpsed the hole. Dead centre.

We began our ascent. I was ill at ease: though the mist was fading, the pale sun growing visible, a sense of deadness lingered, of ghosts nearly drawn. I might have been in that Papuan village again, the pastor warning me of the shadow at my back.

Or perhaps my discomfort was due to the clothes Yves had brought to the gun room and insisted I wear. Plus fours and leather gaiters. I disliked travelling so heavily. In the jungle, I often went barefoot. The first time had been by accident, my boots sucked into mud five feet deep, but I found it made the ground easier to read. This way nature could whisper in my ear, and if I stepped on a snake, it would not bite me. But Yves had said the items were not just about practicality. To dress up, after all, implies a sense of occasion.

We were an hour in the climb, travelling against the wind, my face soon raw. You had to be high to see deer, yet not so high that your shape penetrated the skyline. Ptarmigan flew beneath us. The marshy ground was both soft and unforgiving, moss campion dotting splashes of exposed rock like stars, a galaxy you could fall into if you weren't careful. There was nothing here. Not a pristine nothingness: this place had been stripped clean. Once there would have been forests, great shadows of oak and rowan and dark pine. I was seeing this land's bones.

We stopped and drank from a burn that parted the heather, tumbling clear down black stone. Nearby was a ruined croft. Someone had lived here. There were only a few stones now, blackened where the hearth would have been.

Don't jump over the water, Yves said. The deer have six senses: they'll notice the vibrations. He'd stalked these hills for over a decade. There was skill here, no less than my ability to trace plants – perhaps more so, for no plant was composed of layers of beautiful muscle that might roam wherever it pleased. I liked that he cared enough to be good at it. To kill them, he had to think like them. Had to get inside their minds in order to destroy their bodies. In a low voice he described where to shoot the animal. Not the heart. Go for inside the diaphragm.

Don't worry, he said quietly, after I confessed my ambivalence to killing. The creature would be old, thin. Unhealthy. It needed culling.

We waded and crawled for another hour, maybe two. And suddenly he was right there, sitting on his own on a high plateau. He was magnificent, more so than I could have ever imagined. Grey stone surrounded him like a throne.

We lay on the ground. I put the sight to my eye and saw the muscle in his flank, the very hairs on his neck. My heart was a wire, sawing back and forth.

'Do it,' Yves whispered, so low it was almost beyond hearing.

And I did. The stag convulsed, stood as though he had something to say; swayed, then settled back onto his haunches and bowed his head. Perhaps he did so in grace; perhaps in defeat; or mayhap with something I could never understand.

'I don't want to leave him here.'

'We won't,' Yves said, soothingly, as though I too were a deer he did not wish to scare. He would return later with a local man and his garron, his pony. Meanwhile we gralloched the stag, the hot stench of his insides wafting up and into us. The windswept plateau was entirely devoid of trees, yet the jungle was all around.

After the accident, I had once tried to accompany Daniel to catch trout. But he refused, the first time he had ever done such a thing.

You cannot fish with anger in your heart, he said sadly. The trout sense it.

In my heart I knew he was right. The water would boil around my boots and cook the fish in their secret burrows. As I had lain down to shoot the stag, I had felt the old rage bubbling, bubbling, seeking release. Daniel had thought I was angry at my sister's death, at my father's blinding. But it wasn't that – the church tower was a horrific accident, that was all. No, I raged against what those tragedies had made me become.

One day that final summer, during those weeks of hot sun and cool shadows, of lemonade and gasping streets, my sister went into town. She had spent much time with Daniel of late, and I had begun to take the hint and leave them alone together. I had become used to solitude and did not mind it now, walking out into Butterworth's secretive woods. It was too hot even for the birds to sing.

I heard Daniel's approach long before he found me, conscious of his growing nearness, like a comet nearing impact. He smiled at me even as he looked around for my sister. The leaves of the surrounding beeches were burnished to a sheen.

'She's in town,' I said, expecting to see disappointment in his features, but instead finding . . . relief. No. Pleasure. He fell into step beside me and we walked in silence, neither of us saying a word. When his fingertips brushed mine, we did not talk then either. We paused, breathless, beside the great spreading oak, the oldest tree on Butterworth's estate, and we were silent then too. And when I leaned up to him, and his firm mouth met mine, I felt a happiness that I could never have put words to anyway.

My sister returned from town. That night we lay hot in bed, the sun's warmth still lingering in the trees.

'I am going to marry him,' she told me, across the dark space of our bedroom. I did not need to ask whom she meant. 'I decided today.'

167

I ignored the flattening in my chest. Ignored the little seed whose existence I had barely begun to recognise before I tore it out.

'You should,' was all I said. After all, she was the one who deserved him.

I could not really look at Daniel after that, though he tried to speak to me, tried to tear open that wordless thing we'd shared. Instead, gradually, through that long summer, I withdrew.

Six weeks later, she was dead.

Yves and I spread out the steaming entrails for the corbies, the crows. Blood dripped over my hands; my nails were scarlet moons, and a streak ran through my companion's golden hair. Finally we turned to go.

'Emily. Wait,' he said. Before I could react, he dipped his hands into the red well of blood, brought them to my face and traced two fingers down each cheek. Hot lines of blood settled there like scars. I asked what the hell he was playing at.

'Tradition. You must be blooded for your first deer,' he said calmly. 'It honours the stag, because you cannot hide away what you have done.'

Something broke. I held it in as we made our way back to Pàrras, as the warmth of the blood faded and dried to a crust. I felt branded. Immediately on arrival, I went to the outside pump and scrubbed at my face, hard, harder, until the stained water turned clear. My head spun as I returned to the gun room, Yves unlocking the cabinet and then watching as I removed my plus fours and gaiters. He did not change: after we had locked up the guns, he would go immediately to find the garron man. It was only then that I remembered Hester, and though I wanted nothing more than to turn and run, I forced myself to offer to put the

168

guns away. But he declined. His uncle was very particular, he said. He would have to clean them too.

Lynette appeared. The garron man was at the door. He had heard the gun's retort and was ready with the pony.

Yves sighed. 'There are no secrets in this place.'

I thought him wrong. He went out, and barely holding myself together, I seized my chance. I went to the cabinet and took out the Parker.

It was beautiful, sleek and powerful, the company name finely engraved upon it. I considered the muzzle. The thing *was* a beast, in its way. I turned it on its end and stared directly into the barrel. A curious feeling.

There. Rolled up in the left-hand tube was something thin and pale. I put my blood-rusted fingers inside, and just as Yves' footsteps returned down the hall, I whipped the papers out and replaced the weapon inside its cabinet.

Perhaps he heard the *clank* as I did so. Perhaps not. But he stopped in the doorway and scrutinised me.

'You washed the blood off. Why?'

I could not tell him that I could not bear it. Suddenly I could be there no longer, not with him, not with the guttural stench that lingered on my hands and clothing. Not with those guns, their craftsmanship a cunning distraction from their brutality.

'Emily,' he said, concerned. He reached for me, but I pushed past him, into the cold stone corridor and onwards, not stopping until I reached my bedroom, my breath coming in harried gasps, my heart flapping wildly in my chest. I grabbed the basin and carbolic soap and scrubbed and scrubbed at my cheeks all over again. I scrubbed on even after they were red and sore, even after the soap got into my eyes and I almost howled, though not from pain.

You cannot hide away what you have done.

But that was exactly what I *had* done, for seven long years.

CHAPTER EIGHTEEN

Those ensuing days and weeks were the happiest I had ever known. Every morning Charles would leave to spend the day with Hyatt Frost; every afternoon, after his work, his brother came to collect me. I spent the time before he arrived in idle frenzies. I could not read, scarcely ate. I no longer worked – Charles had seen to that. I was nothing, I did nothing. There was only Henry.

No, not only he. The paradise bird was my other companion, though the man and his gift were becoming the same, blurring into one like my father and the great auk all those years before. I watched it for hours, crooned to it, fed it sweet fruits through the bars of the cage. Sometimes I played it silly tunes on the piano. The species' name was apt. Paradise lay before me. I had not realised how small it would be.

When Henry arrived, the bird's iridescence would by some magic transfer to the wider world, which glistened with an unreal brightness: the sheen on some oily puddle, or a lady's glossy pearls as we passed, arm in arm, perfectly proper, a woman and her brother-in-law taking the air. I felt the weight and shape of that arm in my dreams; the insides of my eyes were papered with the thin, delicate skin on his neck, my own mouth covered by his.

One day we returned to Central Park and released English skylarks for no other reason than Henry's inclination; on another we went to a matinee, and in the crush I luxuriated in our closeness, each of us breathing the other's air. How greedily I crammed my self into his! I arranged him in every corner and felt something close to completion. Usually we went to his rooms at the club, which had a private entrance; on Sundays, when gentlemen fleeing church were most likely to be about, we went to the shuttered emporium. I would touch my cheeks after our encounters, testing for the familiar soreness, but either his whiskers were softer than his brother's, or our bodies were in some way made for one another. I could believe both.

Summer lingered, but I no longer cared for the open air; the outside held no charms for me. It was Henry who insisted upon it, though he was also mindful that we should not be seen idly strolling too often. So one afternoon we found ourselves browsing Bloomingdale's.

We entered that vast temple to commerce arm in arm, the doormen bowing politely. We were the happiest pair, for all the world like husband and wife perusing its many treasures. We passed electric toothbrushes and ivory walking sticks, curtain poles and hair curlers, portières and fans, eventually coming to the famous sky carriages, shooting passengers upwards to further attractions as easily as a saint rose to heaven. We sat on the upholstered seats while the black operator readied himself with the lever; the doors closed and as though by magic we began our rumbling ascent. Instinctively I

171

drew nearer to Henry, who bent his head close, his breath warm against my neck.

'I love you,' he whispered. 'I hope you do not mind.'

I did not mind; I did not mind at all, and though our destination was only the women's department, as the elevator went higher I felt as though I really were ascending to paradise.

We left the operator to his mysterious workings and meandered on through. There were corsets, I noticed with an odd pang – but I was happy, perfectly happy. Henry was all I needed. We moved through flounces of Valenciennes lace and on to the fashions, where rows of dressed mannequins stood to attention. In this place a woman might think she could be anybody.

'They always remind me of bodies awaiting possession,' I said.

'And which would you pick?'

I shrugged. 'Any would do.'

He looked me up and down. 'I prefer this one.'

'Yes, but that was not the question.'

'Oh Hester, if we only ever answered the questions we are asked!' He took my arm and I forgot my responding thought. Being with him was like that: my own personal River Lethe. With him there was no Charles, no company, no empty hours of wasteful, wanting idleness. Nothing beyond pure existence.

We carried on into the millinery salon, French-bevelled mirrors stretching from floor to ceiling. We might have been in the emporium for the sheer breadth and variety of plumage on display. I did not appreciate the reminder, but Henry was busy inspecting one hat boasting the deaths of at least seven birds. I was about to suggest we move on when, to my horror, I spotted Mamie Fish.

Had she seen me? I had not encountered her since the catastrophe and had no desire for that loud voice to boom out commiserations or interrogate me on my companion. I whisked into one of the little curtained kiosks, leaving Henry to fend for himself, and waited, realising as I did so that I had a hat in my hands, a green felt affair bristling with egret feathers. The kiosk was panelled with yet more mirrors, like a funhouse. But any amusement fled as I heard – horrors! – Mamie Fish say, 'Mr Vogel?'

Henry answered in the affirmative.

'But you are not Charles. Forgive me.'

'Not at all, madam. He is my sibling.'

'Ah! At last we meet "& Brother".' She laughed uproariously while I cursed under my breath. 'Mrs Stuyvesant Fish. And what are you doing in the women's millinery department? Or is this where you source your birds now? In truth, Mr Vogel, it might save you a step or two. The number of creatures I have seen grievously maimed or killed by careless ladies – and yet these women call themselves devoted! One supposed fancier friend *would* put her cage outside in summer, though of course the sun is too much for the poor animal. It was a pretty cage, though – a simple square, golden, containing a noble wren.'

'It is a pity indeed, madam. I cannot but think that it is a severe flaw in our race that what we profess to love, we do not necessarily value, nor know how to care for.'

'But not at Vogel & Brother.'

A silence, during which I assumed Henry bowed. I could not take it any longer: carefully I parted the curtains until I had the smallest chink. The unlikely pair were facing one another over a case of Brussels lace fans.

173

'You still have not told me what you are doing in this department,' Mrs Fish remarked idly, and to my horror, the faintest of flushes rose to Henry's cheeks. 'You are married?'

'No, madam.'

'Engaged?'

'No, madam.'

'A gift, then. For your sister-in-law.'

I gave Henry credit: he prevented himself from glancing over at my hiding place.

'Hester is a dear, isn't she?' Mamie Fish rattled on. 'I have felt terribly guilty that I have not visited the emporium since the party – I *know* you will not do yourself the discredit of pretending you are unaware of that unfortunate event, Mr Vogel – but I cannot feel comfortable among all those birds just yet. One cannot help but imagine that they are on the brink of bursting out and attacking, despite – or perhaps because of – their sweet songs. I suppose the terrible thing about cages is they speak at once of freedom *and* imprisonment.'

'You know the Italians have a proverb?' Henry said. '"The caged bird sings not for joy, but for rage."'

Mamie Fish's gaze shifted into something more appraising.

'That is why my brother recommends keeping canaries in enclosures of no more than a foot in diameter. Any larger and they do not sing so well.'

Mamie regarded him thoughtfully. 'Do you know, Mr Vogel, I think I prefer your brother.' Another bow. 'In the summer, we go yachting at Nantucket. I believe there are two kinds of people: those who sail with the wind, and those who decide to set themselves against it. I do not need to tell you who is home in time to catch the best of supper.' A smile. 'Where you see enclosure, *I* see

174

beauty, presented to the best advantage. For that is the function of a cage, is it not? To exhibit?'

'Which is the greater punishment?' Henry asked quietly. 'Incarceration, or display?'

Mamie Fish made an un-societal shrug. 'A ruder observer might note that regardless of your views, you continue to work in your brother's business.' She examined her fan minutely. 'Another might note that Mrs Vogel is extremely pretty.'

I was caught off guard as much as Henry, who could not help himself. Rage and concern flickered as he glanced at the kiosk, at my hiding place.

Mrs Fish did not bother to follow his gaze. 'Good day, Mr Vogel.'

She left; I sat back in the kiosk, hat dangling limply from my hands. I realised my fingers had been working busily upon it: its feathers were shredded. There was no hiding from myself: in that dreadful funhouse, my face was reflected back in every direction, spectator made spectacle.

Eventually I found my way out. Henry and I proceeded to the china department in silence.

'I loathe millinery,' he said eventually, his tone bloody. 'It is the *impression* of nature that I cannot abide. All those feathers. I despise how our capitalist system conspires to give the notion that the world is stocked with a limitless supply of marvels, and money is all that stands between us and them. That the world may be endlessly raided – that it *must* be so. If you only knew the rapacity I have seen!'

'Henry . . .'

'The paradise bird I brought you. Did you never wonder why I troubled to send it alive, not dead? It was the last in its valley. They are so easy to kill. The males return to the same tree, time and again, and those that the hunter does not manage to kill the first day, he simply waits for the next day, and the next, until all are gone. And then they are sold to the so-called civilised world. For *fashion*,' he added scathingly. 'We have chased down Wonderland, slaughtered its curiosities, caged its fascinations. And to say so is to be branded sentimental, merely because people cannot bear to consider pretty things being obtained through cruelty!'

'Henry.' I seized his wrist, then relinquished it, fearful of who might see. 'She knows.'

'Is this all we are? Is this the best of us? It is the fault of our race that no sooner have we marvelled than we wish to possess; and the act of possession is the beginning of destruction.'

I knew what he was really talking about. 'It has barely been two months,' I said, trying to smile. 'I do not think we need to talk of destruction just yet.'

He would not meet my eyes. We had stopped beside a table bearing tureens of all shapes and sizes. Helplessly I lifted the lid of one.

'What do we care about Mamie Fish? She is nothing to us.'

'But you are becoming everything to me,' he said quietly. 'And there, I am afraid, is the problem.'

I bowed my head as though to confirm the emptiness of the tureen. Still a treacherous tear fell, plashing into the silver bottom.

'We are too much for one another, Hester.'

'Better that than not enough.'

'Perhaps it is the same thing. I cannot work; the business suffers. Soon Charles may wish to send me on another sourcing expedition, and what then?'

'I'll come with you.'

'And be pariahs? It is never the *going* one has to consider, my darling; it is the coming back.'

His gentleness made it worse. I was back in my father's office at the corset factory, the cage factory, confined alone while life receded into the distance. With a careless clang, I replaced the tureen lid and walked away, out of the crockery, through the hollow mannequins of the fashions, down the stairs and out of the door into the blasting summer. I wanted the sea so badly then, but there was no ocean here, and no land either.

Henry caught up with me at the corner.

'We are so new,' I managed at last. 'Would you stifle us before we have time to live?'

He opened his mouth to answer, but just then an incredulous voice said, 'Hester?'

I turned: a man about my own age was staring at me, a stack of pamphlets in his hands. '*Robert?*'

We greeted each other with the enthusiasm of old friends. Robert Odlum, my erstwhile swimming companion – my *only* swimming companion, the boy who had helped build my bathing machine. His family had only remained in town a few months, but that was time enough in the long epoch of childhood to become firm friends. He was a superb swimmer. After he moved, we lost touch, though I heard later that he became a tea merchant, and later still began to read reports of his daring athletic feats. He had a habit for jumping from great heights into the water, and had done so to great acclaim at the Occoquan Falls.

'And this gentleman?' he asked.

'Mr Henry Vogel. My brother-in-law.' There was a short silence, Robert looking from me and my red eyes to Henry and back again.

'A pleasure,' was all he said, bowing as he did. Relieved, I asked whether he was living in New York.

'No, Washington. But I find myself here for the summer, and perhaps into next year, depending on business.' He showed me his rather lurid pamphlets: they were for a small touring museum displaying artefacts of the assassin of President Garfield, including his clothes, photographic scenes of the tragedy, and the rope used to hang him. It seemed rather tawdry.

Perhaps catching my feelings he said, 'It is only a pastime, you know, since the closure of my Natatorium.' He gave me a pamphlet for that as well, telling me how, at great expense, he had set it up as a swimming school in Washington for both sexes. It had been a wild success until it ceased to be so, though in the interim it had earned him the title of 'Professor'.

'And shall you perform any more leaps?' Henry asked.

'Perhaps.' His eyes sparkled, as I remembered them doing in the summer sea. With a pang I noted how they outshone his rather faded coat. 'It is the leap itself, sir, the fearful leap. People are afraid they shall be killed by the air, but it is not the falling that does it. Only land properly, and a man might leap from the highest building and be uninjured.'

We exchanged promises to see one another, and after scribbling down his lodgings, he left us. Wistfully I watched him disappear into the crowd.

'So he wants to help people jump from buildings,' Henry said, sceptical.

'Oh no. Robert is much more ambitious than that.' As a child, my friend always swam to the greatest extent of his abilities, and often beyond that. On one memorable occasion I went in and pulled him out before he drowned. 'Nothing but the impossible will do. Why, I do believe that what he really wants is to learn to fly.'

Henry smiled strangely. 'Don't we all?'

I looked at him a moment, thinking of the girl I had been at the cage factory, her head filled with empty dreams. The woman who had married, hoping for a largening of the soul, for other worlds than this. And the creature I was now, her whole being narrowed to the man before her. 'Perhaps. But look at the emporium, Henry. The best most of us can hope for is to find comfort in our cages.'

CHAPTER NINETEEN

'Emily.'

Yves was outside, and I jolted. I'd dived into Hester's diary to escape the roaring in my head, but now that the account had ended, I felt the walls closing in upon her, and me. Who could I disburse my soul to when my own right hand struck me in the breast?

'Emily?' Yves' voice echoed through the door again. Hester had thought that Henry could help her to freedom, but I knew from her death that this was not so. A cage-maker's daughter ought to have known better the workings of entrapment.

As for Robert Odlum . . . I had heard that name before. But where? There was no time to consider as I hid the papers and answered the door.

Yves frowned down at me. 'I came to see if you were all right.' I had noticed that in times of stress, his German accent strengthened, and was touched to hear it doing so now.

'Come in.'

I pointed to the chair, then sat clumsily on the bed. It was barely afternoon, yet I felt heavy and drained. Then again, there is no exhaustion so insidious, so wearying as that from pretence. It was for this reason that, despite the remorseful pain of leaving my father for months, I had chosen the expedition lifestyle. You had to leave yourself behind. Out in the wilderness, I wasn't anyone.

Yves did not sit down, only observing me with concern. The cut on his head still had not healed. In fact, it seemed even larger than when I had first met him. I'd wondered if he was diabetic – it was a signature of my illness that injuries took longer to heal – but did not think that was it.

'Yves,' I said suddenly. 'Why are you not at your school?'

He seemed to choose his words carefully. 'The subjects I teach show my students how to take pride in their past. There are those who disagree with this approach.'

I waited.

'I took my students to a tavern to celebrate after an exam.' He shrugged. 'There were some others there – young men, drinking. Things became, shall we say, excited. There was a disagreement.' He gestured to his temple. 'I tried to break up the fight and received this for my trouble. The school decided I should take some leave.'

It made sense, though it did not answer the riddle of that unhealing wound. Looking at it now, I saw something within it glisten.

'Are you all right?' he repeated. I shook my head to clear it, then realised I had forgotten to inject myself that morning. I'd been caught up in the Parker, and the stalking. I was hours overdue.

'Sorry. I just need to . . .'

I stood and went shakily to the alcove with its glass bottles and syringes. I returned to the bed and, without thinking, rolled my skirt high and stabbed myself in the thigh.

The relief insulin provided was never immediate, but knowing it was coming was enough. I blinked, realising just how far gone I'd been. My doctor, stout old Mr Beedle, would not have been impressed. His office had a medal for bravery on the wall and orange goldfish in a tank. His voice was always calm, but often his hands shook.

We'd been left with a world full of broken things. My sister and I were barely twelve when the war came. Daniel was sixteen, and tried to sign up without his father knowing. Harold found out and was furious. It was the only time I saw him express any protectiveness towards his son. We spent the war at Butterworth, whose racing stables had been repurposed as a remount depot. I think Harold was rather surprised to find his little kingdom annexed by stern, stocky upper-class women who seemed to keep the place up to scratch through sheer force of personality. They treated him much as they did their charges: as something to be bucked up.

Like Hester's father, my own had gone to war. Just briefly, before shrapnel to the leg sent him home and kept him there. Our mother would have been horrified, not by the injury but by the fact he went at all. She was a conscientious objector before most people had even heard of the term, though perhaps she would have found the white feather appropriate. She loved birds, after all. Taught us to blow out eggs, the lightest things on earth, strong and fragile all at once. We dyed them with madder, indigo or one of the concoctions she herself made from nettles or ragwort. My father was obsessed with natural history, but she loved plants in a different way. Not for her this pickling and poking and prying. She assimilated herself into them, enriching the poor soil with her own spirit. When she died, the garden died with her.

She was one of those who know secret things. It is these people who are truly free. Hester and I – we were both trapped, unable to free ourselves through our own resources, relying on another to uncage us. I knew from my own decisions that there were stronger imprisonments than those wrought by iron.

I realised two things: first, that Yves was watching me, and second, that my skirt was still high up my thigh. He came and sat beside me, his warmth and weight settling on the bed. Hastily I pulled the material down again.

'You are diabetic.'

'Yes.'

'Why didn't you tell me before?'

Oh, because.

'Show me.'

I started. 'Why?'

He moved closer. I saw the ice blue of his eyes, the smoothness of his golden skin. 'You see the cut on my head?'

'It has not healed.'

He nodded. 'You are a scientist, Emily. You know this world. Nature shows us that the strongest are always the victors. Wounds show these struggles – and that we have overcome them.' He bowed his head, moving his injury into my line of vision. 'Look again, and see.'

I stared at the wound. Scarlet and crimson twined together in tiny flaps and gristles. A door to a hidden world.

There within was the thing that glistened. It was white, granular. Without thinking, I put a finger to it and licked the tip.

Salt.

He rubbed it in deliberately, he told me as my tongue tingled. His fencing friends valued such things. If they received a *Schmiss*, a duelling cut, they would make it bigger in this manner. I thought of the skin-cutting ritual in Papua; this felt different, but I wasn't sure why.

'An injury shows our strength, and strength is everything. Do not hide your scars, Emily.'

'I do not see strength,' I said at last, gesturing to my thigh. 'I see . . . something to run from.'

'Why run? You have already fought and won.'

I opened my mouth to object, then stopped as my mind filled with the unending rhythm of injections, twice a day, every day. I remembered the near misses, the constant weight of the little glass bottles in my bags, how it racked my nerves when they chinked together, no matter how many banana leaves I wrapped them in. Oh, I knew I was lucky – insulin had replaced the starvation diet that had been the only treatment hitherto. It was a mercy, yet the thing about mercy is that it leaves you a survivor. Insulin condemned me to fight on and on in a life already so full of battles.

'Show me,' Yves repeated softly, and after a moment I lifted up my skirt's edge.

'*That's* it.' He bent over my thigh, fascinated but not repelled by the punch marks that mottled the skin, some old, some new. It was an ugly ailment, and I disliked that I cared about its disfigurements. Some called it the disease of a thousand cuts. There was the dark, dull scar from the jab that had become infected while I was in Sumatra: I'd nearly died, draining out the pus in a fever dream, and was found by a handsome Swede while recovering. He also hunted the corpse lily I sought. We were miles from anywhere and anyone, yet he almost tripped over my campfire ashes.

I usually steered clear of the male botanists and explorers I occasionally encountered in the field, but he was particularly sweet, my Swede, sweet as the candied skin on the yams he roasted for me while I regained my strength. When I'd recovered, we travelled together awhile. None of the men I studied with wished to accompany a woman, a feeling I returned. No, that was not quite true – one had, and after administering a swift knee to the groin, I'd vowed never to travel with any of them. The Swede was an exception, even if he never quite persuaded me of the virtues of making love in a hammock.

At last, one night in that damned hammock, I told him that we had to go our separate ways. Partly because our planned routes were different, partly because I did not want a man discovering the lily with me and being handed all the credit.

I would never do that, he said.

No, I'd replied, but the world would.

'Strength,' Yves said quietly. 'Not weakness.'

My eyes blurred, and I only knew from touch when he put out a finger and, with exquisite gentleness, placed it upon the freshest scar.

CHAPTER TWENTY

As we entered the fourth week, Mr Vogel was growing impatient, understandably so. His words were just as friendly, but his tone had an edge and his flourishing gestures had diminished, as though his energies were turning in on themselves. The solstice was in a month, and while I still did not truly believe he would die that day, it remained a fact that I had found nothing.

Well, not nothing – but I would not share Hester's account until it felt wise to do so. The revelation of her affair with Henry had changed things.

The man I love is trying to kill me.

I'd thought that sentence referred to her husband, but what if she meant the man who was now my employer? Heinrich – Henry – Vogel was ninety-one now. Weakened, yes, but still pursuing a gemstone fifty years later. What if he had eventually tried to persuade Hester to leave Charles? What if she'd refused, and he'd killed her in a jealous rage?

What if, in other words, I was living with a murderer?

Hester would lead me to the truth. In the meantime, I must tread carefully. That meant showing my employer that

I was doing the job to the best of my abilities. I reapplied myself fervently to searching the castle.

Yet my searches came to little. Any castle worth its salt ought to have been riddled with hidden passages and priest holes, yet Pàrras stubbornly defied me. If there were secrets here, it would not surrender them to me.

It was while searching the library that I remembered the rumoured secret chamber, the one that allegedly held the doomed clansman, and an idea occurred.

'Lynette,' I said, entering the kitchen, 'how many tea towels do you possess?'

She gathered as many as could be found, while I nosily peered into a large bucket on the table. To my surprise, it contained ice.

'From the ice house,' she said, pulling open drawers. 'They bring it down from the hills in winter. We'll have lemon ice cream this evening.'

I regretfully declined. Of all the things my illness denied me, ice cream was one of the things I missed the most. Instead, I unstrapped the Thermos flask from my belt. That same illness demanded I stay hydrated, and I liked iced water best. It seemed to be a symptom of diabetes: even before the diagnosis, I had craved it without knowing why.

'Do you mind if I take some?'

'Of course not. There's usually some in the kitchen at this time of year. Help yourself any time.'

I thanked her, scooping a handful and dumping it in. Then, 'Lynette, how did you come to be with Mr Vogel?'

Her expression grew cold as the ice on my fingers.

'You don't have to say,' I said hastily, but she was already speaking quietly.

'I suppose I have my husband to thank. It was a Sunday. God's day. I always did a roast. He liked a roast, did Mr

Macleod. Liked it well done. I always say when the meat is like that, it's not worth . . .' She broke off. 'We didn't have much, but the fishing went well that week and I'd got the best bird at the market. Fat, it was, Miss Blackwood, and golden as I took it out. It was still moist, all the fat bubbling nicely. I went to put it back in, cook it until it was how he liked it, all dried out, but for some reason I couldn't bring myself to do it. Couldn't bear to ruin something so perfect.

'I served it to him, and he realised immediately, of course, and shouted. Then he took the gravy pan and, well . . .' She gestured to her melted face. 'The gravy went everywhere but the chicken.

'He went out, leaving me on the floor. I don't know how long I was there. It was winter, the wind was going, and suddenly the door flew open. I can still hear that bang now.

'Well, I managed to pick myself up and put cold water on the burns. Didn't realise how bad it was – no mirrors in the house; it was vanity, he said. I was about to start cleaning up the mess, but the thing was, the door was still open. Just a rectangle of black. Couldn't see a thing beyond it.

'He'd locked me up, you see. Not just cutting me off from my family, my friends. But where it counted – in my head. Only teach someone to inflict their own pain, and they are yours for life. But all at once I realised: *I did not have to be there.*'

The words were slow, emphatic, as though she'd held them a long time.

'So I walked out. Walked out with my head held high.' A grim smile. 'Well, pride only keeps you warm for so long. You can't eat freedom. No one would help or take me in, not in this godforsaken country. Told me I ought to go back to him, but I said I'd rather die. I *was* half dead when Mr Vogel found me, on the road. But I meant what I'd told the locals. I've never looked back. Never wanted to go back to him. Not once.'

Ten minutes later, I was climbing the stairs of the menagerie, laden with tea towels from a woman I now saw differently. The bravery of setting your whole life down and walking away . . . I admired it. Envied it.

I had declined her offer of help with my hunch. The idea was simple. The family had purportedly built the secret room to save people, not imprison them. There were cellars for that. Therefore it was not improbable that it had a window. So I would go into all the known rooms, bar the forbidden tower, and hang a tea towel from their sills. Then I could walk around the outside of the castle and identify any window missing a cloth.

It took some time. I did the kitchen and the great hall, the library and the pantry and the gun room. Yves insisted on doing his own room and his laboratory, as well as Mr Vogel's rooms.

'My uncle doesn't like anyone to be in there,' he said, smiling. 'It took Lynette half a year to convince him to let her clean.'

I smiled back and passed him an armful of cloths. He stepped in to receive them and our forearms touched.

'Do not use me like a cross,' my father once told me. My arms had been full of cloths then too; I had just declined an invitation to dinner to finish the laundry, along with work due for my doctorate. 'We can hire someone to do that. As I keep reminding you.'

I did not know what he was getting at. 'You're not a burden.'

He let out a small, amused snort. 'That's not what I was saying. I mean, do not brandish me before you to keep others away.'

He was right. After the accident, I'd barely bothered to make friends, let alone entertained the notion of a relationship. I'd told myself I was simply too busy. But for his sake I made friends with Susan Jennings, an American engineering geologist and one of the only other female students. In the classroom she was as fierce as me; we both wore similarly severe clothing and treated our male classmates as necessary evils. Only when we were alone did the facade drop to reveal a kindly, open-hearted soul with a fondness for pink velvet cushions.

'We *have* to be battleaxes,' she said. 'You can have respect or a sex life, but not both.'

It was she who advised me to put Noilly Prat in my gin – a true partnership, we both agreed – while I showed her the walking routes I liked in the wilderness around Sydney. But in the second year, she mysteriously vanished. I visited her apartment several times, but the door was not answered, though I knew somebody was in. Eventually I yelled up, threatening to return with a crowbar. I barely knew the crumbling, tear-streaked creature who answered, but I recognised the swollen stomach well enough.

'Fuck,' I swore bluntly. She tried for a smile, then dissolved again. I guided her back inside and made her tea, shoving in a tot of brandy when she wasn't looking. Her supervisor, she said. A stupid, stupid mistake.

He would marry her, 'But of course my career is over.'

'It doesn't have to be.' We both knew it did. Motherhood – did any cage have stronger bars? She dropped out, and a little while later she and the supervisor moved to Adelaide. I wrote to her for a while, but less than nine months later the replies stopped coming.

I worked away, tucking towels into every window I could find, saving my own tower until last. Eventually I arrived

190

back there and ascended the spiralling stairs, past Yves' bedroom.

A strange sound, like a gasp.

'Yves?'

No answer, only that gasp again, long and drawn out. Suffering.

The door was unlocked: I went in and saw him collapsed on the floor, body contorted and that clear face twisted in pain.

CHAPTER TWENTY-ONE

I dropped the tea towels and hurried to him, calling his name. He could not hear or see me – his gaze was locked in upon itself, empty of consciousness, while his body jerked and twitched as though shaken by some awful puppet master. I yelled for Lynette and Mr Vogel, hoping they would hear. No one came. I moved furniture out of the way so he did not hurt himself as he broke and shook on the floor, his breathing tortuous, his lips blue. He needed help, but I could not leave him, not like this.

Then, just as suddenly as it had come, the fit left him. His body went limp. His eyes rolled back in his head.

The danger seemed to have passed, but I still did not want to leave him. I positioned him so he could not swallow his tongue, and remained close. His hair was plastered across his soaked forehead: I pushed it aside, unpicking a strand from that scar, wishing he would let it heal. My mother had had such a wound: hers was on the inside, but like Yves, she too had been unable to let it close. The tower room smelled as hers had done, full of the sweet, tainted scent of human injury. I felt precisely as I had back then: that I would do anything to take the pain away.

Time passed; the light changed. His eyes flew open.

'It's all right,' I said. 'It's all right.'

'Water,' he murmured. I had not wanted to give him any before – did not wish to choke him. There was a jug on the dresser beside the window. Gently I raised his head from my lap and went to it. I might have ascribed that immaculate room a military air, but right then I had the impression of someone pinning himself together. Tidying himself away. It grabbed at my heart.

The jug was atop a neat stack of papers. I filled a glass and took it to him, only to find him asleep. I set it down and, for lack of anything else to do, hung a tea towel out the window.

Turning back, I was once again confronted by that neat paper pile. I glanced at Yves – still unconscious – then back at the documents again. The topmost page was typewritten on headed stationery. A letter.

I could not look through his things, I told myself, yet my treacherous eyes had already gathered that it was from his school. The school from which he was so mysteriously absent.

I bent over it. No good: it was in German. I was both relieved and disappointed. I looked again, abandoning any pretence of accident, and this time I saw one word I knew. A term I'd heard fall bitterly from the lips of both Daniel and his father. Not a word I'd expected to see.

Jude, it said. And then, in the same sentence, *suspendiert*.

Yves was a Jew? Had been suspended because of it?

No, that did not feel right. But then what? I wanted to cry in frustration. The answer was right in front of me, but I could hardly take it away to study. Quickly, guiltily, I memorised the key sentence. Perhaps I could ask Daniel.

There was a noise from the sleeping man behind me. I replaced the letter hurriedly, but a snapping sound drew my gaze down: a small scrap from the pile had escaped onto the floor. Yves moaned again: he was waking up. I scooped up the paper to put it back, then stopped.

It was a bus ticket to Southampton. My eyes went to the date. The exact day my ship, RMS *Otranto*, had arrived at the port.

Yves had been in the country at the start of the year. Unusual, Lynette had said.

I remembered that January day and that busy quay, alive with pigs and sugar. I remembered the too-thin man who had helped carry our luggage, and how he had been knocked down, the trunk that clearly bore my name stolen by an unknown assailant.

Nothing had been taken, which meant the trunk had not contained what they were seeking . . .

'Yves?'

I jumped. Mr Vogel's voice came echoing, sepulchral from below. 'What is this tea towel doing in my room?'

I stuffed the ticket into my pocket and hurried downstairs.

CHAPTER TWENTY-TWO

I explained to Mr Vogel what had happened, and Lynette was dispatched to tend to Yves. I would have remained, but she was politely yet firmly clear that I was no longer required. I caught a last glimpse of him through the closing door: his pale eyes snagged on mine.

Tea towels. I forced myself to focus on them and forget the ticket in my pocket. I had completed the internal work. Now I simply had to search for the telltale window. It was growing late, the light slanting low. Tonight was the full moon, though just now it was nowhere to be seen. Leaving the castle walls, I began to walk their circumference. A faint breeze had risen, flapping the cloths as though in surrender. Perhaps similar banners had flown the day the inhabitants bowed to their invaders and were massacred for their trouble.

I moved around clockwise from the front gate: every window was accounted for. When I reached the broken tower, where the land crumbled to the sea, I was forced to retrace my steps and go back round the other side. After this I would check the windows facing the courtyard, though the darkening glass was increasingly hard to see. The only lamps shone from the kitchen and Yves' room.

No – that was not true. I stared up. A light moved within the broken tower. The windows were boarded up, but there it was, issuing up through the gaping roof.

It could only be Mr Vogel. The tower, it seemed, was not as dangerous as he had claimed. Then why was I forbidden to enter? What did he not want me to see?

I knew what I had found in Yves' room. He had been there that day in Southampton. The *Times* article that had followed the first interview piece had named my ship: it would have been easy to confirm the arrival date. Easy from my photograph to spot me in the disembarking crowd and follow. Had Mr Vogel sent Yves to steal my bird, and when he failed, employed me as a ruse to get it to the castle?

The tide was coming in, grey waters slopping hungrily at the causeway. The sky had sunk into itself. But every window seemed to have its white flag, save that glowing forbidden tower.

An osprey swept across the thickening horizon, as though brushing away invisible dirt, and then I saw it: a lone window from which no white cloth fluttered. I broke into a run.

'Emily!'

At first, mid stride, I thought I had imagined the disembodied voice calling my name, stroking down my spine. The full moon, rising. It came again and I pulled up dead, peering into the dark . . .

And leaping back in shock as a shadow emerged from the loch.

'Daniel?' I said incredulously.

He came up the path towards me. His shoes were wet, the causeway already disappearing behind him.

'Emily,' he said. 'You're alive.'

*

'Of course I'm alive,' I said tersely. I'd said nothing until I'd brought him into the courtyard, beneath the sallow shadows of the lantern, beside that deep, dark well. I lost my temper so easily around him: the vast thing that I worked so hard to contain sprawled within me, and Daniel's presence always awoke it. It frightened me, making me snappish. 'What on earth are you doing here?'

'You never answered my letters.'

'I . . . Oh.' I had not even read them; the only one I'd opened, I'd discarded when I found Hester's clue.

'You had me worried sick. Your father isn't well.'

I grabbed his lapels. '*What?*'

He disentangled himself and told me my father had caught pneumonia, unlucky for the season. The doctor thought it was too much time outside, caring for his plants in my absence. There was no missing the reproach in Daniel's tone.

'I'm coming back. Now.' I made as though to run off, but he seized my arm.

'Don't be foolish. *Think* for once, Emmy, rather than just rushing in. There isn't a train until tomorrow morning.' He ignored my cry of frustration. 'If your employer will allow me to stay the night, we can go back together.'

The secret chamber would have to wait.

I found Mr Vogel in the low sitting room, beside the fire. He agreed to host Daniel immediately – Lynette had a lamb joint – but his brow darkened when I explained I would have to leave for a few days.

'Impossible.'

I shot Daniel a glance. Tactfully he left the room.

'My father is deeply unwell,' I said.

'And you are running out of time. *I* am running out of time. The solstice approaches.'

'We could extend the deadline.'

'That,' he said softly, 'will not be possible.' And though his expression was as open as ever, it was as though someone had placed one of Lynette's ice cubes against my back. 'I cannot permit you to leave.'

'I'm not asking.'

We regarded one another.

'Does he know?' His voice was cold. 'About the diamond?'

'You told me to keep it hidden.'

The flames snapped in the grate. If he would not release me temporarily, then I would have to abandon the whole enterprise: the diamond and my hopes for its proceeds, but also Hester. Strange how equally I felt the pang – but when it came to my father, nothing was negotiable.

I threw him a bone, a distraction. 'I believe I have something.' I told him about the cloth-less window. 'You and Yves can investigate it while I am gone.'

His features remained immobile but his eyes gleamed. It was a major gamble: I risked them discovering the stone while I was absent, and perhaps trying to deny me my commission. But seeing my father was more important than anything.

It worked. 'One week, then,' he said, and I exhaled. 'We will search your things, of course,' he added. 'To ensure you are not carrying the diamond off our property.'

I stared at him. 'You do not trust me?'

'I trust you plenty, Miss Blackwood. But I have learned the cost of trust. It is not a price that I am willing again to pay.'

The four of us had dinner: Mr Vogel, Yves, Daniel and me. All of us were hungry, I think. I looked carefully at Yves as he entered: he appeared to have made a full recovery, shooting me a smile as he took his chair. He seemed to glow with good health, despite – *because of* – the illness that traced its way through his seams. Whereas Daniel, his skin pale under the chandelier, set off by the darkness of his eyes . . . he was as lost as me. What good could come of us ever being together?

I did not like seeing him here. He was a part of myself that I always left behind on expeditions. This work at Pàrras was no exception.

'You have known Emmy for how long?' Yves was asking him.

'Almost twenty years,' Daniel said pleasantly. 'Although she has been away in Australia for many of those.'

'How many?'

'Seven,' I supplied.

'Like Faust.'

My mouth twisted upwards. 'Let's hope not.'

Daniel was watching us both curiously. 'Your family is German, Mr Vogel?'

Mr Vogel replied that it was. 'But I have not lived there since I was a boy. The Germans do not appreciate success, Mr . . .'

'Loewe. Daniel Loewe.'

Yves coughed abruptly. His uncle continued. 'The Germans do not appreciate success. Only mastery. But I have no skill, unless it is that of collection.'

That was not true. The embroidery on his jacket, this time in deepest indigo, was testimony to that.

It was Daniel's turn to smile. 'As a banker, many of my clients would say that is the greatest skill of all.'

'Ah, but I do not speak of merely *having*. Ownership is generally a passive state, whereas true possession is not so different from loss. Two sides of a coin. In both cases, one is passionately aware of the thing in question. Do you understand me?'

'Yes,' Daniel said quietly. 'I understand.'

So did I. As children, wrapped up in one another, we twins barely noticed our parents. Yet when my mother was having one of her days, it felt like she had died. My father would talk at her of hope and mercy, while my sister and I

199

became suddenly, terribly aware that we had a mother and clung to her like animals. 'Leave me,' she'd say fretfully, but we held on all the tighter.

'Yves took me stalking,' I said, changing the subject.

'Oh yes? Did you bag something?'

'A red stag.'

Daniel blinked. 'Aren't those out of season?'

I turned to Yves, expecting him to refute it. I knew nothing of the hunting cycle, but was vaguely aware that there were specific seasons, tailored to ensure numbers were not over-culled. Surely Yves, an accomplished hunter, would not have broken such rules.

But he said nothing. Daniel frowned in distaste.

'You are German yourself?' Mr Vogel asked smoothly.

'My parents are.' With palpable effort, Daniel focused on his host. 'They left before I was born.'

'Was there a reason?'

Daniel gave a faint smile. 'My father said the Germans scared him.'

'Although he was one of them?'

'Especially. He understood what they were capable of.'

Lynette brought in the next course, and as she clinked about, I noticed that Yves' eyes did not leave Daniel once.

He did search my things. The next morning he offered to bring my bag down to the great hall for me, and I felt a stab of betrayal when he set it down and began to look through it. I'd interleaved the loose pages of Hester's latest account inside *Gray's Manual of Botany*, which I would take with me to Oxfordshire, gambling that Yves would not look inside. The remaining diaries I had rolled up and concealed inside the hidden window compartment for extra security in my absence.

Yves pulled out *The Birdcage Library*. 'Why are you taking this?'

I had expected this – had not tried to conceal it. Less suspicious that way. 'There is a retired antique books expert in the village,' I lied, my tone dry and musty. 'Used to work for a London dealer. I thought I would ask him to see if he can deduce anything from it.'

But Yves, already bored, had moved on to Daniel's case. Finding nothing, he had the decency to look embarrassed.

'One more thing,' he said. 'Before you go, I need you to come to my laboratory.'

Despite the unpleasant revelation about the stag, surprise and curiosity mingled in me equally. I had never yet been to that third floor above the library; there was little possibility of anything being hidden there, Mr Vogel and Yves agreed. The whole chamber had been renovated when the installation was done.

If he had tried to force me, I would not have gone. But instead he held out a hand and said, calmly, 'Come.'

So I went.

The space was so different to the rest of Pàrras that I gaped. The walls were whitewashed, as was the floor, hauling the stubborn light in. There was a long table, scrupulously clean, and a repurposed pharmacist's' cabinet, the printed words upon the drawers covered over with neat labels bearing Yves' handwriting. At the near end of the table was a stack of scientific magazines, and in the middle a microscope crouched. At the far end were test tubes, a quarter full with some thick beige substance and swarming with . . .

'Fruit flies,' Yves said.

'I thought you taught social sciences.'

'I do. Fruit flies are useful for the study of genetics, which in turn has much to teach us about our society. Wait here.'

He went to fiddle with a contraption in the corner. My attention was distracted by a cardboard box containing a mass of cabling, two light bulbs and a couple of small, hand-painted signs.

This light flashes every 16 seconds, marking every time a person is born in the United States.

The second read:

Every 7½ minutes, a high-grade person is born. Approximately 4 per cent of all Americans come within this class.

Something was scrawled beneath it. I squinted. *EUGENICS SOCIETY EXHIBITION.*

'What's this?' I asked.

'Student project.'

I had heard of eugenics: yet another supposed way for mankind to separate the wheat from the chaff. Of course. We all want to be wheat, while suspecting we are chaff. One might hold that gap responsible for an awful lot of pain.

'Come,' Yves said at last, straightening beside his curious machine.

It looked quite simple. Two upright metal poles supported a pane of wood, while two shorter poles were bolted at the perpendicular to their longer counterparts. To these were attached a second, smaller screening pane, glass with a wooden frame. Facing these, attached to wires, was a smallish device with a lens that looked a little like a camera. The X-ray machine.

'I have zapped everything in this castle, looking for the diamond,' Yves said. 'Anything we could get between the frames.'

'How did you get the bear in?' I said, and for some reason he smiled as though at a private joke.

'Oh, we did not need to scan the Kodiak. But we have done so to everything else. Everything but that bear – and *you*.'

'You have to be joking.'

'For all we know, you could be smuggling out the diamond.'

'You already searched me.'

His eyes glinted. 'Not everywhere.'

'Well, I don't *have* it,' I said vehemently.

'I believe you.' His eyes softened. 'But you must see my uncle's point of view. He has already been betrayed once.'

'It is a gross invasion.'

'Come on, Emmy. You are the one breaking the terms of the agreement with this visit. Unless you have something to hide?'

I glanced at the clock on the wall. Less than an hour until we had to leave. I could not miss that train.

'For all we know, you might disappear today and never return,' Yves went on. Then, softer still: 'And I for one would think that a pity.'

I relented. Let him usher me gently into his contraption. It reminded me oddly of Hester's bathing machine: an immersive device enabling a different way of experiencing the world. I had seen Dr Tasker's spectacular X-rays of plants: simultaneously alien and familiar, they showed at once the deadness and the secret life of things. A fuchsia became a diaphanous cluster of shadows; the rather unromantic tube of a philodendron was transformed to a candle wick, dancing in flame.

Yves went to a cupboard and returned in an enormous metal apron. The absurdity of the situation hit home and I found myself stifling a smile.

'Hold still,' he said lazily, winching the smaller frame towards me so that it pressed gently against my torso. 'Put your arms like this.'

He arranged me as though I were a still-life painting.

'Perfect. Except . . .' He bent towards me and smoothed a lock of red hair from my forehead, tucking it gently behind my ear. Then he moved away to where a panel waited,

203

unaware that he had just done exactly the same thing as my mother used to with my sister and me, those days we came in late from the beach, our hair slick and dark from salt spray. Perhaps the last time I was truly happy.

A click. There was no flash of light, but I shut my eyes automatically. Nothing seemed to have changed; I remained there, splayed like one of Lord Rothschild's butterflies, no part of me secret. It was like the blooding all over again. What was it about Yves that stripped me away?

I heard him remove the metal apron, leaving its husk to one side, and disappear with the image into a large cupboard. I kept my eyes closed, scenting that long-ago salt.

'Emmy,' he said at last, returning, but I wasn't ready to look. I had not imagined that snatch of brine. There was salt on my cheeks, salt in this wound that I was beginning to think would never heal.

'Emmy,' he repeated, his voice losing its usual casualness.

I screwed my eyes up, trying to gather myself as I did every morning, scraping together whatever pieces of soul I could find, trying not to consider that each time there was less than before.

Then I felt it. His breath on my cheek – the warm, soft wetness of his tongue.

'Let me take those,' he said. And licked my tears away.

CHAPTER TWENTY-THREE

I could not look at Daniel when I met him in the hall. Yves leaned casually against the door frame as Mr Vogel bade us goodbye, not without a slash of suspicion on my employer's part. But my X-ray had been clear. Just bones.

Daniel was hardly more lively than a skeleton would have been. He tried to buy me a first-class ticket, then, when I told him not to be ridiculous, spent the journey to Glasgow sitting bolt upright in the third-class carriage, hands neatly folded on his lap with the primness of a schoolgirl determined to repel undesirable influences. Perhaps this was to ward against the man who travelled several stops with a terrier and a cardboard box that emitted the occasional squawk – a chicken, I decided – but I rather thought his attitude was directed at me.

I tried not to touch my cheeks and eventually sat on my hands, earning me an odd look, and a glance at the tooth necklace at my throat. I avoided his dark eyes, determinedly thinking instead of my father, hoping that he was all right, and of that curious window, whose secrets I could only hope would stay safe until I returned.

'Why don't you find yourself a drink,' I said at last.

'In third?'

'You never know.'

He took the hint and departed, though I knew he knew it was fruitless. The thing between us was so different from that snatched wholeness I got from Yves: a sick sensation of something wasting away. What was it? Friendship? Time?

'Are they treating you well at Castle Pàrras?'

I turned. It was my laconic acquaintance the conductor.

'Yes, thank you.'

'I remembered who visited the castle before,' he said calmly, as though continuing a conversation that had finished only moments before. 'Right after you left. Another woman, almost as tall as you. A Mrs Briggs. About a year ago.'

Phyllis Briggs. Lynette had mentioned her.

'Smart woman. A hunter, she said, though she would nae tell what she was hunting. You wouldn't happen to know what it was?'

'No idea.'

'Mmm.' He shot me a disbelieving glance. 'Odd, it was.' When I said nothing, he went doggedly on. '*Very* odd. Said she would take the train down again a few weeks later. Well, young lady, I was working extra hard last year. A sick sister to care for, and my colleague down with the fever, I took all the shifts I could get.' He leaned in. 'I saw her walking the moors once or twice. But she never travelled back down again.'

'She probably returned by car. Or by a different route.'

The conductor smiled unpleasantly. 'What car? What route? There isn't a car to be found between here and Oban. No, miss, something happened up there.' He inclined his head towards the window. 'I believe she walks those moors still.'

He left me, proceeding down the aisle in intermittent strides, a bishop traversing his pews. I was grateful Daniel had not heard this little exchange, though he returned a little pale nevertheless.

'What happened? Did someone bite?'

'No. These carriages rattle so. I always thought I should like to be an explorer, but I've learned travel is not what I want from life.'

I regarded him awhile, then said, 'What *do* you want, Daniel?'

'Ah, Emily.' He gave a faint smile. 'What is the point in such a question, other than to make us unhappy?'

I did not smile back, thinking of Hester's words.

The best most of us can hope for is to find comfort in our cages.

I arrived to find my father very unwell but not as bad as I had feared. The case itself was mild, only exacerbated by his poor overall health. On the train down, I had prepared myself to abandon Pàrras altogether to nurse him, even if it meant leaving two people behind: Yves, and Hester Vogel. But now I felt I would be able to return by Mr Vogel's deadline.

It transpired that once the illness had set in, Daniel had insisted on moving my father to Butterworth. The few remaining servants had taken devoted care of him – the milk diet recommended him was administered faultlessly, his bedroom stuffed with small luxuries that I knew its owner could ill afford. I was furious, but quietly so. From my father's faint conversation, I learned that Daniel's business had gone from bad to worse: like bailing out the *Titanic* with a tin can, he said. Of course I did not want my father suffering unduly, but I resented the underhandedness as well as these extravagant exhibitions of guilt.

'Did you open the letters I packed?' my father asked.

I hadn't. I'd tucked away the one from the Royal Geographical Society along with Daniel's correspondence – they were still in my room at Pàrras. Why had I sent the

207

RGS that orchid paper? I'd known all along that it would be rejected.

I went to check on the state of our rented cottage, and spent a savage few hours attending to my father's neglected plants, although like people, each expressed their discomfort differently: some threatened to burst through the glass, while others had dwindled away to nothing. At least I had always found it easy to know what a plant needed. At university, my male peers were only too ready to ascribe motherly motives to this stewardship. But one could not prune a baby.

As I laboured, I could not but think of Daniel and myself in a better-tended cottage not so far away, seven years ago.

I'd loved him. So when I had done with the plants, I did not stop, scrubbing at the windows, ignoring the sweat pouring down my brow, being sure to exhaust myself, until the light shone between the iron bars and I burst out, gasping, into the sultry afternoon.

After the first few days at Butterworth, I quickly realised that my father did not need nursing so much as company, so I sat with him for long hours. He slept much, and I took a great joy in being there whenever he awoke. Despite this, when his eyes were closed, I was restless. On the fifth day, I took out Hester's diary again from inside the *Manual of Botany*, along with *The Birdcage Library*. Hester might have been long dead, but her story meant something to me, and not only as a treasure map. She too had lived a life for other people – there was no stronger cage. But in Henry she believed she had found a door.

Perhaps there were such doors in my own life, if only I could learn to see them.

The first clue had been in the first chapter of *The Birdcage Library*, the second in the second. I would therefore focus my energies on the third chapter. For the first time I considered the fact that there were five chapters in the book, including the introduction. Did that mean there were only five clues?

I began to read.

Empty Cages

There are some birds which fare less well in captivity, and some of these may surprise the keeper. Naturally one would not generally attempt to keep an albatross or an osprey; yet who would have thought that, at the other end of the scale, the little wren would mount such fierce resistance to captivity? No cage will hold a creature that insists on dying. Yet an empty cage need not be a melancholy affair. I have known collectors whose birds have sadly perished to repurpose their enclosures as pretty ornaments. See page 34.

Oh. *Oh.* Subtle. Had it not been for Hester's continuation of the bird theme, I might have missed it.

I had thought it a little unusual that an inveterate snob like Mamie Fish should refer to a wren as 'noble'. They were plain little birds without even an especially sweet song. Now I saw a further discrepancy. As Hester's father had specifically mentioned, the species did not thrive in captivity.

I found the passage Hester had written: *It was a pretty cage, though – a simple square, golden, containing a noble wren.*

No cage will hold a creature that insists on dying . . . I read the rest of the paragraph in *The Birdcage Library*. See page 34, it instructed. I did so.

A drawing of a cage, an ordinary box affair, though made of golden wire.

A simple square, golden . . .

Well, there was the pretty cage. But what about the noble wren? I looked closer and was elated to see something else. Someone had crossed out the page number at the foot and written the number 10. The ink was green.

Eagerly I turned to that page. We were back to the first chapter, discoursing upon the difference of housing for male and female birds. The males, Herman Millar said, being more valued for their song, benefited from larger cages to draw out their music. The females did not sing so well, so they could get by in smaller enclosures.

I reread this passage grimly. What was Hester trying to say? This clue felt different to the rest. I gave an irritated sigh, stirring my father in his sleep; I caught my breath until he relaxed again, then returned to the second portion of Mamie Fish's – Hester's – sentence. If this was the clue, then Hester must have twisted Mamie's words to create it. What did that imply about the rest of her account?

Still, we had come this far together. She had promised to lead me to the treasure. I had little option but to trust her.

A quiet knock: Daniel opened the door, shooting me an enquiring glance. I waved him in. The bed was in a kind of nook, so the chair he took beside me was rather close. He looked tired. These days, he always did. Wordlessly we observed the sleeping patient. My father was so reduced from the man who had once thundered from the pulpit that I wanted to weep.

'What is you are reading?' Daniel asked eventually. I frowned, but he said, 'It's fine if we whisper.'

'Just something I picked up at the castle.' Then, in a flash of decision: 'Daniel, how is your German these days?'

'Fraying.' A wry smile. 'Like the rest of me.'

I decided to ignore this. 'Can you translate this for me?' I recited the sentence I had memorised from Yves' letter.

He stared at me. 'Where did you hear that?'

'I read it somewhere.'

'You are sure you read it correctly?'

'Yes. What does it mean?'

He said slowly, '"The injuries inflicted are likely to take not less than six months to heal; you are to remain away from the school until the survival is certain of . . .' His voice dipped beyond my hearing.

'The survival of what?' I demanded.

'Not what. Who.'

I waited. He sighed and said, 'Of the Jew.'

I sat back, the wind knocked from me. I had not paid much attention to European politics these last seven years, but even in Australia we had heard of the slow stirrings in the Teutonic breast – the awakening of something deep and hateful. My thoughts scraped against my skull as I pictured Yves in all his gleaming ardour. The social sciences he taught. The salt he rubbed into his temple.

A man I had once worked with had had a willow tree in his garden. Not a weeping willow but a corkscrew one, as though someone had taken an ordinary tree and twisted its branches into brittle, unnatural shapes.

The species had another name: the tortured willow. Though fast-growing, they did not live very long.

I closed my eyes.

'Sorry,' I said emptily.

'For what?' Daniel asked.

'For making you translate that.'

He gave a smile as twisted as the willow, and a strange ache spread through me. As though I had travelled many miles only to happen across someone I knew.

Daniel left me, and my father awoke a short time later – so short, in fact, that I wondered whether he had been listening. I asked how he was.

'We maintain, Emmy dear,' was all he said. 'We maintain. Like Daniel.'

'The collapse of his business has hit him hard.'

He frowned. 'I don't mean the business. I mean your sister's death. Do you not see how it haunts him?'

I bit my lip and looked out of the window at the summer snatching at the panes. Autumn would soon come. I hoped desperately that my father would be there to see it.

'Do you know what a noble wren might be?' I said, changing the subject. 'Crossword clue,' I added, to preclude questions.

'Since when did you do the crossword?'

I shrugged. 'People change.'

'No, they don't. But since you ask – I suppose the architect, Sir Christopher Wren.'

I gaped for a second, then quickly closed my mouth. Perhaps that was why the clue felt different. Maybe the next instalment was not hidden at Pàrras at all, but rather at one of Wren's creations.

'I think Harold had a biography in his library,' he continued.

He had loved the library, my father. Harold often joked that it was his only reason for visiting. He would spend hours there, not only among the religious volumes but the scientific texts too. It was there that he showed my sister and me our first botanical illustrations, gorgeous things effortlessly bridging science and art, knowledge and beauty, and made us understand that each was as important as the other. Through those drawings the world opened up: petals were splayed apart, stems cut through, their innards visible. We can only pray that someday, someone will have the love and the courage to open us up too. That they will see us from every angle yet still find beauty.

My father moved on his pillows, wincing. 'It is a funny thing to be a churchman. One is close to death.'

I grabbed his hand. 'You are not close to death.' I wanted so badly to tell him about the diamond, to reassure him that soon we would be all right. But I had given my word to Mr Vogel, and besides, I did not want to pile more burdens on his shoulders – hope, of course, being the heaviest burden of all. I had spent seven years protecting him. I would not yield now.

'You misunderstand me. I have been close to death for decades – it was my profession. That is why we have holy men: we stand between God and the flock, until such time as we become a portal, showing them the way through. It is a beautiful thing – a blessed thing, or so I thought. It is humanity's tragedy that the things that hound us are almost always invisible to other people. Your mother died, and then the war . . .' His voice faded. 'I thought that in the darkness I would see the face of God, yet only death was there. I survived, but I did not change. Not in any way that meant something. These were things to be borne, and I told myself I could bear them, and wrench meaning from them in the process. I came home and preached, never realising that I had experience without wisdom, passion without empathy or understanding. Instead I prided myself that where I had only spoken of sin, I now spoke also of mercy. Mercy, when I had seen the merciless! It was they who had inherited this wretched earth.

'After your sister's death, I removed myself from it all, and I have not set foot in a house of God since. But the Church does not relinquish so easily. In my fever of these last weeks, I felt it in my body still. My ribs turned to buttresses, and upon my brow shone the cross . . .' The breath shook in his chest. 'And though I no longer have a congregation, I find myself thinking more and more of grace.'

I opened my mouth, but could not speak.

'I refer to mortal grace, not divine, if there is such a thing.

Human grace, which we can only grant to ourselves. It is the rarest of qualities, the divine product of ceasing war against oneself. I was jealous of your mother because I saw she had it – not despite her torments but because of them. My jealousy made me preach of sin all the harder.'

I remembered him blasting our small congregation with his fury, the villagers wincing in the pews.

'It is so easy to point at this world's shadows, and so difficult to attend to the real source of its shine. True grace is as rare and miraculous as a diamond – more so. It cannot be strived for, only attained. It is neither an ambition nor a goal; neither reward nor compensation. It is the only gift that cannot be given.' He paused. 'Nonetheless, Emily dearest, I wish nothing so dearly as to be able to give it to you.'

'You already do,' I choked out. It was true. Caring for him enabled me to set my own miseries aside, but it was more than that. I'd thought of late that I might not be able to go on pretending, but to do so would mean giving up my father. If that was the way out of the cage I found myself in, then I could never make myself take it.

'Sometimes,' I whispered, 'I worry that I will never be free of pain.'

My father shook his head, his lightless eyes creased with worry. 'You never will be, my darling. None of us will. There are no answers, only replies. But know that these lie not in our strengths, but in our weaknesses.'

CHAPTER TWENTY-FOUR

Still raw from the conversation with my father, I distracted myself by heading off in search of the Wren biography. Harold Loewe did not really believe in books, but as a gentleman he did believe in a well-stocked library. The place hadn't changed at all, and I was grateful. It was a gorgeous room, double height, late sun pouring liquidly through the tall windows and across the dark wooden shelves with their lounging inhabitants. I crossed the herringbone floor, my own bones alternately warmed by sunlit patches. In country fashion, many of the books were local history and stout volumes on trout, ducks, grouse, et cetera. But there was a good case of biographies, Harold having enjoyed reading the lives of great men, if only to pick them apart afterwards.

With a little searching, I found *The Life of Christopher Wren*. It had been written by a Victorian enthusiast, its sheer length suggesting that this biographer had had a good deal of leisure time to pursue his hobby horse. All I needed was its list of the places designed by the great man.

Unfortunately, these were multitudinous. Wren seemed to have designed half of England. Churches, hospitals, libraries . . . had Hester really hidden a diary in one of these? What if I needed a specific biography of Wren from the castle library? What if it was sewn into the spine like the Audubon?

I took the book and sat on the floor in a patch of sunshine, back to the wall. We had done this as children, the three of us lined up in a neat row. None of us was particularly bookish then, so my recollections of the library were chiefly of rain flowing down the window panes. Only later did I discover how a bottomless hunger might be fed by reading. The joy of books is that adults will not judge you for your rapacity; it is the only vice that may be entertained quite respectably in public. I loved the language of botany, as rooty and voluptuous as the plants themselves. Leaves weren't hairless, they were glaucous. Trees could be fluted, like crystal glasses. I felt myself being lowered into the natural world, the landscape growing riper and richer. My own personal form of possession.

Yes, I remembered this library in the rain, not with gilded rectangles cast upon the floor.

A sudden notion. I pulled out *The Birdcage Library* and turned again to page 34. It showed that boxy gold cage. And in Hester's account: *It was a pretty cage, though – a simple square, golden, containing a noble wren.*

Christopher Wren. Golden squares . . .

I scanned the list of the architect's achievements. Nothing. Turning to the index, I ran my finger down the entries for G, then went directly to a particular page: *Golden Square in London's Soho. While the originator of the design is rather unclear, it was laid out in accordance with a plan that bears Wren's signature . . .*

Warmth spread through me. Hester had not let me down. I had the location of the next clue. I'd been right – it wasn't at Pàrras after all.

Since my sister's death, I'd thought I would never again feel that joyous sensation of two minds intermingling, wrapping round one another like vines. Yet here it was, and all from a woman I would never meet.

'I haven't sat like that since we were children.'

Daniel was there, sunlight spilling across his features, quite in opposition to the strain in his voice. It pulled my chest taut with it as I remembered what my father had said about him. I shut the book quietly, and to prevent questions about it, and more importantly to stop him sitting down beside me in a way that would have torn me in two, I said, 'Shall we go for a walk?'

By unspoken agreement, we headed down to the mirror pond. His mother had organised the garden into nine levels, each different to the next, so one descended through lavender, rue and sariette; then hyacinths and honeysuckle, yew trees and woodbine, and so on, each level criss-crossed by stone parapets and staircases. Everywhere were roses, always roses, buds wrapped around themselves until forced to bloom. Harold had maintained this garden in her memory; Daniel had done the same, though I noted without comment that the plants had grown unruly.

The mirror pond was at the very lowest level. Its clear waters had been overtaken with algae; if he did not do something soon, the fish would suffocate.

A nightingale sang from the trees. Daniel glanced at me askance, omnipresent shadows in and beneath his eyes.

'Why don't you sell it?' I said suddenly.

'Sell what?'

'Butterworth.'

'I told my father I would take care of it. I can't just sell.'

'Why ever not?'

'My father . . .'

'Is dead.' Unfeeling but true. 'I'm serious, Daniel. Sell the place, pay off your debts.'

'And what then? What else do I have to live for? Don't

look at me like that. You have your father. I have no one. I am not so idiotic as to think Butterworth needs me, Emmy, but *I* need *it*.'

Silence. Before I could work out what to say, he spoke again. 'Harold and I went to the Riviera the year before he died. He was growing sicker, and his friends had recommended the Train Bleu. We walked along the beach. I was behind him, and as we walked, it dawned on me that I was unconsciously doing what I had as a child, trying to step exactly where he had. I was trying to fit myself into his footprints without even realising it.'

His voice was despairing. I thought of the last year before Harold died, when Daniel was setting himself up in the City. How I'd catch him gazing at his father with a peculiar intensity that I only later identified as something very like loathing.

'I have never been able to function as myself, Emmy. That is why I lost your money, and why I hate myself so passionately for it. I am but half a person.'

I clamped my teeth into my lip, biting down savagely on my own secret. It did not matter that I reasoned with him, saying it could have happened to anyone; that the recession had wiped out the fortunes of greater men than he. He would neither sell Butterworth nor forgive himself.

'I have nothing else.'

'You have me.'

He let out a strangled laugh. 'I don't have you. Not in any sense.'

There was that sprawling mass within me. I had spent so many years forcing it down. Crushing it. I could not eliminate it – but I could help him

'There might be a way to save Butterworth,' I said slowly. I had given Mr Vogel my word that I would keep the diamond secret, but I could not bear to see my friend so despairing, not on my account. I told him of the stone; told him that if I found it, once my father was adequately cared for, then he and Butterworth could have the rest. The money was otherwise of no use to me. I would return to Australia and my old job, sending samples across the world, sealed tight in their glass cases.

I expected him to thank me, or to protest. I did not expect silence, nor the brittle smile on that full mouth.

'I do not want you to buy me off, Emmy.'

'What do you mean?'

'You cannot purchase my indifference. Not at any price.'

His eyes were deep; unlike the mirror pond, they showed me nothing. The nightingale's song soared again, but I was imprisoned, black bars all around, nowhere to run. I could not allow myself to love him. I was a counterfeit, a parasite, a nothing. The twilight shadows were crowding in, filling my eyes, flinging themselves on my back. I muttered something about having to go, and fled, conscious of his eyes on my back, of my drowning thoughts, of how even while I ascended the garden's levels, I was only descending deeper. Somewhere a bell tolled, rising around me, claiming me, and no matter how far I ran, I knew it would find me again. For it was not Daniel, or my father, or my sister who had locked me away. My jailer was me.

I fall, landing brutally into a twisted mess of stone and bell metal, my neck twisted where I lie, a streak of red before me. Not a bird's feathers, but my sister's beautiful hair, trailing from under the largest of the church beams, other breeds of red colouring the dust around it.

My father is calling, and with great effort I wrench my gaze away, telling myself I cannot see what is before me, plain as day. If I do not look back, none of it is real.

He calls again. Somehow, gasping with the pain, I manage to lift a great weight from myself and crawl to him. His voice grows fainter, though I am coming nearer. He is crying a name.

'Emily,' he says.

But I am not Emily – I am Emma. I am Emma, who killed her mother by failing to grab her hand. I am Emma, watched for ever by green eyes of guilt. Emma, whose sister and father have sidled further and further away ever since. My twin and I used to be the same person. Now Emily is a separate unit, and half of me has been lost – more. We could have grown up together, wound around one another like symbiotes. But with my mother's death, I destroyed it all, and so I became unwanted – unnecessary – a parasite. It is not obvious to the outsider. Together we walk, talk, attend church, hang laundry. But we three all know the great, silent gulf. I do not accompany Emily and my father on their Alpine expeditions – even if they wanted me there, which they do not, I worry that my guilt will stain the very snow.

At these times I go into my father's greenhouse and tell the plants my secrets. He loves them. Why else would I study botany? To be close to these plants is enough, because it has to be.

I look down at my father, this man I love so much yet who is so far away from me.

'Emily,' he says again, ever fainter. Emily, the only remaining comfort of his soul. Emily, the only member of his family he can consider without grief.

His strength is fading. These are his last moments, and there is a flicker of thought, of decision, but only a flicker.

I speak, and the flicker is extinguished. I speak, and everything changes for ever.

'Yes,' I say.

'Emily,' he whispers, slow relief smothering his pain. 'Is that you?'

'Yes, Father. It is me.'

220

CHAPTER TWENTY-FIVE

I lied to my father to bring relief to a dying man. But he did not die. It was a long, slow recovery for both of us in hospital, and his sight never returned, along with the use of much of his left side. Half his body had given up. Well, I knew how that felt.

I meant to tell him the truth. Most of my face was bandaged for the first fortnight, rendering my deception invisible when I went in to read to him, as I did every day, passages from his favourite scientific volumes. Alfred Russel Wallace. Carl Linnaeus. Old friends. Even once the bandages came off, I decided to wait until he was in a better condition, though to maintain the pretence I had to modulate my speech: Emily's voice was slightly lower, more laconic. She wore her hair differently too, tighter around the base of the neck. Soon, both behaviours became habit. My father could not see my hair, of course, but there were other visitors, not least Daniel, and I could not let them spot the discrepancy before I told him. Yet even when the bandages came off, Daniel saw little, grieving as he was for Emma – for me – with an intensity I found perversely touching.

I did not grieve, not yet. After all, it was my very pretence that was keeping Emily alive.

Perhaps it was this, finally, that made the charade so seductive, that fused the mask to my skin. Or perhaps it was the morning when I decided to tell my father once and for all. It was still summer, and the countryside was indecently alive. He was nearly ready to leave hospital. I myself had been discharged weeks ago, but came every day, leaving behind the empty house spattered with my sister's presence, like a crime scene. Unable to bear our bedroom, I slept downstairs. The hospital had diagnosed me with Type 1 diabetes during my stay, and that, coupled with the injuries I had sustained, meant I was cripplingly aware of my body in a way I never had been before. Now something to be injected, monitored and filled with the right foods, it was no longer really mine.

Would Emily have had it too? Would our bodies have mapped our joined lives, in sickness and in health, even if we ourselves did not? I would never know.

'What have we today?' My father's voice had softened since the accident, weak as warm tea. I guiltily adored this time we had together, time we had not shared since my mother's passing. I loved the ease of his manner with Emily, loved his asides as I read aloud, loved being close enough to scent his faint fragrance of earth and tobacco ('finest of all the plants'). Dread choked me at what I would shortly tell him, and how that weak-tea voice would turn cold.

Incidentally, the term for a parasite that cannot survive without its host is *obligate*.

'Humboldt,' I replied to his question, and began to read. Sunlight shone through the hospital window upon us, as though we were the blessed ones about whom my father always preached. At some point he put out a hand and placed it on my own.

'Emmy,' he said at last, interrupting. 'The doctors have recommended warm weather. The bishop has a connection in Sydney. I had thought – well, he has written to Oxford to enquire about the circumstances of a transfer to the university there. They are able to make arrangements for you.' He tried a smile, though such movements still pained him. 'What do you think?'

My confession piled up in my mouth, a jumbled mash. I tried to arrange the words into a coherent order. *I am Emma. I am sorry.*

'Father,' I said hesitantly. 'Father, I have something to—'

'I know it is a big step,' he interrupted quickly. 'Your achievements in this field have already been so great, and I would never hinder you. The University of Sydney allows women not only to graduate, but to become doctors too. Only think of that, Emily!'

No. No, not Emily. Emma. 'Father, I—'

'My darling, I do not think I have ever told you how proud you make me. I have so little left. Your mother gone, and now your sister. I have lost my eyesight, and the enjoyment of my books and plants with it. It is *your* future, dear heart, not mine, that I now live for.' The hand on mine tightened. 'What do you think?'

Dear heart. He had once called both of us that. Not any more. Tears filled my eyes. He believed that Emma was dead, and I knew then that if I told him the truth, not only would it break him, but I would die all over again. His despair and grief at losing his preferred child would kill me in every way that mattered.

But if I kept my secret . . . Emma would be gone for ever, but Emily would live on. She was the laughing pioneer, the bold, crisp apple of his eye. She was the Oxford student, the discoverer of Blackwood's orchid. In every way she was an improvement on me. Emma's death would mean Emily's survival. Perhaps it would even assuage my own grief, keeping my twin alive by offering her my body as a vessel.

Mistletoe disguised itself by taking on the appearance of its host. I could do the same.

I took a deep breath, inhaling a whole new life.

'I think it's a brilliant idea.'

How often does each of us wish to be someone else? Like every child, my sister and I played pretend. Not princesses for us. Adventurous types – Georges Legagneux, Julia Henshaw, Isabella Bird, Harry Houdini. It never occurred to us to play each other. We were, to all intents and purposes, the same person.

It was that bond, twisted and broken though it was, that made my transition effortless. My father noticed nothing. Neither did our friends, not even Daniel, though he hated the new distance between us. I could not trust myself in his presence. He was grieving – grieving for me. Little did he know that the girl he thought he'd lost lived on, hating herself for every moment of his pain. My sister had declared her right to him before she died. With her gone, I *could* have married him. But my own lie had slammed that door shut. It was Emma, not Emily, whom Daniel had loved. The moment in the greenhouse was an aberration.

I gathered up Emily's books and papers and, on the ship to Sydney, learned everything she had learned. I was not starting from nothing: I had embarked on my own career in botany, though not at Oxford, and I was always quick. My new teachers saw no discrepancy. In the ensuing years, I would often be disturbed at how easily I stepped into her shoes. It was Emily who had found the Blackwood orchid, on her third trip to the Alps with my father. This had cemented her acceptance into Oxford, which in turn was the first period we'd spent physically apart, even if the true

224

separation had occurred long ago.

In her first year, I apprenticed myself to a conservationist named Rutherford, the owner of the tortured willow. He was doing what he could to battle the Dutch blight of the elms, which was to say little or nothing. It was a massacre. In dismay we found the fungus's telltale carvings on tree after tree, the alate markings reminiscent of winged men. Touched by angels, but it was the angel of death. It was a discouraging time, and even before Emily died, I buried myself in the books she left lying around, careless treasure. She wore life lightly, did much and cared for little, preoccupied with ambition. She wanted to become an RGS fellow, and I had no doubt she would do it.

In that last summer, she entered to find me looking at the orchid specimen she kept, the one that bore her name. Her mouth twisted in something I initially thought was pity.

'Have it if you want,' she said. Then I realised: not pity, but scorn.

I could not be angry at her, because as soon as the rage flared, it turned upon myself. If my mother had not died, everything would have been different. Emily and Emma would have passed the days side by side, still picked yellow irises, played pranks, jumped the unlucky stair, made a mess, caught newts.

Person. A Latin word that means *mask*. Almost every culture has masks; the ones in Papua were made from woven bamboo canes. Civilised life meant donning faces every day. At least the one I chose I had the advantage of knowing intimately. At least it kept my father's hope alive. There were worse crimes than that.

There was another, unexpected benefit. My guilt over my mother's death lessened. In turning myself into Emily, I was now the faultless sister, the one without blood on her hands. It seemed I had become her so passionately that the deepest parts of myself were half able to forget I was pretending.

In so many ways, it was the perfect mask. So what if I was unable to take it off again?

CHAPTER TWENTY-SIX

I said before that lies are like plants, but perhaps that is not quite true. A plant, even a parasitical one, is a living thing, whereas I was a dead woman walking. The next day, I avoided Daniel, except to tell him that I would be leaving for London early. I was not running away. The Wren discovery had merely changed my plans.

Despite this logic, the waver in his expression was a knife to my heart. Without thinking, I took his face in my hands, my palms warm against his skin.

'What are you doing?'

My hands dropped to my sides. 'You looked upset.'

His dark eyes locked on mine. 'Thank you for your offer yesterday. It was most considerate.'

'But you are going to refuse.'

A wry smile. 'Because you are not doing me a favour – at least not the one you think you are. I do not want you to buy off my guilt, Emily, if such a thing were even possible. I understand that you wish to unburden yourself of me. That is what you would be paying for. Well, I cannot do it.'

I swallowed.

'Don't worry, I do not ask anything of you. I never will.

You have enough weight on your shoulders. But the fact remains . . .' He ran a hand through his hair. 'The fact remains that I love you. I am sorry that is so hard for you to bear.'

I packed for my departure from Butterworth as one who has been hit over the head. I wanted to be angry, to relieve myself with storm and fury; but I could only manage stunned, then later, drunk. Reynolds handed over the bottle with palpable disapproval.

'Don't tell him,' was all I said.

I hadn't emptied so much of a gin bottle in a long, long time. Daniel loved Emma. Not Emily. How had this come to pass? How had he accounted for it to himself? I dreaded to think how this shift in his affections must have tormented him – the guilt and confusion at loving one sister, then, seven years later, falling for the other.

The next morning, painfully, I kissed my father goodbye, making him promise to provide regular updates on his condition. I bade farewell to the few remaining servants, including Reynolds, declining to look the latter in the eye. Daniel was in his office, speaking to a man dressed in clothing so ruthlessly inexpensive that he could only have been a creditor. While he was so occupied, I did what I always did.

I left.

The train was unbearable. The sun beat down mercilessly upon the crammed carriage; I drank from my Thermos, then leaned my aching forehead on the travelling case smothering my lap, incurring askance glances from the man opposite, his hat brim fairly dripping with sweat.

It was for my father that I had pretended to be my sister; Daniel had merely been collateral. Edwin would die one day, but if I accepted Daniel, I would have to go on pretending.

I would have to lie to my husband every day. What would that make me?

The train rattled on, Butterworth retreating farther and farther into the distance. I had escaped.

Why did I feel no relief?

London at last. I hurried from Euston to Soho, damp spreading across my back. Despite the heat, I was grateful for the seething distraction of the metropolis, for the people scurrying along the Euston Road, for the scalding bus fumes and the brilliance of the river I'd seen from the train, solid in the bright light.

That same light burnished Golden Square, which that day lived up to its name. I'd always liked London's garden squares. It must have been delightful for the residents to sit there with their coffee and their newspaper and feel, quite against the evidence, that all was right with the world.

It was then that I realised I had no idea which house I was looking for.

I stared around me, hoping for . . . what? A sign, I suppose. My pursuit of Hester's story was becoming something of a pilgrimage, my faith in her growing by the day. Still, my train to Pàrras was in an hour and a half. There was no time to waste. I had a not-even-closely restorative gulp of water from the Thermos, then took out *The Birdcage Library*.

Mercifully it was not long until I had it. As I'd noted before, the number on page 34 had been crossed out, replaced by 10. I rubbed my finger gently on the green ink, then looked around the square.

Number 10 seemed just like the other houses, a Georgian brick affair with a basement flat below and a green double-fronted door. I didn't loiter. I knocked and prayed for an answer. Or at least a reply.

'Can I help you?'

I turned: behind me was a sprightly lady of perhaps fifty.

229

She had intelligent eyes and a good figure, but that was not what caught my attention. She seemed to have come from the garden, but instead of a newspaper, she sported a massive pair of shears. My eyebrows lifted slightly.

'Do you live here?'

She inclined her head in assent.

'I am Emily Blackwood.' I hesitated. 'It is rather a curious story, and I do not have much time. To cut to the chase, I am here about a diary.'

Her eyes narrowed. 'You had better come in.'

The home of Mrs Heatherwick – for that was her name – was much like the woman herself: stylish, composed, ruthlessly neat. Yet there were curious touches. The umbrella stand was a large earthen pot, while eastern Asian ornaments lined the mantelpiece and one wall bore an elegant arrangement of spears. I thought I recognised the carvings of one, but was distracted by my hostess pouring the tea.

There was no Mr Heatherwick, she told me. 'Of course husbands are mostly nothing but trouble.'

Her tone was mischievous, but I winced, thought of Daniel. 'I am afraid I wouldn't know.'

'Oh, everybody may try marriage once. Just don't make a habit of it. My parents never bothered, and they were more than happy.' She herself wore a ring, I noticed, a gold band with a small diamond, but it was not on her wedding finger. 'You are an explorer, you say? A plant hunter? Perhaps that is enough excitement for one lifetime. You know, my benefactor was a great friend of Isabella Bird. A man named Richard Heatherwick. It was he who passed me this house and the diary. I took his name to honour him.'

Richard Heatherwick. . ..Hester's grandparents' lawyer. He had left the house to Hester originally, not knowing he would outlive her. 'Your parents did not mind?'

'Not in the slightest. They were . . . especially free in their outlook. Richard himself was unconventional. I share his admiration of explorers. Always looking forward, never back. Lot would have approved. You know the Bible story, of course. Though his poor wife . . . I always sympathised with her. To look back, knowing the cost to yourself – well, that seems to me like love, not sin.' She sipped her tea. 'Love traps us if we let it, but my parents taught me it need not. The highest form of love is indistinguishable from liberty.'

She set the cup down and her manner became businesslike. 'Now, I think you had better explain how it is that you are after my diary.'

I told her the brief particulars. I left out the diamond, naturally, and my increasing doubt as to the manner of Hester's death – in fact, virtually all the important details. In my telling, I had merely stumbled across the first papers while conducting research for the castle's owner, and was following the trail to a mysterious treasure.

She poured more tea for us both and took a sip. 'You were invited to this castle for what reason?'

'I discovered an item in Papua. The invitation was from its rightful owner.'

'And that item was . . .?'

I could not see the harm in telling her. 'A bird of paradise. Stuffed, in a glass box.'

I could have sworn for a moment that her eyes gleamed over the teacup rim. Then there was only her clear gaze, fixed upon me. It was all I could do not to squirm.

'I can see that you are under a great strain, dear, which is why I am going to let you off the pack of lies you have just told. No, please do not apologise. I am all in favour of bending the truth when required. I shall do you the courtesy of assuming that it *is* required.'

I blushed to the roots of my hair. 'It is. Sorry.'

231

'Don't be. Life puts the weeds in, and it is up to us to yank them out. I "do" the square, you know.'

I remembered the shears. 'It is very pretty, Mrs Heatherwick.' Something about her demanded manners. I felt myself at the foot of a queen.

'Call me Saxen. I know it is, but like all beautiful things, it takes a great deal of work. Plants, like people, will decide whether or not they wish to grow. And there is very little we can do about it. We just have to do the best we can. Now.' The teacup was set down with a decisive chink. 'The person who gave my benefactor the diary entrusted him with a very great task.'

'Who *did* give it to him?'

'I am afraid that is not for me to say. When the house passed to me, I swore that I would give the diary to the one who asked for it, as long as they seemed of good character, and so long as they had in their possession a particular book.' She shot me a look. 'Do you have it?'

I dug in my bag and brought out *The Birdcage Library*. Her eyes sparkled. She stood and went out. A moment later I heard a whirr and a click, as though from a safe being opened. Then she returned and gently pressed a roll of papers into my hands.

'After all these years . . . I have felt like a gatekeeper, and I suppose I am. It will be a shame to give up my position.'

I gazed at the pages I now held. 'I would tell you more if I could,' I said uncomfortably. 'Only at present, such secrets are not mine to share.'

'Of course, dear. I imagine it will be an enormous relief when that is no longer the case. I mentioned Isabella Bird. My father was also an admirer. He had a favourite passage: "I have just dropped into the very place I have been seeking, but in everything it exceeds all my dreams." He thought it as near enough a perfect description of paradise as he had ever heard. That is the thing about heaven, he said. We never know what it will be until we find ourselves there.

'I haven't known you very long, dear, but I can see that a shadow dogs you. We are fallible creatures, always getting in a muddle, but in some respects we are straight and true. I may not know what you need to do, but I can tell that *you* do. The trick is to let yourself do it. We all know that the entrance to heaven is barred by pearly gates, but my dear father always dismissed the idea of petty Peter loitering outside, waiting to judge us. The only person who can do that, he said, is ourselves.' Her hand brushed mine. 'When we have done so, and only then, do we discover that the key has been in our pocket all along.'

I pressed my lips together to stop them trembling. I'd thought Hester was helping me see the doors in my own life, but Mrs Heatherwick was right. Finding them was one thing. To unlock them was quite another.

'Well, dear. You have your book. If you are ever at liberty to disclose more, I shall be delighted to listen.'

I heard the dismissal. My train left in less than forty minutes. Time to go.

'Thank you, Mrs Heatherwick. Saxen.'

She nodded, and rose to escort me to the door. I bade her farewell. Just as I was departing, she suddenly spoke.

'And if you *do* find the diamond, dear, do some good with it. That is all I ask.'

I gaped. I had never mentioned the stone. But before I could speak, the door was closed, and though I knocked, it did not open again.

Heedless of strangers' glances, I fairly sprinted to Euston, and made the train with seconds to spare. As soon as I had settled, I opened the pages I had been given and began to read.

CHAPTER TWENTY-SEVEN

I waited for Henry the next day, but he did not come. Nor the next day, nor the next. The days turned to weeks; the summer skies gave way to rain, and I sat inside, watching civilisation recede as the streets turned to mud. Sarah returned from visiting her brother, home from seafaring, and shook herself in the hall like a dog, skirts brown up to the knee; Myrtle's puddings tasted of damp. I alternately avoided the small bedroom that had so briefly been Henry's, and went into frenzies for it. Once Charles saw me hovering in the doorway, and his lips went white. For a sick moment I thought he had guessed, but then I remembered the nursery. I had failed my husband on every front.

Otherwise, I fretted over the paradise bird, asking Sarah repeatedly if it looked unwell. To my mind its plumage was fainter, its liveliness quelled.

'It's just the weather, madam.'

I did not want to be one of those ladies Mamie Fish had mentioned, murdering my charge through ill-placed love. Once I had cared for, fought for a workforce of fifty women. Now I could not be trusted with a single bird. Love had brought about my diminishment – it is love that ruins us, love of the damaged and damaging kind. I tormented myself first with Henry, then with Charles, and back again. I even thought of leaving, then dismissed the notion as quickly as it had come.

Had my husband not noticed that our marriage was crumbling in our fingers? Could Henry not see all that we were supposed to be?

At last I heard that the younger brother was coming to our house, though only to see his sibling: I met him as I happened to be descending the stairs, a coincidence I had spent much of the afternoon engineering. Pathetic, and to no effect. He only bowed to me and left.

'You ought to give it a name,' Sarah said of the bird, shaking me from yet another reverie. I already had, though it was one I could never speak aloud.

Henry.

One morning, I received an unwelcome visitor: Hyatt Frost. He arrived unannounced, accompanied by his horrible pipe and an exceedingly rough-looking fellow introduced as Paul Ruhe.

'Forgive me. I was looking for Charles.' As ever, Frost's voice was flat as flat could be, his tone as dry as dry, but his eyes were hungry, and I pictured Charles and me as those innocent young oysters, faithfully trotting on behind the walrus and carpenter. The two men had entered without invitation, and I could not but notice that Ruhe closed the door behind him.

'I thought he was with you,' I said.

'He left early. On an errand for you.'

I shook my head grimly. 'I know of no such errand.'

'Pity.' Then: 'Is that a bird of paradise?'

I did not like them looking at it.

'May I?' Frost had already crossed the room. The bird

235

shrank from him. 'A gift from Charles?' I did not correct him. 'What a fantastic creature. Do you know how rare it is to have one in captivity? *I* have never seen it. Have you, Mr Ruhe?'

Mr Ruhe said that he had not.

'Mr Ruhe is a hunter, Mrs Vogel. Lately returned from the dark continent.'

'I collect mammals,' Ruhe said. There was a deadness to his tone that made me suppress a shudder. 'Infants, naturally. Adult creatures will not stand to be taken, bar the elephants. Everything else will fight to the death. Kill the parent, take the pup.' He gestured to the cage with a paw. 'But perhaps birds are different.'

'I shall never tire of the *romantic* element of this marvellous business,' Frost declared, glancing at me for confirmation. Finding none, he went on, 'I hear from my collectors that with the current fashion for feathers, these birds are increasingly difficult to find in the wild.' He poked a finger through the bars. 'This one's plumage alone could fetch a significant sum. I cannot think why Charles has not sold it already.'

Mr Ruhe sighed lugubriously. 'Collection is a difficult art. Only think of how many hundreds of thousands of dollars have found their way to the dark continent and the Orient. Yet how little makes it out again!'

'Please do not do that,' I snapped, as Frost's finger quested for the bird's tail. 'He dislikes strangers.'

'Nonsense. Beauty lives to be appreciated.' He gazed at me. 'The circus is shaping up nicely. Charles is plan-ning some spectacular fireworks for the opening night next year.' He pulled a thin tube from his pocket and held it up. 'I like to carry them with me in case of opportunity. It is one of life's pleasures, to seek out possibilities for spectacle. Like this bird. Perhaps you could lend it to us. It would do wonders for our ticket hall.'

'No, thank you,' I said stiffly.

'Charles would not mind.'

'That is beside the point.'

He moved quicker than a leopard. Suddenly he was before me, that same long finger reaching for my cheek.

'Yes,' he breathed. 'It certainly seems that way.'

His finger came within a fraction of an inch: upon it was a powder, white and dusty. I said, as fiercely as I could muster, 'I don't know what sort of spell you have Charles under, but it must end.'

He seemed genuinely surprised. 'It is not *I* who have him under a spell, Mrs Vogel.' His voice lowered to a repellent intimacy; behind him, Ruhe had his eye almost against the cage. 'I used to dabble in canaries. At length I decided to try my hand at breeding. Yet suppose you have let loose multiple birds into the room to mate. If you later try to mix the birds in different unions – for example, by putting the male into an enclosure with a different male – it does not work. The male is always longing for his old companion.'

'With a different female, you mean.'

'I beg your pardon?'

'You said by caging the male with a different male. You mean female.'

Something flitted behind his eyes. 'Of course.'

I took a deep breath. 'I think it is time for you both to leave.'

'I quite agree. Come, Ruhe.' Then, over his shoulder: 'Let us hope your circus guests find a more welcoming reception.'

They left, and I collapsed into the armchair. The bird Henry seemed to feel as I did, huddled in his cage. Mr

237

Ruhe's unimaginative brutality frightened me. With men like him roving the world, how long before its stock of wonders was either caged or dead? *No sooner have we marvelled than we wish to possess; and the act of possession is the beginning of destruction.* Henry's words. But for all that, it was Hyatt Frost, the unknown quantity, who made me truly afraid.

I do not know how long the bird and I remained like that before Charles returned. I glanced up from my seat and there he was, gazing down upon me like God. It occurred to me that while I was dazzled by Henry, I nevertheless understood him. Whereas with Charles I was awestruck, and as with any deity, I comprehended so little. Had I truly only chosen him because he was different? What did that make me?

'I brought you something.'

I saw now that he was carrying a large, pretty box. At times I forgot we were well off. The remembrance of it was like burying one's head in our expensive sheets: comforting and suffocating at the same time.

He set the box upon the card table, which had never yet seen a game. I had learned early on that my husband disliked entertaining unless either useful or necessary. The paradise bird cheeped, but he did not look at it; I realised then that he never did.

Inside was a doll of papier mâché. Its design had an Oriental look.

'From Japan.'

'Oh,' I said, then, after a moment: 'Thank you.'

'Wait. I am not yet done.' I watched as he took it up and . . .

And took it apart. I could only gasp as it broke into two pieces, revealing a second doll within. He took that out and repeated the trick, revealing a third, and a fourth, and so on until the ninth, this last one solid and so small it was barely a finger's length. He smiled at my wonder.

'It is called a Daruma doll. My mother had several. I liked the ones I could dress up, but these were my favourite. So many versions, all cooped up in the same body.' He went on, so quietly I had to lean in to catch him, 'She could be so many things.'

'Oh my darling,' was all I could manage, and now I reached out. Not for the doll, but for him.

It was the beginning of a wonderful reconciliation. The rain gave way to snow, yet between us shone a warmth I had not felt since the first few months of our marriage. My husband was far more at home and could not have been more attentive. Rather than both of us disappearing to our respective rooms after supper, he now came to mine, and I would read to him beside the fire while he paced about, inspecting trinkets or, increasingly, drawing up a chair to the paradise bird and observing it closely as he listened.

'A most intriguing creature,' he said on several occasions. Then, a week later: 'May I hold it?'

I was surprised. Though I had often stroked the bird through the bars, it had never occurred to me to do more.

'Why not?' I did not want to upset this love we had dug up from somewhere, the earth hardly brushed off. I undid the cage door while he knelt, ready, lest it should try to fly away. The bird watched us from the side of its eyes.

'Try now,' I said quietly. He reached in and gently withdrew it, the creature uttering a small chirrup of protest.

'There, there,' he said with utmost tenderness, one

239

finger caressing its neck. To my immense surprise (and indeed, jealousy), the bird closed its eyes. From this angle my husband could have been in prayer, and indeed, I heard a murmur, almost a croon. It took me some moments to realise I did not recognise the language; it was one I had never heard him use, not ever.

German. He was speaking German.

It was not a man who knelt there, but a child. A hot pain sprang to my eyes.

My husband's blossoming tenderness found a response in me, and over the following weeks, it grew and grew, not only picking up from before but developing into a whole new conversation, that private language which is at once common to all true partners and yet entirely unique. It is a curious thing, to fall back in love with one's own husband. No longer was it like painting a picture, as I had felt the first time around, feeling one's way across the blank canvas. Now it was like sculpting marble – the shape was in there; I had only to find my way to it. When passing one another we made contact, he taking my hand, I touching his cheek. One evening, as I bent over some needlework, he begged to be allowed to try, and for the first time I saw him be silly. At night he once more came to me, and our joinings were different to even the early months of our marriage: slower, sweeter. Gradually my strength and focus returned; gradually I re-formed myself. Once more he sought my opinions, including on the circus launch in several months' time, which I appreciated deeply.

At no point did he invite me to the emporium or suggest I take on the books again.

The launch was set for late spring and would occur in two stages: a dinner party at our house, then the actual circus opening twelve days later. For this second event, Charles and I sent dozens of special hand-written tickets to the great and good of society. But ever conscious of his rank, he deemed it too presumptuous to invite those people to our humble home; therefore the dinner would largely consist of business connections and their wives, in the hope that their influence would wend its way up through society in time for the launch. Extra staff would be hired especially for the evening, and as the date neared, permanent steam clouds issued from the kitchen as Myrtle concocted pies and jellies of all kinds, odd shrieks and whistles emitting from the steaming pans and indeed from the cook herself.

Nor was I immune to her hysteria. I was desperate to please Charles, spending many hours poring over the guest list and even, I am ashamed to say, an old copy of *Sensible Etiquette of the Best Society*, which resulted – as was doubtless intended – in many fruitless hours of feminine dissatisfaction. I found myself in need of relief, and it was then that I received word from Robert Odlum, saying that he was back in town.

I went to meet him. His rather mean lodgings were at the extreme south of Manhattan, not very far from the emporium, and he greeted me with a delight that warmed me through. I suggested we walk in the opposite direction from Vogel & Brother, along the water, and he consented.

'I never miss an opportunity to observe the bridge's progress,' he told me.

The Brooklyn Bridge was indeed close to completion, its rather Gothic towers rearing above us like a cathedral. Robert pointed out where the eyebars had been set in its trusses.

'Why do you follow it so closely?' I asked, thinking of

the Occoquan Falls and already knowing the answer. The old gleam rose to his eyes.

'Because someday somebody might jump from it.'

'Robert! Surely it is much too high.'

'It is merely a matter of technique. Here.' He showed me a pamphlet, printed again on that cheap, thin paper. It detailed the proper way to leap into water and his personal triumphs in the subject. 'I am circulating it privately at present, but I hope to publish. It is crucial to enter the water with legs together, feet first, at the perpendicular. It is when one does so at an *angle* that one has trouble. And to brace the muscles immediately before impact, that is vital also.'

'You are making it sound so simple.'

'It is – and is not. Oddly, one must not *jump*. Better to step, with the shoulders a little ahead of the body; spread the hands for balance, and look not down, nor up, but at the horizon.'

'But might it not prove fatal?'

'Perhaps. Perhaps not.'

'How can you be so equivocal?'

'A life without testing our limits, Hester, is not worth living.'

'But why not be happy as you are? Why not see out one's days in the ordinary way?'

Robert gave a small smile, not unkind. 'Is that what you were doing when I met you at Bloomingdale's?'

I could not look at him. He went on, gently, 'We all of us must find our boundaries at some point. Better to choose to do so than be forced to it. I am only doing with gravity what others do with alcohol or opium. Everyone needs an escape from the humdrum pain of living. The trick is to do so in a manner that enlivens, rather than diminishes, the soul.'

I took him in then: his coat was faded but his smile was not. Even his gait was lighter than mine, less bound by the earth's forces.

'I cannot work out if I envy you, Robert.'

'Do not, Hester dear. Anyone may do what I do. All it requires is a step over the edge.'

We carried on along the river, glowing beneath the early May skies. I left him at the corner and watched as he walked into the crowd like a man wading into the sea. A scarlet and yellow omnibus clattered by, and then he was gone.

The stage was set for the dinner party; all was ready. The footmen had laid twenty-four impeccable places, cutlery shining on the white, white linen. Charles's expression was one of careful composure, though he was wound tight as a pocket watch. I had noticed that about my husband: the bigger the turmoil, the profounder the calm. At teatime that day, I took hold of his hand and we ate that way. I could not have said whose grip was tighter, for I had nerves of my own: Henry was due to attend. A few months ago this would have occasioned agonised excitement. Now, with the distance he had placed between us, and the closeness that had bloomed between Charles and me, I did not know what I felt. Agony, certainly, but of a different kind. I had seen my husband's seating plan and noted with relief that Henry was not beside me. Nevertheless, I felt like one of the tightrope walkers at the upcoming circus, and as Josephine helped with the green dress Charles had bought me (Sarah was assisting Myrtle), buttoning it over my corset, I gazed down and hoped I would not slip.

She finished, and together we put up my hair. There

was a knock: Charles came in. We were in my dressing room, which my husband had furnished in pretty silks. My sitting room would not be used during the party, but I had taken the precaution of moving the paradise bird into Henry's former bedroom, telling Charles I was afraid it might be disturbed. In truth, I did not wish to share it.

'Mrs Roebling is here this evening,' he said.

I nodded. Emily Roebling was the wife of Mr Washington Roebling, an invalid who also happened to be the chief engineer of the Brooklyn Bridge.

'Do you think it would be imprudent to ask her for a good spot to watch the bridge opening?' He toyed with a brooch which lay on the table. 'It is the day after the circus launch. I should like to see it.'

'I think that is an excellent idea.'

He smiled and left us. At seven, the guests began to arrive: I was upstairs with Henry, stroking him through the bars as the first hansom pulled up below. I watched the horses pant and was struck by the completeness of our dominion over living things.

As the lights dimmed, I gathered myself and went downstairs.

I had not been among a large party for a long time, and had forgotten the heady helplessness of participating in a choreographed scene. Charles was everywhere, splendid in a deep red tailcoat. If he could have had a whip to crack, he would. From the moment the guests stepped out from their cabs into the spring night, the dance flowed seamlessly in one long orchestrated movement: they passed first under the awning erected over the door against undesirable elements (striped, like a circus tent), and were funnelled through the front door, the valet taking the gentlemen's coats, Sarah assisting the ladies with their wraps and primping; then on in a perfect wave to the rooms where footmen circulated with champagne. I glided to and fro on the bubbles of small talk, avoiding Hyatt Frost, who nevertheless greeted me with a cryptic smile. In the mantelpiece mirror I glimpsed an elegant woman in smooth discussion, and it was a moment before I recognised this perfect character as myself.

But a sharp blow was dealt to my facade when Henry arrived, dressed almost as well as Charles in a coat of green. He did not come to greet me, but his presence burned as he moved about the room. He seemed intimately familiar with the daughter of a lawyer, a very beautiful girl who could not have been over twenty. I ignored him, leaning in towards Mr Havely, who seemed flattered by the attention.

To dinner. Myrtle had done us proud: hors d'oeuvres and soup were followed by fish of every kind, and crab, and oysters, and shiny lobster claws. Then came the entrées and roasts of poultry, venison and game; French side dishes and salad; and dessert, where half the calves' feet in New York must have been boiled for the jellies. I was at one head of the table, and for the first half of the proceedings I spoke to the gentleman on my right, a tea merchant, never glancing at the man three seats down, nor his pretty young acquaintance. The moment came to switch sides, and I turned to the woman at my left.

'Your bridge looks to be very near completion, Mrs Roebling.'

Emily Warren Roebling was not pretty, but a firm mouth and direct gaze made her striking. It was well known that her husband, the bridge's chief engineer, had been an invalid for many years, racked by a debilitating case of decompression sickness after diving beneath the

245

East River to work on the bridge's foundations. Since then, Emily had become her husband's eyes, ears and tongue, liaising with and directing the workmen. Not content with mere ventriloquism, she had trained herself in the cunning, clanking science of engineering, and was now generally regarded as chief engineer in all but name. The puppet had become the master. I could not but dwell on the fact that *she* had not been shut out by her husband – quite the opposite.

'It is,' she was saying calmly. 'I do not know what I shall do with myself thereafter. The launch is hardly a week away.'

'The very day after the opening of Charles's circus.'

'Perhaps then you feel as I do.' Pride glowed from her face.

I said only, 'It has been wonderful to observe how you and your husband have become one, your capabilities merging to serve so great an enterprise.'

'You mistake us, Mrs Vogel. We have not merged. We are each of us independent, but together.'

'But . . .'

'This project could not have been done if I were merely an extenuation of my husband, or vice versa. To be *whole*, Mrs Vogel. That is the trick.'

The volume at the table had risen as the glass levels fell; the room was warm, the candlelight intense. I felt a great yearning within. 'It has been the work of a dynasty, has it not?'

A brisk nod. 'Washington's father invented a new way with wire. He took the hemp ropes of old and replaced them with wrought iron, then developed a method for stranding and weaving.' She paused as though to assess my interest, or perhaps my intelligence. 'You see, a bridge is under constant pressure from different forces,

246

which would distort the body if they could.' She demonstrated, twisting her napkin round itself and stretching it in a long, taut rope. 'Therefore, if it is to survive, the structure must *absorb* these forces. In other words, all these pressures must be in equilibrium.'

I stared at her hands and swallowed. 'And if it cannot? If one force should overpower the rest?'

The hands caved; the napkin collapsed upon itself, falling to her lap in a crumpled heap. Her voice was calm. 'Then, Mrs Vogel, it is the death of the whole enterprise.'

At the other end of the table, my husband rose: it was time for everyone to break off before coffee. My cheeks were flushed; I excused myself and hurried up to my living room. But no, I might be interrupted there. After a moment's hesitation, I went into Henry's old room.

It was blessedly empty, other than the paradise bird, which cheeped in welcome. I checked the clock. Only nine thirty. In the corner was a small basin: the water it contained was old, but it did not matter. I crossed to it and splashed my face.

'You must give it to me.'

I froze, water trickling down my cheeks: Charles's voice, faint but clear, had sounded just outside the door. It was a peculiar quirk of this room that it lay some distance away from the rest, at the tip of the L-shaped landing. Had I been in my living room, I would not have heard him.

'I had intended to,' Henry's voice came in reply. 'But not for this folly, Charles. I will not.'

'It is only to sustain us for the first few months. The ticket sales . . .' My husband's words became inaudible. '. . . Frost's man underestimated —'

'He is sucking you dry, Charles. I warned you of this from the first.'

'It is only these first few months! Or perhaps the year. Henry, this is *our* venture.'

Despite the solid door between us, I could see my husband, pale but determined, hand in his pocket. I could not bear the desperation in his voice. All our warm encounters of late, all our soft confessions to one another – I had lost my carapace, and with this realisation of how much he was keeping from me, every word was a wound.

'No, brother. You undertook this knowing full well my disapproval. I cannot hand it over now.'

'At least *show* it to me. Let me ascertain its value.' I recognised Charles's acquisitive tone, the same he used when inspecting a new shipment. I longed to know what *it* was. A rare animal?

'Not unless you give up this venture.'

'It is too late for that.' A short silence, then his voice came through even clearer, as though he had moved closer. 'I *need* it, brother. Do you know how much this evening alone has cost me? If I have to ransack your apartments, I will.'

'Then do so. You will not find it there.'

My husband swore.

'You had better go down, Charles.' Henry's voice was curt. 'Your party is waiting.'

Footsteps on the stairs; I looked down at my trembling hands.

Then all at once the door opened and Henry was there, slicing off the end of a cigar, evidently seeking a quiet room in which to smoke it.

Our eyes met. Each of us was as dumbfounded as the other.

'You heard,' he said at last.

'I could not help it.' The silence was sharp between us, its edges doubly felt for the sweet softness with

248

which Charles and I had been so recently enveloped. The softness which, it transpired, had been no more than the swaddling of a lie.

Not just his – but mine too. I had betrayed him with his own brother. The guilt that I had held at bay these last months came roaring in.

Whether Henry understood my emotions I cannot say, but after a minute, he gestured to the paradise bird.

'Did you ever name it?'

His lively eyes beheld me. Choked, I told him. At first he looked confused. Then a smile broke across his battered features.

'You named it so . . .'

'Because I love it. Yes,' I said quietly.

All at once the last months with Charles dissolved, giving way to memory's sweetness.

'Hester,' was all he said, and the last of the distance crumbled between us. I met him in the middle of the room and we tore at one another, our mouths meeting with warm breath, crushed lips, his teeth at my neck and my hands seizing his hair. He slammed my back into the wall and I pushed my dress up between us, his hands on my thighs, then higher, higher still, and then he was inside me, and with every movement I loved him, I hated myself, loved him all the more.

But there were footsteps, close, closer, and in the seconds before the door opened, we thrust ourselves from one another and whipped round to see who it was.

Mr Havely. The plumassier's jolly round face peered in at us, the hubbub of downstairs drifting past him. My clothing was barely reassembled. I squashed down my fury.

'I do apologise,' he said. 'I was looking for the smoking parlour.'

'You will find it downstairs.'

'Ah.' He paused, and with terror I thought he had noticed Henry's lopsided collar, the flush in my cheeks . . .

But no. His eye was fixed on the bird of paradise. Unlike Mr Frost, he did not comment on it; but just like Mr Frost, I saw the hunger that rose in his expression like a beast from the jungle. In that moment, he did not seem jolly at all.

He left, and I turned to Henry, who seemed stunned. The heat of these last minutes had faded into that cold, fireless room.

'I cannot do this any more,' he said.

A long silence. I tried to find the words but could not.

'Charles has asked me to go on another sourcing expedition. Africa again. I leave in ten days.'

I stared at him, at the alien words issuing from that mouth so lately on mine. Neither he nor Charles had mentioned it. 'Will you accept?'

He hesitated, then finally nodded. I restrained a sob.

'I cannot remain here,' he said quietly. 'It is agony.'

'I had thought it ecstasy.'

'Do not do yourself a disservice, Hester. This is half a life. Who would seek out such a thing?'

To be whole. That is the trick. 'My life since you came has been more complete than it has ever been.'

'Has it? I know we have been happy, radiantly so. But look at you, Hester. You are brave, and clever, and kind. I know you ran your father's company for years when he was unable. I have looked through the Vogel books: you have a brilliant mind for business. I cannot imagine Charles knows even a fifth of how much you have helped him. *You* are the reason he can suddenly afford this circus. I know you know it. You are the most capable person I have ever met, and yet during our time together you were reduced to . . . what? Reading silly books and awaiting your lover's visits?' His voice was low, sad. 'You deserve so much more. Perhaps it is your father's dependence that is at fault. Did you want to spend thirteen years – your best years – operating a corsetry business, alone? Do you always mould yourself around what the men in your life demand?

'You are a good person, Hester. You have always been obedient, done what was asked of you. That may be what is demanded by society, but it ought not be answered with the surrender of your own humanity. Believe me, I know how obedience sits heavy in the soul – how it applies a grey wash to everything one does, gradually leaching life's brightness. It was only on my voyage that I learned what it was to think and act for myself. Do not tell me that you have not at times thought of more.'

The green half-frozen sea rose before me. I gulped, an odd kind of sob sounding from me.

'The freedom of original thought. *That* is true liberty, Hester. *That* is true life. Anything else, however well disguised, is just a cage.

'I love you, dear – please don't cry – I do, of course I do. But just now that is not enough. Oh, do not mistake me. It is enough for *me*. But it is not for you, though you may not know it yet. I see you wasting yourself upon me and I cannot bear to be the culprit of your diminishment.'

'You are not diminishing me.' I was desperate. I stepped towards him, pressing him into the corner. 'You *augment* me.'

He would not meet my eye. I repeated myself, pushing in, tilting my face up to him, seeking any contact I could.

'Stop,' he murmured as my hands sought his brow, his chest. 'Stop.'

'Take me with you.'

'That solves nothing. You would only be doing it for me, with me. It would have nothing to do with yourself.'

'*Take* me.'

His breathing grew short, his eyes wild. He grabbed my wrists, hard enough to hurt. I saw for the first time the hunter. The man who captured younglings and killed their parents.

'Do not. Push me.'

I could not stop the tears. 'You took over my heart, Henry. You cannot simply withdraw.'

His chest heaved, hard, despairing. He let go of my wrists. 'This is precisely what I mean. Do you see everything in terms of conquering, and collection, and control? Because those who see the world that way are destined to be owned. You call that bird Henry, but it is not *I* who is incarcerated, Hester. The strongest cages are those we make for ourselves.' He looked so sad. 'And I fear I am just the latest model.'

'Henry. Henry, please.'

'When you are free,' he whispered, 'come find me again. Until then . . .'

There was nothing I could say, no mould I could pour myself into. He rejected it all.

I managed to muster dignity enough to leave the room, and though he reached out to me as I passed, I evaded him so he caught only a button, which came away with a snap of threads.

I returned to the party, hurrying downstairs without the faintest notion of where I was going. Charles was there. Briefly his eyes locked on mine. I gave a bright counterfeit smile.

The next morning was grey and lifeless. I awoke before Charles and lay there staring at the ceiling. The streets outside were quiet. Even the newspaper seller seemed to have taken his business elsewhere, or perhaps the world had ended and there was no news, nor any newspaper men left to sell it.

Charles and I breakfasted together in silence. Of my husband's dispute with Henry or the money troubles implied, there was no trace. I watched as he ate up his cantaloupe, his muffin and his bacon, but refused everything for myself but the coffee urn. I could not eat. Too busy consuming guilt, or perhaps it was consuming me.

'You looked beautiful last night,' he said finally, finishing his bacon. 'A credit to the business and me.'

I managed a smile. *Which is the greater punishment?* Henry had asked Mamie Fish. *Incarceration, or display?*

Charles departed; I sat there while a red-eyed Sarah tidied away the things, reluctant to go up to my living room, to retreat once again into never-ending solitude. Oh, it was so easy for Henry, a man, to inveigle against a woman's weakness! What could I have done? I could hardly have abandoned my father and the factory with all its workers. Besides, I had enjoyed the work – been good at it too. So what if I was lonely, in the factory and here in this house? So what if I could go all day and night without communicating with another soul? Was that not what people did for those they loved – they gave of themselves? And therefore did it not follow that the more one gave, the more one loved?

And what about when there is nothing left? a little voice said.

I drained the coffee to the dregs, deliberately scalding my throat, and went up to my room anyway. After all, I had nothing else to do.

*

It was very quiet as I ascended the stairs. Sarah was in the kitchen. Myrtle had the day off. I realised I had yet to return the paradise bird to my living room, so I headed up to the failed nursery. The carpet (chosen by Charles) was new and thick, so my feet sank with every step; the polished banister was cold beneath my finger-tips. On the landing, I paused, overtaken by an odd feeling of dread. I continued on with increasing effort, like moving through treacle. The doorknob glinted as I took hold. I turned it, and almost before the door had finished swinging open, I knew.

There was the cage. In it was my paradise bird, dead, its neck snapped in two.

I must have fainted, because the next thing I knew, I was in my armchair, Charles cradling my face.

'Hester dear.' I heard his relief.

'He is dead,' I sobbed out. 'Henry is dead.'

'Henry? No, dear, you are mistaken. It is your bird, I am afraid. I am so very sorry.'

Gradually I came to my senses. The bird was nowhere to be seen, but it made little difference: still I saw that incandescent plumage, that noble head, so unnaturally twisted. A spur of bone had protruded through, horribly white in a creature composed entirely of colour, the once bright eyes empty.

I could not be in my living room, not with that vacancy by the window. Charles thankfully understood. He carried me to his own study and instructed Sarah to build up the fire, for the day was unnaturally cold. Once he had assured himself that I was in no danger, he left.

'Only for a few hours, dearest. I shall return as soon as possible.'

I lay on his sofa, unable even to read, assailed by a

grief that appalled me. My bird was dead. Who had killed him? And why?

I do not know how long I remained there, lost in my reflections. Gradually the deep well of grief was iced over by something else: dread.

What if Henry's death had not been a random act of violence? What if it had been a message to me, or another in our household? A statement of future intent; a *warning*. The assassin had struck in our own home – had slaughtered a beloved, defenceless pet. They must have known that their deed was not merely a murder, but a violation. I pressed at my bosom, feeling its corruption in my very soul, my chest cold with its menace.

Whatever they wanted, I would not let them take it. All those hours of reading detective novels would not be wasted. I did not have to accept Henry's death. I could track down his killer. And I could avenge him.

CHAPTER TWENTY-EIGHT

'Didn't request your stop, did you?'

I looked up from the diary: the carriage was virtually empty, the conductor looming over me. 'I took the liberty of doing so.'

'Thank you.'

'Going back, are you?'

'Of course.' My tone was stiff; I had not forgotten his dour pronouncements previously.

He sucked his teeth. 'We're overdue a storm. Do me a favour. Keep a route open for yourself somehow. An escape. Just in case you should need it.'

I might have ignored him had I not been in a state of shock from the killing of Hester's bird. I'd been expecting a death, but not this one. There was a difference between shooting a creature in the wild and killing it in its cage. That was not hunting; that was murder. I thought of the bird as I knew it. There was stitching around its neck. Now I realised why.

Its killing seemed such an *aberration*. Unnecessary. It would have made sense if it had been slaughtered for its feathers. I'd heard of the wholesale massacre of species in that era, egrets, the great auk, the dodo. We'd improved very little as a race since then, still mistaking nature as solely a resource to be tapped. We forgot the earth's incalculable magnificence in our rush to turn ourselves and the living world into measurements and machines. We reduced a whale to so many litres of oil, a forest to the minerals beneath. I wanted to believe that in the future things would be different, but it would take millions of people to remember what we had allowed ourselves to forget. To recognise that we had never left Eden.

Christ, but I wanted a drink. I drank from my flask instead. The day outside was grey, lowering, with an insidious drizzle, fine drops that I knew would soak to the bone.

The bird was dead; Hester's own death must be fast approaching. History would catch up with us both. The dwindling number of remaining chapters in *The Birdcage Library* confirmed it.

Yet with all I now knew of her, I could not believe in her suicide. A caged nightingale might beat its own brains out trying to migrate, but people were not birds. What – who – had truly put her in her grave?

The grave at Pàrras . . . I forced a sudden, unpleasant idea from my mind.

My father had said there were no answers, only replies. Nevertheless, I had to hope that Hester would show me the way before it was too late.

CHAPTER TWENTY-NINE

Now, reader, we come to the finial act; I can only hope
that in the land of my birth, we may all heal. Beginnings
have become endings. I am run out. Pay attention – I
have learned that it might just save your life.

I sat up, determined. I would not cower, despite my
grief, despite my fear. I would become a lady
detective.

First I must make a list of suspects. No – first I must
work out when the crime had occurred. I went to
Charles's bureau. He kept it locked, the key hidden
beneath a vase on the mantelpiece. I retrieved it now,
unlocked the bureau and took out pen and paper; a blue
ledger book fell out, and I replaced it before sitting
down again. The window for the crime was not large,
but nor was it small. It had certainly occurred after my
. . . encounter with Henry. After that, but before my
going up to the living room that morning. Charles always
finished breakfast at eight o'clock. That was the outer
limit. As for the other side . . . I had checked the clock
in the small bedroom, not wanting to miss coffee. Nine

258

thirty. When had I left? My cheeks grew warm at the thought of what had passed, but I pushed it aside. I had to be dispassionate. I wrote down 'ten o'clock', and added a small '?' for good measure.

That left ten hours for the murder to have occurred. The last guests had left before midnight. If it had occurred before that time, the assassin was likely a stranger. If it had occurred *after* – the sense of violation sharpened – it had to be someone in the house.

Despite myself, I felt something long submerged rising to the surface: *purpose*, and the opportunity of using my brain. I had not realised how I had missed it.

Time to draw up my suspects. I ought to cast the net widely. I asked Sarah to bring me the guest list, and a list of the hired staff also. Thirty people in all, though that excluded our household. I wrote down

Self
Henry
Charles
Sarah
Josephine
Myrtle

I drew a line immediately through my own name. One down, at least. What about Henry? I had left him in the bedroom, but I could not believe him a murderer. Still, no one must be above suspicion. After a moment's hesitation, I put a bracket around his name and Charles's. Henry loved animals, and Charles loved owning them. Neither seemed a likely killer, and if we were in as much financial trouble as Charles thought, why would either brother slaughter a valuable creature? The memory of that overheard conversation opened a sick little hole in my heart. Oh, this suspicion and counter-suspicion was horrible work.

I hastened to reapply myself. Who else? Myrtle was in the kitchen, Sarah likewise busy. I trusted them completely, and in any case, they were always home – if they wanted the bird dead, why wait until a party to strike? The same went for Charles and Henry. I put brackets round those names too. Of Josephine, I was less sure. I left her as she was and moved on to the guest list.

Who had definitely been present after I came down, and remained so, with no opportunity to sneak upstairs? After my arrival, Charles had brought over Mrs Thomson, wife of a wealthy physician, a bustling, bosomy woman who had embarked on a lengthy lecture. I could cross *her* off. Ah, and the pretty girl with whom Henry had been so intimate – I had been particularly aware of her. I eliminated her, and her father, who seemed very protective and from whom she had hardly been parted. I struck off the pork merchant and his wife, who had hogged the canapé table all evening; and the two officers, who had been talking rather loudly by the end, entertaining their corner with military tales.

My pen paused at a name. Hyatt Frost. Oh, of all those there, I could believe it of *him* the most. Nor could I definitively say he had been there all the while. I put a small cross by his name and carried on.

But try as I might, I could eliminate no one else. I was reasonably sure every guest had been in the saloon at *some* point – but as to whether they had gone upstairs, I could not say. The footmen of course had been in and out constantly, while the valet was stationed in the hall, out of my sight.

I sighed. What I needed was something thornier: motive. *Why* kill the bird? Perchance the power of its killing lay in its very lack of reason. There was no possible purpose in murdering an innocent creature other than to send a message. They had snapped its neck. It was brutal, yet also contemptuous. The cage was not locked, yet they had not even bothered to open the door. Nor had they stolen its body, though it would have been perfectly possible to do so: as Frost had said, its feathers were valuable. What were they trying to convey? Anger? Spite? That swift violence seemed to me a man's, though I knew from newspapers as well as novels that the female sex was just as capable of savagery. Could this be something to do with the circus? Were Charles's business dealings so troubled as to result in this crime? Was the wicked Hyatt Frost responsible – but then why not merely smash or thieve one of Charles's possessions? Why target *my* bird? Exhaustedly I contemplated the Persian rug Charles had recently purchased. The room was full of new things: a man trying to make, or remake, himself.

A knock – Sarah's, two smart raps. She entered, a folded note in her hand.

'From Mr Vogel.'

'Charles? Is he on his way?'

'No, madam,' she said with a curious expression. 'Henry.'

'Oh!' I hoped desperately that my blush went unnoticed. I put out my hand, but instead she set the note on the coffee table, as though it bore some contamination, and went out.

My trembling fingers took hold. *Dear Mrs Vogel*, it read:

As discussed, your husband has engaged me to travel
to Africa. I shall be busy making preparations in the
interim; therefore it is unlikely our paths shall cross
again. I have left you a parting present in thanks for
your kindness towards me. A gift from South Africa.
I have left it with your bird – I trust he will ensure
its safety.

Yours,

Henry Vogel

I did not let the paper fall from my fingers, as heroines
in novels do; nor did I scrunch it up and hurl it into the
waste-paper basket.

I only hunched over, as a child receiving a blow, and
wept.

I did not want Henry's parting gift, whatever it might
be. Yet once I had recovered myself, cold cream erasing
the watermarks from my cheeks, I went up to my living
room. The body had been removed, but I'd assumed the
cage had been returned to its original location. I opened
the door, bracing myself.

The cage was gone.

In vain did I question Sarah and Josephine as to its
whereabouts. 'You are overtaxing yourself, madam,'
Sarah said at last, Josephine eyeing me cattily. They
thought I was fixated on the cage from sentiment, and I
could hardly tell them the real reason. I had to await
Charles's return in the late afternoon before I knew its
fate.

'Darling,' he said, his tone gentle, as if he were
tending to a nervous animal. 'I hope you have rested?'

I reassured him that I had passed a quiet afternoon.
Another lie. My face ought to be quite black with them,
though when I caught it in the mirror, it looked the same

as ever – paler, even. How we belie our appearances! Only when he had lit his pipe did I judge it safe to ask the location of cage and occupant.

'Oh darling, do not distress yourself with that now.'

'But I *do*, Charles.'

'It is at a safe place, I assure you.'

'Where?' I pressed, but he was unusually recalcitrant, and I knew tears would only convince him of my need to be quietened. At last, seeing I would not rest, he relented.

'I have sent it to a friend.'

'Which friend?'

For a moment he looked as though he would not answer.

'*Which* friend, Charles?'

'William Hornaday at the United States National Museum. He recently accepted the position of chief taxidermist.'

'But why?'

He sighed. 'I had hoped to have your creature stuffed and returned to you in its original condition. Good as new.'

I gazed at him. At last I said, 'That is very thoughtful, dear. Thank you.'

On my insistence, it was arranged that I should go to Washington the next day to instruct Mr Hornaday on my wishes for the bird's preparation. I would be accompanied by Sarah, since Charles was entirely occupied with preparations for the circus. The city's wide, wide streets took some getting used to – after New York, I was not accustomed to seeing the sky. The cab deposited us outside the museum, an imposing Gothic structure of red brick with turrets and a bell tower.

263

'They call it the Castle,' the cab driver said, and I could not but think of my grandparents, and my mother, and that place she had once called home.

Could I really hope to find the murderer? And if I did, would that end the threat they presented, or merely aggravate it? I suppressed a shudder.

We disembarked and joined the herds of respectable-looking gentlemen, all seemingly preoccupied with great scientific thoughts, though as we followed, I saw them crowd into a hall that looked decidedly like a canteen. Sarah and I were greeted by a secretary in the white arched lobby; I thought we would be taken up to an office, but he led us out the back and, with an air of quiet disapproval, directed us to the model and taxidermy shop. It was little more than a large shed.

Oh, it was a curious sight that greeted us. To be sure, the emporium had accustomed me to animals – living animals, that was – and with taxidermy all the rage, I was also used to the other state. But this in-between stage was a shock. Tiger skins hung from the rafters; there were bloodstains on the floor, and bison skulls and stuffed sharks gazed from the walls. Most striking of all was a skinless, eyeless monster that might one day be a leopard, its tail like a whip, snarling fangs calmly ignored by the man tending to it.

'Mr Hornaday?'

He flapped a hand to a shadowy corner, where a second individual busily scribbled. Rills of bald skin already lined either side of his head, like gills, though he looked approximately my own age. I approached and repeated myself.

'And you are?'

'Hester Vogel. Wife of Charles. And this is Sarah, my maid.' Sarah bobbed politely. 'I believe you received a

264

bird of mine. I was wondering if I could just see it for a moment. That is,' I added, looking around, 'unless it is disembowelled already.'

'Oh, that – no, I am not nearly there. I wish Charles had *asked* first. I have my exhibition to plan and much, much to do.' When I looked blank, he repeated, 'The exhibition. My Society of American Taxidermists. You are aware that I am a founding member?'

'Er – yes. *Yes*, of course. We are very much looking forward to it, are we not, Sarah?'

Sarah, bless her, indicated that she was.

'Then you know the greatness of the undertaking. It would be better if you took the creature back with you. Or perhaps to Ward's in Rochester. They take all sorts there, and conduct all kinds of scientific examinations.'

'Where is my bird?' I repeated firmly.

He pointed to a distant corner, where a dirty piece of sacking had been drawn over something the approximate size of the cage. I went immediately to it, motioning to Sarah to stay put. My fingers trembled as I took hold of the cloth.

There it was. That beautiful broken body, the colours still bright. It was as though a part of me had died: that innermost piece that in childhood forms the greater part of us and dwindles as we enter adulthood; the part of us that feels most truly and is nobody but ourselves. I swallowed the hot coal in my throat and opened the cage. Henry had said his gift was within – I could only hope it had survived its journey. I put my fingers into the layer of gravel and sawdust, trying not to touch the body, praying that the thing, whatever it was, did not lie beneath it.

Nothing, only grit under my fingernails.

I took a deep breath and picked Henry up; in that

265

same moment, I noticed something that angered me. I confirmed my discovery, then tucked it away for later, focusing wholly on the body I held. It was like holding a child. The corpse was so light, so soft, yet already a hardness gathered beneath the flesh. I allowed myself to stroke his head, just once. Tried to avoid his poor bent neck, but it was impossible, its grotesqueness bursting in my vision.

There was something upon him, a residue . . . I forced myself to attend to it. A sort of white powder dusted his feathers. I brought them to my nose, sniffed. A faint whiff of sulphur, reminiscent of something.

Thinking of my detective novels, I took out my snuff box – it had run out the day before – and brushed what powder I could into it.

At last I set my poor pet aside. Now I saw that he had been lying on top of a large pile of sawdust. Putting my fingers into it, I met a curious lump, about the size of a gobstopper, and brought it out of the cage.

It was a diamond.

CHAPTER THIRTY

I awoke as though from a stupor. Hester's bird murdered.
The diamond found. The game was well and truly afoot.
In Hester's telling, Henry had refused to give it to Charles.
I had been wondering at what point it would leave his
hands, and whether it would do so willingly. Apparently it
had.

I became aware that the train had ground to a halt. The
conductor bade me farewell, and I stepped out of the carriage
into the heavy air. I lugged my bags to the horizon, yet
cresting it I saw the tide was up, completely covering the
causeway. I cursed my way down the slope. How would I
get to Pàrras? The ground was slowly turning to mud, the
loch half concealed by a grey mist the same colour as the
water itself, so it seemed as though the waters were rising,
droplet by droplet, into the air.

Then I saw the boat. A single broad-shouldered figure
was rowing from castle to shore: Yves, his muscled back
crunching in and out of itself. I hurried down towards the
stony beach, remembering the line that Daniel had translated
for me.

Nazi. I'd first heard the term in Australia, a black, bitter seed in Germany's soil. Suddenly so much about Yves made sense. The hunting. The cicatrice. In botany, the word meant the mark left on a stem when a leaf was torn away. But for a person to exaggerate their own scars . . .

I knew what it was to render oneself falsely, aggressively whole. It made you more certain than you might otherwise have been, dug your heels into stickier mud than you could otherwise have imagined. It trapped you. I understood Yves, and that was what made the realisation such a punch in the throat.

The boat was closing in, his back still towards me. He would be here in a minute or less.

It took a certain step to see other human beings as animals. A fearful leap, as Robert Odlum might have said.

Keep a route open. An escape.

I took a single insulin bottle and a spare needle from my bag, tucking them behind a boulder shaped rather like a small church. And had the Church not been so thoroughly excised from me, I might have offered up a quick prayer.

'Emmy.' Yves' smile was wide, despite the rain glistening on his cheeks. I wanted to ask whether he and his uncle had found the diamond, but did not do so, instead unhappily observing the athleticism with which he leapt from the boat, thinking of Daniel and the religious holidays he kept like a secret. Of the bruise Emily and I had seen him with one afternoon, where a university peer had struck him. Daniel did not need to rub salt into his wounds. The world did that for him.

Yves helped me with my bag, not minding that the grey waters swirled around his ankles. He would have carried me into the boat, but I refused, wading out instead.

'The tides are high for this time of year,' he was saying. 'Lynette says the waters rise when Pàrras is trying to preserve

268

its secrets.' He observed me a moment, then added, 'I never thanked you. For looking after me so well.'

'Don't mention it.' Please.

He asked about my trip, and I answered, though my replies were rote. I was too busy trying to see him for what he was.

I had thought this man was teaching me strength, but what he really knew was how to crush weakness.

We arrived on the island's west side, where the slipway ran from the shore, vanishing into the loch. I helped Yves drag the boat up and into the small boathouse. He locked the door with unusual care and pocketed the key.

'Who would steal it?' I asked.

'Oh, someone has tried.'

We wound our way around the shore to the main gate, the waters lapping. At the entrance, I turned and looked for the causeway, but it was still nowhere to be seen.

Mr Vogel's welcome was muted. 'We have not much time,' he said. 'It is barely three weeks until the solstice.'

So they had not yet found the diamond. I took him in. Had he killed Hester? Had they had another dispute before he left for Africa, an argument gone horribly wrong? I could only hope that Hester would tell me the truth – and do so in time. Meanwhile I would have to pretend normality, or at least this twisted version I was living.

The tea towels had been removed in my absence, but I knew the window we needed. It was in the menagerie tower, facing east. I went there: Mr Vogel insisted on following, though his breath came in lurching gasps as we went up to the second floor, heading for the point on the solid wall that I thought approximated the location of the window I sought. There were a few other windows in this room, though blocked by animals of varying shapes and sizes.

Mr Vogel watched impatiently. 'Yves searched the walls and floor while you were gone.'

'Did he move the animals?'

'He lifted up each. What more can you hope to find?'

I glared. 'Let me think.'

I inspected the east side. No window. I ran my hands over the wall, prodded the stone, then took out my knife and began to probe the mortar. Nothing. Behind me, my audience wheezed distractingly.

'Mr Vogel,' I said, 'it would be easier if I could think about this alone.'

'Absolutely not.'

'You do not trust me,' I said flatly. I remembered the X-ray, Yves' warm tongue on my cheeks, and shuddered.

'What do you expect, Miss Blackwood? Your terms were strictly to remain here for the duration of the project. You broke those terms.'

If that was the way he wanted it, so be it. I turned my attention to the floor, what I could see of it, anyway. Could there be a lever hidden beneath one of these innumerable animals? But clearing the room for a full inspection would take days – days, it was becoming obvious, that Mr Vogel was neither willing nor able to afford. I began to circumvent the room as best as I could, clambering over glass cages and fragile predators. Even with the electricity, the light was grey, dulling the old red sandstone with its splashes of lichen.

The lichen . . . I stopped short. Bent down.

For a period at university I had thought of making lichens my specialty, until I met the rather myopic denizens of the enthusiastic lichen community and decided that, on balance, there was more to life. The organisms were surprisingly interesting, however, principally because they were not one organism at all, but rather two or three: a fungus and an algae joined together in such a close relationship that when

270

separated, they could not exist. An association that, if nothing else, I understood. By the time I turned from symbiotes to parasites, I had picked up a fair bit. And that was how, as I peered at the speckly grey-black marks on a particular section of wall, I recognised that I was looking at something rather unusual.

Opegrapha areniseda. Quite rare. It liked coasts and church walls, north-facing ones, preferably exposed. It was all over this section – except on one plane of the hexagonal room.

Something about that part of the wall, therefore, was less exposed than the rest.

'What is it?' Mr Vogel asked sharply. I made a distracted answer as I crossed to the corner. The stone here was raw, red, like an unhealed wound. I pressed my fingers against it, feeling its age, its crenulations.

Lynette had said that the unlucky occupant of the secret room had never come out again. So it was likely any entrance had been sealed.

I took out my knife once more and stabbed it through the crumbling mortar, twisting. The stone loosened but did not withdraw. I needed a lever.

A condor was perched on an iron bar. I lifted the bird away and wrenched the bar from its position. Mr Vogel did not protest. Carefully I dug it into the stone's edges: it fell out with a crash, and I hastily stepped back to avoid it crushing my toes. Then I approached again and placed my hand through the resulting gap.

The hand met wood.

'Open it up,' Mr Vogel commanded, his voice tight with excitement. Somehow he had made his way over and around the animals. They say that the mind wields more power over the body than we know. But how much? This man thought he knew the date of his own death . . .

I began removing the stones. It did not take long – the wall had been built hastily. Guiltily. I piled them up around the disbelieving eyes of a lemur, until I had revealed a narrow door.

It was old; moss writhed across its surface, as though in pain. My employer and I exchanged glances. He put a hand on the latch. Locked.

'Break it.' His voice carried the slightest tinge of hysteria. Heedless of the damage, as eager as he to get inside, I threw my shoulder against it. There was a shriek of metal and decaying wood, and then I was through, smashing straight into the opposing wall.

The room was tiny. Coffin-sized, really. A space for surviving, not for living, and in the end, this pitiful chamber had not even supplied that. There was the window, cloth-less. There too was a single narrow bed frame, the wood old and cracked. Upon it was something that had once been human.

I gazed at the wasted thing, forcing myself to look, then turned away. Mr Vogel seemed unable to do so.

There was nothing else in the room, not even a water jug. That comforted me. Perhaps it had not taken long.

It was actually otherwise not an unpleasant place. The sun had come out, vanquishing the shadows, warming the stones. The view showed the hills in all their loveliness. I wondered how many hours he had stared at them before he realised no one was coming – that no one ever would. For all that Lynette loved her ghost stories, evil is incurred by the living, not the dead; and phantom tales, for all they purport to scare us, are really told for comfort. Gather round the fire and pretend the darkness lies without, not within.

I inclined my head towards the bed in respectful salute. Then I gently steered Mr Vogel from the chamber and closed the door behind us.

*

272

He seemed to come to his senses.

'Go back in,' he snapped.

'What for?'

'You know very well what for.'

I gazed at him. 'Nobody has been inside for a very, very long time. Your diamond is not there.'

'You do not know that.'

I gathered up some of the remnants of the mortar, crumbled it in my fingers. 'This is old. It has not been disturbed for years. I don't mean decades. I mean centuries.'

Something in his features leapt and snapped. 'First Phyllis Briggs,' he spat. 'Now you. You have found me nothing.'

I said, as calmly as I could, 'That was not nothing.'

He made a derisive sound and pushed past with surprising force. I watched him disappear down the stairs.

He was right: I had not found the diamond. But Pàrras had given up one secret. I knew the next was just a matter of time.

Returning from the menagerie via the great hall a short while later, I heard two things at once. First, a horrible rending noise. And second, Yves' shocked tones:

'Uncle!'

I hurried through. Yves was in the doorway of the kitchen. Mr Vogel was inside, panting, face ghastly. He held a knife. On the table before him, like the centrepiece of a surreal and dreadful meal, was the bird of paradise.

He had removed it from its glass box and torn it apart. Lynette had been making ice cream again, and ice and sugar were scattered across the table along with straw and feathers. I watched in horror as my employer began questing among the dismembered parts, poking into the stuffing, digging into the wings, the shredded tail, and now the head, bony white fingers forcing out one of the black glass eyes, which fell onto the table and rolled hideously.

The fingers paused – snatched amongst the cotton entrails. They had found something. A fragment of paper. Yves stepped forward to look, and despite myself, I did the same. I could not see what was upon it, so I watched Mr Vogel's face, the eyes grown black as the loch, unnamed things swimming within. No one spoke.

Then, wordlessly, methodically, he tore the paper into tiny pieces.

CHAPTER THIRTY-ONE

In the shocked silence that followed, Mr Vogel's hand went
to his jacket pocket, furiously rubbing, rubbing within. The
motion failed to return him to himself. He hurried from us,
leaving behind the destruction he had wrought. Yves and I
looked at each another.

'What was it?' I asked, sure that the paper must have
shown him something terrible.

'Nothing,' Yves said. 'That is the problem.'

'Are you sure?' If the bird was a clue, it would make sense
if something had been concealed inside. Something that had
not shown up on Yves' X-ray.

'I don't like things that hide within other things,' Yves
said, then added, with an odd amusement, 'Though sometimes it is necessary.'

'It might have been a clue.'

His mouth twisted. 'Like in a detective novel?'

I did not like his faint mockery. 'No more ridiculous than
a treasure hunt.'

'Ridiculous,' he repeated softly. 'Is that how you see us?
There is something different about you.' He moved closer.
'A change.'

'There is no change.'

I resisted my instinct to back away. The lazy smile still played around his mouth, but now I saw the cruelty in it. One who saw the world as hunter and hunted, hero and weakling, predator and prey.

'What about your friend who was here?'

'What about him?'

'Does he think we are ridiculous too?'

'I don't know what Daniel thinks.'

His lips were no more than twin slashes. '*Gut.* Best to keep it that way.'

I would have asked him what he meant, had I thought the answer would make me anything other than sick. Instead I began to pick up the paper shreds. He watched for a while, then left me to it.

I was fortunate that while Mr Vogel's fingers had been frenzied, they had not been particularly thorough. I was able to gather up almost all the fragments of paper. Several ice cubes were scattered across the table – these I dropped into my Thermos. Then I brushed together the stuffing, returning it sadly to the box, along with the bird's torn remains. Slaughtered all over again. I was fairly certain it was past fixing.

Had the paradise bird's killer murdered Hester too?

I took a long, cool drink from my flask, then got to work on the fragments. It took almost an hour to piece together what I could. To my surprise and disappointment, it was an advertisement.

A Splendid Natatorium at the National Capital

The only SWIMMING AND DIVING SCHOOL in WASHINGTON. The Natatorium is being put in first-class order for the coming season, which opens April

276

15, and a limited number of lesson and season tickets will be sold by the management. Ladies and Gentlemen are equally invited to make use of this splendid opportunity. For particulars apply at the Natatorium on E Street, between Sixth and Seventh.

R. E. ODLUM & CO.

Robert Odlum. Hester's friend. Again the name tugged at me, but it was hopeless. I'd heard it before but could not recall where.

Why had she kept this advertisement? How had it ended up in Henry the bird – and how had the bird, so lately murdered in her account, come to be in Papua? I wondered at the violence with which Heinrich Vogel had destroyed his namesake.

I had to solve the next clue, had to find the next diary, but there was something else I wanted to do first.

It was time to dig up Hester's grave.

I'd been mulling it over, and though it was repellent, I could not let it go. It wasn't just that I was trying to solve the mystery of her life and death while the woman herself lay close by, under the soil. That was like studying a plant only from textbooks. It was also the fact that I was not just trying to find the diamond any more. Mr Vogel had said had Hester died in a fall: if true, her body might tell me so. Fractures. A broken neck. If it showed different kinds of injuries, well, that would tell me something else.

The man I love is trying to kill me.

Hester had made it perfectly clear that Charles was no longer the only man she loved. She had also shown me that justice mattered. She was hunting a bird's killer – how could I not do the same for her? How could I not find out what had happened fifty years ago?

*

I vowed to do it that very evening, but it was not to be. Mr Vogel had added another element to his routine: he now walked the castle late into the night. I heard him before I retreated, pacing back and forth along the corridor that led to the great hall and which was the only way out of my tower. The footsteps were ceaseless, without rest. How the old man had the energy, I did not fathom. Something quite out of the ordinary must drive him.

I went down every night for a week; every night I was driven back. I worried that the weather would break and the storms would come before I got my opportunity. I tried to use those late hours to locate Hester's next clue, but found nothing, possibly because my thoughts were distracted.

At last there came a caesura. Mr Vogel complained of a headache at dinner. My hopes rose, and after midnight, I crept down the winding stairs, past Yves' darkened bedroom and into the corridor. I peered into the lightless gloom. No one there.

Quietly I walked along it. The way was narrow, the stones here even colder. The castle's residents must have run along here in their terror hundreds of years ago. I thought I heard . . . but no, there was nothing. Only the old red walls. A slight pressure in my head and I suddenly found myself wishing the corridor was shorter – that the courtyard door was not quite so far off. The long-dead thing I had found in the secret room seemed less pitiful in the dark. It grew in my mind, swelling, the flesh pushing out and taking on a life of its own. His supper companions had been slaughtered, but there were worse ends still . . . death not quick, but slow. I pictured the terrible emptiness of realising he was alone in a narrow chamber; that nobody was coming, and no one ever would. Of knowing it was hopeless but breaking his shoulders against the door anyway, tearing his fingernails to bloody shreds and wearing his voice to ashes; then, at last, lying upon the miserable bed and condensing down into a white-hot star of rage and vengeance. Then, nothing.

No – not nothing. The villagers thought he stalked these halls still. He was hungry, always hungry, would have eaten himself up but there was nothing left, so he sought nourishment in others. The weak ones. The minds that were cracked in some crucial way, letting in not light but darkness. He would curl in through the gap between the eyelids, the space between a clenched fist, and wait. Wait for the solstice.

I fell through the door and out into the waiting night, the horrors of my imagination lifting as I leaned against the wall, my breathing gradually slowing as the monster dissolved from my veins. The stars were out, bright piercings in the Milky Way.

When my father and I were recovering in hospital, there'd been a patient with schizophrenia. The disease often manifested in diabetic patients, and there had been a time when I was terrified I had it, until Dr Beedle firmly told me that the hallucinations I occasionally experienced were entirely due to my failure to take my insulin on time. That had been no hallucination, however. Just my imagination, running wild in the shadows.

I gave one last glance at the night sky, then set off shakily towards the cemetery. I didn't need the electric torch in my tool belt. The moon was bright, both friend and enemy. As I stole past the castle, keeping to the shadows, I glanced up at the high windows. Nothing, and no one, though anything could be watching from behind those dark panes. The window of the secret room seemed a deeper black than the rest.

There was a small lean-to affixed to the eastern wall, once used by the groundskeeper. I had already peered in through the grimy window and ascertained that 1) the lock was old

and breakable, and 2) it contained a spade. I retrieved it
without incident, the trees susurrating against the walls
helping to mask the sound. It would be windier still at the
cemetery.

The gravestones gleamed in the moonlight, faces shining
like an expectant crowd. I hoped not to disappoint. They
seemed an unforgiving audience, and indeed why would they
be otherwise when they had paid such a price for entry?

A low wall ran around the cemetery, too low to keep the
living out but perhaps high enough to keep the dead in. I
allowed myself to touch my tooth necklace, just once. Then
I stepped over the wall and found myself among the graves.

Her headstone was on the north edge. I felt as though I were
going to meet an old acquaintance, one I had not seen for
a long time and was unsure whether they would be friendly.
I knew the Hester on the page, but the Hester in her grave
was a different matter.

The ground was unpleasantly knobbly. Most of the head-
stones were simple, but here and there were the white forms
of a marble sarcophagus or a weeping angel. I wondered
how many ancestors were buried here, a long marching
column stretching back in time. I used the spade as a walking
stick until I realised its tip was slicing into the soil. I held
it firmly aloft after that. I could not leave traces.

As for the mess of grave soil I would inevitably create, I
had a plan.

There it was. Hester and Mr Vogel had loved one another,
yet her grave was neglected. He had pushed her from him.
What if, after all, she had not been murdered – rather killed
herself because of his withdrawal? I was momentarily, ruin-
ously sad.

I allowed myself a moment, then raised the spade.

Oh, it was a dreadful business. Nothing but extremity

could have driven me to it. I had let the vine of Hester's fate tangle up in my own: I *had* to know what had happened. The spade bit greedily into the dank dark soil and my nails became black crescents, filling with earth, as though by disinterring her I was burying myself. My shoulders began to scream, but I did not rest.

Thud. A dead sound, deader even than the rest of that expectant place. I had hit something.

I kept on until I had fully exposed it. A coffin.

Well, it was hardly the least likely thing to discover in a grave, but it was shocking nonetheless. If only my God-fearing father could have seen me then. Gingerly I bent to it and switched on the torch, trusting the hole to conceal the light. Nothing out of the ordinary, if any of this could be called ordinary. Mouthing a silent apology, I slid down into the grave. Took hold of the damp coffin lid. Heaved. With a groan, it came away.

Heart in my mouth, I flicked on the torch – and promptly dropped it into the coffin in shock at what I saw.

CHAPTER THIRTY-TWO

'I believe we should examine Hester Vogel's grave.'

It was a strange utterance for a Wednesday morning, but Mr Vogel only gazed at me over his kippers as though I were talking of the weather and not his lover's final resting place.

'I do not believe the diamond is there.'

'Think about it, sir. You say your brother buried his wife at the same time as he hid the stone. Is her grave not the perfect hiding place?' I paused, pressed harder. 'Fifty years, sir, and you have nothing. There is little time remaining. We must try something new.'

I wanted so badly to tell him that I knew of their affair, but I could not do so without revealing the diaries' existence. The doubt over Hester's fate, and the violence she had seen in him – that *I* had seen, when he tore the bird apart – had put paid to that. He might be old, but he was beginning to frighten me.

'Very well. But I must accompany you there.' I looked at him doubtfully, and his expression flared. 'I am more than capable, Miss Blackwood. Fifty years, as you say. I have strength enough for this. You go ahead and I shall follow. Yves?'

I jumped – I had not seen him enter.

'Please go with Miss Blackwood. Help her with the excavations.' *And see she does not take anything she shouldn't.*

I panicked. I could not allow Yves to come. The principal reason that I had asked Mr Vogel about the grave was to have an excuse to dig it up all over again, explaining the disturbance of the soil. I'd meant to do it myself, then show my employer afterwards. If Yves came, he would see the truth.

'Sure,' I said, smiling brightly. 'Let's go and change our shoes.'

We returned to our tower in silence. I went upstairs and changed into my other pair of boots. I didn't need to – I was playing for time – but mercifully on the walk over, an idea had formed.

'Yves,' I said, knocking on his door. He opened it, and I injected my smile with extra brightness. 'I've been meaning to speak with you.'

It was particularly pretty, the island that morning. The air was fresh and salt-swept; birds cried on the shore. The visibility was good, and whenever I looked up from digging, I saw all the way out to sea. I also had a good long time to observe the lone figure picking its way down to me.

'Where's Yves?' Mr Vogel asked, frowning as he leaned tiredly on his cane.

'He said he had to see to something. Don't worry.' I indicated the mess I had carefully created, erasing the traces of the first upheaval. 'I'm barely halfway.'

Digging up a grave was one thing. Digging up that grave a *second* time was quite another. 'Sorry – sorry!' I whispered. It was easier this time round, in daylight, without worrying about leaving evidence.

The pine coffin became visible again. Mr Vogel watched

as I jumped down into the hole I'd re-created. Slowly I inserted the spade and levered the coffin open, making a fuss of it. I didn't want the lid lifting too easily, having been prised open less than twelve hours before.

I had readied myself for a performance over seeing the inside of the coffin, but in the event, I did not need to pretend. Its contents were even more shocking in daylight.

It was empty.

Mr Vogel gasped.

'She is not here,' I said redundantly. Last night I had been both thrilled and appalled. Hester was not here.

'She jumped . . .' Mr Vogel's stare bored into the pine. 'She jumped and was never heard of again. Until her family's lawyer wrote to say her body had been found and was to be buried here. When I came to Pàrras and found the grave, and my brother's traces, I assumed . . .' His voice was no more than a whisper.

I climbed up beside him and stood awhile in respectful silence. The depth of his shock seemed genuine. Despite his neglect of her resting place, perhaps he had had no hand in her death after all.

Gently I said, 'We may need to consider an unpleasant notion.'

He turned a ghastly face to me. 'Miss Blackwood, I have just discovered my sister-in-law's grave to be empty. If there is a time for unpleasant notions, now would be it.'

'You believed Charles to have buried Hester here, correct?' I took a breath. 'What if she did not kill herself? What if he murdered her and hid the body elsewhere?'

'Then why bury an empty coffin?'

'Perhaps he did it as a decoy. Who would look twice at the grave of a suicide, especially one thousands of miles from where she lived?'

284

'My brother,' he only said emptily.

'We ought to call the police.'

His attention snapped to me. 'Never.'

'But what about justice?'

'What justice? She is dead. My brother is also, and I am nearly so.'

'The law will demand—'

Fury flared in his voice. 'Hang what the law demands! This is my family, my property! You are not here to chase ghosts, Miss Blackwood. You are here to *search*. The solstice approaches. Are you going to find my diamond or not?'

I regarded him.

'Yes,' I said at last. 'Yes, I am.'

Yves finally reappeared at dinner, looking a little pale. I had not seen him all day.

'Where have you been?' Mr Vogel demanded.

'Another seizure. While you both were out.'

I murmured my concern.

In my bedroom that morning, I had put on my boots, pinched my cheeks and twined some locks of hair around my fingers so they fell in curls. Then I met Yves in his doorway. I'd put on scent especially.

'What is it?' His tone was curt.

'I wanted to apologise.'

'For what?'

'About Daniel. You were right about him.'

His lip curled. 'I know.'

'And,' my voice lowered to barely a whisper, 'about other things.'

I lifted my face: he bent down to hear me.

'What you did,' I murmured, 'in the laboratory . . .' My hand went to the back of his head, guiding it gently down so my mouth was at his ear, his lips almost touching my neck, his breath on my skin as my scent rose about us, bittersweet.

'What I felt . . .' My voice dissolved further into honey. His breathing was uneven, in and out.

'I wanted to tell you . . .'

Another breath. Sharper. And another.

'You make me . . .'

But his eyes had rolled back in his head.

'Yves?' I said, stepping back as his body began to shake. 'Yves?'

I guided him back into the room, manoeuvring him onto the bed just as he collapsed. I moved away any hard objects, made sure he was well surrounded with pillows, then watched for a few seconds as he fitted.

Susan Jennings, my geologist friend, had been epileptic. She'd come over once and my father, excited that I had a friend, showed her his greenhouse and the various botanical concoctions he liked to make – or rather, that I now made for him, under his instruction. He never let me go on expedition without taking a few of his creations with me. The trip to Pàrras had been no exception.

'You never know,' he always said, 'and it makes me feel like I'm helping.'

Essential oils were a favourite. Bergamot for stress. Eucalyptus and tea tree to fight infection.

'Try,' he said to Susan, holding forth a vial of eucalyptus for inspection, but I stopped him.

'She has epilepsy. It can bring on convulsions,' I explained. I'd learned its properties in class the year before.

It was a nice smell, eucalyptus, I thought as I lavished it on my wrists and neck that morning. Medicinal, yet with a wood and citrus aroma. I was not surprised Yves had inhaled it so deeply.

I left him unconscious on the bed. I would go find Lynette and tell her she might want to look in Yves, since he was not answering his door. Before I did so, I paused on the threshold.

'I really did have something to tell you.'

He let out a low moan.

'What I wanted to say,' I murmured, 'is that you make me sick.'

CHAPTER THIRTY-THREE

The days were stretching longer – time rolled out, thin, thinner. It was running out. I searched for the diamond through the day and late into the night, finishing the fourth tower, which contained dusty guest rooms, unused for decades. Mr Vogel still kept his routine, though I saw it less and less as a sign of health and more as a figure on a clock helplessly maps the hour, pinned to its wheel. We all of us took to dining separately, speaking little as the solstice loomed. Ten days. A week. Then six days, five, each swallowed up as though by the loch. It would be a day without shadows, yet when I looked, I saw them everywhere, chasing me through the cellars, coiling up the spiralling stairs. Violet crescents appeared under my eyes. The only transparency was in the gin bottle, though even there, when I swallowed, darkness lingered in my throat.

I had searched everywhere there was to search – everywhere, that was, except Mr Vogel's rooms, and the northern tower. I tried to suggest both, and was met with a blast of ferocity. I'd seen the light in that broken tower, its lock as impenetrable as ever. What went on in there? What was he so keen to keep hidden that he would risk missing out on the diamond's discovery? It obsessed me, even as I sometimes detected him watching me with a different light in his eyes. As though he now had a new plan, one that I doubted led to my receiving a fat commission. I could not but think that the gemstone was lost to us all.

As, it seemed, was Hester. For I had found nothing in her account that would lead me to the next clue. Night after night I went over and over the diary and *The Birdcage Library*, each fresh failure driving me back to that bottle of spirits. My body cried out in complaint, the diabetes bruises blossoming yellower, darker.

It was while reviewing the blueprints for the umpteenth time that I noticed an oddity.

The towers on either side of the great hall – mine and the one that held the guest rooms – were accessible only internally. The rest were entered via the courtyard; one could not move inside between them. Or so I had thought. I now saw a thin line, added later, quietly drawn over the boundary between the broken tower and Mr Vogel's apartments. The addition had been designed to make it appear as though it was a solid wall.

I knew what I had to do. All I needed was the opportunity.

But none came. Four days left; then three, then two. Just as I was preparing to take drastic action, finally, on the eve of the solstice, Mr Vogel broke with his routine.

He was going to the village, he said, to make some purchases for tonight's dinner. The delivery boy would take him on his cart. Lynette had told me there was a special meal planned that evening, diamond or no diamond, and meaty smells pervaded the hall at breakfast.

It was now or never. I watched him leave, crossing the black waters. As soon as he was over the causeway, I headed to the courtyard and for the door that led to his rooms.

But Lynette was there in the doorway. Lynette, skin shining, busily mopping the floor of the entrance.

'Mr Vogel wants all the towers spick and span,' she said, panting slightly, wetness about her mouth. 'I've had to polish everything. I just about talked him out of getting the finials done.'

Finials. The sculptured ornaments atop every tower.

'Were you wanting anything, Miss Blackwood?'

I made something up. 'I wondered what I ought to wear tonight.'

'A nice dress, I think. Perhaps some jewellery.'

'I'm not sure I possess such things.'

'Just do your best.'

'You don't think it strange that Mr Vogel should celebrate the eve of his death?'

'He told me once that Faust did as much.' Before Mephistopheles came to claim him. 'Books,' she said, shrugging. 'My husband used to say they were nothing but pretty lies.'

'Lies to tell the truth.'

'A roundabout way of doing it. I never learned to read. There was always something else to do – something more useful.' Another shrug, as though shaking something off. 'I always thought they looked like doors, though. Books, I mean. You open them up and . . . step through.'

I left her cleaning. I would wait until she was done, and hope Mr Vogel did not return in the meantime. Outside, the wind had whipped into being, eddying round the courtyard. A storm was coming.

I spent the wait casting a torch down the well's eye, looking for irregularities. There was only greasy black stone, and far below, the faint gleam of tainted water. I'd already descended into it days ago, inspecting the slimy walls. Now, with the road run out, I decided to take a second look.

I collected my equipment from my bedroom and secured myself to an abseiling rope, tying it to an iron ring set into the courtyard stones. Then I clambered down inside.

Cool air enfolded me, dank and dark. I descended piece by piece, the walls gradually rearing up. As the rim slipped over my vision, my eye was caught by the golden sunlight gleaming from the roof of a tower.

Those finials.

I stopped my descent abruptly. I had abseiled since childhood: it was no difficulty now to pause, bracing my feet against the mossy stones. I'd read Hester's last diary and *The Birdcage Library* so many times now that I could virtually recite them by heart: *Now, reader, we come to the finial act; I can only hope that in the land of my birth, we may all heal.*

The finial act. I had dismissed it as a rare spelling mistake. But in the same paragraph, Hester had made a command. *Pay attention*, she had declared. *I have learned that it might just save your life.*

I pulled *The Birdcage Library* from its now-permanent place in my pocket. There, in the fourth chapter, on Antiques: *Now, reader, we see the finial: a common adornment, visible on this English mahogany hanging cage with four turned sides. Observe the architectural details . . .*

There were five finials, one for each tower. For each chapter. Lynette had told me what they were when I first arrived. Pineapple, thistle, mistletoe, rose, heather. *If* I was correct, could I hope to search each before dinner, as well as Mr Vogel's rooms, all without attracting attention?

There must be a closer hint. I focused on the first sentence. What helped with healing? A medicine box? There was one in the kitchen. I had searched it weeks ago.

My legs were beginning to cramp. 'I'm trying,' I said through gritted teeth. 'I'm trying.'

The land of her birth was Scotland, obviously. If she meant it in relation to the finials, Scotland would point to the thistle, or the heather. Classic native plants.

Or was she merely reminiscing, thinking back to her childhood as the walls closed in?

Footsteps passed overhead: I recognised Lynette's heavy tread.

The clue would have to wait. Painfully I began to drag myself up, up towards the light.

I freed myself of the rope and looked around. The door to Mr Vogel's tower was now closed; Lynette had disappeared. Yves, I knew, was on the moors. I hastened to the door, but paused on the threshold. Despite everything – his age, my experience, the knife in my tool belt – I felt horribly like one of the yellow flies above the Papuan river, hovering before a fish reared up and swallowed me whole.

Before I could change my mind, I put my hand to the latch and pressed. It was not locked, the hinges swinging open with an impressive creak.

'Mr Vogel?' All was dark within. Once, in Sumatra, I had entered a cave, intending to spend the night. It was only when the light had already dwindled to a dot that I caught the acrid stink of leopard.

I switched on my torch and went inside.

At first I thought I'd made a mistake. I was in the menagerie tower – no, I was at Tring at midnight . . .

The chamber was crammed with canaries. Dead ones. Thousands of eyes seemed to turn towards me in the torch-light. Each was in a small cage, the enclosures clambering the walls with sawn-off fingers. The room was dark because the cages completely covered the windows.

Mr Vogel had said that canaries were the first creatures

he ever sold, imported from the mountains of his homeland. He'd said the gold-rush miners were homesick and desired their song, but as I stood among that silent host, I remembered the real reason why miners liked such birds. Canaries sang in the shafts. They were watchmen of death.

Other than the cages, there was only a bed, a desk and, in the corner, a large glass cage. I could not help noticing how *very* large it was, far bigger than my Wardian cases, or the bird of paradise's box. Even with my height, I could have fitted inside. Reluctantly I moved towards it, my skin buzzing as though crawling with flies.

Within, contained by the glass, was an antlered head. A red stag's. The same one I had shot? It looked a little different now. Partly because it was no longer attached to the rest of the body, and partly because the decaying flesh was being busily stripped to the bone by a writhing brown mass.

Dermestid beetles. I'd seen them before at Tring. They cleaned the skeleton so it could be used for taxidermy. No wonder Mr Vogel would not allow me to search this place – he could not reveal his passion as what it really was.

Madness.

It was at that exact moment that I heard footsteps.

I extinguished the torch, plunging me into a horribly crowded dark. I had to hide, but I could not move. Fear froze me, as cold and deep as if I had dived into the loch.

I wrenched myself from it and did the only thing I could: I threw myself under the bed.

A second later, the door opened and I watched the shoes of Heinrich Vogel enter. His wavering lamplight sneaked into my hiding place, as though it would rat me out. A soft croon escaped him as he set something unseen on the low table opposite the bed. I noticed how polished his shoes were, polished to such a degree of shine that the leather had worn through in places. This was where he spent his time, tending to his stuffed companions, sewing his intricate clothing, his mind conspiring to create those fantastical shapes. *Papillotage* – that was the word I had sought for his embroidery, the eye constantly moving from shape to twisted shape, the attention unable to focus, the mind unable to rest.

The shoes shuffled further in, toes pointing towards me. My eyes swept towards the door, as if I could drive them there, but then – oh, horrible! – the bed creaked, a weight settling above. He was no more than a foot from my head. I tried to keep my breathing quiet and controlled; his was rasping, as though passed through a grater. A wild desire to laugh surged in me. What if he went to sleep? And had the room always been so cold? Silence spread itself amongst his breathing, wreathing in like smoke. A deeper darkness trickled through the clammy air, as though the loch itself had crept in between the stones.

Heinrich Vogel spoke. 'Please.' His voice crawled low. 'The solstice. It shall happen as promised.'

Another black silence. As though the void was listening.

'I am so close. *Más é do thoil é,*' the man above me breathed. Some disused part of me blinked awake. Gaelic? *Please.*

The darkness flexed around us – whispers out there, in here, as Heinrich Vogel cried out.

'Tonight!' A gasp, serrated with desperation. 'I promise you. Tonight!'

CHAPTER THIRTY-FOUR

I lay in the darkness, calming myself down. Heinrich Vogel had left, scuttling out quicker than I would have thought possible. I forced myself to wait a full minute before scrambling out from under the bed.

The unheard voice . . . the haste with which he had departed . . .

No, not departed. *Fled.* I thought of the pastor in Papua, gazing over my shoulder at unseen things. I knew what it was to split one's mind in two, but surrounded by those canaries, I knew that the psyche I had seen bore witness to a darker abyss. Schizophrenia. I remembered that patient who had shared a ward with my father and me – his delusions, his sighting of death in strange corners, his complaints of a vacancy in his chest . . .

I wanted nothing more than to leave this cursed place and never return, but I could not. Mr Vogel's outburst had stirred up the language silting my childhood memories. Gaelic had given me the location of Hester's next clue.

I forced myself deeper into the dark.

*

I had read the blueprints right. At the other end of Mr Vogel's chamber there was indeed a door. It was old, but the hinges were freshly oiled, swinging open without a sound. Clutching the tooth necklace at my throat, I went inside.

Unlike the chamber behind me, the broken tower was streaked with natural light, leaking in through the shattered roof. After the horror of my employer's lair, I had expected . . . well, I had tried not to expect. But this place was merely filled with junk. Cabinets, curtains, a wardrobe, a lady's dressing table and mirror and some other feminine-looking furniture pieces. There was a pianoforte, the teeth hanging off, as well as (I blinked) a stuffed bear. A Kodiak, unlike the grizzly in the menagerie.

Hadn't Yves talked about a Kodiak? I'd thought he'd been in error, yet here it was.

There was no time for idle wonderings. *The land of my birth*, Hester had said. I'd been right, she did mean Scotland – home of the Gaelic tongue. My mother's tongue. Once more I was beside her as she worked with her plants, dried leaves rustling softly. She did not have favourites, but there was one species she particularly found useful. It helped soothe the thing that thrashed within her on her bad days, a plant that wound itself as easily around myths and legends as it did the oak trees of which it was so fond. A plant I had learned in my studies to refer to as *Viscum album*. A plant that was a parasite.

Mistletoe. Or in Scots Gaelic, *uil-ioc*. All heal.

I had to get to the roof. A staircase wound up the wall to the next levels. The wind whined as I clambered over the room's detritus towards it, brushing against some dusty bolts of velvet, coughing at the resultant cloud. The place contained little menace. But like the loch, it was old and expectant, its motives similarly obscure. Hester's grandfather had half destroyed this tower in his rage. I shuddered to think what magnitude of wrath could have caused such ruination.

I walked up towards the lowering sky. The light had grown strange, billowing gold and shadow-blue. Storm light.

Here was the second storey, and the third. No junk here: the floor was barely more than a few ruined planks, and I forced the bell tower from my memory. An ancient ladder brought me onto the roof.

It was half in pieces, but the finial I had come for was undamaged. Mistletoe, carved in lead. I ran my hand over its leaves and berries and found a metal nut holding it in place.

It was removable.

I reached to the small pair of pliers in my tool belt. After a few creaking rotations, the mistletoe came away, whole, in my hand. Within it was a lead-lined hollow, and within that . . .

CHAPTER THIRTY-FIVE

I gazed dizzily at Henry's gift. Why had he given me a diamond? Charles was having money troubles and Henry had refused to help him. *I cannot hand it over now*, he had said. Now I knew what he had meant. Charles had threatened to search his apartments for it. Presumably Henry had imagined that the one place he would never search was his own home.

But he could have just hidden it himself. Instead he had given it to me. Did he have some idea of what I should do with it? Because *I* did not. I stared absently at the cage and noticed something else protruding – a white translucent lump, about the same size as the diamond, but crude, misshapen; beneath that poked the corner of a piece of paper. Gently I drew the paper out.

It was a letter. The handwriting was the same as the stiff, dreadful note I had received the day before, but the tone was markedly different.

Darling Hester,
    I know you believe that I have abandoned
you. I know you think that my love for you is

insufficient. Nothing could be further from the truth.

I was given this stone on my travels. Given – not sold. We had stopped at Port Elizabeth, on the southern cape of Africa. I came onshore to restock our supplies and receive some specimens from our collectors. As I walked the docks, I saw a black man sitting in an exhausted attitude upon the quay, wearing an expression such as I had never seen. I stopped to ask if he was all right and offered him some food and water. In return, once he had recovered himself a little, he told me this story.

He was from the Transvaal. He had grown up poor but happy and married a woman whom he loved. They moved into a small but adequate dwelling. Daisies grew around the door. They lived contentedly for some while, until diamonds were discovered in Kimberley. My acquaintance had a deep desire to see his wife in comfort, and although she attempted to dissuade him, he determined to go and seek their fortune.

Well, he toiled for years. His money ran out earlier than anticipated and he could never afford to visit home. He had also vowed that he would not do so until he had some success to show for his labours. He loved his wife intently and could not bear to disappoint her, nor see her denied the worldly comforts he was so desperate to provide. At last, when he was close to giving up, he turned aside a heap of debris and discovered the stone you see now, enough for several fortunes. Ecstatic, he hid it about his person and hurried back to his wife, whom he had not now seen for seven years.

Alas! Tragedy had visited in his absence. She had

been struck down by a vicious disease common to those parts, and died but the previous month, alone.

My acquaintance was undone. Inconsolable, he left his home town once more and wandered aimlessly, cursing the stone he still carried in his pocket, knowing it had done him evil. Knowing that he had let worldly riches obscure the real treasure.

After some months he found himself at Port Elizabeth, where the land turned to sea. He could go no further. The only thing to do, he determined, was to rid himself of the diamond. It had brought him only unhappiness, and though penniless, he had no desire to taint himself further with its riches. He considered throwing it into the waters, but after some thought, he decided he would give it to the first person who spoke to him with any kindness. The situation and treatment of his race leaves much to be desired, and so he was there three days with neither food nor water before I came along. He told me his tale, fixing me as he did so with a look and manner I have never experienced, neither before nor since.

Naturally I said I could not accept, but he would not be refused. He had made a pact to free his soul and could not break it, in the manner of a Faustian bargain. I shall never forget his words. His parents had been enslaved to cruel masters, he said, and even after their freedom was granted they had remained imprisoned nevertheless, in the only place it counted: their heads. True liberty, he concluded, was only to be granted by ourselves. That was why he would give me the diamond. It was the exact price, not more, not less, of his freedom.

So why, Hester my darling, am I presenting it now

to you? For my freedom? For yours? I do not know exactly. But what I do know is that you and I are tying knots around one another, unhappy knots that constrict rather than secure. If I give it to Charles, he shall never learn from his folly. I love my brother, but he views me as another of his emporium creatures. I used to be content with this arrangement, but after these months with you, observing how this same situation has tamed you, altering your very nature, I have realised I cannot bear to be so any longer.

On my travels I heard of a Chinese Buddhist custom that grants honour to those who gift captive creatures with freedom. I have no use for this diamond – but I hope you do. Perhaps it will buy you liberty, if such a thing can be bought.

I also leave you a second stone, this from my own childhood. It is my mother's paste diamond from her pearl necklace, the same she treasured for many years before realising it was counterfeit. The discovery killed her, which in turn led to us fleeing to America. When we did so, I took the stone with me. I have kept it all these years, though whether for love or loathing I could not say. My mother, wonderful as she was, lived in a fantasy. She could no more acknowledge her imprisonment than she could act against it, choosing instead to maintain appearances until the last. Her life was as much a falsity as that stone.

How shall you live, Hester? Shall you choose truth or falsity? Reality or verisimilitude? Our species is ever poor at valuing what is truly worthwhile. Always we are drawn to appearances, surfaces, more concerned at what we display to the world than

301

what we experience in our hearts. To prioritise the latter takes courage, which I know you have, and knowledge of the self, which I believe you have only forgotten. Rediscover it, my darling, and when you have, never let it go – not for anyone, and certainly not for me.

The rest of the letter I shall not re-create; suffice to say that by the time I had folded it and placed it in my breast pocket, my eyes had fogged with tears. I could barely see the two stones I set beside one another.

The thing I had taken for a diamond was in fact only a charming counterfeit. I could see why Henry's mother had clung to it all those years: it *seemed* so impressive, but now, turning it in the light, I saw its falsity, its lack of sparkle. I discarded it and picked up its unimpressive sister, rubbing my fingers over its inscrutable features.

This was the real gem, this misshapen lump I had dismissed. It was uncut, I realised now, its fire lurking beneath the surface. All it needed was for someone to unleash it.

I would find my bird's killer. I would confront them and learn what they wanted, and in doing so Henry would see that I had regained my independence. For the first time in more than a year, I would *do* something, and then I would find Henry before he left port in nine days' time, and he would see me again as someone capable. Someone worthwhile.

As for the diamond, the real one . . . I would decide what to do with it in time.

I bade my bird farewell and, with some difficulty, convinced Mr Hornaday to see to it post-haste. Outside, the Castle's shadow loomed long, covering the ground in fantastic shapes. There were so many other worlds, out there, in here. I felt as though I were moving back and forth between nightmare and dream.

I returned home, but I did not rest. I sorely wanted to seek Henry out, but resisted the temptation. I would go to him once I had found the bird's killer – and of this I was hopeful, for the diamond was not the only discovery I had made in Hornaday's workshop. When I'd inspected the paradise bird's body, I'd found that several tail feathers were missing.

Mr Havely. He had seen the bird when he interrupted Henry and me. There was no time to waste: the next day I sent Sarah on a certain errand, then paid a visit to his store.

Well, the plumassier's place of trade shocked me. Dozens of small avian corpses hung from the rafters; everywhere were piles upon gorgeous piles of feathers. It was nothing like the taxidermist's workshop – those creatures had died for science, or at least for curiosity. These had been slaughtered for *fashion*. When I had worked in the Vogel & Brother emporium, it had been easy, surrounded by such natural abundance, to imagine it was infinite. Now I became abruptly, brutally conscious that the human race was ransacking a world unable to defend itself from our onslaught; that our species possessed an illimitable capacity for sustained ferocity, particularly when done in the name of profit, which acted as a sort of magical invocation to legitimise the wickedest of deeds. We had reduced nature to what we could extract from it; eternal growth was portrayed not as a fantasy but as the mightiest of pursuits. I touched the pheasant feather in my own hat and, despite its gossamer lightness, felt its weight. For in truth it was not the plumassiers who were to blame, nor the hunters, nor the wealthy collectors. No – it was me. Me and all those

303

other millions of ordinary people who moved carelessly through the world, not knowing – not *caring* to know.

'Mrs Vogel.' Mr Havely's sprightly tones chased my thoughts away. 'To what do I owe the pleasure?'

He was as smiling and kindly as ever, but then a breeze curled in and those dangling corpses swung from their gallows.

'I must speak with you.'

His smile remained, but the warmth disappeared. He cast a quick eye around his employees, all female, all bent over their work at an angle that made it easy to imagine a whip. 'Come to my office.'

It was a small room, cramped and pictureless, and he seemed too large for it. We each took a chair, and his plump hands steepled. 'What can I do for you?'

I took a deep breath. Suddenly, alone with this man, I felt less sure of myself. Once more I saw Henry's splintered neck.

'Charles and I were delighted to host you the other evening,' I said at last. His eyes watched me. 'You may recall that you were unable to find the smoking parlour. You may recall a certain paradise bird.'

He shrugged his meaty shoulders. 'Perhaps; perhaps not. I see many birds in my line.'

'Quite. But I wonder if you picked up something of mine. Accidentally, of course. Because the next morning, that same bird was discovered with several tail feathers missing.'

He said, carefully, 'That is unfortunate.'

I gave a thin smile. 'Quite unfortunate. Particularly when a plumassier is among the guests.' I produced a newspaper advertisement from my pocket. Charles kept newspapers, sending bundles to the emporium for use in lining cages. 'As I am sure you are aware, paradise-bird

304

plumes are rather hard to come by at present. The notice from this auction, the most recent one for your trade, says so. Yet when an associate of mine enquired after such plumes this morning, your store told her that some have recently become available.'

Sarah, dressed in richer-than-usual attire, had done her task well.

Mr Havely's face had darkened. 'I am not sure of what you are accusing me, Mrs Vogel, but any plumassier at any time may stock such feathers. It is not a crime.'

'No, but theft is.'

He suddenly stood and stepped out from behind his desk. I forced myself to my feet, conscious for the first time of how *large* he was, how beneath those layers of jolly fat were more of muscle.

'This is interesting work, madam. Your husband must be so proud.' He paused, licked his thick lips. 'And your brother-in-law too. Hmm?'

I froze under those pale eyes.

'I would be grateful if you would allow me to return to business. As you allude, the plume trade is not so easy at this moment.'

'I can understand you stooping to theft,' I spat. 'But why did you have to kill my creature too?'

'I beg your pardon?'

'Do not pretend. You stole my bird's feathers, and then you wrung its neck.'

Shock sprang to his features. 'I did no such thing. I adore birds.'

I laughed bitterly. 'So it would seem from your store.'

He passed a hand over his brow, the muscle subsiding. 'Do you not think this industry pains me? We all have to make a living, madam, and this is the only one I know –

the only one I am fit for, and sometimes not even that.'
He sighed. 'Very well. I saw your bird. I returned and
took some feathers. My customers never pay, and my
competitors are fiercer than ever. But I did *not* kill it.
Why would I?'

'Why? Because of your profession.'

'Precisely. I needed only the tail. My employment
wreaks destruction enough. I personally will not even
harm a fly.'

I considered him; it was dubious morality, but was it
any more so than my own? Than Charles's?

It was the very inconsistency of his principles that
convinced me of his humanity. He was not the murderer.
I left, but as I did, he insisted on pressing a packet into
my hand.

I did not need to look inside to know that it contained
poor Henry's plumes.

Mr Hornaday returned Henry to me by courier five days
later, days that Charles spent at Coney Island with Hyatt
Frost. I used that time to search through the suspects with
increasing desperation, the clock ticking down towards
Henry's departure. There were just two days left, and
with Mr Havely eliminated, Frost was now my prime
suspect. He was the only other guest who definitely knew
of the bird. He was bound up in business dealings that
were apparently troubled, and I could easily believe he
had the petty brutality to engineer its death. But I had no
evidence against him beyond my own dislike; and since he
and Charles were always at Coney Island, I had no opportunity to interrogate him. In truth, even the thought of
doing so made me sick with anxiety, and more than a little
fear. I had asked Josephine and Sarah about his movements, along with those of several other guests, even going

so far as to interview the valet hired for that evening. I came up with nothing. There was no time to waste: I vowed that the next day I would go to Coney Island and find Frost myself.

Without asking, Charles returned Henry to his original site by the window. Doubtless he believed it the right place for him. I gazed at my dead pet, now mounted within a glass-fronted wooden box.

Still caged.

I could not bear it. I left my sitting room and went to Charles's. I needed a fresh place of work, a fresh approach, fresh paper. I went to collect the key to the bureau from its usual hiding place.

It was not there.

Peculiar. My husband was a man of habit. Why would he have moved it? I looked for it, idly at first, then with frustration that began to morph into suspicion. Where had he hidden it, and why? I stopped and tried to think like him, a man who loved to see everything in its proper place. A man who kept his secrets where they ought to be: inside.

The Japanese doll was on a shelf. Despite it being a gift to me, he had kept it here. I had not complained. I opened it up now, then did the same with the successively diminished creatures within.

The ninth and smallest had been removed. Instead, hidden inside the penultimate figurine, was a key.

The bureau opened quite easily. Once more that blue ledger fell out, as though replaced in haste. This time I picked it up.

At last, numbly, I returned the ledger to the bureau. It contained the latest accounts pertaining to Vogel & Brother: the emporium, but also the circus venture.

307

I buried my head in my hands. No wonder Charles was so worried. No wonder he kept this ledger locked away. No wonder he wanted – *needed* – the diamond. Profits from the emporium had been in steady decline since my departure, but the real issue was the costs of the circus. These had skyrocketed. They would need to pack every seat, every night, for months – years – to even begin to hope to recoup their costs. Profit was by this time out of the question. They could only attempt to evade ruin.

My husband knew my capability with numbers. Yet in his pride, his stubbornness and his secrecy, he had treated me as no more than one of his pretty birds.

Coldly, methodically, I went through the other documents in that bureau. Most pertained to humdrum affairs. All except one.

It was for a policy of life insurance taken out for one Mr Charles Vogel. And another for Mrs Hester Vogel. The paper was thick, spanking new. It was dated from just a week ago. The day after the dinner party, when I had overheard Henry refusing to give Charles the diamond.

Sarah knocked. 'Madam.'

She had just returned from the South Street docks, where her brother's ship, the *Freedom*, was being prepared for departure. She had encountered Henry, whose ship was being readied nearby, and told him of the paradise bird's death.

'He sends his deepest consolations, madam.' Then she told me what he had told her: that his ship's captain wished to leave early in order to catch a favourable wind. They were leaving that very day – would have left by now already.

He was gone, then. I sat for a long time in Charles's

drawing room, the light drawing in too, closing upon me like a hand about my throat.

My husband returned late. He looked old, tired, doing his best to hide it. We ate woodcock from Myrtle's kitchen to the gentle chinks of good crockery and silver. I drank our equally good wine, thinking on how long such luxuries could endure. Well, I now knew that answer: until one of us died. Then the other would receive a sizeable pay-out, enough to begin assisting with those circus debts. I did not wish to conceive what desperate imaginings had driven Charles this last week; I had read too many detective novels not to be alarmed. Even afraid. I gazed at the dead meat on my plate. The diamond was upstairs. All I had to do was give it to him, and our troubles would be over.

And why not? Henry had abandoned me. *Do something*, he had told me. Well, I could at least do this.

I took a deep breath. 'Is everything well with the venture?' My voice was tentative, thin under the weight of my thoughts. If he would only allow me into his troubles, I would give him the stone in an instant.

'Naturally.' He was bent over his woodcock, not looking at me. Frustration rose. How could he *maintain* so? Who was this man, really – my husband, or someone playing that role? Were his kindnesses of the last few months sprung from love, or appropriate behaviour?

'Darling.' I forced as much tenderness into the word as I could. 'If anything is wrong . . .'

'Nothing is wrong.'

'Listen, dear. If there is anything I can do to help – if that man has hurt our affairs . . .'

His face shuttered. 'Hester, I am not willing to entertain your irrational dislike of Mr Frost.'

'It is *not* irrational. I . . .' But I could not ask him about the ledger – could not reveal my snooping. Instead, I said, 'I think he killed my paradise bird.'

A clatter. Charles had dropped his knife and fork, and the quality of the silver did not prevent bird meat and gravy spattering the table. 'What?'

Thinking I had shocked him into listening, I said quickly, 'I have been attempting to trace the murderer. Mr Havely stole some plumes from it, but it wasn't him, I went to his workshop and he told me so.'

I produced the list of suspects from my pocket and pushed it towards him. 'Of those remaining, Mr Frost is the only one who makes sense! He had seen my bird on a previous visit and he coveted it then, I *know* he did.'

My husband said nothing, only staring at the slip of paper.

'We cannot trust him. What breed of wickedness leads one to slaughter an innocent creature? We cannot do business with such a man. We cannot—'

'*Enough.*' The voice was in no way raised, but the coldness in it froze me. Frost, frost everywhere. 'Hester, I had thought you had spent these days recovering from shock. Not on some lunatic goose chase. What on earth has possessed you to take up this foolish notion? Who do you think you are? A *detective*?' His scorn penetrated my heart. 'No. You are my wife. You accused Mr Havely of *murder*? How do you think this makes me look? A man who cannot control his wife is no man at all. No wonder Mr Havely withdrew the order he had made with us. And now you would do the same with Mr Frost.' A bitter smile. 'I am your husband. You are my wife. Yes, I will confess, I took your help at the beginning, and gratefully too. I should not have done so. I have been too free with you, but no more.'

310

He picked up his cutlery again, gripping the knife so tightly his knuckles swelled through.

'You will give up this nonsense. Now. No longer will you question and jeopardise this venture. Particularly not over some *pet*.'

He spat the word: a fleck of spittle landed before me, just visible through my burning eyes.

I could not speak. I had been so foolish. Foolish to think I could find my own footing. Foolish to believe I could ever do something worthwhile.

I had pretended to myself that I was embarking on the first steps to liberty, but really I had simply been trying to earn the approval of the men around me.

A small dark stain blossomed on the napkin on my lap, then another, pattering down like rain. I excused myself; my husband said nothing as I went.

There were three days before the circus's opening night. Even had I forgotten the fact, the newspaper sellers outside were yelling it. I put the pillow over my head. Charles had left before first light.

At last I roused myself and went to my sitting room, alone. My bird was still there. Still dead. The tea in the cup I held was warm, but I felt nothing but cold to my very bones.

I do not know how long I was there before someone knocked. Sarah again. I rose slowly, like those unfortunate sailors who, stricken by scurvy, discover the disease has opened old wounds, as though they had never healed at all.

'Please, madam, an elderly gentleman just came by. He left this.'

She handed me a folded note.

To Mrs Vogel

As a reminder that some things are never finished

The hand was unknown to me, but its words tingled down my spine. With shaking fingers I opened it. A single paragraph. No – a poem.

Did we count great, O soul, to penetrate the themes of mighty books,
Absorbing deep and full from thoughts, plays, spec-ulations?
But now from thee to me, caged bird, to feel thy joyous warble,
Filling the air, the lonesome room, the long forenoon,
Is it not just as great, O soul?

Beneath it was written the initials *WW*.

My breath caught. I had asked the old poet whether he had completed his compendium. Here was his reply.

I had read Mr Whitman as a young woman – a girl, really, managing a factory on her own, holding up the weight of all those livelihoods when the man who ought to have done it had proved unable. I had come so close to being crushed by that responsibility, by my own love for my father and the duty I had felt towards him and the company he had built. Then Charles had come along and I had let him nearly crush me too, only to repeat the routine with Henry all over again. The latter had spotted the pattern before I did. That was why he had left: to save me from it. To save me from myself. Tears blurred my vision as I realised how he had loved me as none of those other men had. No sooner than we are conscious do we go searching for hands to remove our freedom.

I clutched that paper to me like a life raft, hands

shaking, remembering what Mr Whitman had said in the
emporium.

*Just because a thing has been made does not mean it cannot
be remade again.*

In the cage factory I had been sometimes afraid, often
desperate, and always lonely. But that did not mean I
must always be so. I'd grown up among cages. The time
had come to leave them behind.

Slowly – so slowly – I drew myself in from the furthest
corners. I gathered pieces of myself from places I had
either forgotten or no longer cared to visit. That part that
loved the freezing sea; the part that conversed with an
extinct auk. The part that could tame a page of numbers
effortlessly, and the part that guiltily enjoyed new shoes.
The part that had walked with Henry, and that which had
walked with Charles. The part that had come to cherish
the paradise bird; and that small part that still dreamed.

I mustered all of me, all these Hesters congregating
together; like diamonds, each of us has a thousand facets,
and the dark room grew brighter and brighter in our
presence, until finally we shone.

As one, we rose and crossed to the bird of paradise.

I had not been able to look at it since its return, not
properly. But now I took it from its box and turned it
this way and that, the plumage still iridescent, moving
under the light. Hornaday had worked his magic: the
bird was whole, though its flesh was now wadding and
wire, its characterful eyes only black glass.

I clasped it to my chest as I never had done in life.
And then I remembered the snuff box.

I retrieved it and inspected the white residue within.
I had no idea what it was, or how it had got there.
I sniffed it – sulphur? What for? I did not think it
had been left by Mr Hornaday. He had not had the

313

opportunity to work on the bird by then. I could ask him about it, but he had seemed terribly focused on that exhibition of his. Nor did I know any other men of science. Unless . . .

You could take it to Ward's in Rochester, Hornaday had said.

It was a desperate idea. But to remain here, in ignorance, waiting for the clock to tick down, would be more desperate still.

Yet when I descended to the hall, my path was blocked by Paul Ruhe.

'Sorry, ma'am,' he said, not sounding sorry at all. 'Your husband prefers that you remain here.'

I stared at him. 'I cannot go out?'

He only shrugged. So Charles had caged me like one of his creatures. Fury flared in me. I would not be a docile, doe-eyed gazelle. I would be the alligator. I feinted as though to return upstairs, then, in a sudden rush, charged past Ruhe towards the door.

I was seized by hands like iron and flung back against the frame, hard enough that my teeth jarred in my skull.

'I am a hunter, Mrs Vogel,' Paul Ruhe said quietly. 'And just now I have little enough to hunt. If I were you, I would make sure that does not change.'

He released me, a feeble quarry, ready to be tamed. I did not have to feign my trembling. With downcast eyes and gritted teeth, I returned to my room.

Perhaps the residents of the graveyard opposite our home found it strange that a woman should be clambering out of the window and down a rope of bedsheets, particularly in the broad light of day. But the wonderful thing about the dead is they know how to keep silent.

314

I had let Ruhe see what he wanted to see: a terrified bird, all too willing to be trapped. It was late by the time I arrived in Rochester. The paradise bird was with me in a carpet bag, wrapped carefully in a cloth.

At least Ward's was not hard to find. The first cabbie I asked knew of it, though he looked at me curiously and said, 'Are you *sure*, madam?'

It was not long before we pulled up before the building. It was dark; only one window was lit, like a great eye, watching as I walked to the entrance. And what an entrance! Two massive whale bones had been set into the ground: they reared above me, ghostly white, meeting at the top like a great skeletal maw. Like every whale, they carried the aura of prehistory, of a bottomless ocean trench of time. The surrounding darkness seemed to mutter with wicked things, of knowledge ill-gotten and worse-used. But I forced back my fear. I had come too far to turn back now.

Quickly I stepped forward – headlong into a man who had just come in the opposite direction, as though fleeing hell itself. The eerie aura dissolved into an ordinary profusion of apologies; I was momentarily afraid that my bird had been damaged, but upon inspection found him intact.

'Akeley,' my acquaintance said. 'Carl Akeley.'

'Mrs Vogel. You are employed here?'

He was.

'I am in need of help.' Seeing his hesitation, I added, 'Of a *scientific* kind.'

'Ah!' His eyes sparked in the darkness, then clouded again. 'Only we are about to close for the day . . .'

'Please,' I said. 'I have come rather a long way.'

He sighed. 'Well, Mr Ward *does* say that science never sleeps. Which is just as well, lately. Come with me.'

I followed him into the building's shadows.

After my visit to Mr Hornaday, I was accustomed to the grisly marvels of a taxidermy workshop. Mr Akeley explained that they were readying for an exhibition of Central American curiosities: dotted about, in various stages of vivisection, were odd spotted cats and black weasel-like creatures with white necks, like priests. Skunks of many kinds snarled odourlessly from the shadows. While full of animals, the place was fortunately devoid of people, and we assembled ourselves beside the nearest lamp. I showed him poor Henry's body.

'This was prepared by Mr William Hornaday.'

His brows rose, but he said nothing. I brought the snuff box out and showed him the white residue.

'This was found on its neck. I want to know what it is.'

'Hum! And you have no idea?'

'No.'

'You believe it to have been left by Mr Hornaday?'

'No.'

'Then by whom?'

'I have my suspicions. But I wish to ascertain their validity.'

'Most commendable. Do you have any theories as to the nature of the substance?'

'No.'

'You are aware it could be any one of a thousand things?'

'Yes. Can you help me?'

He regarded me seriously. 'Yes.'

I tried not to sag with relief, only watching as he withdrew a magnifying lens from his coat and bent close to the snuff box, studying it from every angle. His expression gave nothing away.

After a minute, he murmured, 'If the substance does not yield itself to initial examination, I am afraid identification could take days. Weeks, even.'

My relief faded. 'I need to know tonight.'

'Tonight! Hum!'

'*Please.* It is important.'

He said nothing, only continued his visual examination. When he had done so to his satisfaction, he took a small dusting on his fingertip and sniffed.

'Sulphur.'

'I thought the same.'

'But what about . . .'

Before I could stop him, he had dabbed it onto his tongue. He began to smile.

'What? What is it?'

'I believe I know already.' I began to talk excitedly, but he cut me off. 'We need *proof.*'

I followed him through the wavering shadows to a laboratory of sorts. I held the lamp aloft: glass bottles filled with mysterious liquids lined the walls, while pipes and machines of opaque design and opaquer purpose dotted the tables. What a destabilising world these men of science occupied, where everything was open to question!

Mr Akeley was already collecting the residue from the snuff box. Once done, he deposited it into a small glass beaker. Then he uncorked a bottle and dipped a wire inside.

'Hydrochloric acid,' he explained. 'For cleaning.'

He left the wire there while he went to a small metal contraption along the table. To my utter surprise, a flame sprang from it, lighting his face from beneath. He removed the wire from the acid and plunged it into the flame, then back into the acid, and then the flame. He repeated this ritual several times before carefully poking the wire into the white residue.

'Now,' he said, returning to the burner, 'we shall see what we are dealing with. Watch for the colour of the flame.'

Hungrily I watched as he plunged the wire, residue and all, into the fire.

It flared. Only for a fraction of a second, but it was enough.

'Lilac,' I burst out. 'I saw lilac.'

His features showed grim satisfaction. 'As did I.'

'What does that mean?'

'Potassium nitrate. You might know it as saltpetre.'

I frowned in confusion. 'The meat preservative?'

'It has other uses.' He did not elaborate immediately, instead tidying the laboratory table while I fidgeted with growing impatience.

'Which are?' I burst out at last, unable to bear it a moment longer.

'Taxidermy, for one thing.'

'Oh.' It was the worst possible answer. All this, only to discover it *had* been left by Mr Hornaday after all!

'But,' he went on, and I looked up. '*But*. You said this was prepared by Mr Hornaday?'

'Yes.'

'Hum. He trained here, you know, at Ward's. A very excellent student. He uses the same techniques as we do.' A pause. 'At Ward's, we do not believe in using saltpetre for smaller carcasses. It may damage the skin, and in any case, a smaller animal is not in need of drying in the same manner as larger bodies.'

'So . . .'

'So I do not believe that this residue came from Mr Ward's workshop.'

'Then what are the other uses?'

'This is the curious thing.' He paused again. For a man of science, Mr Akeley carried a touch of drama. 'There is one other major use of saltpetre, although how it would have come from there into contact with your bird I cannot guess.'

'What is it?' I exclaimed. I could wait no longer.

'Gunpowder, Mrs Vogel. Saltpetre is one of the chief ingredients in fireworks.'

New York rose up into the train windows like Atlantis dredged from the greedy deeps. A day for buried things to be dragged into the light. I disembarked into the glass and iron cavern of Grand Central Depot, and as I pushed my way through the crowds and towards the exit, I saw him.

My husband. He stood beside a column, frozen like an iceberg in the sea. We regarded one another, the crowd sliding around us. How he had found me, I had no idea, though later I would learn that Ruhe, hunter that he was, had tracked me as far as the station.

Mr Akeley had discovered saltpetre on my bird's neck. There was only one person it could have come from: Frost.

I had to tell Charles that he worked with a murderer. I had to bring an end to this circus folly, which had led to that blue ledger and those thick new documents I had found in the bureau. For the first time in a year, I would *do* something and be fearless of the consequences.

My husband made no greeting. In his eyes burned that cold fire I had seen in my father's gaze all those years ago, though this was not born of determination. This was the child of rage.

He slipped around the side of the column. Helpless and afraid, I could do nothing but follow.

'You defied me.' His voice was quiet. We were in a corner beside an iron truss. Across the way there were stores and a billiards room, but here there was only the two of us. I began to explain, to tell him where I had been, what I had found, and what he needed to know about Frost.

'You defied me,' he said again, and something dead settled in his eyes. He sprang towards me and spun me around, throwing me up against the truss so my head cracked against iron even as his hand went to my throat. Terror leapt through me as his fingers began to tighten.

'Charles,' I got out. 'Stop.' His grip only tightened further, a terrible crushing pressure against my windpipe, my pulse pounding as I choked and choked, trying and failing to breathe, my eyes fixed on his unmoving face. The man I loved was nowhere to be seen. And just as blackness threatened to overtake my vision, I spat out a single word, one I had heard in the Germanic quarter around the emporium.

'*Bitte.*' Please.

Slowly he released his grip. I slid down the wall, my breath coming in ragged gasps, tears streaming down my cheeks. He allowed me a minute's recovery, then hauled me up and out into a waiting cab.

CHAPTER THIRTY-SIX

A sudden ringing sound had me back in the castle tower, the page before me aglow in that unearthly golden storm light. It tolled again.

The dinner gong.

I had been crouched on the roof, but now went quickly down the stairs, down to the ground floor, lest anyone emerging into the courtyard should see me. And in the shadows I read, faster than I had ever read before.

Charles brought me home and pushed me into our bedroom. Just before he closed me in, he paused, as though to consider. I said nothing, trying not to tremble, my throat painful and knotted. Was he about to change his mind?

He made that habitual gesticulation, his hand sliding into his jacket pocket, fingers closing round the thing within. Then he brought it out into the light.

His canary bird. Growing worn now, the vivid yellow of its feathers fading from repeated caresses in times of discomfort or difficulty. I knew he carried it always but had not seen it since Mamie Fish's ball. He examined it like his jeweller father might have inspected a gem, and whatever he saw there made his face close as surely as the door he shut and locked in my own.

What was the difference between keeping something safe and imprisoning it? Was there one at all?

I lay in bed for long hours, the light and the bruises around my throat deepening to shadow. It was late before someone knocked and unlocked the door. It was Sarah, carrying a tray, worry etched across her features.

'You don't need to knock when the key is on the other side,' I said to her, trying to sound light-hearted. But my voice emerged as painful ashes.

'Oh *madam*.' Setting the tray down, she rushed to me, embracing me not as a servant but as a friend. I clung to her, pressing my face into the warmth of her dress, her familiar scent.

'Well now,' she said at last, her smile belied by the choke in her throat. 'You can't let this get cold.' She picked up a bowl of turtle soup. I shook my head, unwilling to try my voice again.

'You must eat,' she said softly. 'It's the only reason he allowed me to come.'

I could not. The circus was the day after tomorrow. I imagined he would keep me prisoner until then. As for the launch night itself, Charles valued appearances above all else: probably he would wheel me out then to perform like one of his beasts. After that? My hand went to my throat as I thought of that life insurance document. How long would he resist its call?

Sarah's mouth had wobbled at my refusal, but whatever she saw in my face made her expression set like one of Myrtle's puddings. Pulling up a pouffe, she sat before me and dipped the spoon in the soup. Then, with infinite gentleness, she put it to my mouth.

322

That gentleness undid me. I let the spoon in, the warm liquid slipping down my injured throat, soothing as it went. She fed me in that way, like a child, and I closed my eyes as another, clearer liquid slipped from beneath my lashes.

When the bowl was empty, she set it down. 'There now.' She touched my cheek, just once, then stood again to re-dress the bed, her manner suddenly no more than a dutiful servant. I was not fooled for a moment. She lifted the blankets high, cold gusting in, but then, before the material could settle, a curious thing happened.

'Madam,' she said, in a strange little voice. I twisted, and saw . . .

Nothing. I scrambled up, revealing the whole bed. There was nothing to see, only the unstained cleanness of the sheets. It occurred to me that they had been so for some time now. Well over a month. Our eyes met.

'Oh *madam*,' she said again, her voice crammed with a tight little multitude: happiness – no, joy – and sadness, and something a little like fear. I knew all this because I had the same emotions, a plunging sensation deep within, as though I was submerging in the Boston sea.

I, Hester Vogel, was going to have a child.

I knew exactly what I had to do. And for the first time in my life, it would not be for anybody else's sake but mine.

Under pretence of bringing me a sleeping draught, Sarah smuggled paper and ink into the bedroom, along with a particular document that I requested be brought from our lawyer's office in Harlem. I amended it under the solemn eyes of Sarah and her brother, summoned from the South Street docks. His ship left the day after next.

'You are sure, madam?' Sarah said, as the ink dried and her brother prepared to depart with the items I had given him, begging him to look after them. I trusted Sarah as I did no one else. I could trust her brother.

I was never so certain of anything in all my life.

With equal surety, I began to write. I wrote all night and into the next day, eyes and hands burning, though this was nothing to the fire that now burned within, this flaming calm. I stopped the next evening for sustenance and to sleep for a few hours on the sofa, then continued on into the next day. Nobody disturbed me but Sarah.

Finally, as the shadows lengthened and the time neared, I set the pen down with a sigh. Sarah had already dressed me for the opening night, lacing my corset and affixing my crinoline, the material crackling as she did so. When she wrapped her hands around my middle, our eyes had met in the looking-glass. Already the clothing felt tighter.

I did not know if the child I carried was Charles's or Henry's. It did not matter. What was certain was that it was mine. For the first time I had something completely of my own, and already I loved it with a painful sort of hurt indistinguishable from joy.

No, not for the first time. The ink on the pages before me was green, green as the plumage on my bird's snapped neck. Tonight I would avenge him as well as myself. Because I'd loved him, and because justice mattered, however smally served. As Paul Ruhe rudely elbowed into the room to fetch me to the circus, I glanced again at the figure in the looking glass. I saw not a lonely girl, nor a desperate lover, nor a caged wife, but a grown woman, calm and resolute.

Here the writing changed. Still the same hand, but messier, as though it had been written later and in haste.

We arrived at Manhattan Beach an hour before the show began. The night was dark, but Coney Island glittered. I had never even visited the circus site, and was stunned. It was situated on the ocean front beside the bathing pavilion and between the Oriental and Manhattan Beach hotels, whose huge castle-like structures flanked the great tent, striped like a tiger. Charles had built a city – and what a city! The crowd snaked back and forth before the ticket booth, faces alight with savage excitement; beyond, where the great tent multiplied into smaller versions of itself, I heard the chatter of monkeys and the genteel cough of lions. The line between human and animal seemed to blur.

The evening was a double bill. First was the circus, its star names thrusting out from the posters pasted everywhere: Maya the Aztec Beauty, Carlos the Knife-Man, et cetera. Then the entertainment, produced by James Pain's famed firework company, in association with Vogel & Brother, whose display would explode above the expectant black sea. The Brooklyn Bridge was somewhere in that darkness, ready for tomorrow's opening.

Ruhe, perhaps judging the risk of my escape to have diminished now we were within the crowd barriers, left me to go find Charles. But I had no wish to see my husband, and set off in a different direction altogether. My nerves were tight as wires, dread mingling nimbly with anticipation. I knew Frost would not be in the main arena, but rather in the wings, dictating from the shadows. I skirted the big tent, heading for the smaller versions, leaving the crowd behind. The silence rose like vines. I lifted the flap of the first tent and peeked through: someone met my gaze.

It was a lion. Male, enormous, caged alone in an otherwise empty tent. Its mane was black, its eyes huge and golden. Later some fool would place his head into its mouth. As if such a magnificent creature could be 'tamed' in any meaningful sense. I could have wept for humanity.

'You and me both,' I said softly, and closed the flap again.

Sounds issued from the next tent, both human and animal, commingling to produce an unnatural tongue that was neither one nor the other. This time I was more careful, creeping around until I found a small hole in the canvas that I could peer through. The moment I saw who was within, I dropped down, out of sight. I had been less afraid of the lion.

Hyatt Frost was there. So was my husband.

Charles was talking animatedly, fingers working away. I thought of the hideous emptiness in his features in the train station, my feeling of being as trapped and helpless as my paradise bird while his hand wrapped around my throat. I would never let myself feel that way again.

'I shall have it this evening.'

Did he mean the diamond? I dared risk another peek, but Ruhe had arrived, and he and Charles moved away, conferring in whispers. My husband accidentally dropped his glove as he went.

326

Frost let them go; then, stooping, he picked the glove up. I watched as he held it a moment, then – strange, so strange – raised it to his face. I had the bizarre thought that he would sniff it like an animal, but instead he did something even more unexpected. He pressed it to his lips. I ducked down again. Did Hyatt Frost harbour an unnatural passion for my husband? I rose to take another look, my mind churning. If this was so, why did he seek to bankrupt him?

I put my eye to the gap – and a hand grasped my shoulder while another clapped over my mouth, severing my scream. Powerless, I was dragged into the shadows.

Frost. I had come for him, but he had also come for me. This was the end – I must fight. I kicked, I struggled, I did everything a woman ought, but his strength was too much. In desperation I bit down, and was rewarded with a savage curse.

'I am trying to *help*. Oh, have it your way, d— you!'

We were in the amphitheatre of the bathing pavilion: later the audience would spill forth from the tent and come here for the fireworks show, but now it was dark, empty. Frost released me and we regarded one another, panting. The circus would shortly begin, and then it would be too late for Charles and me. At the thought, my fear flamed to rage.

'You,' I seethed. 'How can you pretend that you are *helping*?'

He gave a thin smile; upon his cheek was a scratch I had inflicted on him. I was not sorry.

'Charles is furious for your absence today.' His tone was perfectly composed. 'I did not think it useful if he caught you eavesdropping on his affairs.'

327

'Since when have you concerned yourself with my well-being?' I said bitterly.

'Since always.'

'You killed my bird.'

'What?'

'Do not pretend! You murdered the bird of paradise.'

He leaned against a pillar, so the shadows swathed his face. 'What evidence do you have?'

'The evidence of my own eyes, and more. You coveted the creature from the moment you set eyes upon it. Do not deny it. Only *you*, Mr Frost, go about with saltpetre on your fingers: residue from the fireworks you love so much – a testament, doubtless, to your destructive nature – and which I discovered upon my bird's neck.'

'And why would I do such a thing?'

I shrugged. 'Because you are wicked. Or because my husband has tired of you sucking him dry. Perhaps he told you as much, and you could not handle it.'

All at once he was before me, moving with that sinuous quickness. I was suddenly conscious of how alone I was, how empty the pavilion and how black the sea.

'You believe me capable of such an act?'

'Yes.'

'You have laid out your case,' he said quietly, 'and it is a good one. But there is one problem, Hester: I did not kill your bird.'

'Liar.'

'It is the truth.' His lips had twisted in thought. 'What time do you believe your bird was murdered?'

I told him, and he nodded.

'Ask Richardson, the pork merchant. I have been pursuing him for some time about a venture. I hardly left his side that evening, except to speak to Charles.'

328

'And why was that? To torment him further, doubt-less, and lead him into deeper folly.'

'You believe that it is *I* who have ploughed so much capital into this venture? Far from it, Hester. I have tried to dissuade him.'

I stared.

'You imagine it was I who approached Charles. Not so; it was the other way around. I was not the first, mind you. It was the talk of our business that an animal dealer was looking to enter the industry and willing to pay ludi-crous sums. I will admit that initially I was perfectly ready to relieve him of his funds. I have been in this business a long while; there are many charlatans. We cannot help it. Show business empties one of substance, leaving only the glitter.' He pulled a thin tube from his pocket and turned it in his fingers. 'Why do you think I carry fireworks, as Charles carries that canary he believes I do not know about? They remind me that this existence is no more than empty spectacle.' Exhaustion crept into his face, as though he could keep it from there no longer. 'And that I shall not have to suffer it for so very long.

'A successful circus is like a successful love affair. One must know how to give it enough, and yet keep it returning month after month, year after year. One must measure out novelty and pleasure without giving too much, lest you find yourself with no more to give. Does this sound familiar? Charles, for all his brilliance, does not know how to do that. It is my error. I mistook his single-mindedness for focus, his obsession for determina-tion. Something whips him on, and either he cannot stop that force or he does not want to. At every turn I have attempted to save expense; at every turn he has denied me. It is no longer about business, or profit. He must have the greatest show the world has ever seen – no more, no less.

'That is why he has neglected his emporium. Why else do you think I insisted my man be installed? I wished to keep an eye on him from the first. It gives me no pleasure to report that we have failed.'

'Pretty words,' I said at last. 'But this has nothing to do with my bird.'

He gave a tired smile. 'I said a good circus is like a good love affair. Whence do you think the comparison came? Why do you think I begged Charles, that night of your party – took his hands and *begged* him – to show more prudence? You must have guessed my sentiments towards your husband by now, Mrs Vogel, or are you even blinder than he?'

And suddenly, beside that open sea, I realised.

I swallowed. 'Is Charles aware?'

'Of course not. I have my pride. And' – that smile again, sad and tired – 'my sense of survival. You think me one who dwells in the shadows, Mrs Vogel. Believe me, if there were another way to live, I would live it.'

My eyes blurred. 'What happened with Charles?'

'That afternoon we had been at the firework shop together. He wanted to sample the latest and best arrangements. More money. More wasteful expense. Upstairs I tried to reason with him, but he would not listen. Not, for once, because he disagreed, but because he was fixated on something else.'

'What else? Where were you? In the library?'

'We were in that little unused bedroom. With your bird of paradise, which I swear to you was very much alive. I was trying to talk to him, but he was too busy turning something over and over in his hands. His brother had dropped it, he said. He would not show me what it was, but I caught sight of it in the mirror and could not think why he was being so strange. I left him to it.'

'What was it?'

He shrugged. 'Just a button. A little green thing.'

My mind flew to the words Henry and I had exchanged in that same room. How he had reached for me, how I had torn myself from him, and the sound of breaking that had ripped between us.

Even in the shadows, Frost must have seen me change colour.

'Are you all right?' he asked, but I was not listening, my thoughts instead racing back to my initial surmisals about the manner and motive of my bird's death, the notion that it must have been driven by rage and spite. Frost and my husband had been upstairs. Frost had implored Charles to curb his expenditure – taken his hands, gunpowder on his fingers, and begged. And then he had departed, leaving my husband alone, and that meant the killer was . . . the killer was . . .

'Charles,' Hyatt said. I jerked with shock as a hand landed on my arm.

'My wife,' my husband said. 'I have been looking everywhere for you.'

CHAPTER THIRTY-SEVEN

I had not heard the footsteps. I was still in the broken tower, leaned against an old wardrobe with my eyes still fixed on the page, and it was only in the bare millisecond before a hand seized my shoulder that I dropped Hester's account to the floor, hiding it under my boot.

'And what,' Yves whispered in my ear, 'are you doing in here?'

He spun me around, fingers digging into my flesh. I gazed at him in defiance, hardly believing that I had ever seen him as an answer. If Yves was the response, I did not want to know the question.

He half pushed, half dragged me from the room. I should fight him, run from him. As if knowing what I felt, his fingers tightened to the point of pain.

'Come, Emmy. It is rude to be late for dinner.'

The great hall had never looked so cavernous as it did then. The fire was lit: above the mantel, the stuffed buzzard danced, dead wings raised above a table laid with gleaming silver. I remembered those butchered clansmen, slaughtered so that the blood ran into the puddings.

'Miss Blackwood.' Heinrich Vogel appeared, knowing and cunning as Faust. He wore a jacket of embroidered night, and his salesman's smile.

I smiled tightly. 'Mr Vogel. I am sorry I have not found your diamond.'

He waved a hand as though it did not matter, as though there were greater prizes, and pulled out a chair with energy. 'Come.'

I glanced at Yves. His expression was a ghastly blank.

'Come,' Heinrich Vogel repeated. His hands were either side of the carved wooden back, knuckles pushing through thin skin. I sat, and he pushed the chair in with a deft movement. For a moment those hands hovered in the corner of my vision, level with my neck; then they withdrew.

He seated himself at the other end of the table, so we faced one another. There were no other places laid.

'Yves shall wait on us this evening,' he said, noting my gaze.

A bang like a gunshot: I whipped round in alarm. The man in question was holding a bottle of champagne.

'Whoops.' I followed his gaze: the champagne cork had hit the buzzard. There was a gaping hole in its flank, and as I watched, several feathers fluttered down, drifting into the fire with a faint sizzle.

'So you found your way to the tower,' Heinrich Vogel said, watching them burn. 'As I had predicted. The fulfilment of prophecies is a curious business. They do not always come true in the way one thinks. Fate is sometimes literal. At other times, metaphorical. Sometimes even . . . transferable.'

His eyes gleamed in the firelight, and I saw the madness within.

Transferable. What did that mean?

Yves poured and handed me a glass. He seemed careful not to touch me, like one avoids an infected person.

333

'A toast,' Mr Vogel said, raising his own glass, bubbles seething within.

'I thought you did not drink.'

'To prophecy,' he said, ignoring me as he threw it back with sudden thirst. I did not touch my own.

'If it is true, then are you not afraid?'

'Why should I be? We all get what is coming to us, Miss Blackwood. In the end. Come, you are not drinking. Or would you prefer we hide the bottle under the bed first?'

Blood rose to my cheeks. I said only, 'Yves told me that life was the one possession you would be forced to yield.'

'If life is an artwork, then DEATH is the frame. You have seen my menagerie. Those animals now are more perfect, more complete than they ever were alive. After I had finished the last creature, a great exhaustion and euphoria came upon me. I knew what it was to be the Lord, labouring on his creation. And what did He do, on the seventh day?'

'He rested.' My voice was flat.

'Rested, yes, but no relaxation came. He knew that it was too much – that he had made the world too beautiful. It was in that moment of realisation that he created the Devil. I felt the Devil as I rested, coiled at the foot of the tower . . .'

He broke off, his hand sliding into his jacket pocket. 'You have spent time in Papua and New Guinea. I have read of the cannibal tribes of that region. You know, perhaps, of the *khakhua*. It is their word for a sort of witch. It comes in disguise, in the form of a relative or a friend. But it is *not* your friend. The creature has eaten the insides of its victim, replacing them with fireplace ash as it does, so he is never aware that he is being consumed. When he dies, the *khakhua* takes up residence and pretends to live as the man did. He talks with his friends. He embraces his women. And all the while its presence corrodes the life of the village.'

I shuddered, remembering the unseen presence to which

Mr Vogel had spoken in his chamber, Gaelic hissing off his tongue like pan fat.

'You know what those savages do to *khakhua*? They kill them and eat the body. It is their revenge, because such a betrayal can be met with nothing else. It is not the killing of their friend that concerns them. It is the deceit that follows.' He leaned in. 'Can you imagine what that is like? True betrayal can only come from someone close to you. That is what makes it so damnable.'

Behind me, a door swung open; I tasted roasting meat.

'There can be no relief from treachery. The traitor is a parasite in your heart that may never be vanquished. Grief fades; love dwindles; only betrayal remains. It burns hotter, not colder, as time goes on, against the betrayer but also against one's own self, because it is *you* who allowed yourself to be deceived.'

He tilted his head, scrutinising me. I felt like one of those condemned men, the bamboo shoot already lodged deep in my skin. 'When you first arrived at Pàrras, I told you there was one rule. Only one. Tonight you broke it. Your Papuan villagers would react in the only way they know how.'

I sprang from my chair, cutlery cartwheeling across the table, making for the door. But there was Yves. In his hand was a carving knife.

'Miss Blackwood,' Mr Vogel said reproachfully, 'do not mistake me. We are very far from savages. Still, they have a practice of which I approve: the pig feast.'

As if on cue, the kitchen door opened with a blast of air, hot like an oven. Lynette came forth, bearing a vast platter. Upon it was a whole suckling pig, glistening and eyeless, grovelling on a bed of its own flesh.

'Please,' Mr Vogel said. 'It is time for dinner.'

Slowly I returned to my seat. Yves, after a long look at me, held forth the knife. Mr Vogel removed his hand from his pocket and took it, setting down as he did so the thing he had been caressing within. He began to carve, but I did not pay attention to that shining blade. I was rooted to my chair, staring at the thing on the table.

It was a canary. Stuffed, long dead, and in a terrible state of repair. The stuffing poked through, and most of the feathers were missing, as though they had been worn away. I had just read of it in Hester Vogel's account: it belonged to a man she loved.

Not Henry – Heinrich – Vogel.

Charles.

A roaring filled my head. Charles. Charles all along. Was it possible? My employer's hatred of Hester, his vivid sense of betrayal, his grasping, possessive character . . . My breath came in quick blades. It was all Charles. Charles had found out about his wife's affair with his brother and killed the paradise bird in fury. Hester had begun to write her diary in those last pages I had read. She had *known* a confrontation was coming, and had laid her trail. But Charles had got the better of her. He had killed her – my eyes ran hot at the thought – but never found the diamond's true location. At some time he came to believe that Henry had hidden it at Pàrras. Hester had changed her will, leaving the castle to Henry – that was the document Sarah and her brother had witnessed. With his business collapsed, his debtors and perhaps the law in pursuit, Charles had fled there and assumed his brother's identity.

The canary in his pocket – the same one that Charles had tried to protect from his father long ago. The odd fact that Mr Vogel had never described the diamond to me: because *Henry* had found it, never showing it to Charles. And my employer's odd allusion, right at the beginning of our acquaintance, to his brother's impressions of the jungle. An inadvertent slip, because Charles had never been to the jungle:

336

it was *Henry* who went on collecting expeditions. The man before me was a counterfeit – a fraud – a parasite. I might not have detected it had it not been everything I was myself.

'Please.' Charles Vogel had finished carving and swept the canary back into his pocket. 'Eat.'

I did so, fork rising automatically from my plate, hardly tasting the food. 'Hester didn't fall, did she – *Charles*?'

For the first time, he seemed taken aback. 'Very good, Miss Blackwood. Very good indeed. A true detective. No, she did not fall.'

'What happened?'

'My *brother*' – he spat the word – 'my own brother had refused to give me the diamond. Then Hester told me he had given it to her. Yet another betrayal. But she said she would hand it over to me, saying that it was at our storage facility in the bowels of the Brooklyn Bridge. We went there, but rather than take me to the facility, she insisted on walking first onto the bridge itself. I was so angry I could hardly see. There, with the city spread beneath us, I confronted her. She denied nothing.

'"I loved you, Charles," was all she said. I responded by saying I would never forgive her or my brother, that thief of my most prized treasure.

'"Tell me one thing," she said. "Do you mean me, or the diamond?" I said it did not matter. Both, after all, were mine.'

Dizzily I swallowed the lump of pork in my mouth. 'Then you pushed her.'

'No. I wanted – *needed* – that stone. What good to me that Hester should perish? I searched the facility afterwards. No diamond. She had lied to me again. Henry had never given it to her – he had brought it here, to Pàrras, which she had left him in her will.' He did not believe, then, that Henry would ever have entrusted Hester the diamond.

337

Another sign of the low esteem in which he had held his wife. 'That note we found in her rooms: I did not tell you it was addressed directly to my brother. *Henry: the path to the treasure lies in Paradise.* The two of them taunted me to the end.'

'You cannot expect me to believe that she fell.'

His eyes glittered. 'She did not fall – she jumped.'

'I don't believe you.'

'Neither did Mrs Briggs.'

'What did you do to *her*?'

'You shall soon discover.'

'The same as you did to Hester, you mean,' I said bitterly. 'You killed her.'

'I did *not* kill my wife. I admit I was tempted. But I have told you many times: I never, ever relinquish what is mine. She jumped and took my life with her. I could not remain in New York without the diamond, not with the debts piling ever higher. The life insurance policy I had taken out for us both was invalidated by the manner of her death. Without it, the circus collapsed after barely a month. I could not even afford to feed my animals, and Henry had gone, abandoned me as my wife had done.

'He is dead, you know. He returned to America but once, a few months after my own departure. I heard he kept on collecting, supplying my rivals. I had a report that he disappeared in the mountains of Papua, where you found the bird, six years after my wife's death. Probably struck down by disease. I assumed his identity, shaking off my creditors in the process.'

Whereupon, like a parasite, he had taken up residency in the castle that should never have been his. Hester and Henry, both dead. It saddened me more than I could say. I'd hoped for their love to find another way; apparently it never had.

'And the animals?' I asked at last.

'Everything I owned had been taken from me. I could not relinquish them too.'

I stared at him, eyes blurring. 'You killed them.'

'I *saved* them. They would have starved or been sold to some trifling showman at a knockdown price. A little poison in their last feed before the supplies ran out. That was all. Then I took them across the sea, and spent the next twenty-four years restoring them to their glory.'

'Living things are not possessions.'

'What is love if not ownership?'

Lynette re-entered. She neither spoke nor looked at me, only heaping more flesh onto our plates. Light-headed, I noticed I had finished mine.

'Lynette,' I said. Her half-destroyed face showed no emotion. 'Lynette, please.'

Mr Vogel laughed softly. 'I do not think you will find help in that quarter. Lynette is in my debt. She understands betrayal as well as I do, along with its necessary consequence: revenge. An elegant equation. It was with my help that she killed her husband for what he did. My beetles saw to the rest.'

He sighed and waved his hand; I felt Yves glide into position behind me. 'Well, Miss Blackwood, the hour is late. It is a pity that you could not meet your side of the bargain.'

'What about the day of your death? Or was that a lie too?'

'I did not lie.' He appeared irritated. 'Unlike my fellow German, Dr Faust, I have cheated the Devil once already. This is in fact the second summer solstice on which I was doomed to die. The first occurred during Mrs Briggs's time, and do you know, Miss Blackwood, I survived.' He leaned forward, and in his eyes I saw that dancing flame. 'It was then that I realised the clansman does not care whose soul he takes. I imagine he shall accept yours equally well. Did you enjoy your meal?'

And in that moment, I tasted it. The tang of sugar on my tongue. I had avoided it so long, I had forgotten its savour. My insulin was in my bedroom – I had forgotten to take it before . . .

'I am afraid we shall be depriving you of your little glass bottles,' Mr Vogel said. 'Yves, I think the broken tower, don't you?'

And as the room spun and went black, golden hands seized my arms and bore me off, I supposed, to heaven.

CHAPTER THIRTY-EIGHT

I awoke into a raging quiet, my tongue sickly sweet. Outside, the wind whipped the walls. The storm was closing in.

No, not Heinrich, nor Henry. Henry was dead.

Charles.

My eyes snapped open; my vision swam. I was lying on the stone floor of the broken tower, my tool belt and Thermos flask digging into my back. The circular room was freezing, and I was clad only in a pullover and trousers. I sat up, automatically inspecting my belt. My knife and chisel were gone.

Painfully I hauled myself upright, dragging some dusty curtains to the floor in the process. How long had I been unconscious? I tried the heavy wooden door, but it was locked. Obviously. The stairs across from me led only to that derelict floor and the roof beyond, far above the loch. I was owed an ending, and Charles Vogel was confident I would get it. He was right: without insulin, ketoacidosis would kick in in a matter of hours. Perhaps not even that long, given the sugar-laced pork they'd fed me. I would die without them having to lift a finger. A hiss escaped me as I cursed my body's insufficiency. I drank deeply from the flask.

Little good it would do me. I would soon be just like poor Mrs Briggs, wherever she lay. Like her, I had been lured into this castle that was nothing so much as the giant corpse flower I had tracked in Sumatra, enticing flies with its stench of rotting meat.

I drained the flask and was about to discard it, but then, purely from habit, affixed it to my belt again. I tried the door once more, throwing my shoulder against it. Again. Again. On the third attempt, my shoulder cracked in sudden pain. I gasped and stumbled backwards, tears springing to my eyes, and collided with something unexpectedly furry.

It was the stuffed bear, snarling upright in that crowded chamber, its eyes level with mine. The Kodiak, its glass eyes glimmering in the dying gold of daylight. One of the creatures Charles had slaughtered.

I turned away, then looked back again. The fur had torn around one of the creature's paws, and something that was neither wadding nor wire poked through. A terrible thought awoke in my mind. I leapt away, causing a black miasma to rise behind my eyes. Blinking furiously, I gazed at the creature before me. Yes: about my height.

I don't like things that hide within other things, Yves had told me. *Though sometimes it is necessary.*

Mrs Briggs had been another tall woman, the conductor had said.

I cast about for something sharp. There was a vase nearby: I swept it onto the floor and picked up one of the resulting shards, approaching the bear as warily as though it were still alive.

Then I stabbed the knife into its head.

With a dreadful ripping sound, I wrenched my hand down, fur and stuffing coming away, opening up a long scar. I struck again, and this time something met my hand with horrible resistance.

342

Inside the bear's head was a skull. Not of a bear, but of a person.

I had to get out, get away. I climbed the stairs in a scramble, the wind rising as I left the shelter below. The storm was approaching and I heard the landscape moan and crack; it would be here in an hour, no more. Bent low, I picked my way across the shattered roof until I was at the edge closest to the loch. The height was obscene, my vision plunging down to shatter on the toothy rocks. The waters writhed lazily around them.

Do it, they seemed to say.

I braced myself on the battlement. This was the only place to jump – anywhere else I would hit the courtyard. How far down was it? Sixty feet? Ignore that part. All I had to do was make the leap, then swim for land before the storm hit. Reach the beach, find the insulin I'd stashed, and flee through the hills to safety.

Move.

But I could not. My mother was clinging to the cliff below, gazing up at me from an impossible vantage. Her upturned eyes were empty. I was eleven years old, and she was about to die because of me.

I pulled away, gasping, and sprawled back onto the mocking stone. Somehow I made it back down into the tower, head pounding. My legs were shaking by the time I reached the ground floor and the waiting bear. I thought I glimpsed the white of bone in its ruined face, and I turned and vomited onto the flagstones.

Slowly I slid down the wall. Hester's account was on the floor between me and the wardrobe where Yves had grabbed me, the mark of my boot upon it. My fingers crept out and picked it up, bringing it to my chest. I was exhausted, but I could not let myself sleep. The onset of ketoacidosis would see me fall into a coma from which I would never wake.

Time passed. I tried to summon up my sister's essence, to absorb strength from her character as I always had, but every time I did so, I saw Charles, his mask stripped away. He was an imposter, just like me. I had not lived as myself, and now, with the chips down, I did not know what I was and where resilience could be found. I was nothing. I had spent my life running, and despite it – because of it – I had ended up in a cage.

A cage . . . There was one in front of me, set carelessly on a table against the wall, half lost in the shadows. It had a finial on top, in the shape of spread wings. Hester's father had won his wife with a creation like this. Perhaps it was the exact same cage. Her mother had died when Hester was small, cut off by her family. How had she felt in her last hours? Had she grieved for the choices she had made? Or had she rather been grateful that she at least had made them – her life dictated by herself and no one else?

So it was that despite my weakness, despite my blurred vision, I swept up Hester's account for the last time.

CHAPTER THIRTY-NINE

I accompanied my husband as obediently as a lamb. Did an animal know when it was destined for the charnel house? Did it feel it in its bones, as I did?

Charles had killed my bird. I should have known it the moment he grabbed me by the throat with that same possessive violence. He had seen me come downstairs, seen Henry with the torn button, and in his rage, in his contempt, he had snapped the animal's neck. Then he had sympathised with me, and arranged to have it stuffed, and all along he had *known*, keeping the truth from me as he always did. No wonder he was so furious about my hunt for its killer.

Wordlessly we returned to the circus tent, his hand never releasing my arm. I blinked, adjusting to the light and heat, conscious all the while of the cold darkness without. The attendants welcomed us; a red cord was moved aside. I tried to step away, but the fingers around my arm dug into the bone, and it was all I could do not to gasp in pain.

'My wife shall go through now,' Charles said to the attendant. His tone was one of perfect courtesy, that same blankness of expression as in the train station. It was terrifying.

I took my excellent seat – ringside, beside a pillar, so I was blocked in at the end of the row – and the show began.

It was magnificent beyond description. It really was. A man rode a cantering horse, first on his feet, then on his hands, then flipping through the air to land again. Tigers leapt through rings of fire and pirates fought with cutlasses, swinging low enough that the audience was forced to duck. Indian men juggled, first with diabolos, then with swords. Carlos the Knife-Man flung blade after blade at a beauty who did not move a muscle as they thunked into the panel beside her head, between her fingertips, in the V of her legs. A three-legged person jumped rope and an invulnerable man inserted swords through himself. Oh, how I wished for the same gift!

Towards the end of the show, Charles disappeared. I stood immediately, thinking to escape, but was prevented by Paul Ruhe, who had taken his place.

'The show is about to end,' he said slyly.

Indeed, the lion had been tamed; the dancing girls came on, and suddenly that was it, a standing ovation, flowers flung to the stage where a figure stood, bowing and smiling in a red tailcoat. My husband.

He did not look like a bankrupt. He looked like a man entirely confident of his success. A man who was confident the universe had fallen into step at last. I thought of that thick document and shuddered.

The crowd were instructed to head to the pavilion: the fireworks were about to begin. People surged for the exits, the tent emptying around us. With a final sneer, Ruhe departed.

In the silence, Charles and I faced one another at last.

'My wife,' he said quietly. The circus lights had been mostly extinguished: in the gloom, he seemed a stranger. 'Come up to the ring.'

I did so, the wooden steps creaking beneath me as an invisible audience watched. Sawdust and glinting spangles covered the floor.

'Stay there,' he said, and I realised I had come to a stop before a wooden panel painted with exotic beasts.

When I looked back, there were three knives in Charles's hands.

'You and my brother,' he said, ruminatively. It wasn't a question, but I answered it anyway, my voice barely above a whisper.

'Yes.'

Before I could move, he flung the knife. It slammed into the panel to the right of my head, the silver of the blade flashing in my vision. Shock clenched my veins; it was all I could do to prevent my hand flying to my stomach, trying to protect what slept within. I had already vowed that Charles would never know. He did not deserve to. I made to step forward, but . . .

'I would not move, if I were you.' Already he was wielding the second knife. 'Carlos is always very clear with his subjects about that. He has taught me much these months, when we have had spare moments.'

'Charles. Do not do this.'

'How long?' His voice was cold, alien.

'You have every right to be angry . . .'

'*How long?*'

'Months.'

On my left, the wooden panel sang out, my blood screaming in my ears. He had thrown the second knife:

it shuddered now on the other side of my head. I wiped a splinter from my eye, half sobbing in fear, and when my vision cleared, I saw he held the third knife ready.

I watched him weigh it in his hands. Saw again that thick document, spanking new. When at last he looked up, meeting me dead in the eye, I knew what was coming.

We had loved each other, but we were both of us too broken for love to be enough. With his hands around my throat, part of me had thought I'd deserved it, for cheating on him with his brother. But as that third and final blade rose, glinting in the ersatz circus light, I understood that was not the real betrayal.

Charles had trapped me. Caged me. Kept me small. Not just these last days, not just this physical incarceration, but long before that. Strange, what it takes to make us see, and in that shadowy tent I saw at last how thoroughly Charles had removed my freedom. In his paranoia and his secrecy, his thirst for society and hunger for propriety, he had taken away my independence. He had taken my livelihood, my skills, my self-respect and ultimately my humanity. One by one he had removed my reasons for existing, and in fortifying his own walls, he had built my prison. Perhaps he had not done it consciously. But every cage is a cell, no matter how well meant. And I, lonely creature that I was, had let him do it, and counted it love.

Henry had recognised this even when I refused to. Love was not the same as liberty, and you could not have one without the other. To pretend otherwise was among the most damaging lies one could tell oneself.

And so, as the blade reared up, as his hand shifted into the throwing position . . .

348

'I have the diamond.'

He paused at my words. Did not lower the knife. 'I am afraid I am past trusting you.'

'It is true. Henry gave it to me before he left. He . . . he loved me. And he did not want you to have it.'

Silence.

'I can take you to it.'

The quiet stretched; the invisible audience leaned forward in their seats. Then, at last: 'Where?'

'The Brooklyn Bridge.'

I write this in the jolting dark of the hansom cab. Charles rides upfront; he has no desire to be near me, only to ensure I do not escape. I add these pages to the others I have written, as my time, at last, runs out. I said from the first that this was a treasure map. Henry, my darling, it is a map for *you*. I know I have not made it easy; I have had to be necessarily obscure, for the sake of the child I carry. I cannot risk Charles following the trail. Cannot risk him finding us.

But dearest, know that I changed my will for a reason. That I have left you Pàrras for a reason. I have no way of finding you, but perhaps one day you will find me – after all, you did it once before. Come join us, Henry; come meet the child whose name I have already chosen. Dearest, this has all been for *you*. You are my true reader; you the only person who ever looked at me and understood. I hope beyond hope that one day you discover these pages and learn the truth. I hope that you can understand; and that one day you may forgive me.

Henry: the path to the treasure lies in Paradise. Those are the words I have written for you, for when you return to New York after I am gone. *The Birdcage Library* represents the very beginning of this unmixed chapter of our freedom. And remember: X marks the spot.

CHAPTER FORTY

The words ran out. Hester's account ended, unmet by the yearning hope that Henry would find these pages.

I pictured her and Charles arriving at the bridge, a vast raptor spreading its dark wings over the East River. She had told him the diamond was stowed in the facility deep in the bridge's bowels, yet if I was to believe Charles, before taking him there she had led him onto the structure itself. I saw the cables rising high above them, the black river spread below; felt the sheer unnatural dimensions of the Roeblings' creation. Now she turned to look at the man she had once called her husband, as he shrieked his fury at the missing diamond, as he accused her of betrayal, even as his cheek was illumined by the circus fireworks soaring from Coney Island, a reminder of how he had abandoned her long before she ever thought of deceiving him.

Hester had not given up the diamond. Perhaps she had never intended to. Yet in taking him to the bridge, she must have known how it would end. The explosion of anger, of possession. The sudden step, her arms seized, dragged fighting to the edge, the horror of the waiting drop, and then the hard shove into the screaming air.

After that, pain. And then nothing.

She *had* committed suicide, in a way. The moment she had refused to give the diamond to this man who saw a human being as another thing to be owned, only one outcome could have been possible. All that determination and passion and intelligence and *zest*, and in the end she had simply surrendered. I hated it.

In the tower, the moonlight shifted. The empty cage was still before me, but to the left, its glass box illuminated as though lit from within, was the mangled body of the bird of paradise. Charles must have brought it here after tearing it apart. He had destroyed it, seeing only its uselessness and none of its wonder. But obsession is not appreciation, and beauty has nothing to do with perfection.

I crawled to it. Paradise lost: the creature was maimed, broken, its stuffing all in pieces. I opened the box and ran a finger down that beautiful sunset tail, remembering the strange leaflet hidden within it.

The Natatorium, run by Hester's friend Robert Odlum.

And then, at long last, I remembered where I had heard that name before.

Daniel. I pictured him now, his kind eyes, the faint worry that always lurked within – not for himself, but for those he cared about. He was talking about his trout, their fishy environment and the human beings who had, for different reasons, loved the water. Swimmers. Daredevils. Underwater adventurers. Lord Byron, Gertrude Ederle, William Beebe . . .

'And Professor Odlum, of course. He once swam eighteen miles each way along the Virginia coast, including against the tide. Remarkable.' Daniel sighed. 'Nowadays, though, people only know him for jumping off the Brooklyn Bridge and dying in the attempt.'

Astonishment spread through me. Hester had described

her friend's love of dangerous jumps. The fearful leap, he'd called it, hinting that he would attempt the bridge. But the bridge remained unfinished at the time of her writing. Odlum had not yet had the opportunity to attempt his feat.

Yet someone had placed his pamphlet inside the taxidermied bird . . .

I had not believed Mr Vogel when he claimed he did not kill Hester. But what if he was telling the truth? What if she *had* jumped?

My thoughts swelled, pressing against my blurry vision. Hester was a capable swimmer, a friend of Odlum's since childhood. Henry had met him with her: he knew what Odlum was capable of. What if she had studied his methods? What if she had faked her own death? What if, in short, *Hester had survived*?

Scenes from her life unspooled before me, my heart pounding as the connection we had built these last months assumed an unearthly clarity. She had given Sarah's brother several items before she left for the circus: these must have been the paradise bird and the diamond, as well as the key to her beloved Pàrras. Suppose she had jumped, using Odlum's technique to land safely in that cold black river. Henry was gone, but Sarah's brother's ship was not due to leave the South Street port until the following morning. It would have been a simple matter for one of her abilities to swim to it. Then, along with her few possessions, she had crossed the Atlantic.

Henry was gone, but she'd wanted him to find her. To find *them*. He'd already sailed – she had no way of contacting him. No way of telling him of the child she carried, or the diamond's fate, at least not while keeping both secret from Charles. So she did the only thing she could: she left him Pàrras, hoping that one day he would visit and discover the trail of clues so carefully laid for him.

As for the concealment of the diaries . . . Mr Vogel had believed that the Pàrras intruder was Henry, acting on Hester's wishes. But I knew from Hester's account that this was impossible. It was likewise risky for her to return to Pàrras herself, but there was one person in Britain she trusted, and who knew the castle well. Richard Heatherwick, her grandparents' solicitor and friend of her mother. Hester must have left the diaries to him, along with the castle key and precise instructions on where to hide each account, including one in his own home. He had dug the counterfeit grave, whether on Hester's instructions, to prevent Charles ever thinking to look for her, or on his own initiative. Hester could only hope that Henry would find his way to Richard, who would be able to tell him the truth.

From there – well, Sarah's brother worked in the eastern Orient. Hester had crossed the ocean she loved so much, a woman alone but not for long, not with the child she carried. She'd voyaged until they arrived where she had always meant to go: Papua, home of the birds of paradise. She had brought her bird Henry home.

The chieftain who had gifted me the glass box had said it was given him by a ghost. He'd said the ghost had remained with them some years – staying as long as it desired, departing when it wished, loving whom it loved.

I could not think of a better definition of freedom.

I hauled myself to my feet, a great burden lifting, energy pouring through me. I knew it sprang from a source far more powerful than insulin: hope. If Hester had survived – if she had found a way out – then maybe so could I.

I examined the door again. It was solid oak, and I was weak, growing weaker. The walls themselves had been built to withstand marauders, several feet thick.

Which left . . .

Shakily I packed up Hester's account, along with *The Birdcage Library*, folding them tightly into the small vasculum that hung from my belt. It ought to be watertight. At last I turned to the bird of paradise.

'Thank you,' I told it. And: 'I'm sorry.'

Then I turned away and climbed up to the roof again.

Night had at last fallen. On the horizon was a patch of deeper dark, rushing in. The storm was minutes away.

I crawled over that rubbled roof, stones digging into my knees, acid fear rising in my throat. Tonight there would be a death, Mr Vogel had said. I had no intention of it being mine, but despite my renewed determination, the height was no less hideous than before, the black loch contorting in the rising wind like the *papillotage* on Charles Vogel's clothing.

He had stolen his brother's identity, just as I had stolen my sister's. The horror of his charade had forced me to reckon with my own. It was time to drop the mask and examine what lay beneath.

Someone who had failed to save her mother. Someone whose lie had saved her father.

Perhaps the moment had come to accept both. To live truthfully, no matter the cost, because as I had seen, the price of *not* doing so was far higher. I was not Emily, not any longer. I did not know who Emma was, or whether she even still existed.

But the time had come to find out.

The courtyard clock struck, working itself through its midnight tolls. The solstice was beginning. Panic spiked; from somewhere rose a dreadful shriek. The black patch of sky suddenly rushed towards me, closing in, the trees moving in a long ripple along the shore. I had to move, despite the edge, despite the rocks, despite the terror. Despite myself, whoever that might turn out to be. And as the midnight strokes neared their summit, I reached into myself and found

355

a kernel of something that felt a little like truth. Something that felt a little like *me*.

Despite the storm, despite the dark, a great calm descended. And, as though I had known how all along, I jumped.

CHAPTER FORTY-ONE

I hit the water feet first, just as Robert Odlum advised, plunging into a freezing black underworld. The loch swathed itself around me, plugging my ears, blocking my eyes. It wanted me so dearly.

But I wanted me more.

I surfaced, gasping, just as the storm hit like a wall. The waves whipped themselves into a frenzy, leaping to terrifying heights; the shore vanished. I did the only thing I could: I swam, using the waves' fury to propel me towards land, freezing cold stabbing at me and seawater barrelling down my throat. My hair was plastered to my face, my tool belt and flask banging against my thigh, threatening to drag me down.

But I made it. The waves shoved me onto the stony beach, the rocks clawing at my hands and knees. I stumbled away from them, from the water, which shrieked and writhed as though possessed by the Devil himself.

I was weak now, very weak. My vision was going, the sugar sickness tightening its grip. I crawled and staggered and crawled until I found the rock shaped like a church.

Beneath it – thank God, thank God – was a little glass bottle and a needle.

I stabbed myself in the thigh and passed out.

CHAPTER FORTY-TWO

Butterworth lived up to its name on my return that long afternoon. The solstice sun spilled gold over the old house and the vines rubbing their backs against the walls. The French doors were open.

Daniel was not around when I staggered up the lime-tree drive, but my father was.

'Emmy,' was all he said.

It had not been a moment for conversation. I was wearing a train conductor's uniform and carried nothing but my tool belt and a small but essential glass bottle, which Reynolds had to prise loose from my fingers. Then Daniel flew in and, rather than asking questions, wrapped me in about six blankets, made me some surprisingly competent cocoa – I had not thought he even knew where the kitchen was – and telephoned the police. For the next few hours, he and Reynolds fussed about, bringing me enough food to equip an army while occasionally providing more details to the telephone.

I sat beside my father, both of us quiet as the breeze blew in through the French doors, bringing with it the scent of verbena and roses. He had not let go of my hand for some time. A letter lay beside him, bearing the Royal Geographical

Society's emblem. Briefly I wondered why they'd felt the need to reject my paper twice. He was in a deep brown leather armchair that I recognised as Harold's; I noticed it was positioned to face the window, so the sun illuminated his lightless eyes.

I'd grown up watching his sermons, the stained-glass light drenching him in kaleidoscopic hues. Then he had been not our parent, but God's agent, separated from us by the pulpit. It had been a long time since I had trusted any force that rendered invisible a person's humanity, their frailty. No species was so defined by its weaknesses as man. Human uncertainty, fear, love, avarice – they all comprised our cruel yet beautiful failure, our fallen sublimity, this race that had nothing and everything to do with paradise.

It was time.

'Father?' I said tentatively. 'I have something to tell you.'

But Daniel entered with the news that Yves and Lynette were under arrest.

'The officers discovered human remains in some outland-ish place,' he said. I could imagine what that was.

'And Mr Vogel?'

His mouth contorted. I'd told him a little of what had passed: not all, but enough. 'He has not been arrested.'

'*What?*'

'They did not arrest him,' my friend went on, 'because he is dead. The officers broke into his rooms and discovered the body. And . . .' He grimaced. 'Are you *sure* you want to know? All right! All right! He was found lying on the floor, his neck . . . his neck completely broken. Twisted almost the whole way round.'

I gazed at him, then out of the window at the long drive, the lime trees full in their splendour.

'No sign of a diamond either,' Daniel said. 'Sorry, Emmy.'

It had all been for nothing. Perhaps I pitied Charles Vogel

then. Had he ever been happy? Perhaps during those years as a boy, when his mother let him play in her bedroom, surrounded by the rustle of dresses and the mushroom puffs of mysterious powders. When she died, he must have locked that softness away somewhere very deep. Paradise, or something like it. Too often the accepted sacrifice of adulthood is to spend our lives hiding from our own joy.

I thanked Daniel, waited until he had left the room, then turned once more to my father.

I told him everything. I told him about my decision as he lay amid the church tower's ruins; I told him about Emily, and about Emma. I told him how I loved him, and how I had deceived him.

When I finished, there was nothing to do but tremble in the long silence that followed, bracing for his disappointment and his alienation. He still looked out of the window, and I wondered – really wondered – what those sightless eyes could see.

Finally he spoke. 'I already knew.'

I stared at him. 'Wh-what?'

'I've always known.' His tone was calm, matter-of-fact. 'Well, not always. But certainly a few days after I regained consciousness. I'm your *father*, my darling girl. Even without my sight, do you really think I could mistake you for your sister?'

Sadness swept his features. 'I did not tell you because it was not long before I worked out *why* you were doing this. The accident tore a veil from me, and though my eyesight had gone, I saw so many things. You did not want to disappoint me; did not want to remind me any more of your mother's passing. Oh, my dear heart, how I hated myself for that. Hated myself for the distance with which I had treated you. Hated how I had allowed *my* guilt, *my* pain to overtake my own daughter.'

I could not speak; could not breathe. My hand gripped the tooth necklace at my throat.

'Your mother's death was not your fault, my darling. It was *never* your fault. For almost as long as I knew my wife, she wanted to die. The ferocity of her joy, the intensity of her pain . . . she could not shut the world out, as most of us learn to. Life whispered too much in her ear.' His hand gripped mine. 'I knew for years that we were on borrowed time. I loved your mother and tried to save her, but I only ever helped her in the way that *I* saw fit, which had nothing to do with what she needed. Every ounce of the divine salvation I offered was only another weight on her back. Eventually it grew too much. I am so, so sorry you were there when she broke.'

Something tore in his expression, and through it, just for a moment, a pair of green eyes fixed upon me. Not in accusation, but with resignation.

'I know that I withdrew from you after her death. But I never *blamed* you. Everyone said that you and your sister were so similar, but it was you who had your mother's kindness, her bravery, her natural optimism in our race. Oh, it galled me. *I* was supposed to be the man of God.'

He closed his dear, unseeing eyes. Forced them open again.

'But like her, you were willing to see what the world contained, whereas I had only ever looked for what I could take. *That* was what drove me from you. Not how she died, but how she *lived*. You reminded me of her, and I could not bear it.

'But I never had the courage to tell you, and after your sister died too, I had no reserves left. While you – you, as Emily, were doing so well holding up what remained of our family. I was not strong enough, brave enough to upset that balance.'

A sob came from my clenched mouth.

'Selfishly, I went along with your pretence. Selfishly, I watched you step into Emily's shoes, making her life *your* life, her dreams *your* dreams, because you thought it would make me happy. I watched you work so damned hard to look after me.' Water leaked from those eyes and I was dissolving. 'I let you feel like you did not deserve me, but it was *I* who did not deserve *you*.'

'Father,' I choked.

There was a noise behind us. Daniel was standing there. The shock and grief in his eyes told me that he had heard.

'I'm sorry,' I began. But he turned on his heel and left. A moment later, I heard the front door close.

Funny how it is exactly when we are trying not to hurt others that we tend to injure them most. I ran after my friend to see his car disappearing down the drive. Hours later, he still had not returned. The force of my betrayal winded me – I could only guess at how Daniel must have felt.

My father had said that the only gift we could not grant another was grace. But perhaps grace was just another word for living in truth. I was not Emily. I had tried to give the two people I loved most the one thing I could never give. And even as my father and I cried together, my tears seeping onto his shoulder, I was drowning in guilt as cold and dark as the loch I had so recently escaped.

Much later, as dusk fell, I jabbed myself again, shuddering at the blissful ability to do so. Reynolds had laid out my tool belt on the garden table to dry properly in the sun. I took a cloth and went to rub it down to prevent salt corrosion and rust. I needed to take care of something.

The Thermos flask had somehow acquired a dent. I shook it out over the grass: it rattled.

I frowned, did it again. It rattled all the more. Ice from

Lynette? But I had not topped that up for days now. I upended it and tried to shake out the hard unseen object. No result. Peering in, I saw only darkness.

I found Reynolds in the dining room, carefully arranging the forks. The shine in his eyes when he'd heard I was staying for a few days had both moved and pained me. 'Can you help me with something?' I asked.

With his assistance, I located some tweezers from the kitchen. He watched curiously as I delved into the flask.

'We could bash it open, Miss Blackwood.'

'No thank you, Reynolds. As I always say, if it isn't broken, don't break it. Ah! I think I have it.'

I held the thing with the tweezers; with a delicate contortion of the wrist, I was able to bring it to the bottle's neck and begin worming it through.

'Emmy?'

The shock of Daniel's voice in the hall nearly made me let go of the tweezers entirely.

'Go on, Miss Blackwood,' Reynolds said encouragingly. And with a yank and a twist, I had it. The hidden thing practically leapt out at us, clattering onto the table.

It *was* an ice cube, albeit a misshapen one, rough-hewn and oddly cloudy.

'Oh,' I said faintly.

Charles Vogel had never been able to describe the diamond to me because Henry had never shown it to him. I thought of the counterfeit stone he had found inside the bird of paradise. He had thought it real at first. So had I. It had looked like what you expected a diamond to be: a large sparkling stone, just like the one Charles's mother had had in her pearl necklace. In other words, a *cut* diamond.

Yves had easily spotted the stone on the X-ray. Too easily. Susan Jennings, as an engineering geologist, had once talked of the low atomic mass of true diamonds. Unlike paste, which showed up clearly, a true stone's presence was faint, shadowy. Easy to miss.

Charles Vogel had destroyed the bird of paradise, scattering its insides across the kitchen table where Lynette had been labouring to make ice cream, ingredients dotted about. It was I who had tidied everything up, collecting the ice cubes without a thought, dropping them into the flask containing the chilled water that helped assuage my diabetes.

The path to the treasure lies in Paradise.

What could be more paradisial than a paradise bird?

'Daniel,' I said quietly, holding out what I had found.

He crossed the room in a few quick steps. I handed the stone – the diamond – to him. He regarded it a moment.

Then he tossed it back onto the table.

'Oh,' he said indifferently. 'You found it.'

Then, with far more enthusiasm, he took hold of my shoulders and kissed me.

CHAPTER FORTY-THREE

I tore myself away. Reynolds had tactfully disappeared. '*What are you doing?*'

'I don't care about the diamond,' he said. 'I don't care about Butterworth, or the money, except for what I lost you both. I don't care about any of it. I just care about *you*.'

I swallowed. 'You don't even know who I am.'

'Yes, I do.' His certainty grabbed at my heart. 'You're the woman who makes me feel alive. Who makes me feel *free*.' He expanded his hands like a pair of lungs. 'That is not because of any pretence on your part. When I overheard you, I was . . . I hated that you felt you had to deceive us. But suddenly the guilt I've been feeling, the confusion, it all went away. It all made *sense*, after seven bloody years.

'I've loved you since that day in the woods. Long before that, really. And when I thought you'd died . . . it was worse than my father's passing. I couldn't believe how much it hurt, and then seeing you in the greenhouse, the way you looked at me – I didn't know how, but suddenly it was Emma looking back. I couldn't help myself.' He closed his eyes a moment, remembering. 'I vowed to sort myself out after that, but then you came back from Australia and it was just the same, my head telling me you were Emily, that you were the wrong person, while everything else screamed at me that you were *exactly right*.' His voice grew choked. 'That you were home.'

I could not stop the tears then.

'I've spent too much of my life wishing I was somewhere else, wishing I was someone else.' A small grin. 'I suppose I didn't have your conviction. But now you're here, I won't waste a minute of it. Emmy. *Emma*.' He said the name as though it were a key to a long-held prison. As though it were in itself liberty. As though he never wanted to say another ever again.

'That was why I left you just now. All the uncertainty, all the difficulty of this last year . . . I have never possessed your courage. I knew if I did not do it right away, I never would.'

'Do what?'

'Sell Butterworth. Get rid of it. There was an offer a few months ago but I was too stubborn to take it. I just instructed my agent.'

I stared at him. 'Why?'

'I don't want to live a life shackled to . . . to *brickwork*. This is my father's idea of what life should be.'

'But you swore to him you would never sell.'

'Yes. And do you know, I think he waited his whole life for me to disobey him.' A small smile. 'He died disappointed. But as I am learning, it is never too late.'

I could not speak, though my eyes and mouth brimmed. Within me was a plant, a parasite, old black leaves that for seven years and more had forested every part of my being. Under his light I felt it shrivelling away.

'So, Emma Blackwood. Adventuress. Escaper of castles. Finder of treasures. What are you going to search for next?'

I looked at him, then back at the enormous stone on the table.

367

Yves had told me that he hated things that concealed themselves within other things. But we all of us hide inside ourselves. We can only pray that someday someone is able to unlock us and find the treasure within.

'I think I have an idea,' I said, and leaned over and kissed him.

I don't know how long we were there before Butterworth's doorbell sounded. Reynolds appeared from nowhere as we sprang apart.

'Shall I answer it, Mr Loewe?' he asked. His tone was as respectful as ever, but from the shine in his expression . . . perhaps we had been there for quite a while.

'Please,' Daniel said with utmost formality. I laughed. I couldn't help it.

A tough-looking gentleman entered. He bore an envelope and a substantial moustache.

'I am seeking a Ms Blackwood?'

I came forward, curious. 'Yes?'

'At *last*. We have been trying to track you down. I am a council member at the Royal Geographical Society.' He handed me an envelope, which I tore open. 'Don't you read your letters?'

'No,' Daniel answered wryly.

I would have made a tart response had I not been so busy staring at the letter I held.

'Daniel,' I said at last. 'The RGS.'

'What about them?'

I stared from the sheet of paper to the man smiling in my direction.

'They want to offer me a fellowship.'

Three weeks later, an embarrassingly lavish dinner was held in my honour at the Kensington headquarters of the Royal

Geographical Society. I gave a lecture beforehand on parasitic plants in Sumatra and the Territory of Papua and New Guinea, which was very well received, though I had to work hard not to be distracted by my father and Daniel in the front row, beaming out at me like lighthouses throughout. At dinner, I was seated at the head of the table and expected to be entertaining, and to my surprise, I found it not difficult to be so. It was as though the creepers I had been describing had withdrawn from inside me, leaving me at once emptier and fuller than I had ever been.

Afterwards the party decamped to the New Map Room, where the fellows' book lay open, awaiting my own small signature among those many luminaries. The entire room watched as I made my way towards it, suddenly nervous for the first time that evening.

The pages were creamy, the writing therein a midnight blue, dark as a loch. As I took up the pen, I felt a presence just behind my shoulder – the weight of someone watching.

I had kept her with me a long, long while. Too long.

It was time to let her go.

My signature, though unpractised for many years, was swift and decisive, like all exorcisms must be. For just a moment, as I gazed at the ink, it seemed to shimmer into green.

Emma Blackwood, it said.

EPILOGUE

Two months later, I was back to my usual self. No, not that – something far better. Daniel and I were at the trout stream together; it was a golden autumn evening, sunlight woven through the late leaves. I'd taken off my shoes as we walked, digging my toes into the heaped freshness of the cold grass.

'Let's see if you've remembered *anything* I taught you,' he said, grinning, and I hit him lightly with my rod. We were dusty from the day's labours: I was helping him pack up the big old house before he moved to a small farm not far away. I'd visited and thought it beautiful. And even though Butterworth was emptying around us, the last months had felt like a homecoming.

Perhaps that was due to my own new residence. Even after seeing to my father's care, there had been money enough from my commission on the diamond's proceeds to buy a cottage. (Or a castle, had we wanted one, which we didn't. I'd had enough of castles to last a lifetime.) I had told the newly appointed executors of Pàrras about the diamond. It felt only right. They were still searching for a rightful heir; if they did not find one, the whole of the stone's proceeds were mine to keep. Meanwhile, our new house was clean and bright, perfectly suited to our needs, and crucially without a slimy cushion in sight.

As for the funds I had left . . . I could not forget the woman who had led me here, and nor did I plan to. Henry had given Hester two stones, one real, one fake, the implication being that she must choose. It gave me great satisfaction to know that she had picked neither. She had found her own way, leaving the stones inside the bird of paradise in Papua. I remained sad that there had been no reunion between her and Henry, her lover who had disappeared six years after her own vanishing.

Perhaps one day you will find me.

That had never happened, but I would try make up for it by not failing her. In some ways we were so similar: she was an animal dealer's wife, I was a plant-hunter. We'd both played our parts in the ransacking of the planet; we both knew how humanity tended to value nature only if it could be collected or incarcerated. She'd wanted more. Wanted better. So did I, because one day, in future generations, it might be different. There had been a deluge of letters in the wake of the RGS fellowship: offers of employment from Kew, Oxford, Sydney's Royal Botanical Gardens . . . I'd ignored them all, instead writing to my old acquaintance Rutherford about a number of conservation projects. I no longer wanted to rifle through the world for wonders. I wanted to look after the ones we already had.

Still, something nagged at me as I unspooled the fishing line, the same tug that kept me awake as I lay beside Daniel at night, listening to his breathing, tracing the dim patterns on the wallpaper. It was the same thing that made people read detective novels. To coax meaning from chaos, resolution from disaster. To finish the story.

Had I done that?

'Emma? You're supposed to put the line into the water, you know.'

I blinked and did so. The stream ran and ran, its gentle song filling my ears as Daniel eased himself into position beside me.

'I know it's troubling you,' he said, kissing my ear. 'But you did it. You solved the mystery. Hester was alive all along.'

'But she didn't lead me to the treasure. The diamond happened entirely by mistake.'

'No. Well. Doesn't mean you can't be happy.'

We sat in silence for a few minutes with the autumn sun on our cheeks, letting the brook do the talking. Gradually his words sank in, and as they did, I remembered the words of somebody else.

That is the thing about heaven, Mrs Heatherwick had said. *We never know what it will be until we find ourselves there.*

'Daniel,' I said slowly, my thoughts pulsing on my tongue. 'You are quite right.'

He laughed. 'Say that again. I don't think I've ever heard it from you before.'

'Sorry, it was a one-time thing. But it's true. Happiness means different things to different people.'

'Well . . . yes.' He looked a little confused. 'Take fishing, for example. I've heard *some* people find it boring.'

'Then it follows,' I said, chucking him the rod, 'that so does Paradise.'

I ran back to Butterworth and yanked open the drawer where I had temporarily stashed a number of treasured items while builders did work in our cottage. There was Hester's last diary, and *The Birdcage Library*, piled beneath the tooth necklace I no longer needed. After all, I had learned to protect myself.

I took out the two books, thankful that the vasculum had protected them.

Henry: the path to the treasure lies in Paradise.

I'd always thought Hester's words ambiguous, even for a treasure hunt. The castle was not made explicit – but nor, I realised, was the diamond. What if, therefore, the treasure was something else?

I paced up and down. Hester's last account had been something of a dead end. There had been no clue to follow, though at the time I'd been rather preoccupied, too busy trying to survive Charles Vogel to notice. It also seemed strange that there were only four diaries. *The Birdcage Library* had five chapters, and each clue had answered to each succeeding chapter. Hester was an accountant by nature, for goodness' sake. She knew how to count. There ought to have been something in her last papers that led me to the final chapter, and from there to the treasure.

But there had been no such thing. I'd found the diamond on my own. So to what had Hester wished to lead me? It was interesting that in her last words she had referred explicitly to *The Birdcage Library*: The Birdcage Library *represents the very beginning of this unmixed chapter of our freedom. And remember: X marks the spot.*

Freedom. The name of Sarah's brother's ship. Coincidence?

Hester had set out to create a treasure map. A treasure was simply something that one valued highly. To Charles Vogel, it had meant a gemstone, but I had seen first-hand how he valued the wrong things. *The path to the treasure lies in Paradise.* Charles had interpreted Hester's words as a taunt. But she had left this trail not as a curse on her husband, but as a gift to his brother.

This unmixed chapter . . .

I took up *The Birdcage Library* and flipped to the chapter list.

Crossing the Line – An Introduction
Styles
Empty Cages
Antiques
New Cages

What now? I went to the start of each chapter page. Wrote down the first word of each. Got gibberish.

'What are we doing?' Daniel came up behind me.

'I thought you were fishing.'

'The fish can wait.'

I smiled and showed him what I had – essentially, nothing. Then a thought occurred to me. The *very* beginning . . .

I went back to the list of the chapter headings themselves. Then I wrote out the first words of these too.

Crossing
Styles
Empty
Antiques
New

Nonsense, no matter how I ordered the words. I sighed and sat back. I'd been so convinced I was right.

'Well?' Daniel asked.

'Nothing. Let's have dinner.'

Daniel, having hardly set foot in the kitchen in his life other than to swipe leftovers, had somehow become quite the cook. But rather than heading there, his mouth quirked. 'You're not giving up, are you?'

'There's nothing here.'

'Perhaps you haven't gone far enough.'

I rubbed my eyes and looked again at the clue. The *very* beginning. Maybe that meant even earlier than the first word. The first letter?

I wrote out:

C
S
E
A
N

Still gobbledegook, but . . . My attention shifted to that word 'unmixed'. An anagram? I tried scrambling the letters every which way. The only whole word I got was 'canes', which meant nothing to me.

'Really, let's eat,' I said again. Daniel kissed me on the nose.

'The gravy is still too warm. Keep at it. I'll fetch you when it's ready.'

I returned to the half-baked words I'd scrawled, combing them for missed meaning. Oh, this was hopeless. I began striking them out, slashing my pen back and forth. Then I sat back and looked despairingly at what I'd done.

A page covered in crosses. X's, even.

And remember: X marks the spot.

'Dinner,' Daniel called, but I did not reply, every thought humming. I looked back at the first chapter heading. *Crossing the Line.*

Slowly I wrote:

X
S
E

A
N

'Emmy?' Daniel was at the doorway, a tea towel over his shoulder. I beckoned him over and he watched as, pulse beating, I reordered the letters before us. A reordering that knocked the breath from me.

S
A
X
E
N

I sat back in helpless wonder, thinking of a woman I had once visited in a house on Golden Square. A house gifted to her by a gentleman named Richard Heatherwick, who had died childless but had never forgotten a certain beloved ward; a gentleman who was the only person on earth able to supply details of Hester's location, if only the right man came looking.

That man had never gone to Pàrras; Charles had already taken up residence there. Nor had he ever come to that house in Golden Square. But he had gone back to America, just once; and more importantly, he had understood the woman he had loved. He was a hunter by nature; he knew how to track that which was not easily found. He had not needed a series of diaries to work out where she was – only a scrap of paper mentioning Paradise, and a name. *His* name – but also that of the bird he had given her, and which she had loved. A bird that he himself had brought her, from a certain valley in Papua.

I thought of the distinctive nature of that house in Soho – of the exotic umbrella stand and the overwhelming flavour that here in the genteel heart of London I had stumbled across something quite wild. Something cared for but not tamed, loved but not barred. And I recalled a spear I had seen there, whose carvings were identical to those used by a certain Papuan tribe: a tribe whose chieftain had been entrusted with a stuffed bird of paradise.

For many years, the chieftain had said, the ghost had visited periodically. As though it were expecting something, or someone, its small companion spirit always at its side. Until one day, another ghost *had* come, setting the first ghost aglow. By then, half as many years had passed as there were feathers on a paradise bird's tail.

A bird of paradise's tail always had twelve feathers.

They had left the village, those white-skinned ghosts, two large and one small, and never returned. As though they did not need the bird any more. As though they had found another way, one that had led them to happiness.

Henry had kept on collecting, Mr Vogel had said, until he disappeared in the mountains of Papua. Had he returned to New York before then, to find Hester gone and only her last clue left for him? Had he heard that his brother had gone to Pàrras, but it did not matter, for he knew her well enough to realise what she'd meant?

Hester had realised that Charles was incapable of valuing what was in front of him. She had known that the treasure could be right before his eyes and he would never see it.

I thought of that green front door in Soho and the shining silver number 10 upon it. Ten in the Roman alphabet was . . . X.

And as I laid down the pen, the corners of my mouth lifting – as I was engulfed by the homeliness of the room, the warmth of the waiting dinner and the fresh-water scent of the man beside me – I knew that while a diamond was just a diamond, a daughter . . . well, a daughter was everything.

HISTORICAL NOTE

It was pure chance that led me, three years ago, to a country house containing the desk of famed explorer Freya Stark. My father had met her while travelling in Yemen in the 1970s; Freya was in her eighties and still adventuring. He was so taken by her fearlessness, her *aliveness* that he named his first child after her. The desk was heavy and solid, yet round, like a map of the globe. I knew then that I had to write about a female adventurer, and Emily Blackwood was born.

It's a strange thing to write about explorers when you yourself are locked down at home. I travelled extensively to research my first novel, *The Dictator's Wife*. This time was necessarily different. To create Emily's expeditions, I read many explorers' and botanists' accounts: 'Take with you paper and ynke', runs one piece of sixteenth-century advice to adventurers, and fortunately for my purposes, that is what these men and women did. As well as Freya Stark, I was particularly inspired by Isabella Bird, and Harriet Hemenway, founder of the Audubon Society, who went on birding expeditions dressed – shockingly – in white sneakers. Also useful was David Attenborough's account of Papua New Guinea, a nation 'characterised by the image of the bird of paradise'. I spoke with Christina Dodwell, who in her twenties explored that country alone on foot, horseback and by canoe; and indeed my own mother, who went while filming for the BBC's natural history department. (The locals, used by now to white visitors, were utterly confused by her Indian skin, and watched curiously as she washed her face and arms in a river to see whether the colour would fade.)

It was two real-life adventurers of a different ilk who sparked the idea for Hester Vogel. Charles and Henry Reiche really did emigrate from Germany as teens and make their fortune selling canaries to Gold Rush miners, before expanding the business and eventually dominating American circus animal dealing. P. T. Barnum, the greatest showman, purchased $300,000 worth of creatures from their Manhattan emporium; it is thought that Walt Whitman bought his canary there. Hyatt Frost did work with Charles Reiche (as well as Isaac Van Amburgh, the first man to put his head in a lion's mouth). Frost was not, as far as I know, either a pyromaniac or a homosexual. Robert Odlum did jump off the Brooklyn Bridge; unlike Hester, he died in the attempt.

The actual events of this novel are, of course, entirely fictional. There never was a Hester Vogel, but for the liberties taken with real lives, I can only plead forgiveness. Historical fiction allows us to grasp at the past; it is only to be expected that sometimes the past grabs us back. Nothing is so rich as reality, and this is particularly true for the Gilded Age. Mamie Fish really did throw outrageous parties, once renting an elephant for the purpose, while she and Caroline Astor shunned the new Vanderbilt money (though she was not quite yet installed in Gramercy Park in Hester's time).

Interwar Britain has its own quirks. The 'hungry thirties', when H. G. Wells remarked that 'saving the world' was a common dinner party topic, must have felt rather short of consolations. St Kilda's residents abandoned their archipelago then, one Bible left open – with a Scottish flair for drama – at Exodus. Castle Pàrras is partially based on Eilean Donan (whose founder, legend has it, could talk to birds); its shape is based on the corpse flower, a curious parasite that has emptied out its own genetic material in favour of stealing it from other plants. Lord Rothschild, the great collector who once took delivery of two bear cubs at his enraged father's bank, really was forced to sell his birds; it emerged later that he was being blackmailed by an unnamed peeress. Today Tring houses the Natural History Museum's bird collection, many specimens being saved from Hitler's bombers by smuggling them to various mansions. They remain immensely valuable to science.

In an era in which the natural world is being eroded, it's difficult to conceive that one could once buy a hippopotamus on the Bowery, but the Gilded Age seems like that to me: outrageous, wonderful, and with an undercurrent of wrongness. Charles Reiche recommended keeping canaries in tiny enclosures to improve their song, while birds, including birds of paradise, were slaughtered in their millions for hats. It's a truism that any book set in the past says just as much, if not more, about the period it is written in, and that uncaring extravagance feels familiar. As William Hornaday – who would go on to become first director of the Bronx Zoo and save the American bison from extinction – said, 'No unprotected wild species can long escape the hounds of Commerce.'

Of course, most Westerners no longer wear hats, nor keep caged birds, yet the ferocious pillaging of our natural world only grows more brutal and efficient. Many birds of paradise species are now threatened not by hunting, but by deforestation. By some estimates, looking after all animals everywhere would cost us just $80 billion a year.

'We all love Birds – Song birds especially. How can we help it?' So Charles Reiche wrote in *The Bird Fancier's Companion*, a work not dissimilar to Herman Millar's *The Birdcage Library*. He's right. That should give us reason to hope – and more, to act.

ACKNOWLEDGEMENTS

To misquote Oscar Wilde completely, to undertake writing one book may be regarded as a misfortune. To write two looks like recklessness. It's traditional to thank nearest and dearest at the end, but I must say upfront that I could not have written *The Birdcage Library* without my husband, Rory. You have been everything I needed you to be and far more over these weird, difficult eighteen months. Thank you.

Lockdown obviously restricted so many things – book research included. Sadly I couldn't make it to Papua New Guinea, but I had the next best thing in Christina Dodwell, real-life adventurer, pioneer and all-round badass. It was incredible to hear your recollections of PNG among other lands, and about the unique experience of being a female explorer. I am eternally grateful to Elle Larsson, for being so generous with her thesis research on Lord Rothschild and Tring Museum; and to Sylvie Hood, Abbie Shaw and the staff at Tring for your boundless helpfulness in my research of that wonderful institution. Thank you also to Lachlan Maclean, whose experience of life in a real Scottish castle was extremely useful – and to Giles Mounsey-Heysham for facilitating.

I don't think a novel can come into being without using

and abusing one's friends. The list of people who have gone above and beyond in their kindness and support through my first novel and into this second is too lengthy to count, but special thanks must go to a few. First, Tom Bird, for the much-needed help with cryptic clues. I hope you know I am being sincere when I say I am grateful for your twisted mind. To historian and co-library (ma)lingerer Tim Bouverie for the ready-made research of 1930s Britain. You saved me many hours, though we probably spent just as many yakking. And a toast to Emma, Hannah, Lucy and Marjan for the endless sympathy and questions on how the writing was going, and for plying me with wine when the answer was inevitably dour.

Thank you to Sally, for seeing me through.

To the people who brought this book into being. Sherise Hobbs, my editor at Headline – whew! Second time round! What a ride. I cannot thank you enough for putting your faith in me. You've been there from this book's earliest inklings, and your sharp mind and unfailing judgement have spurred it far beyond where I could have taken it alone. Thank you, thank you for your patience, your trust and your enthusiasm. Thank you also to Joe Thomas for his tireless publicity efforts, and to the whole team at Headline for your amazing support and commitment all over again. It means so much.

Major thanks also due to Flora Rees, who didn't let me get away with *anything* – thank you for your incisive eye.

To James Wills, my agent. You are blooming marvellous. I mentioned the seed of this novel on our very first meeting, and you've nurtured it all the way. Thank you for being on hand at every twist and turn of the last few years – I rely on your wise words and niche film references more than you know. Huge thanks as well to the endless support from the Watson Little team.

384

To my family. Ma 'n' Pa, I might not have made you read this one *quite* as many times, but when you did, you told me you knew once and for all that I really was a writer. (About bloody time.) Thank you. Your encouragement and interest and love are everything to me, as are the emergency photos of the cat when things get tough, again. Whatever I do, I know you're there with bells on. I couldn't ask for more.

Bringing things full circle, because I guess that's what you do with homes – you come back to them – Rory, you scraped me up on countless occasions. You leapt into action when things were hardest, and took on so many burdens to give me the freedom to write. Thank you.